Into the Sun and Shadows

Lisa D. Jones

This book is a work of fiction. Names, characters, places and incidents are either the product of the writer's imagination, or are used fictitiously. Any resemblance to actual events, locales, or persons, living or dead, is entirely coincidental.

To Oscar Jones, the love of my life, soul mate, best friend, husband, and "the smartest man alive". You came into my life shortly after I finished writing the manuscript for this novel, and here we are over 12 years later, finally getting it published. Thanks for always encouraging me and pushing me to reach my goal. Thank you too for being a wonderful husband.

To my son, Alex. I love you to the moon and back. Thanks for always telling me I could do this.

To Kelsey, I miss you more than anyone can know. Thank you for the gift of Alaina. I wish you could be here to see the joy she brings to us, and to celebrate this big accomplishment with me. Keep watching over us Goose.

To my "daughter", Alaina. You are my bright and shining star. You are such a precious gift, and gave me a reason to keep on living when my world collapsed. Thank you for being such a great toddler, playing contentedly at my feet, or sitting on my lap as I edited this. I love you so much.

Chapter One

"Yes officers. Can I help you?"

"Are you Wanda Newton?"

"Yes, but I didn't call the police. What do you want?"

"Ma'am we have a warrant for your arrest. Please step outside."

"I'll do no such thing! I told that detective what happened, and that's the truth. Now get out of here, you have no right to be here!"

"Ma'am, step outside now with your hands up. We have a warrant for your arrest, and you're going to jail. You can call your lawyer from downtown."

"I'm in my own home, and you're not taking me any damn place! Y'all can go to hell!"

Forcibly the officers entered the house, and grabbed Wanda as she tried to slam the door on them. The first officer continued to read her the Miranda Warnings as the other officers secured the premises. All the while, Wanda put up quite a struggle for her freedom. The officer continued, "You have the right to remain silent. Anything you say, can and will be used against you in a court of law. You have the right to an attorney. If you cannot afford an attorney, the State will provide one for you. Do you understand those rights?"

"Fuck you!"

"I'll take that as a yes. Let's go!"

"Y'all are gonna be sorry you messed with me."

"Whatever, lady! I'm already sorry. You ripped my shirt," Officer Webster exclaimed.

"I would have ripped more than that if I had gotten the chance you stupid flunky!"

Officer Grady yelled to Wanda, "Lady, shut up! We're only doing our jobs. You broke the law. Not another peep."

"Don't think you can keep me in this car and tell me what to do! I'll make as much noise or say whatever I want. I didn't break any laws! I'll sue every last one of you! You broke into my home, harassed me, and roughed me up."

"Lady, we didn't break in, we didn't harass you, and there is no way in hell that anyone would believe we roughed up some middle aged woman!"

"Brian, shut up! Let her be. There's no sense arguing with her. She's mad and she's going to jail. Stop trying to reason with her. Just pretend she isn't here. Too bad they never invoke their right to remain silent at this point."

Several months later O. J. Simpson is being charged with the brutal murder of his ex-wife and her friend, and Wanda Newton was placed on probation for writing bad checks. Only time would tell how similar these two people were.

Prior to being arrested, and even after sentencing, Wanda continued to deny the charges. She explained all along that it was just a misunderstanding, but coupled with her prior record and blaming a seemingly non-existent person, her story was completely unbelievable. Try as she might to forget it, the record that they were able to locate, would just not go away. Although it was only petty offenses, it lent credence to the fact that Ms. Newton was a schemer, a liar, and a thief.

Wanda initially explained to the detective assigned to the case that had her future son-in-law not been so inept, and she had owned a car, she would never have been in such a predicament. She claimed that because she had no car, her daughter's fiancé had offered to take her to the bank, but she was too busy and asked him instead to make the deposit for her. She said he agreed and, without question, she assumed he had done what she asked. She went on about her business, never even giving a second thought to the deposit that he had supposedly made.

She continued by saying that she apparently had enough money in the account to cover the first check she wrote to pay for something long since forgotten. She claimed it was a complete accident that she had overdrawn the account which then led to a domino effect of bounced checks. She claims that it was not until she was arrested that she realized he had "made off with her money" and not deposited a dime into her account. She told the detective that he could verify her story if he would only call her daughter. The detective took down the daughter's phone number, but made no promises.

Later, the detective decided to call Wanda's daughter, Cynthia Reynolds, only to learn that she did not have a fiancé, and she wished she didn't have a mother. She informed the detective that she and her mother had been estranged for quite some time, and she wished that the police would stop calling her every time her mother was arrested. She refused to give him any other information, and hung up on him.

The security department at the bank also gave a different account of Wanda's story. Apparently, Ms. Newton came into the bank alone and opened a checking account in her name with $200.00. Within a few days she had written several checks totaling over $5000.00. Having completed what little investigation was necessary the detective filed felony charges against Wanda Newton.

When the detective went back with the warrant to arrest Wanda, he confronted her with the information he had uncovered. Wanda was not only humiliated that her daughter didn't confirm her bogus story, but was aghast that she was now facing felony charges, and a prison term, for Forgery and Theft. She did not back down on the story she told, and continued to blame her estranged daughter's non-existent fiancé. She had hoped to be long gone before authorities caught up to her, but a change in plans had caused her house of cards to tumble.

Although all this information was in the detective's police report, the Pre-Sentence Investigator had left out the unsavory comments made by Ms. Reynolds. Most likely Wanda knew exactly how her daughter truly felt, but chose to overlook it, and the Pre-Sentence Investigator saw no reason to include it in the report. Therefore the Judge would not know of the relationship between Wanda and her only child when he sentenced her. After reading the report and accepting Ms. Newton's reluctant guilty plea the Judge placed Wanda on probation for two years with several special conditions. She was assigned to Marisa Spencer for probation supervision.

Marisa liked to review the whole file and get some idea of the person she was going to be supervising, prior to actually meeting them. Although she tried not to 'judge a book by the cover,' after reading her newest case file she was sure that Ms. Newton was going to continue denying any illegal intentions, and she would most likely continue her lies throughout her probation period. Most con artists operated in this fashion, and this con artist was not going to be any different, she could just "feel it." Marisa was puzzled by the daughter's comments in the police report, and wondered why those remarks didn't make it in the PSI. Marisa figured that Wanda Newton has been using Cynthia her whole life, and this time was just like any other.

Marisa believed that when Cynthia was old enough to live on her own she bolted from her mother's grasp, trying to put as much distance as she could between them. But if this were the case Marisa thought it was odd that they still lived in the same city. Although Cynthia had refused to talk to the detective, she wondered if Cynthia might enlighten her on their relationship. While Marisa was unaware of it now, later she would seek Cynthia's help; it may turn deadly for them both.

The probation case started out as any other case would have, except for Marisa's foreboding thoughts about this woman. She just could not stop wondering why she felt such distrust and animosity for Wanda Newton--a woman she did not even know. Although she decided this was a gut instinct, it wouldn't be until months later that she would realize these thoughts were there to protect her.

Marisa Spencer is a 27-year-old college graduate that worked for the government, not a glamorous job, a Probation Officer at the county level; long hours, low pay, with benefits that included nightmares, obscene phone calls, and constant harassment. It was a very intense job that Marisa just loved. Not the job she had always dreamed of, or even a dream job, but at least she considered it to be in the field of law enforcement. The first few years went smoothly, but as time wore on, the crimes and criminals worsened. Her parents wanted her to do something else, but no one really had any idea what the "something else" should be. She continued in this thankless job with no upward mobility, and very little pay. Though, she did like the control it gave her. She was demanding of her probationers, and although most of them didn't like her approach, they had a certain respect for her honesty and her willingness to see their side of things. Certainly, most people would not choose to be on probation; even fewer liked the prospect of going to jail or prison. So, reluctantly, most followed the rules. She knew instinctively, and immediately, that this case would be different from all the rest.

Marisa had a sense of commitment to the job and to the probationers she supervised that no one seemed to understand. She didn't care what the others thought of her, or of the way she did her job. The Judge's and the DAs admired her tenacity; the defense attorney's hated it. She never backed down when she knew she was right, and she wasn't usually wrong about her clients.

She had an instinct so keen that it sometimes scared her. She could sense when one of her probationers was going to violate the terms of their probation; it was as if she knew before they did. Where did she pick up this intuition? It scared her, but it scared them even more. Other officers said it was merely luck on her part; others just wished she could teach them about her instincts. She didn't understand it herself, but what a better world it would be if we could all look into the future and save the world. Wouldn't it be nice if Marisa could have looked forward into her own life and spare herself the despair she was headed for? Of course she would probably not change a thing. Soon she would experience danger, intrigue, and heartache. But, she would never regret the choices she was going to make. Her motto had always been "never look back, and have no regrets!"

The only thing the Judge had ordered Wanda to do was make restitution to the victim, pay her court costs and probation fees, and find a job. Wanda never missed her appointments, but she just couldn't find a job, and therefore claimed she could not make her payments. She would weave stories about how good her interviews were, but they just never hired her. She claimed she didn't know why she couldn't find a job. Marisa began asking her to complete a job search list. This list would assist Marisa in figuring out what Wanda was doing wrong. Wanda gladly took the list indicating that she really wanted to find employment. And, she would thank Marisa profusely for all of her help. But, Marisa knew that this was all just a game with Wanda. In the end, she knew that this was a game Wanda was going to lose.

Because of her risk to re-offend and because she was unemployed Wanda had to report weekly for her probation appointments. Wanda would act like she enjoyed these appointments, but inside she was seething with rage. Wanda could tell that she was going to have a quick-witted adversary in this little setback. She did not think that Marisa would be quite as good as she was, however. Wanda mistook Marisa's youth as a sign of incompetence. This would prove to be Wanda's undoing. Wanda forgot one very important detail: Never underestimate your opponent.

Week after week Wanda reported without fail to her probation appointments, but she didn't make any payments, nor did she have any type of employment. Many times Marisa asked her how she was supporting herself, but Wanda danced around the subject, never really answering the question. Finally, Marisa decided to do a home visit. Home visits were just extra things that had to be done on all cases. Officers went out in pairs to do these visits, or took with them a Warrant Officer assigned to the department.

Wanda was ill prepared for this unscheduled visit. Marisa could see that Wanda did not feel in control of this situation. She was renting a room in a boarding house. It was well kept and nicely decorated. Even though it was not Marisa's taste in decorating, she could tell that Wanda had a good eye for detail and nice furnishings. Wanda did her best to seem hospitable, but anyone could see that she was very uncomfortable with Marisa there unannounced. Marisa knew exactly what she was doing when she planned this visit. She knew that Wanda had weaknesses, and she would do everything within her power to make this woman comply with the rules of probation and the laws of the state.

Wanda was controlling her anger, but it was there, roiling just under the surface. Marisa decided not to press her luck today, so she didn't stay long. Wanda was reminded of her office appointment for the very next day just before Marisa and the other officer left. Wanda questioned why she needed to come in the very next day since she had just been seen for the week in her own home. Marisa explained that the home visit did not replace the regular office visit; rather it was in addition to her regular supervision level. Wanda went on and on about not having transportation and how much it cost to take a cab downtown. Marisa said perhaps she should get a bus pass, and it would be much less expensive than a cab. Wanda bristled at this suggestion. As Marisa and the other officer walked down the steps outside she heard the door slam behind them. She couldn't help giggling. She knew that Wanda was furious with her, and the situation she had gotten herself into.

A few weeks went by and Wanda indicated that she had been unable to pay her rent and was evicted. She was able to rent a room from a woman that had advertised in the newspaper. Wanda stated that it was just a bedroom in this woman's house, but she would be able to cook and entertain if anyone came to visit her. She also said it might be company for her to have someone else around, and maybe she would be company to this elderly woman. Marisa asked if she had told her landlord she was on probation.

"I don't think that's anyone's business but my own!" Wanda exclaimed.

"Well you are living in her house, and she has a right to know who and what's going on in her house."

"There is nothing going on in her house. I think this system is meant to harass people and you get some kind of sick thrill out of making me miserable!"

"Well Wanda, we can bring in my supervisor, but I'm sure he will tell you the same thing, and then maybe we can ask him if he gets a perverse kick out of making people miserable too. Sit right still and I'll call him."

Thinking better of it Wanda said, "No, don't call anyone else into this; I'll talk to her about it later. I just hope I'm not looking for another place to live because of it." Wanda tried to act as if it was not a big deal, but inside she was full of rage.

Marisa told her that she had twenty-four hours to tell her new landlord. She also informed her that she would be verifying this directive, so she really shouldn't put it off. Wanda indicated she would tell the landlord when she got home.

Although Marisa knew it would probably add insult to injury she asked her about her employment situation again before the appointment was over. It had been nearly three months since Wanda had been placed on probation and she still had not obtained a job.

Wanda gave her standard answer, "All I can do is fill out the applications. I can't make them hire me."

"No, you're right Wanda, you can't make them hire you, but you can try some different types of places. All the places you have applied to seem to be office type settings. Perhaps you should try cleaning services, restaurant work, telephone sales, or retail," Marisa offered.

Wanda told her that she was too old for the cleaning and restaurant jobs, she didn't like talking on the telephone, and she didn't like customer service oriented jobs. Wanda thought she was narrowing the field of choices down, but this only seemed to spur on Marisa.

Marisa then said, "Well Wanda, sometimes we all have to be with people that we don't like, and do things that we don't want to do. But, I am telling you now that you have thirty days to find some type of employment or I will be forced to file a violation with the Court."

Wanda gave her a look of indignation, but then thought better of it, and tried to show a half-hearted smile. She knew that if she went back to Court she could go to jail, or come out with more sanctions. She would have to show Marisa that she was really looking for employment, or at least make her think she was. She knew she was forcing Marisa's hand. Wanda had no intention of finding a job; however, if she could convince the Judge of her efforts, Marisa would have to back off.

Marisa called Wanda's new landlord, Mrs. Snow, two days later to verify that Wanda had told her of the felony conviction. Mrs. Snow indicated that Wanda had told her and she would keep an eye on her, but she gave Marisa the idea that she believed Wanda was the true victim. She expressed pity about her family situation. Moreover, she indicated that it was hard for people over the age of forty to find decent jobs, so she would just have to be patient with her new tenant. Although Marisa wanted to warn her, tell her the gut feeling she had, she knew she couldn't. She could really get in hot water over that, and she wasn't risking her job for anyone, least of all Wanda. Marisa had done what she could to protect Mrs. Snow from Wanda, now she would feel no responsibility when Wanda messed up. She was certain of one thing: Wanda would mess up. Marisa's favorite saying was, give them enough rope and they will hang themselves. She truly believed Wanda would be hanging very soon.

Before ending the call, she gave Mrs. Snow her office number. Marisa told her if she had any questions or something she thought Marisa should know she could call it any time, day or night.

The month passed and Wanda still did not have a job. Marisa had already typed up the violation report before Wanda reported for the last scheduled appointment within the grace period. Marisa went over the report with her, explaining that she would rather have resolved this matter without going to Court, but Wanda had left her little choice.

Wanda agreed, stating, "I told that Judge I would never be back in his Courtroom again, and now look what happened. He's really going to throw the book at me."

Wanda really thought she had Marisa fooled, but Marisa could see right through her charade. Marisa knew all along that Wanda never intended to find a job, but how was she going to convince everyone else what a horrible person Wanda was? She also wondered how Wanda was supporting herself.

A hearing was scheduled three weeks away. Marisa mailed the notice to Wanda's new address. The next day Wanda should have reported as indicated, but she didn't appear for her appointment, nor did she call to cancel or reschedule. Thinking this was odd behavior just before a Court hearing Marisa called her the next day. Mrs. Snow answered and said that Wanda was out with her "gentleman friend, Mr. Randolph." Mrs. Snow stated that Wanda spent a great deal of time with Mr. Randolph, and that he was the one paying her rent.

Mrs. Snow gossiped to Marisa for about twenty minutes, with Marisa taking notes as quickly as she could. She knew she might not want to use them at this hearing, but they would certainly come in handy for the next. Marisa asked Mrs. Snow to relay the message that she called and that she wanted Wanda to return the call as soon as she got in.

"Dear I can take a better message than just telling her to call you back. Isn't there something else I should tell her?"

"No Mrs. Snow, just make sure she knows I called, and thank you for telling me about her friend. Just remember not to tell her we discussed anything. Also, are you sure that she received the paperwork I sent through the mail?"

Mrs. Snow said she always makes sure her tenants get their mail and their phone messages. In fact, she recalled telling Wanda that it looked important, but Wanda just smiled and went back to her room.

Marisa said, "Mrs. Snow I want to thank you for all your assistance, and I want to remind you again that I don't think you should tell Wanda that we talked about her date with Mr. Randolph, or how much time she spends with him. I don't want to get you in any hot water with her or Mr. Randolph. I do so enjoy talking with you; you sound so much like my aunt that lives in Wyoming."

"What city does your aunt live in," Mrs. Snow asked.

Quickly Marisa lied, "Cheyenne, but I don't get to see her much. She's about your age I bet. She's about fifty."

Marisa knew full well that Mrs. Snow was probably pushing seventy-five, and she didn't even have an aunt in Wyoming. She did, however, want to be on Mrs. Snow's good side.

"Well thank you honey, but I'm going to be 73 this year. And, those cold Wyoming winters are not my cup of tea," Mrs. Snow replied.

"I would never have guessed you were that young! You just seem so full of energy and all. Well listen Mrs. Snow, I have another call, but thanks for talking with me. Maybe we can chat again sometime soon. You take care and call me if you need me. Thanks again," Marisa said as she hung up.

She thought to herself that this woman's kindness and gossipy nature might be just the help she needed to show Wanda's true colors.

The next day Wanda returned Marisa's phone call. She questioned the need to continue reporting since a violation was already filed.

Marisa shot back, "Well Wanda if you want I can add non-reporting to the violation, but I thought you didn't want to be in anymore trouble than you were already. You were violated on only two conditions: failure to pay and failure to find a job. Should I give you your next appointment or update the violation to include non-reporting?"

Wanda was angry. Marisa could hear the anger rise in her voice as she answered, "Fine, I didn't understand the situation, and you didn't bother to explain the reporting part to me. When is my next appointment Ms. Spencer?"

"Well Wanda, I thought since I gave you a business card with your next appointment date on it you could probably figure that out. Perhaps next time we will go over reporting procedures again. Your next appointment is at the usual time, next Wednesday. That would be at 1:00 p.m. in case you don't remember the usual time," Marisa stated emphatically.

As soon as the words were out of Marisa's mouth, the phone went dead. Wanda had hung up on her. Marisa just laughed. She thought to herself that Wanda really had a bee in her bonnet, and she didn't like it when she was wrong. Moreover, she didn't like it when someone caught her being wrong. Marisa also found it amusing that now Wanda was referring to her as Ms. Spencer. Up to this point, Wanda had always called her by her first name. Marisa let all her probation clients call her by her first name, although some of her co-workers and some management staff didn't think it was a good idea. She believed it made them feel more comfortable, and usually they weren't as defensive when they talked to her.

Later in the day, Marisa continued to receive hang up phone calls at work. They would ring through the receptionist, and when Marisa would answer, the caller would just hang up. Marisa didn't really give it much thought until driving home. It was then that she thought Wanda probably had something to do with them. Marisa just laughed and wondered why Wanda would expend so much effort to harass her, but wouldn't expend any effort to get a job and stay out of trouble. Although there was nothing she could do about the telephone harassment, she could call Wanda's bluff at the next appointment.

During the rest of the week before Wanda was scheduled to report again, Marisa received about four or five hang up phone calls per day. It was getting to be a little irritating, but she would just keep her cool until she could talk to Wanda about it. Finally, the day had arrived for Wanda to come in. Marisa was tense all morning wondering how she would convince Wanda she knew it was her calling and then hanging up. She discussed her predicament with Dani. Dani told her there was a gadget on the market that notified you of the caller's name before you picked up the phone. Although they really didn't have one, Wanda would not be the wiser. Marisa would just concoct a story that would lend credence to belief. She and Dani worked on the plan over lunch. Dani was Marisa's best friend, confidante, and co-worker.

Wanda appeared almost thirty minutes before her scheduled appointment. The receptionist informed Marisa that Wanda had indicated a need to hurry along and wanted to be seen as soon as possible. Marisa informed Joyce, the receptionist, to tell Wanda that she would do her best to see her early. Then she told Joyce the truth; Wanda was not going to call the shots here. Wanda would be waiting because Marisa had other work to do. Joyce then hung up and told Wanda that Marisa was going to do her best to see her early. Wanda thanked her profusely, and then she said that she didn't think that

Marisa really liked her that much. Joyce told Wanda that the officers had a lot to do and had a very stressful job; she shouldn't take anything personally. Joyce knew, in this case, that Marisa really didn't like Wanda.

Joyce was asked several times by Wanda in the next twenty minutes to call Marisa and remind her that she was here and needed to be seen early. Joyce called Marisa once telling her of Wanda's request. Marisa listened and then without hesitation said that she was sorry for putting Joyce in this sticky situation but she had to let Wanda know who was in charge. Joyce said she understood. Joyce then informed Wanda that Marisa was aware of the situation, and she was doing her best to see her early. Finally, at 12:55 p.m. Marisa went to the waiting room to retrieve Wanda. Wanda tried to act nice in front of the other clients, but Marisa could feel the rage building.

Once they got to Marisa's office Wanda demanded to know why Marisa left her there so long. Marisa then pointed to a stack of client files on her desk and said, "Contrary to your popular opinion, I do have other clients Wanda. Those other clients have needs and problems just as you. My office time is also time spent making phone calls to therapists and other agencies. And, if you look at your watch, I am seeing you a bit before your scheduled appointment. It's the best I can do today. Really, if it bothers you to wait, perhaps you should find a job so you wouldn't have to report as often.

Wanda didn't utter another word; she merely nodded her head yes or no to Marisa's questions. Marisa finally set up her next appointment and gave her the card. Wanda stood solidly and waited for Marisa to escort her back to the waiting room; however, Marisa wasn't quite finished. Marisa told her she should sit back down as she had one more question. Angrily Wanda complied.

"I just wanted to know why you have been calling me so often this past week? For some reason we keep getting disconnected as I answer," Marisa said.

Wanda spat, "Call you? Why would you think," but Marisa interrupted her before she could finish.

"Well the calls have all originated at the front desk, and they have a system that tells them who is calling before they answer. I just can't understand why all your calls keep disconnecting, unless perhaps you are hanging up on me on purpose?" Marisa said. Without missing a beat Marisa continued, "If you are wasting all that energy on me, maybe then you do have more time than you think to look for a job. But I'm sure I don't need to tell you that."

Although Wanda never acknowledged any wrongdoing, she didn't deny it either. Marisa knew that she had called her bluff and won this round. On the way down the hall Marisa was thinking, *'if looks could kill I would be dead right now.'*

As she opened the door to let Wanda pass she said, "Wanda do have a nice day, and try to put a smile on that beautiful face, you wouldn't want to wrinkle prematurely."

Wanda didn't even turn around or try to respond she just kept walking. Several people in the waiting room laughed among themselves and said she was wasting her breath. They laughed, but Marisa ignored them.

The next two office visits with Wanda were icily still. Wanda didn't want to get in any further sparring matches with Marisa for the time being. She could tell that Marisa was holding the cards now, and she would rather be silent than risk another verbal attack by her at this juncture. She had already figured out that it was no use trying to put on a show for Marisa. Marisa could see right through her so she would just bide her time until the hearing. Maybe then, she could convince the Judge that Marisa just didn't like her, and he would reassign her to another officer. She knew that she could wrap another officer around her finger. She had had no problem convincing the Pre-Sentence Investigator of all her lies. It was clear, however, that Marisa wasn't going to budge.

Marisa was always prepared for Court, but this time she left nothing to chance. She had always gotten along with this Judge; he really seemed to respect her opinions, and her drive. Several days before the hearing she contacted the D.A. handling this case, Tom Roberts. She told him of her complete and total distrust of Wanda. Further, she told him that she believed Wanda had no intention of finding a job, or repaying the restitution that was ordered. She also advised him of Wanda's living situation, and that she was certain Wanda would try to take advantage of this elderly woman. She described her conversation with Mrs. Snow, and her feeling that this woman really just wanted a friend, not a tenant. The D.A. told her she had done all she could do ethically, and for the time being she should just keep taking notes. He also told her that he really didn't think the Judge would revoke Wanda's probation, but he might add some additional sanctions.

Marisa gave him an evil grin and said, "Well, you know, Wanda can't seem to find a job that will pay her, but perhaps she could do some volunteer work. Yes, I think Community Service Hours would be just the thing for dear Wanda."

She and Tom thought this would really get her goat, help the community, and impress the Judge at the same time. They would wait for her to violate these terms in addition to the old ones, and then recommend revoking her probation. They were certain too of one thing, Wanda would not win this round, and she would be fighting mad.

Wanda appeared alone at the violation hearing. Marisa wondered why her new friend, Mrs. Snow, didn't accompany her, or why her "gentleman caller" didn't tag along. Marisa figured that Wanda was going to state to the court that she was all alone and play on the Judge's sympathy. The D.A. and Marisa already had their plan worked out. They were just going to let Wanda do all the whining and moaning about Marisa and the rules, and they would be magnanimous about it. Then, Marisa would only request that Wanda complete Community Service hours since she was not working and ask for a compliance hearing for a later date. This would make the Judge see that she wasn't being too hard on Wanda, only that she wanted her to work. Marisa would also point out that many of the probationers learned new job skills at their service placement, and some had even obtained permanent positions there once they had completed their hours.

As is customary, the Probation Officer would read the violations to the Judge, and then the Judge would ask the defendant's attorney whether his client wished to admit or deny the charges. As Marisa read the charges against Wanda, non-payment of restitution and fees, and not obtaining employment, Wanda just shook her head. Wanda appeared to be trying to impart that she was making the effort but Marisa was just expecting too much. Wanda really put on one of her better shows, but Marisa held her ground. The Judge seemed to see that Marisa had a steely glaze about her, and he too had a hard time buying into Wanda's accusations.

Finally the Judge asked, "Sir, is your client admitting or denying the charges brought against her?"

Wanda's attorney, Donald Martin, a small, bespectacled, young man, being paid by the citizens of the state calmly rose to address the court. He was a public defender fresh out of law school. He had not yet signed on with a law firm, and judging from his courtroom demeanor wouldn't be anytime soon. He was a public defender working in an over-burdened system barely being paid as much as a kid working at McDonald's. He was no match for his client or for Marisa. He stammered around the issues at hand, but finally said she would admit with explanation. Marisa just gave the D.A. a knowing nod; they knew exactly what was coming next.

Mr. Martin then asked the Judge if his client could relate to the court her explanations. The Judge said as long as the State had no objection, he didn't mind. The D.A. and Marisa both said they had no objections, so Wanda started to speak--her voice quivering and low. Marisa had difficulty hearing and so did the Judge. Judge Taylor told her to speak up or have her attorney speak on her behalf. Wanda realized she had better get her point across to them so she spoke up. First, she started with the fact she had always worked in office settings, but now that she was getting older it was becoming increasingly difficult to obtain employment. She told the Judge that she had completed many applications and that the jobs had sounded promising, but she never was called for a second interview.

She told Judge Taylor just as she had told Marisa earlier, "All I can do is fill out the applications, and I can't make them hire me. And, I can't repay the money if I don't have any money coming in."

The Judge didn't like this tone, he could see that she was used to getting her way. He knew that Wanda had probably met her match when being assigned to Marisa.

Not wanting to seem uncaring, Judge Taylor asked her if she was having any other problems. Falling right into his trap, Wanda told him that she felt that Marisa just didn't like her, and was being too hard on her. She told him that Marisa didn't show her any respect at all, and always seemed to make her wait for her scheduled office appointments. Further, she said that Marisa was rude because she appeared on occasion at her home without first calling to announce herself. The Judge gave Marisa a look of contempt.

The D.A. whispered to Marisa without even moving his lips, "Don't take that look personally, I've seen it many times. He's playing with her, not you. Don't show any emotion."

Marisa wrote 'OK' on her note pad. Wanda went on and on about how horrible she thought, Marisa was. She placed blame on everyone and everything but herself. Finally, she thanked the Judge for listening and then suggested she needed just a bit more time, and perhaps another officer might be more understanding. Wanda shouldn't have even gone that far. Marisa knew that Judge Taylor didn't like being told what to do in his own courtroom and certainly not by some common felon.

Just when Wanda and her public defender thought the air was clear; Judge Taylor's voice crashed down on them loud and clear. He pointed his finger at Wanda and told her to rise. The crescendo in his voice was deafening as he told Wanda just how things were going to be. He told her in no uncertain terms that Marisa worked for him, not for her. Further, he stated he had no problems with the way Marisa conducted herself with her clients in or out of her office. He told her that making an appointment to see a client in their home was not of much use; it was the element of surprise that let the officer's see just how their clients lived.

In addition, he told her that if she wanted to work she had had many months in which to find a job, any kind of job. He told her that she was not a stupid woman, nor was he a stupid man, and he knew that she didn't want to repay that money. But, if she didn't pay the money she owed she would find herself behind bars for a very long time. He told her she should think what her life might be like then, and that might inspire her to find some type of job. He then asked her if she needed a taste of the lock-up or a weekend in jail to get her attention. She did not want to seem impertinent, so she just shook her head no. Wanda tried to stand erect and without emotion, but Judge Taylor's words seemed to make her cringe with his every blast. She was definitely not going to get any sympathy from this man.

The Judge then ordered Wanda to complete eighty hours of Community Service Work by her next hearing which was scheduled a month from today. He ordered her to perform no less than twenty hours per week, and the remaining free time he wanted her to search for and obtain gainful employment. He told her that she might have to lower her expectations in her search, but that the local fast food places were always hiring. He also ordered her to submit copies of her applications to Marisa, and once she obtained a job, he wanted copies of all her pay stubs. He then wished her good luck and called the next case. Wanda had wanted to ask him questions, but the young, public defender had told her now was not the appropriate time. He advised her to just do what the Judge had ordered and be grateful that she didn't land in jail. The public defender had never felt Judge Taylor's anger until today; he knew he didn't want to feel it again.

In the corridor after the hearing Tom told Marisa to be on her toes; Judge Taylor was really going to be keeping an eye on this case. After Wanda spoke with her attorney she started to walk toward the elevator. Marisa called to her and told her that they needed to talk and she needed to get her next appointment. Wanda was consumed with bitterness and anger. Marisa knew that she was not helping the situation, but she did have a job to do.

They walked to her office in silence. Marisa had already decided that she was not going to make small talk with this woman ever again. She would state her business and answer Wanda's questions, but she would not engage in conversation with her. She knew this tactic was probably just what Wanda wanted, but she knew that killing her with kindness wouldn't work either.

As Wanda filled out the usual paperwork, Marisa started to write down her next appointment. Marisa then asked Wanda if she remembered everything the Judge ordered her to do. Wanda didn't speak but nodded her head affirmatively. Marisa then told her there were a number of work service sites near her home, and also asked her if she had any special interests. Wanda nodded again, this time negatively. Wanda was not going to make this easy on herself.

Marisa then stated, "Well we can do this the hard way, or the easy way. It makes no difference to me; you're the one doing the work. And, Wanda do remember although this is free labor to the agency, we hope that you get something out of it too."

Wanda just raised her eyebrows and had a slight smirk on her face. Marisa then asked her if she had any physical limitations or special abilities that she should consider before finding her a placement. Again Wanda just nodded her head no. Marisa told her that by being uncooperative she was not hurting anyone but herself.

Marisa made a call and asked a few questions; Wanda sat quietly listening to every word. Finally, Marisa hung up the phone and began filling out some forms. Wanda could see that it appeared to be a contract of sorts. Marisa finished and handed Wanda the documents.

"Here, you need to read and sign this, and then you can be on your way," Marisa stated.

Wanda put on her reading glasses and studied the document. Without uttering a word she signed her name and gave it back to Marisa. Marisa then told her she would be working at a soup kitchen near her home, and it was on the bus line in case she thought transportation might be a problem. She then gave her basic instructions on whom to contact and the time she was expected tomorrow. Marisa then gave her a copy of the paperwork and her next office appointment. Wanda took the papers and stood to leave never once uttering a sound. Marisa thought to herself if only all her appointments with Wanda could be this pleasant. At least if she were silent there would be no arguments and more importantly, no lies.

Marisa called the soup kitchen just before it closed the next day to see if Wanda had arrived, and how she had behaved. The lady in charge, Miss Millie, spoke well of Wanda and said she thought she could be quite an asset there if she was willing to give of herself. Marisa told Miss Millie if she experienced any problems that she shouldn't hesitate to call her. Miss Millie told Marisa she had raised twelve children, she didn't expect any trouble she couldn't handle. Marisa knew that Miss Millie had a grip on the situation; she had had her share of tribulations raising those twelve children single-handedly after her husband left her. At least that was part of the story Marisa had heard about Miss Millie. Wanda and her syrupy sweet put-on would be no match for Miss Millie's keen senses.

By Wanda's next appointment she had completed fifteen of the requisite twenty hours of service work. Rather than make an issue of those five hours, Marisa just made a note of it. Wanda was an adult; she knew exactly what the Judge had ordered. Still though she was no closer to finding employment than she was when she came on probation. Again this was a very one-sided appointment. Marisa would ask questions, and Wanda would just shake her head yes or no. When Marisa requested copies of employment applications Wanda just handed them to her. It appeared at first glance that there must have been twenty or more completed applications. Marisa glanced at them. Nothing seemed out of the ordinary, so she just put them in Wanda's file. She set up the next appointment, wrote in on a business card and escorted Wanda out of her office.

This whole thing was rather amusing to Marisa and some of her colleagues. Marisa's supervisor, Charles Bond, wondered how the Judge would deal with this behavior, but Marisa assured him it was only going to backfire on Wanda. Marisa also assured him that she was taking excellent notes; every minute detail was written in Wanda's file. Somehow he knew that Marisa could take care of herself, and fight her own battles, but he too had misgivings about this case.

Wanda came to her next appointment with more completed applications, and her time sheet had now only accumulated twenty-seven of the required forty hours she should have worked at the soup kitchen. Again, Marisa initialed the time sheet, and accepted the copies of applications. And, again there was no spoken words from Wanda, just nodding of her head to the questions Marisa asked. Finally, Marisa had her appointment time written down and escorted her out. They were getting this down to a science Marisa thought as she was leading Wanda out. They had gone from a twenty-minute session of arguing down to about five minutes of gesturing.

Marisa talked to Charles about Wanda's progress or lack thereof. He told her to just treat this as any other case, and let it be until court. She could report the information to the Judge, it was up to Wanda to comply with the Judge's orders or not. He reminded Marisa of one of her own mottoes, 'give them enough rope and they will hang themselves'. Marisa knew he was right. The Judge wasn't going to be mad at anyone but Wanda.

Wanda's third appointment came and went without incident. At this point she had now only worked forty-one of the required sixty hours, but she had now turned in over fifty completed applications. Marisa decided she had to know what was keeping Wanda from being hired by these prospective employers. Of course she wouldn't even question Wanda about this, she knew she couldn't nod the answer. Furthermore, she knew that Wanda had something up her sleeve or she would have been hired already. Whatever the reason, Marisa knew that she would figure it out before they went back to court next week. Wanda was due into Marisa's office two days before her compliance hearing. That meant Marisa had only five days to figure this out.

Chapter Two

Marisa decided she would rather not be distracted, so she took all of Wanda's completed applications home with her. Once she started flipping through them she noticed that they were all alike. This was odd she thought, but decided to go on looking at each one. She knew she would not get through all of them tonight but she would continue taking notes long into the night. She was not going to lose this battle with Wanda. Wanda was devious that was for sure, but Marisa was quite skilled in her investigative abilities.

Marisa believed that most of the forms had been completed elsewhere and probably copied because the only real difference in them came in the date area, and the position for which she was applying. She detected that the ink was different in these two lines. It was darker in those areas than in the rest of the document. She also noticed that she had listed three references: Mrs. Snow, Ms. Marisa Spencer, and Cynthia Reynolds. Beside the name of Marisa Spencer it stated, "My probation officer", much to Marisa's surprise. It was no wonder she wasn't getting called for an interview. Although Wanda could argue that she was being honest, there were other ways of bringing this bit of information up at the interview. Marisa believed it was clear that Wanda was sabotaging her own efforts to find employment. This would not bode well with the Judge.

The final appointment with Wanda before the hearing came and went without fanfare, as usual. By today Wanda had now only completed fifty-five hours of the assigned eighty hours. She was now twenty-five hours behind in what the Judge had ordered. Marisa knew there was no way she could finish those hours before court. The soup kitchen had certain restrictions on hours available to probationers. Even though most places would take volunteers any time they were available, probationers were not exactly volunteers; and safety and security had to be considered.

Marisa told Wanda to have her time sheet in court with her, and if she had any money to pay, she should do it before the hearing. Marisa knew she was wasting her breath. She just wanted to cover all the bases in case the Judge asked her at the hearing if she had informed her client what needed to be done. Wanda had no intention of paying toward the money she owed. Marisa then gave her an appointment card with the hearing date and time, and the Courtroom number on it just in case she had forgotten. Again, Wanda uttered not a word.

Marisa went to Charles after the appointment with Wanda was over. She told him what she had been doing at home after work with all the applications that Wanda had given her. He told her that she should be prepared for a fiery blast if the Judge didn't like the interest she had taken in this case. She told him she wasn't worried, she was only doing her job. Charles knew she was a good investigator; he always thought she had missed her calling. But, he also knew that she was a good Probation Officer, and he didn't want to lose her. He told Marisa to go on home after she had finished with her clients, and work on the applications and her notes. He knew she would be ready for this hearing. He planned to watch her and use whatever he could on her yearly evaluation.

Marisa went home about two hours earlier than normal. Dani stopped by the apartment after she got off work to see if she could offer any assistance. Dani looked at the papers that were strewn all over the table and the floor of the living room. Marisa told her they were in piles of various job types. She had done this to see if Wanda was backtracking or if they were actually all different places. What she found was not a surprise. It seems that Wanda had gone to several convenience stores, restaurants, discount stores, and office buildings; however, she apparently didn't think that Marisa would be researching each application. It had been a tedious process, but Marisa had persisted, and had started calling everywhere that Wanda had applied.

Marisa explained that after she had looked at all the applications she noticed that some were very similar. She decided to stack them according to job type, and then she put them in date order. After doing all that, she began the tedious process of calling all the potential employers. Wanda was devious enough not to write down the same telephone number on each application. On some of the applications she had written only the address of the business; on others she had written only the telephone number. However, once Marisa started calling the places and looking them up in the telephone directory she knew that Wanda had intentionally tried to mislead her. When Marisa started making the inquiries she stated that she wanted to verify if someone had applied at this business. Marisa took copious notes; writing down the name of the business, the manager, and any other details they wanted to share about the applicant.

After making a few calls she would start to recognize the voices that were answering the phone. Sometimes the person answering would say to another worker "hey someone else is calling to verify if that lady applied here again." So, the calls went on until Marisa had to go to court. Because there were so many places to call and re-call, Dani and Charles pitched in just to get them all called before Marisa had to go to the hearing. Most of the potential employers remembered Wanda, only because she had come in on more than one occasion to apply for jobs that were not available. And, most of them also said they thought it was odd that she always had her own application to give them. Marisa had never heard of taking in your own completed application to a potential employer. Most often, if a job was available, the manager would have you complete their specific application, not a generic form obtained from a copy store. Marisa felt she had enough proof for the Judge that she would win this battle of wits with Wanda.

Prior to the hearing Marisa met with Tom again to tell him that Wanda had been scheming as usual. She also informed him that Wanda had still paid no money, and she was behind in her work service hours. Both decided to let the facts speak for themselves, and let the Judge decide how to handle this matter without offering any unsolicited opinions about the disposition of this matter.

Judge Taylor began this session by telling everyone he had a matter to attend to outside the Courthouse in one hour and he was not in any mood to be late. Marisa knew this was his standard greeting when he had an important golf game scheduled at the country club. She knew this hearing wouldn't take long. How long could it take to tell him that Wanda had not done as he had instructed and for him to lock her up?

He began first by stating on the record that all parties were present, and indicated that he knew they were here for a compliance hearing. He then asked Marisa if her client was in compliance. Marisa stated that in fact, Wanda was not in compliance. She noted that she had not made any payments, she was still not gainfully employed, and she had not completed her community service hours.

The Judge gave a harsh glance at Wanda and asked her attorney why she wasn't in compliance. The pathetic little man cleared his throat and quietly stated that he had not heard a reasonable excuse from his client about why she did not do as the Judge had instructed. He then offered that his client might better make the Judge understand. Everyone could see that he did not want to tangle with Judge Taylor, and he didn't get paid well enough by the State to take what was rightfully due his client.

Judge Taylor then pointed his finger at Marisa, and motioned for her to approach the bench. A million thoughts were swimming through her head. *Why didn't he just throw this old broad in jail for her contempt? Why isn't he yelling at her, why me? What am I going to say about everything I have found on those applications? How can I interject about her lack of cooperation in office visits?* Finally she reached the bench.

"Yes sir?"

He covered the microphone and said, "Marisa, you know and I know that I can't throw her in jail for the remainder of her sentence just because she isn't in full compliance. And, as you know I have an important meeting in less than an hour, tell you what I'm going to do. I will briefly hear what you have to tell me, then I will order whatever is necessary and we will have another compliance hearing in a month. Okay?"

"Sure Judge, but she is up to something and I want at least a little leeway and I want it on the record."

"Make it brief, I tee off in 45 minutes."

Marisa was not happy, but she put a smile on her face when she glanced over at Wanda. Before she sat down the Judge asked her to state Wanda's non-compliance. Marisa hurriedly stated that no money had been paid toward the rather large debt, that she had only finished about two-thirds of her work service hours and she was still not working. Then before he could say anything, she stated that she believed Wanda was sabotaging her own efforts at becoming employed. Raising his eyebrows he looked at Marisa and asked her how her client was doing that. Marisa indicated that Wanda had been writing down Marisa's name as a reference on the generic applications she was completing and next to the name she would write, 'my probation officer. She didn't get a chance to state anything further before he asked Wanda if this was true. She stated in her phony, little girl voice that she was just being honest on the applications.

She started to tell the Judge that she could not complete all the work service hours because she was spending so much time looking for a job. She then said she knew how important it was to repay the restitution to the victim. Marisa let out an exasperated sigh that even the Judge heard. Wanda shot a glance her way and kept talking before the Judge told her he had heard enough. Wanda was a bit surprised. Judge Taylor asked his bailiff to call the jail and ask them if it would be too inconvenient to put Wanda in overnight and let her go by noon tomorrow.

As the bailiff started to leave, Wanda jumped up and said, "Your Honor, I am not a well woman. I am trying my best to get a job, and do what you told me, but that woman just won't help me like she should!"

"Ms. Newton sit down and speak only when you're spoken to or I will have the deputies put you in the lock-up right now. Mr. Martin keep your client in check, or I will hold you both in contempt!"

The bailiff came right back stating that she had spoken with the jail commander as the Sheriff was not available. The commander stated that they could provide a cell for her in the holding area in the jail's basement, but she would be in a general population environment. She would be with all new detainees that had not yet been formally charged. The Judge looked at Marisa and the D.A. then he looked at Wanda. Marisa thought he was just toying with them both.

Then he said, "The easy thing to do is lock you up and throw away the key, but I don't usually do the easy thing. I am now ordering you to complete an additional eighty hours service work, and to make up whatever amount it was that you didn't do, and to find a job. We will have another compliance hearing in one month. This time Ms. Newton you better do as I say, or bring your toothbrush with you the next time you walk through my doors."

He then stood, and left the bench without another word or glance in their direction. The Bailiff loudly stated "we are adjourned." Although Marisa wasn't very happy with the outcome she knew that Judge Taylor had just given Wanda more rope.

Wanda was shaking her head and pointing her finger at her attorney. Marisa decided not to wait for Wanda this time; let Wanda come to her office or phone for her next appointment. Marisa walked away a little mad, but pleased at the same time. She knew that Judge Taylor was right. He couldn't just lock her up; he had to show that she was not really making an effort to comply, or better herself.

By the end of the day Wanda had not appeared, nor had she called to schedule her next appointment. Marisa left the office as usual, but today she was physically and emotionally exhausted. She had been burning the candle at both ends for almost a week, and it was catching up with her. As she came closer to her car she noticed it didn't appear to be sitting level. Her step quickened. When she reached the car she could see that both of her driver side tires had been slashed. This was not an accident. She just knew that Wanda had something to do with this. Of course she could never prove it, and it was just too much of a coincidence, but she knew Wanda was trying to tell her something. Marisa also knew she wasn't interested in anything Wanda had to say.

Marisa went to the lot attendant and asked if he had seen anyone around her car this afternoon. He told her he was a busy man and a lot of people are in the lot milling about. He asked her how he could be responsible for anything that happened in that lot. She could feel her anger rising, so she just went back to the building and called the road service; she needed to be towed home. She would call Kate, her sister, and ask for a ride home.

When Kate arrived she wondered why Marisa wasn't driving herself home. Marisa told her she had two flat tires. When Kate gave her a funny look, Marisa told her she had parked in glass. Kate bought that story, and drove toward home. On the way they stopped off for Chinese food. Over the course of the meal Marisa confided in Kate that she had a big case today and she was just not really happy with the way things had turned out. She also told her she had poured a lot of time and energy into this case and it didn't seem to matter. Kate could tell that her sister was just really tired and needed to take her mind off work. She suggested that they go get Dani and go out for drinks. Marisa declined stating she really just wanted to go home, relax and go to bed early. Kate didn't want to interfere and she knew that maybe the best thing right now was to leave Marisa alone. Marisa had always enjoyed being alone with her thoughts, and although most of her family didn't like it, Kate respected that need.

Chapter Three

Although Marisa was several years older, she and Kate had become very close, and they relied on each other very much. They had a special bond that could never be broken. Marisa had so much wanted to involve Kate in the case she had been working on, but she knew she would never forgive herself if anything ever happened to her younger sister.

For a time, Kate and Marisa lived together, a very short time. They were both very headstrong and total opposites in every way. With all that going for them it is little wonder why they couldn't live together once they both left home. After Marisa graduated and began living on her own, Kate expressed a desire to live with her when she started college. Although their parents, Cliff and Tina, weren't thrilled with this idea, they were happy that at least their girls would be together. Tina told them it would never work, but they insisted they were no longer petty little girls and they would learn to compromise.

Tina wanted both of her daughters to stay in town and live at home while they went to college. Marisa had no problems with that arrangement, and what could she really say when her parents were footing the bills for college. Kate, however, was adamant she was going to live on her own. Tina said Kate was on her own financially if she wouldn't live at home, so Marisa tried to negotiate a deal to keep peace in the family. The deal was that she and Kate would share a two-bedroom apartment, and Kate would work part-time while attending school full-time. In that way, Kate would pay her own way for the apartment, their parents would still only being paying her tuition, and she would be living under the watchful and protective eyes of her sister. What could go wrong with that plan?

Once the girls were under one roof, their collaboration lasted only three months. The biggest clash was space and privacy. While growing up they had always had their own rooms. Marisa was a neat freak and Kate liked clutter. Kate liked the stereo or television on all the time; Marisa liked peace and quiet. They opted instead for adjacent one-bedroom apartments in the same complex. Both still very close in proximity, but no more arguments. Cliff and Tina weren't happy about this, but they knew they couldn't keep Kate's wings clipped forever. This arrangement seemed perfect. The girls often dined together, watched television together, and swapped clothes, but they no longer had to be mad about the way the apartment looked, sharing the bathroom, or their need for privacy. Both of the girls had call waiting. Tina would often laugh because whenever she called Marisa, Marisa would have to end her call with Kate, and vice versa.

Marisa went into the bedroom and took off her clothes, and started a long hot bath. She grabbed a book she had wanted to read, and fixed some hot tea. She relaxed in the tub for over an hour, afterwards she really just wanted to sleep. It was only eight o'clock in the evening; she never went to bed this early. Marisa climbed into bed and tossed and turned for an hour. Just as she was about ready to drift off to sleep the phone rang. She knew it was probably her mother. As she picked up the phone she heard a man's voice talking to someone in the background.

Calmly she said, "Hello, who's there?"

The voice on the other end of the line stated, "Your tires are just an example of what can happen Miss Spencer if you don't leave things that don't concern you alone. Next time it might be you or someone you love that gets hurt. Don't mess with things that aren't your business."

The phone went dead. Marisa didn't recognize this voice, but she knew who was behind it. Now what was she going to do? She couldn't talk to the Judge about this, and she didn't think that her superiors at work would do the right thing. She figured they would just reassign the case to someone that didn't care about anything, and Wanda would just continue getting away with things. No, she knew what she would do. She would keep working on things and she would bring this woman down. And, she would do it on her own. Marisa was not going to be bullied or terrorized by Wanda or by anyone. Marisa was calling the shots in this game, and this was a game she intended to win.

The next morning Marisa arrived to work a bit early. She wanted to check out a few things before she actually started seeing clients. She consulted the criss-cross directory that the office kept for locating people. She looked up her address and her telephone number, but her name did not appear. She then looked into some old directories, but again her name did not appear in them. When she had gotten her own phone several years ago, she had been unlisted and non-published to protect her privacy. She was amazed how someone had gotten a hold of her number and called her last night. She knew that someone had given her number to someone else, but she couldn't imagine anyone doing that to her. She had always told people that she liked her privacy, and when she told them her phone number or address she told them to give it to no one else. If she wanted her number given out, she would be the one to do so.

Immediately she went to Dani and accusatorily asked if she had given anyone her phone number or address recently. Dani looked at her like she was crazy and told her she would never do that. Satisfied she went to the Chief Probation Officer, Jansen Oliver, and asked if anyone recently had requested her phone number or address. Jansen told her that if they did she would have told them to contact her for that information. Jansen then asked her why she had asked such a silly question. Marisa told her that she had received a weird phone call at home and she didn't recognize the voice.

Jansen said, "Marisa maybe you're making more out of this than you should. It was probably some creep, or a teenager, making prank phone calls."

"Yeah Chief, but most of those creeps don't know your name."

Wanda still had not called to schedule an appointment, so Marisa decided to go out to her house again and ruffle some feathers. She asked one of the special deputies assigned to the department to accompany her. She told Charles what she was doing and told him she didn't know when she would be back. She informed him that she had given the front desk staff instructions on what to do with her clients, and she would let him know when she was back. She grabbed her calendar, and her gun, and told Dani that she didn't think she would be back in time for lunch.

On the drive over to Wanda's she told the deputy what she really wanted to do. He listened intently as she told him about the slashed tires, and the weird phone call. She told him that the landlord had indicated that Wanda had a boyfriend. She knew that she was going to have to wait to meet him, and today seemed like the day she should try. He agreed, but told her she wasn't paid well enough to risk her life. Marisa laughed and told him she had always wanted to be a cop, so this was right up her alley. Once they arrived on the block where Mrs. Snow lived they parked some distance away. Marisa used her cell phone to call Mrs. Snow, but she let the deputy do the talking in case Wanda answered the phone.

A woman answered the phone and the deputy said, "May I speak to Mrs. Snow please?"

"This is she, who's this?"

"Please hold the line, Ms. Spencer needs to speak to you Mrs. Snow."

Marisa took the phone and said, "Mrs. Snow I'm sorry to bother you this early in the morning, but I have a big favor to ask of you. I only want you to answer yes or no to my questions, okay?"

"Yes."

"Mrs. Snow is Wanda still living with you, and if she is can you tell me if she is home?"

"Yes, yes."

"Mrs. Snow is she in the room with you night now, or can she hear you talking on the phone?"

"No, but well maybe."

"Okay, Mrs. Snow is her gentleman caller with her now?"

"Yes."

"Are they awake ma'am?"

"Maybe."

In the background Marisa could hear Wanda talking to Mrs. Snow.

"Mrs. Snow just say that it's a home repair person calling about some work you might have done, and please do not tell her that I called. I'm sorry for putting you in the middle of all of this."

Marisa then hung up the phone but she could hear that Mrs. Snow was acting like she was talking to a salesman before she disconnected. Marisa then told the deputy that she needed to hear Wanda's boyfriend's voice to see if that was indeed the person that had called her last night. Although he wasn't thrilled with the prospect of a confrontation, he knew that Marisa would come back without him if he didn't agree to let her do things her way now. He convinced her to watch the house for the time being and take notes. He thought this might buy them some time and she would get bored and wait until another day.

They drove up the block slowly and wrote down every license plate of every car that was parked on it. Marisa then told the deputy that she wanted to wait and see if Wanda and her boyfriend would leave any time soon. He agreed to wait a little longer.

Finally, a break occurred. It appeared that a man in his 50's was leaving Mrs. Snow's house and going to a car. He was digging around in the trunk when Marisa decided she would walk casually down the block and say hello to him on her way to Mrs. Snow's house. The deputy didn't like this, but Marisa told him she was well protected as she showed him her gun. Marisa jumped out of the car before he could utter another word. As she approached the car the man was getting ready to go up the sidewalk.

She had caught him off guard and said, "Well hello there." He mumbled hello but didn't make eye contact.

Marisa wondered if he had ever seen her before

Finally she said, "Are you Mr. Snow or just one of the tenants here?"

The man looked at her and said, "I am not Mr. Snow, I'm a friend of one of her tenants but I don't believe that is any of *your business*."

When he uttered those last few words Marisa knew that she had given him enough rope to hang himself too. He had said those words to her just last night. Now she knew that this was the creep that was trying to intimidate her, but she acted nonchalantly and kept on walking. He noticed that she was going to the door and he followed suit. He brushed past her and left her waiting outside. She patiently waited at the door as he grumbled something to Mrs. Snow. Mrs. Snow hurried to the door and let her in.

Mrs. Snow acted like she didn't remember her name, but said, "You must be here to see Ms. Newton, I'll go get her. Please wait right here."

As she left the room she gave Marisa a wink. Marisa smiled.

As Wanda entered the room she said, "What are you doing here again?"

"Well hello to you too Wanda. What a way to start a conversation. I'm here because you didn't stop by my office the other day after the hearing, nor did you bother to call. So, if you don't like my little unexpected visits perhaps you should follow the rules."

"No one told me I had to continue to report to you, and if you needed to speak to me you should have said something after the hearing. All you want to do is have me locked up."

"Wanda, I don't know why you think like that. All I want to do is help you, but you just won't let me do my job."

"Well I'll tell you what, I'm not going to keep coming in and being harassed by you or any of those other flunkies. Do whatever you have to do, but as long as I do my service hours and find a job you better get off of my back!"

"Wanda I think you are making a big mistake, but it's your life, do whatever you think is best."

With that said Marisa turned to leave. Mrs. Snow was not in the room, and the boyfriend just sat stone faced, as Marisa left the house. The deputy was waiting just outside the door, and had heard every word.

"Well now Marisa what are you going to do?"

"Well Frank, I think I'll let Wanda think she has won this round. I won't file any paperwork with the court until the day of the next hearing. I will then cite that she has been non-compliant with the reporting aspect of her probation too. We'll see what the Judge thinks of that little jab at his orders."

By the time they finished with this brief repartee from Wanda it was past lunchtime. They stopped off at a burger joint and had lunch together. Marisa told him that she knew this was going to be a difficult case from the moment she set eyes on the file. She told him she wasn't a worrier, but her instinct was strong and she would need to stay on her toes. She confided to him about the idle threats that had been made. He told her she really should make a police report of both incidents; she told him she could handle it and swore him to secrecy. After they got back to work he went to his office and made a note about what he had learned, and what had happened today. He thought it might just come in handy one day; he only hoped he wouldn't need it.

Back at her desk she started checking her voice-mail and reading her mail. The phone rang, it was an outside call, and she answered, "Criminal Probation, how may I help you"?

"Ms. Spencer this is Mrs. Snow. I just wanted to tell you that I hope I didn't hurt anything by not staying in the room when you were talking to Ms. Newton, but I didn't want her to think I was prying. She and Mr. Randolph left right after you did, so it's okay for me to talk to you now."

"Mrs. Snow, no, no you did the right thing by leaving the room. I don't want anything to happen to you, and you did a wonderful job on the telephone. I don't think she suspected a thing."

"Well honey I think you should also know that Ms. Newton doesn't stay here most nights. I think she stays down at Mr. Randolph's place out of town. I think that is where they're headed now."

"How do you know that Mrs. Snow?"

"Well this is my house you know. I don't want anything illegal going on in here, so sometimes I check out their rooms when they're away. I think I'm entitled to do that, and I don't feel bad about it either. I won't lose my house because of someone else doing something wrong."

"Well Mrs. Snow I think you have every right to do that, but if the tenants found out they might have a problem with it."

"Well then they could just leave, I don't need that kind hanging around here." Marisa laughed at this woman's spunk. She knew the old lady was just nosy, but Marisa didn't care what she did to Wanda or Wanda's privacy.

"You know I have found some really interesting stuff in her room. Would you be interested in seeing anything?"

Marisa could barely contain her enthusiasm. She knew that the Judge or a good attorney might have a problem with her snooping through Wanda's things, but to have something dumped in her lap was hardly within her control. She told Mrs. Snow that she would be interested in hearing about it, but she didn't think she should come out and look at it.

"Fine then, can I come down and see you sometime?"

"Sure Mrs. Snow, but I don't want you to get in any trouble with your tenants."

"Nonsense, what they don't know won't hurt them. I'll stop by sometime in the next few days. Bye honey." Marisa just shook her head, this was just plain dumb luck.

About an hour later the front desk buzzed Marisa and stated that someone was there that didn't have an appointment.

"Can you please see who it is and ask them why they don't have an appointment?"

"Marisa, she says her name is Mrs. Snow and that you were expecting her."

"Yeah, sorry. I'll be right there. Thanks." She thought to herself that Mrs. Snow just couldn't contain herself and whatever it was that she had stumbled upon.

She escorted Mrs. Snow back to her office. Mrs. Snow was carrying a large box, full of papers. Marisa wondered how Mrs. Snow had managed this, but she decided she didn't really care, she just wanted to nail Wanda to the wall. Mrs. Snow apologized profusely for showing up today without an appointment. Marisa indicated she was not really that busy, and she was definitely interested in the information that Mrs. Snow had uncovered. Mrs. Snow was thrilled with herself.

Inside the box there were numerous bank statements in Wanda's name, Cynthia's name, and in another name that neither recognized. There were also stubs from unemployment benefits in a different county within the state. Those were in Wanda and Cynthia's names only. There was identification for a Barbara Harris and a Velma Higgins; however, both had the picture of Wanda on them. Most of the paperwork was dated after she was placed on probation; this could only mean that Wanda had not learned anything by being in jail briefly or by being placed on probation. This infuriated Marisa.

Marisa asked Mrs. Snow if she could copy everything in the box, so she could look at it more closely and without distraction. Mrs. Snow said she didn't mind, and even offered to help with the copying. Marisa took her up on her offer, and the pair took the box and headed to the copy room. It took about an hour to copy everything in the box. Marisa was satisfied though that she would find something of major importance in this box to help put Wanda away.

Marisa also made another copy of the pre-sentence report. She had always had a problem with the lack of investigation that was done on these reports. She knew with all the crime and criminals, the officers were doing the best with what they had to work with. Marisa decided to start with the information in the report and start her own investigation all over again. Maybe she would uncover something that the other officer had missed.

It was Friday afternoon, and Marisa already knew what she was going to be doing all weekend. Wanda had taken over her whole life.

Marisa told Charles that she had uncovered some documents that might be very incriminating against Wanda and she planned to work on it all weekend. He told her she really shouldn't be working on this stuff at home, but he wouldn't tell the Chief if she promised to go out and have some fun this weekend. Marisa told him she would work on one of her hobbies a little while just for him. She just didn't tell him that one of her hobbies happened to be research. She put everything in a large box from the copy room, and carried it out to her car.

After the flat tire incident she was more cautious, however. She would go to the building doors and look all around, she wasn't quite sure what she was looking for but she looked nonetheless. After she was sure the way was clear she went straight to her car, but kept an eye out for Wanda and her boyfriend. Once in the car she drove straight home. She could hardly wait to dig into this treasure trove of information today.

As soon as she arrived at the apartment she kicked off her shoes and began pulling out the contents of the box and placing them in neat stacks. She began stacking bank statements in one pile, unemployment papers in a pile, identification papers in another pile, and so on. Finally the box was empty, and her living room was a mess. She decided to go through each stack one by one and take notes.

Before she began her quest, she wanted to call Mrs. Snow and see if she had gotten home safely and put everything back. She dialed the number quickly and decided that if Mrs. Snow didn't answer the phone in four or five rings she would just hang up. After a few rings Mrs. Snow picked up.

"Hello."

"Mrs. Snow I think you know who this is. Use only yes and no answers. Is it safe for you to talk?

"Yes, but only for a minute."

"Okay, is she home now?"

"Yes, but they're still outside. Hurry."

"Okay Mrs. Snow please stay calm. Did you get the papers back in place before she got home?"

"Yes dear, no problems."

"Mrs. Snow please don't take any more chances. Call me next week whenever you like if you have anything we need to discuss. But please try to stay calm. I'm going to do all I can to see to it that she gets just what she deserves. Without your help today I don't think I could have done it, but please don't take unnecessary chances."

"Well no, I don't have any rooms to rent just now, maybe in a month or so sir. Thanks for calling. Yes, I have your number I'll call you if anything comes up. Good-bye."

Marisa knew that Wanda had just come inside, and Mrs. Snow was telling her she would call her again. She felt better for calling her, and warning her about Wanda.

Going through all those papers was going to be an arduous task, but Marisa knew if she didn't do it Wanda would continue wreaking havoc in people's lives.

Marisa started with the identification paperwork. It seemed that all of it had the same basic description, but with three different social security numbers, and at least the four names. Marisa wondered if Wanda Newton was in fact an alias, or her true name. She also wondered how she was going to figure this out in such a short time.

Marisa decided she should start with the Pre-Sentence Report to see what information had been verified. Of course Wanda indicated that her parents were both deceased, and that she was raised outside the city limits in a town several counties away. She claimed that relatives raised her after her parents died, but those relatives were also now deceased. Further, she asserted in the report that she had attended various schools because she was moved between relatives so often. She claimed that she had graduated from a rural high school that no longer existed, and she was unable to provide her diploma because it had been destroyed in a house fire after she left home. Marisa could only laugh. Wanda had given the pre-sentence officer a major 'snow job' and wrapped them right around her crooked little finger and they didn't even realize it.

Marisa knew that the school records had to be somewhere. She decided to call the town hall in the city where Wanda supposedly went to school and find out anything she could and any other assistance they were willing to provide. If she were really lucky maybe she would get one of the old town ladies that liked to gossip.

It may prove difficult tracking down anyone that remembered Wanda or her seemingly non-existent family, but Marisa wasn't known for giving up easily. At this point it seemed that any information would be a long shot, but perhaps Wanda hadn't really covered her tracks so well that someone with Marisa's instincts and drive couldn't uncover. Marisa was just glad she had an odd hobby of investigation and research. It wasn't a hobby that one could share, and there were no social clubs she could join to be with others like her, but at this time hopefully it would serve her well.

Marisa continued reading the report which stated that Wanda had been married briefly just out of high school, but he was in the military and died while he was stationed out of the country. Wanda had indicated in the report that she was unable to be with her beloved husband, Henry Reynolds, for almost a year before he died. However, her daughter was apparently born to this union, but by looking at her birthdate it was obvious to Marisa that the person that died was not Cynthia's father. Apparently because Wanda was legally married to him though her daughter was given his surname. It appears until now no one has even questioned this. She wondered if Cynthia really knew anything about her real father, or if she even knew of this facade.

So, if this part of the report was true, maybe Marisa could find this Reynolds family and start asking some questions. She doubted that they had any use for Wanda at this point. Making a note of this, she decided she would need to see if there were any living Reynolds family members in Wanda's old hometown. Perhaps one of Marisa's contacts at the Naval Investigative Service would be of some assistance in locating Henry's surviving family. Maybe if all went well when she called the town hall they may know something of the Reynolds family too. Marisa knew that the odds were against her, but she decided if she was going to bring Wanda down she was going to go after her with everything she could find.

The next item on her agenda would be to check out was those three social security numbers. A former sorority sister from college, Amanda McGregor, now worked for the Social Security Administration. They were not really friends in college, but they were 'sisters' and perhaps she would help. Amanda and Marisa saw each other about once a year at alumni activities, and always caught up with each other's lives. The last Marisa remembered was that Amanda had married a boy from a fraternity on campus several years earlier; did some modeling and had put off having children.

Marisa knew that Amanda was always very aware of professional ethics and may not give her any information. Somehow Marisa would coax the information from her, begging if necessary, and refuse to give up her source if she could just find out to whom these numbers were assigned. She would appeal to Amanda's sense of duty to the community in order to find out as much as possible about Wanda, or whoever she was. This was another phone call to add to her list to take care of on Monday. First, she would need to figure out all the questions she intended to ask; leaving nothing uncovered, because she knew that friend or no friend, Amanda would give her only one shot at this. She would start a list of questions tomorrow. Tonight she just wanted to give all the documents at least a cursory glance; tomorrow she would sit down and study it all at length.

By midnight her eyes were getting tired, and her attention span was dwindling, so she decided to call it a night. She would go to bed and sleep in late. After a shower and a walk around the complex she would start in again. She would of course go over everything that she did the night before just to make sure that she didn't overlook anything. There were so many pieces to this puzzle that she just wanted to make sure every aspect was thoroughly covered.

In the morning over coffee Marisa wondered how Wanda would respond if she knew that Mrs. Snow had a hand in all this. She wondered if Wanda or her boyfriend were capable of murder. Marisa thought about this a long time. She was a bit worried about her safety, but she knew she had to do this. It was as if she was on a mission to search and destroy Wanda.

Before her morning walk around the complex she looked for the little kitten that had adopted Kate as its mother. Because Kate was out of town this weekend Marisa was the designated caregiver for the kitten. The apartment management didn't allow pets, but what could they say if you didn't take the animals inside and only fed and watered them on the sly? So, today Marisa fed and took care of the kitten that Kate had named Rufus. Although it liked anyone that gave it attention, she could tell that it was looking for Kate. After she played with Rufus for a while she decided she needed to go for her walk and get busy with the paperwork she had brought home. It was already almost eleven o'clock.

When she got back to the apartment Rufus was sitting near Kate's door; she talked to him and held him a few more minutes. She told him she would check on him later, but Kate would be back in the morning. She just knew that he understood her as he purred when she put him down.

She finally showered and took the phone off the hook so she wouldn't be bothered by anyone. She knew that Dani would be calling later today to see if they could go out tonight; however, right now she didn't want to think about anything else but the task at hand. She wasn't even going to turn on the television. She was only going to listen to classical music today, so she wouldn't be tempted to sing along with the radio. It would be hard to stay focused if she was interrupted by phone calls, the radio, or the television.

She started today by looking at all the bank statements. None of the statements were anything to be real proud of for a woman of Wanda's age, but at least they all showed that there was money in the accounts. And, if all the accounts were combined and tallied together there was at least enough to pay off the restitution and probation fees. Of course she would first have to prove that Wanda managed and had access to all of these accounts. This would prove to be a daunting task.

She didn't have connections at any of the local banks; however, maybe the security representative from the bank that was victimized would be of some assistance. The victim in this case was a bank itself. Therefore, the security department had become involved, and they wanted Wanda to pay as much as anyone. Any money recovered from Wanda would be paid to the bank as restitution. She decided another phone call to the security representative assigned to this case would also need to be made on Monday. She would try to connect with Amanda at the Social Security Administration first. Whatever Amanda would divulge may give the bank representative more information to go on, provided he was willing to help in Marisa's quest for knowledge about Wanda.

She took notes about each of the accounts that were at three different banks, and each very far from one another. She would need to find out when the accounts were opened, and the last transaction dates, and what the current balance was, if any. She also wondered if anyone at the bank would remember the description of the account holder. She made a note to have more arrest photos of Wanda made. She also thought it might be nice to have the various ages of Wanda on hand. She would request the photos that were taken from each of her old arrests. Wanda may have changed her appearance over the years, so old photos may come in handy.

Next, Marisa decided to tackle the last few pieces of paper in the box. These were unemployment benefit check stubs made out to Wanda and Cynthia. These stubs listed a city about three hours away. She knew that a person on unemployment had to go in to pick up the check, and prove that they were actively seeking employment in order to continue receiving benefits. Marisa now wondered if Cynthia really was a part of Wanda's game, or if Wanda was somehow using Cynthia's name to receive two checks. Somehow Marisa was going to have to contact Cynthia before this game was over. She may hold the key to a lot of information.

Marisa looked at the police reports to see if Cynthia's phone number or address was listed. To her surprise it was listed, so she took a chance and called it. She got an answering machine that sounded like a woman in her twenty's stating that she wasn't available. The machine then beeped and Marisa hung up. For some unknown reason she just knew that this was Cynthia's voice. This was a local number so that in itself proved that Cynthia should not be receiving unemployment benefit checks in another county so far away.

The afternoon had gone by quickly, and Marisa was tired of looking at all this paper. She replaced the receiver on the phone, and turned off the classical stuff. She switched on the radio, and went to check on Rufus. He was sleeping near Kate's door.   The phone rang as she closed the door. Dani was making her usual weekend call to set up the evening's plans. They decided to eat out then go to the sports bar not far from Marisa's apartment. Dani said she would be over in about two hours. She gathered up the stacks of papers with her notes on top of each stack. She then paper clipped each stack individually and put them back in the box. She put the box under her bed so it would be out of her way, and out of Dani's reach. Marisa knew that she couldn't let Dani in on all that she was doing. Dani could sometimes ask too many questions and Marisa didn't want to drag anybody else in at this point. Marisa knew that the only people that needed to know anything about this would be Charles, and Tom.

    She decided she was going to have some fun tonight and she wasn't even going to think about work. She knew that Dani always had work on her mind too, but tonight it was going to be different for both of them. They always had a good time when they were together, but they always talked about work, the people that they worked with or recent incidents involving something work related. Tonight Marisa just wanted to be free from those thoughts. She would inform Dani of her agenda before the night got underway. Maybe they would meet some nice guys and have a good time getting to know them out on the dance floor or over a few beers. She knew Dani wouldn't have a problem with that.

    As she continued to get ready her mother called and asked if she had remembered to take care of Rufus. Since her parents no longer had any animals and they didn't yet have grandchildren they had started to ask about Rufus like he was part of the family. Marisa told her that she had fed him twice and played with him several times, but that he seemed content to wait for Kate at her doorstep. The other tenants acted like he was invisible, but only because they knew that Kate and Marisa had adopted him. No one would complain, because they were making sure he didn't make a mess in the common areas.

Dani arrived right on time. The first thing Marisa said was, "Okay girlfriend, tonight is just for fun. No talk of work, co-workers, or anything work related. I'm tired of all work and no play. Tonight we are party girls."

"Sounds good to me, but what brought about this change?" Dani asked.

"I've been working too hard all week, and I brought home some files to work on for next week. I'm tired of having no life. So, tonight we're gonna party, and have a great time! So speak now or forever hold your peace if you have anything work related to talk about. Once we leave this apartment we will pretend that we don't even have jobs."

"Well, okay, but the only thing I've been thinking about lately is you and Elliot. He just seems so alone now. He isn't the same as he was before."

Marisa said, "There is no "me and Elliot". He made a choice, I made a choice, and it's over. I have to get over it, I can't keep thinking about him and you shouldn't either. I'm a big girl and there are plenty of fish in the sea. And, tonight I'm goin' fishing!"

Both of them laughed at that remark, and Dani asked, "Can I be your first mate on that fishing expedition?" They were going to have a great time tonight.

They had a nice dinner at a local seafood restaurant just to make sure they were on a fishing expedition, but both were anxious to get 'out on the town'. After paying the bill they both went into the restroom to check their look in the mirror. Satisfied with what they saw they were on their way. They headed out to a sports bar frequented by Dani. Although Marisa wasn't much of a sports fan, Dani knew her stuff. She could talk about any sport and she really knew what she was talking about. Marisa, however, was just there for the scenery. A sports bar always had a lot of male clientele. They decided to grab a table in the middle of the place. This way they could see all around them, and more importantly, everyone could see them.

They ordered drinks when the waitress came by, and watched the action at the nearby dartboard. Tight jeans and cowboy boots were abundant. They both liked the scenery tonight, and a really good band was scheduled to start in about an hour. Marisa was having a good time but she felt uneasy for some unknown reason. She didn't say anything about her feelings to Dani because that would just start a conversation about work. She decided she was just not used to having so much fun without thinking about work, so she let it go.

A short time later two younger men approached the table and asked them both to dance. Even though these guys were too young for either of them to be interested in, it would be fun to get out on the dance floor. They danced a few dances and went back to the table. They told their dance partners that maybe they would catch up to them later, but they just wanted to finish their drinks and talk. Dani was smitten with her young man, but when they were dancing she learned he was barely the legal drinking age. She decided she needed someone just a little older to keep her company.

Marisa could feel someone watching her, as she glanced around the room. It was dark, very crowded and full of smoke, so she couldn't see everyone. She didn't notice anyone in particular watching her, so she didn't give it much more thought at the moment.

"What's the matter Marisa? You seem preoccupied."

"Oh, nothing, I'm just checking it out. Looking to see if we might meet any of the other unattached males."

A few minutes later the waitress brought over a refill for Marisa. As Marisa started to say she hadn't ordered another drink, the waitress informed her a man sitting in the booth by the back corner sent it over. However, when Marisa looked in that direction, there were only two girls sitting there together.

The waitress glanced around and said, "Hmm, well he was there just a minute ago, and now I can't see him. Well enjoy it anyway, he already paid for it."

Dani said, "Wow, that's odd. Maybe he went to the restroom to check himself out before he comes over and asks you to dance."

Marisa thought to herself that she knew now that he was the one watching her earlier. She wondered who he was and what he wanted. After about twenty minutes and no one approached them Marisa suggested that they go to another bar. Dani agreed but still found it odd that someone would send a drink over but then would not come over to talk. Marisa didn't let on that she felt uncomfortable in there tonight.

They went out to the parking lot and Marisa was more cautious than usual. She wondered if he was waiting for them in the lot, or if he was going to follow them to the next place. She didn't say anything to Dani about her concerns. They went to the bar where Marisa used to work; she still knew several people there and if anyone sent her a drink she would be able to find out about them. Tonight this bar was full. They had recently put in a karaoke machine and the bar was turning into the new place to be seen and heard. Although neither of them wanted to try their hand at singing along with some of their favorite bands they did have a good time listening to others try. Some of them were very good, while others sounded like wounded animals. They laughed at some, sang along with others and just had a good time tonight. Marisa excused herself from the table and went to talk to the bartender. They had been friends a long time now, and he knew all the regulars.

"Hey man, whatcha' know Chad? I haven't been in here in a while. This place is really hopping."

"Yeah Marisa, you wanna come back? The girls have been making some killer tips since that machine went in. Of course we have a lot more new people coming in now, but maybe this machine will put us back in front again."

"No babe, not me. I have a job, and although I don't make killer tips, I do sometimes get to work with killers. I was just wondering how you were doing. My friend and I just stopped in to have a few and see if there any nice looking guys in here."

"Dear, I'm the best looking guy in this place, but I'm busy right now."

"Well I know you are, but that's always been our problem, you were always too busy for me," Marisa said jokingly. "Hey, I better get back to my table, but I just wanted to say hello."

"Well dear, maybe when I get off work and if you're still here we can have some fun. But with the outfit you're wearing I think someone will beat me to you. Have fun and come back soon, we don't see enough of you anymore."

Marisa smiled as she went back to the table. He always knew how to talk to the ladies. Dani told her that she had missed some really good-looking guys at the microphone. Marisa just smiled. This place had always made her feel good. The people were nice, everyone that worked here got along well, and she had made some good money here. And, the hours suited her just fine. She could sleep in late, go in to work in the evening and stay up to the wee hours of the morning. She only left this job because of getting the job in probation. She was the only one that worked at the bar that was already out of school with a college degree and not putting it to good use. She felt guilty working at the bar after she graduated. Her parents had paid a lot of money to see that she went to a good school, but she was making more money at the bar than she did working in a professional office. Her parents were happy about her decision to leave the bar scene and getting a "real job" as they so often called it. Now all they ever said was that they wished she could find another job because this one was too dangerous. If they only knew the half of it she often thought.

Before the night was over the bartender had coaxed a few of the waitresses, along with Marisa and Dani, to sing as a group at the karaoke machine. They laughed through most of the songs, but they sure had a lot of fun. By the time they sang, most of the regular bar patrons were the only ones left, so Marisa didn't feel too embarrassed. Finally, it was almost closing time and Marisa didn't want to have to explain to the bartender why she wasn't going home with him tonight. She and Dani decided to slip out without saying goodbye to him before he had a chance to ask them back to his place, or invite himself over to Marisa's. Of course Dani said she wouldn't mind having him share their evening, but Marisa kept telling her he had shared his evenings with too many women to ever think about dating him.

"You know Marisa, sometimes you just have to take a little risk."

"Geez Dani. Do you realize that taking a little risk in this day and age could get you killed? Frankly, I'm not willing to die for a good piece of ass."

Although Dani was not promiscuous, she had had her share of men, but it had been awhile since she had been with anyone. "I don't know how you can be so strong willed when it comes to sex, and so many other things."

Marisa just shrugged her shoulders and said, "Hey I'll be the first one to say that sex is wonderful with the right person, but I'm not going to give into the feelings and catch some horrid disease just for a brief period of pleasure."

When they got back to the apartment Rufus was nowhere in sight. After Dani left, Marisa put out a small dish of food, and went to bed. Rufus was not her responsibility and she wasn't going to go chasing around the complex in the dark just to bring him back to Kate's doorstep. He knew the way and he wandered around all day without Kate worrying about him. If he wasn't back by the time she woke up she would go look for him, but now she was going to bed.

Marisa finally pulled herself out of bed at noon. She could hear Rufus meowing outside her front door. She went outside and brought him in to cuddle for a few minutes. She didn't want to admit it but she was getting attached to him too. He purred and cleaned himself while she rubbed his ears and the top of his head. He had eaten all the food she had put out last night, so he must be hungry now. She wondered where he was when she got in this morning. He was probably out chasing mice or staying at some other person's doorstep. Finally she put him out with a new dish of food and water. He ate like he was ravenous. Marisa switched on the television and ate a bowl of cereal.

After sitting there for a while she decided to get up and shower and get back to the grind of figuring out Wanda's schemes. She wanted to go over her notes, making a list of questions to ask the people she would be calling tomorrow. She also made a chronological list of people she planned to call. Hopefully in doing this she would begin compiling the information that the next person would need in their search of records and information. She knew that whatever she found may or may not be used when she went back to court in a few weeks, but she didn't want to leave any stone unturned. She also wanted to compile as much information about Wanda as was humanly possible so the next time she got arrested it would be available to whomever needed it. Marisa knew that Wanda had been a crook too long to stop now and go straight.

When Marisa first started this job, an older, more seasoned probation officer had told her that sometimes criminals decided that they were just too old for the crimes and the jail scene, and decided to go straight. For some reason Marisa didn't see this happening with Wanda. If anything, Marisa believed that Wanda would just move out of state and start her scheming over again with another new identity.

Marisa's list of questions and people to call was very detailed. Although she didn't really have that many people to call, she did have so many questions to ask. She knew this was going to take a lot of time, so she would need to talk to Charles about how to handle her caseload for the next few days. He would probably tell her to see her clients first, and do this last. Perhaps she could go in early and try to reschedule some of her people for next week. This would make next week more difficult, but the payoff would be worth it if she could prove Wanda was still up to no good.

Kate got in late in the afternoon. She stopped in to tell Marisa she was home, but wanted to unpack before she told her sister all about her weekend. This gave Marisa a chance to put all of the paperwork away, so Kate wouldn't ask too many questions. Kate returned with Rufus in her arms just as Marisa was putting the box in her bedroom. Marisa told her that Rufus was a good kitty, and she had even brought him in a few times over the weekend to let him know he was still loved.

Kate and Marisa talked a long while about how wonderful Kate's weekend of shopping in Chicago had been. Kate had met some friends there and they spent the weekend shopping, sightseeing, and just generally catching up on old gossip. Most of these girls were friends from high school that had gone away to college. Kate was the only one of the group to remain in town to study. It was way past dinner, so they decided to order take-out from the Chinese place down the street. When they went out to the parking lot a car was pulling out with its lights off. As she started to get in the car, Marisa noticed a slip of paper under her wiper blade. She pulled it out and looked at it, but tried to remain calm. It said:
BE CAREFUL WHAT YOU LOOK FOR YOU COULD GET HURT!

Kate grabbed the paper from her and with a startled expression said, "What is this about? What have you been up to this weekend? Does this have anything to do with work?"

Marisa just laughed and said it was probably just Dani playing a prank on her. Then she explained that they had gone out last night and when they got back Rufus was missing. Although Marisa knew this was partially true, she knew that Dani would never do anything like this. Marisa then wondered if the car leaving the lot without its lights on just a minute ago had anything to do with the note. If all this was tied together, the drink last night, and now the note, what did it mean? How did anyone know she was researching Wanda now? Had someone been following her all along and just speculated that the big box she was bringing home was about Wanda? She would have to be more careful.

The girls ate and talked late into the night, but finally Marisa told Kate she had to leave because she had to get up early in the morning and go to work. Kate obliged, and said she might let Rufus come in tonight. She said she had been thinking that she might just start keeping him in all the time. Marisa warned her that she could get evicted for having an indoor pet. And more importantly, she would have to move home with her parents if she gets evicted because management would never let her move in with Marisa with the cat.

Kate turned up her nose and said, "Whose side are you on anyhow?"

"Well little sis, I'm on your side of course, but I'm just playing devil's advocate with the possibilities."

Kate said she would definitely have to think about this wrinkle in her plan as she went out the door to her apartment. Marisa double locked the door and then went to check all of the windows and patio door locks. Afterwards she shut off all the lights in the apartment and went to the patio door and watched the parking lot. She wondered who had left this note, and if they planned to come back to visit tonight. She was becoming a little frightened, but she would not be intimidated into stopping what someone should have done a long time ago: putting a stop to Wanda Newton's criminal behavior.

The first thing Marisa did when she got to work was to make duplicate copies of everything in the box. She had gotten to work about forty-five minutes early, so no one else was there yet. She also made copies of her notes and planned questions for the calls she would make today. She wasn't quite sure why she was doing this, but something inside her told her to. She would take this information to the bank and put it in the safe deposit box on her lunch hour today. She had made two sets of the same information. She knew that one day she may need to give the information to someone else, and she didn't want anything mysteriously happening to it.

Next, she got out her appointment calendar and started pulling files of her appointments for the day. She would start with the morning appointments and try to catch them before they started trickling in. Within minutes of her picking up the phone the other officers and clerical staff started getting to work. She wasn't usually so perky in the morning, but she was on a mission now. She was able to contact all but three of her clients. She rescheduled the others for the next two weeks, spacing them out so she wouldn't be so burdened next week. The three that she didn't get in touch with would be able to just fill out report slips and receive new appointments unless they really needed to talk to her. She decided to wait until later in the day to call all the people for tomorrow's appointments. It would really depend on how much she accomplished today before she would know what her tomorrow would look like.

After about an hour on the phone she had cleared her calendar for the day and checked her voice-mail, and mailbox. She then informed the front desk staff not to put any calls through to her unless it was an emergency. Marisa then stopped by Dani's office and told her she was going to be tied up most of the day, and at lunch she had some errands to run. Dani asked if she could tag along at lunch because she was sick of the standard lunch fare. Marisa told her that she had to stop by the bank and put some papers in her lock box, but that it would be fun to go out rather than eating downtown today. Both had busy days, so they cut their conversation short and agreed to talk more at lunch.

Marisa went back to her office and closed the door. Her first call was to the security division of the bank. She identified herself as the probation officer for Wanda Newton, and asked to speak to whomever was handling the Wanda Newton fraud case. She was told the representative on that account was William Danielson, and he had just arrived so she would need to hold for a minute or two. Finally, Mr. Danielson picked up and asked her if she had good news to report. She laughed and said she only wished she could do that, but she actually was stumped and wondered if he could be of any assistance to her.

"Mr. Danielson some things in this case just don't add up, and as you are aware I have filed a violation against the defendant in this case. I don't know anyone at the area banks aside from you, and I don't really even know you, but I have heard of your reputation."

"Well first Ms. Spencer let's cut the formality, please call me Bill. Why don't you tell me the problem and I'll see if I can help you or know of someone that can."

"Ok Bill, please call me Marisa. Okay, here goes. You may need to take notes because this is all very confusing."

Marisa didn't tell him every sordid detail, but the essentials were covered. He didn't ask many questions, and he certainly didn't want to know how she had obtained the information with the other bank accounts.

"Well Marisa this is a delicate issue. You have information about someone that may have been illegally obtained; however, she committed an illegal act and owes a lot of money to my employer. I do know the other security people at the banks you mentioned, and I'm sure they would give me the information. It wouldn't necessarily be illegal for them to give it to me, perhaps unethical, but I know they wouldn't give that information to someone outside the banking system. How about if you provide me the pertinent information only? I need names on accounts, account numbers, statement dates, address of account holder, and the social security numbers on each account. I'll see what I can come up with and get back to you hopefully later today?"

"Bill that would be excellent, but I don't want to put your job in any jeopardy."

"Nonsense! I'm trying to protect my bank, don't you worry about my job."

"Well if you're sure you don't mind I'll give you whatever you need. Just remember, don't talk with anyone else about this but me. No one else from here should be calling you, but just in case, don't divulge any information to anyone, I don't know who to trust at this point."

"No problem Marisa, now give me your direct number and give me the information on each account."

Marisa gave him all the details, and he promised to get back to her as soon as he knew anything. Before he hung up he told her that he hoped that there was money in these accounts that the bank could attach and hold as payment for restitution. He promised not to do anything without telling her first, however. Marisa felt a great deal of relief with this part of her investigation. She knew that Bill would know exactly what questions to ask, because she didn't have a clue. She also knew that he was right about the bank probably not giving her any information about any account holder without a warrant. After this phone call she figured the rest would be much easier.

She got out her notes about Wanda's beginnings in the small town almost two hundred miles away. She knew she would need to talk to someone in the town hall, so she concocted a story about why she was calling. She settled on the story that she was working on a family tree, and she had run into a dead end that led to their town. She decided that she would be one of Henry's long lost relatives by marriage. This way, if she happened to get someone that really liked Wanda she wouldn't give herself away right off the bat. She called directory assistance and requested the number for the town hall in Long Pine. The operator gave her the number and connected her directly to the general offices in that building. Marisa got her notes ready and was quite hopeful that this would not be a futile effort.

A younger woman answered the phone with the standard greeting of "City Hall, this is Jenny, how can I help you?"

"Hi, my name is Elise Morgan," she lied. Marisa continued," and I'm not quite sure what department I need, but I would like to speak to the most knowledgeable town historian that is employed there. Do you have anyone there that might be of assistance?"

Jenny giggled and said that there were a few older women that worked in Vital Records, and she could connect directly or give the extension. Marisa asked for the extension but also that she be directly connected. Marisa was thankful now for Jenny.

"Vital Records, this is Bernice."

"Hi Bernice, this is Elise Morgan. I'm working on a family tree, or genealogical record to be more precise, and I have run into a dead end that leads to your town. Do you think there is anyone there, maybe a knowledgeable town historian so to speak, that might be willing to answer a few questions?"

"Sure honey, hold on I'll get Miss Henrietta, hold please."

A few moments later Bernice came back to the phone and said that Miss Henrietta knows everyone past and present that ever graced Long Pine. Henrietta finally came to the phone and Marisa restated her purpose in calling.

Henrietta said, "This is Miss Henshaw, but everyone calls me Miss Henrietta. I've lived my whole life in Long Pine, and I have worked in Vital Records for over forty years. I'm sure I can help you if the person you are looking for ever lived or conducted any business here."

Marisa thought Henrietta sounded a bit like a no nonsense schoolmarm, yet gossipy, but this was exactly the kind of person that would have what she was looking for.

"Well Miss Henrietta the person I'm researching was actually married to the person I am doing the family tree on. I just can't seem to find out anymore information on them so I decided to try going farther back like high school and the early part of their married life. From what

I have already gathered it seems that I may not be able to find out the school information because other family members have said it burnt down a very long time ago."

Miss Henrietta interrupted Marisa and said, "Well the old school did burn, but they were going to consolidate with the adjoining town anyway so all the records had already been moved. The new school is called Pine Wood Consolidated High School. She laughed, "Listen to me, the new school, that school is nearly thirty years old now. Why don't you give my friend a call over there? Her name is Mrs. White and she is in charge of the school records and such. I'm sure she would be happy to help." She then gave Marisa the phone number.

Marisa indicated that would be most helpful, but her inquiry has become most difficult because this person has used some different names and no one in the family really knows much about her.

"Do you think I could give you some of the names I have run across in connection with her and you could see if any of them ring a bell?"

"Honey, like I said, if she spent any time here at all I will know her, or something about her. Go ahead and give me the names."

"Okay, well I think her real name is Velma Higgins or Barbara Harris, but the last anyone heard she was going by something else. Do either of those ring a bell Miss Henrietta?"

"Well dear there was a Velma Harris and a Barbara Higgins. They were cousins or something.

The story goes that Velma Harris left town after having a bastard child, a daughter, and her husband had died. Velma Harris was married to Henry Reynolds. The poor man died in the war. It was probably her that really killed his soul though."

Marisa was writing furiously. It would seem then that Wanda had just switched around some family names. And, this story was getting too interesting to focus on anything but the story pouring forth, and Marisa certainly didn't want to miss any details. She would ask questions later. Miss Henrietta asked if she wanted to know any more of this sordid story, and Marisa told her that it might bring something else out, so she should please continue. She could tell too that Miss Henrietta liked the attention and gratitude she was now receiving. Miss Henrietta continued weaving this interesting story with colorful details as Marisa listened with rapt attention.

She stated, "It seems Velma married Henry right out of high school when she was probably about 18 years old. I could look it up, but I am pretty sure it was in 1967. The war was going then you know. Well about a year later Henry was shipped overseas to Viet Nam. Soon after Henry left Velma was out messing around in the bars and all. She got pregnant, but no one ever knew who the father was. She tried to pretend that it belonged to Henry, but he had been gone some time before she came up pregnant. Some say she was working as a prostitute because she never worked while they were married and she didn't work after he left. But, she was able to keep the place they lived in and didn't appear to fall on hard times like some of the other women here in town. And, then that bastard child was born and she never told anyone the real father's identity. Well, she had that baby while he was in Viet Nam."

Miss Henrietta went on, "Everyone believed he knew about the baby although he never saw her. Velma didn't write to him or anything while he was gone, but people were sure he knew about that child and the way his wife was acting. The Reynolds family was humiliated by what she had done to Henry and their family name. They had nothing to do with Velma after she got pregnant. Then Henry died and she came to the family home with that bastard child. Velma just left her there. They did take good care of that baby for about four years and didn't hear anything of Velma. They wanted a grandchild desperately, and that baby needed a family. Then one day Velma just came back to town and took the baby away. The family then grieved again. First they lost their only son to the war, and then the grandchild they had so desperately wanted taken away by that awful woman. Their daughter, Bess, went away to college, and then Mr. Reynolds died shortly thereafter. Mrs. Reynolds stayed in town awhile. She finally moved out west to be near Bess, and she got remarried about three years after that. Ain't no one left here in town related to the Reynolds family except me now. So, dear I don't know who you are really trying to research, but I know it ain't poor Henry. You see Henry was my nephew, and I don't know any Elise Morgan."

Marisa was stunned. She was amazed at the story she had just heard. But, she was bewildered by the fact that this woman went on and told her the family saga knowing full well that she wasn't who she had told her she was. Finally Marisa apologized for lying to her.

"Miss Henshaw please forgive me. I'm a probation officer investigating a woman purporting to be Wanda Newton. I believe from the information I have already found that she is in fact Velma Harris. I couldn't risk telling you what I was after in case you or any people there were still friends with her. Please accept my apologies."

"Well dear, you now know the family story that we are not too pleased to share, but when you said you were researching Henry, the poor man, I knew it had to be something bad with his wife or that bastard child. Can you at least tell me that?"

"Miss Henshaw, I believe that Wanda, or Velma, is involved in a lot of criminal activity, and her daughter really appears to have no use for her. Her daughter's name is Cynthia Reynolds and seems quite appalled by her mother's actions."

"Well dear I will tell you again, I am Miss Henrietta to all that know me. And, maybe that girl got some of the Reynolds values in the short time she was with them. Maybe though she can just see what a piece of work her mother is, and doesn't want to be associated with that. Dear I must get back to work, but if I can help you again, please call me. And by the way what is your name again?"

"I'm sorry Miss Henrietta for lying to you earlier, but I'm going to do everything within my control to put Velma behind bars. My name is Marisa Spencer. Maybe someday you can be helpful to Cynthia like you were to me. You know she probably has no other family. Thank you again for your information and your time."

Marisa could not believe the luck she was having today. One day, she thought, someone should write a book about this woman. Marisa was so excited when she got off the phone she didn't even stop to check her voice-mail. She went right to Dani's office and said they could leave for the bank and lunch whenever she was ready. She really wanted to share this information with someone, but doing that could compromise her investigation. She would just have to settle for talking to Rufus when no one else was around. She grabbed the large bulky papers that she was putting in the lock box, and headed out the back door with Dani.

Dani asked what she was putting in the bank box, but Marisa couldn't risk telling her the truth. She told her that her parents had rental properties and it was deeds and leases. Because it was in her name too, she put them in her lock box instead of keeping it at home. Dani bought this story without question. She knew that the Spencer's did have rental properties. Of course she always wondered why the girls didn't rent from them, but she never wanted to be intrusive and ask.

After running in and out of the bank quickly they headed over to a little storefront diner. The food was good and the atmosphere was quaint. The small talk stemmed around their night on the town and of doing that again. Both of them started reminiscing about Ian too. He loved to go out on the town with them before he got sick.

They both loved Ian, he was a good friend to both, but he was Marisa's best friend and soul mate. Everyone speculated that if he hadn't been married he and Marisa would have been together. Even though he was in a loveless and unhappy marriage, neither of them would cross that line and commit adultery. Some people assumed that they were having an affair, but they both knew the truth and that was all that mattered to either one of them. Marisa had never been a person to care what others thought about her. She knew when she went to bed at night and said her prayers that she had always tried to do the right thing and been the best person that she could be. Dani and Marisa laughed about some of the pranks he had pulled, and how alike he and Marisa were. Before either of them got too melancholy they changed the subject back to work and decided they better get back while they both still had jobs.

When Marisa got back she decided to go on and try to reschedule her clients on tomorrow's calendar. She didn't have that many people scheduled. However, it would be less hectic if she could just reschedule those that didn't need to be seen and leave a report slip and appointment date for those that really needed to come in. Most clients didn't mind missing an appointment to talk with their officer, even though it was sometimes a hassle to find transportation to the office. These calls took about another hour, and Marisa still had not checked her voice-mail. One of the front desk receptionists came back to Marisa's office with an urgent message "*to call Bill at the bank immediately*". Marisa thanked her and dialed the number. When she identified herself to the secretary she was immediately connected to Bill's cell phone.

"Marisa why haven't you gotten back with me? I have called your voice-mail several times today. You aren't going to believe where I'm going as we speak."

"Bill, you aren't going to believe all that I learned either. I don't think her name is really Wanda Newton, but then you probably already knew that."

"Sweetheart I told you I wouldn't do anything to those accounts without telling you first, well, I tried to tell you. I hope that counts."

"Bill, what have you done?"

"It's okay Marisa. What I'm doing is completely legal. I'm just having the account frozen so she cannot access any of the money. But you should know that there is enough money in one account that she could pay off all that she owes to my bank and her fees to the court."

"Bill, this could really cause me some problems. I want the money repaid to your employer too, but I think we need to slow down and let the Judge in on this new information."

"Look Marisa, that money is owed to our bank. It is under Wanda's control and it isn't her money. We will attach that money and she won't get away with any more of it. I'm not out to hurt you or your case, but I want back what is rightfully due my employer. Capisce?"

Marisa didn't know what else to say. She told Bill she needed to get back with him, but she first needed to speak with her supervisor. "Okay, ciao babe."

Now she was being forced to divulge to Charles some of what she had learned and what she had been doing for the past few days. She contemplated how he might respond, but she knew that she had to involve him now. She would not tell him everything she had uncovered, or how she had obtained the papers she got from Mrs. Snow. She rang his office and asked him if he was terribly busy. He told her had a little while before he needed to be in a meeting, and she could talk to him in his office while he prepared his files. Marisa said she would be right there. She grabbed Wanda's file and the notes she had written about the bank statements, and ran to his office.

"Charles, I've been working on this Newton file since I got it, as you are aware. And, as you also know I just don't think we have all the information that we need on this person. She is in violation status currently, and I've been turning over some rocks to try to find out more about her. Well, her landlord stumbled on some papers and gave me a call. Apparently her landlord doesn't trust her either, and must have been snooping around when Wanda was away. This woman, Mrs. Snow, has met me on just two occasions and I guess she figured that she should call me and share what she found."

Charles had stopped looking through the papers on his desk and was giving Marisa a disapproving look. He said, "Marisa, you cannot expect landlords and anyone else you might run into to do your dirty work. You know that what she has done is an invasion of privacy. There are laws against that kind of stuff and I know you are aware of them. Truly, I don't think the Judge or any decent attorney will allow this stuff in as admissible evidence at the next hearing, or any hearing in the future."

Before he could finish lecturing Marisa stated, "Look, I didn't ask her do anything. I didn't even hint at it. But what am I supposed to do, when something incriminating is dropped in my lap, look the other way? I know the law, and I also know that Wanda is continuing to break the law and thumb her nose at the legal system. I will do whatever I have to do to make people see what a threat she is to the community. She knows I am onto her, and after today I'm sure that things are going to heat up between us. But I will not give in, and I will not be intimidated by her or her weirdo friends!"

"Marisa has something happened that you have not shared with me? If something is going on outside this office and it involves a threat to your safety I need to know."

"Look, I'm a big girl. I can handle myself, and I don't want any office involvement. I'm just telling you that something has happened that I cannot control, and I think you should be aware of that. Perhaps you can help me with that aspect of this case."

"What has happened Marisa; tell me everything, and I'll see what we can do."

Marisa didn't fully trust what he was saying, and she certainly wasn't going to tell him everything. She would share what had happened with the bank accounts only.

"Okay. I was given a few old bank statements that the landlord found in Wanda's room. Well, I didn't know what to make of them. I mean, they were several months old, but they did have account balances. In fact, when I added them all together it was enough to pay off the restitution and our fees. I didn't have a clue where to start because I knew that any bank would not give out account holder information without so much as a warrant. So, I called the victimized bank and asked to talk to someone in the security department. I was told William Danielson was taking care of this case."

Exasperated that no one seemed to understand what she was doing and why, Marisa continued, "I spoke to him and asked where I should begin, and what questions I should ask. He then offered to take over that task for me. He said that they would definitely not divulge that information to me, but they might to him. He also said that it was in the scope of his duties. I had no problem with that, so I gave him the information on the statements that I had. He told me he would only inquire, but he wouldn't do anything without telling me first. That's it. Well, that was it until I was busy doing other things today and didn't check my voice-mail. I finally received an emergency phone call from him while he was en route to one of the banks in question. He said he had good news to report, and then he said he had the accounts frozen. I was dumbfounded by what he has done. I can't stop him. What he has done is completely legal he assures me. But apparently he found more money than I did. He was just so excited. I tried to tell him that we needed to speak to the Judge, but he says he is taking care of his bank. So, now what do I do?"

"Well first I think you better call the D.A. that prosecuted this case, and see if there is anything that we should be doing. I mean, we can't stop what he has already done. Perhaps we could have the account unfrozen, but who knows if she knows this has happened by now. And again, if anything or anyone has threatened you or your safety I need to know about it."

"Thanks for listening Charles and I'll keep you posted. I have a few calls to make now."

She was out the door before he could say anymore, and he had about one minute before he was late to the meeting with the Chief Probation Officer. Sometimes she did drive him crazy, but she was an excellent officer.

Marisa did as Charles said and called Tom. He had prosecuted the case against Wanda and was still working with Marisa on the violations. Although he didn't really care that the accounts had been frozen, he was a little upset that it was done without his knowledge. He was also wary about how they would need to proceed in order to protect Mrs. Snow, and not be sued or charged with invasion of privacy. He knew they really needed to let the Judge in on this, but he didn't want to taint his opinion on this case. He knew that Judge Taylor was a 'by-the-book' Judge, and wouldn't be happy about how this new information was obtained. Tom told her that he was glad that the victim was potentially going to get their money back, but he wasn't sure this was the route he would have taken. He told Marisa to stay by the phone because he would call her right back.

Tom then called Judge Taylor's secretary and asked if he and Marisa could stop in and talk a few minutes. She told him to come on down that the Judge was just reading some briefs and watching television. Tom called Marisa back and told her to meet him in Judge Taylor's chambers, and to bring the file with her. Marisa scooped up the file and headed out the door. As she ran out of the office she told the receptionist that if anyone was looking for her she would be in Judge Taylor's court.

Just as Marisa was entering the court office she spotted Elliot. He winked at her and started to approach her. "Elliot. Hi. I can't talk right now, I have a meeting with the Judge."

"Darlin' it has been so long since we talked. How about if I wait for you?" Marisa could hardly resist his charm, but she knew that she wasn't ready to spend any time with him today.

"Elliot I have no idea how long I'll be, and I'm really swamped today. How about I give you a call soon and we can chat?"

"Well I guess that will have to do won't it? Whatever you say Marisa, but I won't be holding my breath while waiting on that phone call."

Chapter Four

Marisa had fantasized about Elliot for many years, but she never attempted anything more than a little flirtation because he was married. When he separated from his wife, Marisa still kept her distance. He had a few brief affairs with clerks and a few court reporters, but nothing of any substance. When he finally asked Marisa out, she was stunned. She knew part of the attraction was the thrill of the chase, so she didn't let herself go for quite some time, but he continued to pursue her.

Their relationship started slowly, a real courtship, but after a month Marisa knew she had to have him in her bed. Of course, he didn't put up a fight. She was flattered he had waited this long. When they finally made love, it was as she had hoped her first time with him would be. Elliot was romantic, gentle and very passionate. They held each other all-night and made love again when the sun came up. Both called in sick to work that morning and stayed in bed all afternoon. They talked of their feelings for each other, but neither of them said the word love. She knew he still wasn't over his wife, and she was certain she couldn't tell him she loved him until she knew he was in love with her. Marisa was convinced she could win his love; she just wasn't sure how.

Over the next few weeks Marisa spoke of wanting to settle down eventually and have children. He said he had already done those things; how could he be expected to start over at his age. Elliot Green was 41 years old, and had already seen the world. Elliot was always very honest with Marisa. And, although he could feel himself starting to fall in love with her, he never told her. The only problem with his love for Marisa was that he thought he still loved his wife.

Their love affair lasted nearly eight months and the night he told her he was going back to his wife Marisa was devastated. She knew that is where he belonged, but she wondered what would happen to her. She was mad, too, because she knew it was her fault she felt this way. He had never told her he loved her. Just before he left, he turned to her and told her, "Darlin' you're so much like that girl that I married. I never intended to be a man that didn't love his wife, and fall in love with another woman. I also never intended to use you, but I'm afraid being with you has made me see that girl again that my wife used to be. She has my kids and they want me to come home."

Marisa was afraid to speak. Afraid that what she said might make him stay, but she would not be the home wrecker. She knew she should never have gotten involved with a married man. She stood there numb and scared.

"Marisa, please don't hate me. I left so I could find out what was missing in my marriage. Instead I found you. I love my kids, and I know that I can be a husband to her again." He walked toward her, and the door she held open. As he brushed away a tear from her cheek, he kissed her and told her he loved her.

She knew she had to stay strong and not break down in front of him, but she really needed a shoulder to cry on now. After he gathered up his things and left, she called Dani. Dani, too, was crying after Marisa told her about the good-bye scene. Marisa wondered how people at work would react, hell she wondered how she would react when they were in court together. Dani said the best way for Marisa to behave at work was to act as if nothing had happened. Be professional, not emotional. Well, for about a month she did just that and no one ever questioned her about the break-up.

Elliot knew that their break-up was tough on her. It had been tough on him too; this was something she probably didn't even realize. He did still have feelings for her. He loved her still. He wished he could tell her that it was her face he saw now when he was making love to his wife. Of course she would then wonder what he was doing with his wife instead of her. And his wife would probably be wondering the same thing. He was miserable. He had hurt all the people that had meant the most to him, and he didn't know how to fix it. His wife seemed to be happy now, but he still didn't trust her completely; he knew she didn't trust him either. He would just have to get on with things and quit pining away for Marisa. He had made his choice, now he just needed to like it.

Marisa entered Judge Taylor's chambers and Tom was already there. She could hear that they were not discussing the Newton case. As soon as the Judge saw her he said, "Well I bet you've got some trouble brewing if both of you need to see me. Let me guess which case it is? Hmm, maybe Wanda Newton?"

"Yes sir. We have some problems here and it may have to be addressed in Court," Tom stated.

"Well aren't we due back in court in a few weeks for that compliance hearing anyhow? Can't we just take care of it then? By the way Marisa, is she doing any better?"

"Well Your Honor I'll be filing an additional violation with the court soon because now she has stopped reporting altogether. But, on the other issue I think I'll let Tom tell you what has happened."

"Well sir, it appears that some little bird that wishes to remain anonymous has dropped some papers in

Marisa's lap. The little bird most likely illegally obtained those papers, so that is problem number one. The papers that they gave Marisa were bank statements. Secondly, in trying to find out all she could about Newton, Marisa contacted the bank and spoke to someone in the security division. That person then made some calls to the banks in question and did his own research and in the meantime had the accounts frozen."

"Well now that is a dilemma isn't it? How much money did they freeze Marisa?"

"Sir I only know that on the old statements there was enough money to repay the restitution debt and the probation fees. I have no idea how much the account balances are now. I do know that there were three banks in question, and we believe that she had control over all of them."

"Well Tom, I don't think I want to hear anymore of this, but I'm sure that her public defender will be filing a motion with the court. Maybe not our court, but one of them in the building, to get those accounts back under her control. And, someone may have some explaining to do about illegally obtained evidence, or invasion of privacy. You need to tell the person in security to get their lawyers working if they aren't already. Have fun kids, I've got to get back to work. Could you turn the volume back up before you leave Tom?"

Tom and Marisa left the court, and went back to his office. She called Bill from there but he was still out. She confided to Tom that she was a little worried because Wanda's boyfriend had already threatened her.

"Marisa you need to be careful. Have you told anyone else about this? What was the threat?"

"Don't worry Tom, the Smith and Wesson family are regular visitors at my house. And, no I haven't discussed that with anyone else. Please keep this to yourself Tom. But, if anything happens, make sure you nail her ass to the wall!"

"I wish you would let us help you, she could be charged you know."

"I'll be fine. I'm not stupid, and I always watch my back." Marisa told him she would be in touch when she knew more, and she hurriedly left his office. She didn't want to talk anymore about her safety, nor did she want to run into Elliot again.

Once she got back to her office she decided she better check her voice-mail. There were four calls, all of them old, from Bill. He told her that he had really gotten more information than he had hoped for, and he was going over to each of the banks to have those accounts frozen. He also told her that he had obtained Wanda's latest arrest photo to take with him. Each bank had given him a basic description of the account holder, and it seemed to match Wanda. Each bank had different birthdates of the account holder, but they were within a year or so of each other. And, more importantly, each account holder had a signature on file. He was planning to take some documents that she had signed in court and compare them to the signature on file with the bank. Although this was a not a scientific or legally admissible way to compare handwriting samples it would be worth a try. She had several other phone calls from her mother, and a few clients that needed to reschedule appointments.

By the time she finished with this she had only about an hour left at work and she really needed to contact Amanda over at the Social Security Administration offices. She looked up the number in the telephone directory and dialed the number. While waiting for them to pick up, she said a little prayer. She prayed that Amanda would be willing to help her, and quick. Finally, the voice activated operator came on and gave a list of selections. Marisa stayed on the line waiting for a real operator because she didn't know Amanda's extension. A real voice came on the line and asked Marisa what she needed. Marisa told her that she needed to speak to Amanda McGregor, but she was not sure in which department or division she worked. The operator connected her without another word.

"Amanda McGregor's desk."

"Amanda, this is Marisa Spencer, from college. How are you?"

"Oh hello Marisa, long time, no speak. Well for a pregnant woman I'm doing just fine. How are you?

"Oh congratulations Amanda! When are you due and do you know what you are having?"

"Well I'm due with twins in about six weeks. We don't want to know the sex of the babies, but we're very excited. So, any changes with you?"

"Twins! Wow! Will you continue with that modeling career after that? Everything is pretty much the same with me since the last time we talked. I'm still single and working for Criminal Probation. Amanda I need to keep this call short so let me get right to the point. I don't want to take up too much of your time, but I could really use some help."

"Hmm, Marisa what on earth could I help you with?"

"Well to be quite honest I don't know if you can or will help me, but all you could say is no, so I thought I would give you a call. I hope you don't mind."

"Go on. I'm listening."

"Well I have this case and everyone thinks I'm nuts, but I know that this person is not who she says she is, and I know that she is still doing illegal stuff. I had some documents dropped in my lap by an anonymous donor, and it is quite incriminating to my probationer."

"Okay, so where do I come in?"

"Well, I have three different social security numbers and they are attached to two different names. I know it is probably highly unlikely that you would want to get involved. But I really need to hear that from you before I go about this another way which I haven't quite figured out yet."

"Well we could play a little guessing game I suppose. I won't give you any information directly, that would be unethical to say the least, and quite possibly I could lose my job if anyone ever found out."

"I understand completely. How about if I give you a number and see if it goes to a name that I have?"

"Sure, that might work, hold on a sec and let me get where I need to be on my computer." Marisa hoped that this would turn up some good information. "Okay Marisa, go ahead."

"Well the first number I have is 501-66-4212, and it's attached to Wanda Newton, but I believe that is a fictitious name."

"Well it is not assigned to that name. Do you have any other names that it could be?"

"How about Velma Harris or Velma Higgins?"

"Nope sorry, you want to try another name?"

"Sure. How about Barbara Higgins?"

"No, sorry again. Any other names?"

Marisa was stumped. These were the only names she had been able to dig up. Then she thought of something. "Wait, what about Velma Reynolds?"

"Bingo! You have a match."

"Can I try another number?"

"Sure, go ahead."

"Okay the next number I have is 506-52-6178, and it again is attached to Wanda Newton."

"Hmm, are you sure that's the correct number Marisa?"

"Hold on while I look. Yeah it is what is written down on the document I have."

"Well that number has never been issued, so I don't know why someone would want to use it. No one will be able to collect from that account until it is assigned."

"I don't think she was planning to collect from any of these accounts. Okay I have one other number, but it has a different name."

"Go on when you're ready."

"Okay the number is 413-16-8207, and the name is Barbara Harris."

"Well that is the wrong name. Give me those names again."

"Okay. Try Wanda Newton, or Velma Harris."

"Nope, not even close. Try again."

"Velma Higgins or Barbara Higgins?"

"Nope. Try again."

"Barbara Harris?"

"Nope. Remember the first name you hit on."

"Hmm, okay. Velma Reynolds?"

"No, but you are getting warmer. Hurry I have to go soon."

"Okay, how about Cynthia Reynolds?"

"No. Again."

Marisa couldn't figure this out. She had used every name she had run across. She had even transposed names, but this still wasn't it. Amanda had hinted that it was close to Velma Reynolds.

Quite exasperatingly she said, "Amanda I don't have any other names to give you. I know you can't give me more information and I'll just go with what I have."

"Marisa I can't give you anymore information, but think. You are so close. Look at the first name that hit, and think about it."

Marisa looked and looked at the name Velma Reynolds. Then in a questioning tone she said, "Henry Reynolds?"

"Bingo again! Marisa I have to go now, my supervisor is coming this way. I'm glad I was able to help you. I hope you're successful in whatever it is you're working on. Talk to you later." She hung up before Marisa could utter another word.

Marisa grabbed a small piece of paper and wrote, *write thank you note to Amanda send with box of diapers,* and stuck it on her calendar for tomorrow. Things were coming together. She just hoped she could put a stop to Wanda before she did any more damage.

It was getting late, but she decided to call Bill one more time before she left today. His secretary said he had left, but she connected Marisa to his cell phone and said that maybe he was still in his car. Bill answered on the first ring.

"Bill, it's Marisa. What did you find out?"

"Well sweetheart I froze all three accounts, and Ms. Newton, or whoever she is, already knows about it. Have you spoken to your supervisor about this turn of events?"

"Oh yes, and I've spoken to the D.A. and the Judge. I hope you have a good legal team at that bank where you work. The Judge says he fully expects for her to file charges against someone, namely me I suppose. I won't give up the source of those documents, and I hope you won't either."

"What source? Marisa calm down and don't get all worked up over this. She will have to prove in court that she is rightfully due that money, and then she will have to explain why she used bogus social security numbers and alias names on those accounts. She may be pissed off, but you know what they say. Look Marisa, I'm pulling into my driveway a happy man tonight. Take it easy. Everything will work out."

"Goodbye Bill, we'll talk again soon I'm sure." As she replaced the receiver she wondered if she would be pulling into her driveway a happy woman. For some reason she just didn't think so.

When Marisa left tonight she was very careful of every move she made. She really wanted to go by and see her parents, but if anyone was following her she didn't want them to know where they lived. She would just settle for going home and trying to relax. She kept looking in her rear view mirror, but it seemed that no one was following her. She had her gun near the top of her purse. When she pulled into the apartment parking lot she didn't find anything out of place. Marisa knew that Wanda had to know she was somehow involved in this and she figured that something would happen soon.

Marisa fixed herself a sandwich and a salad, but she didn't really feel much like eating. She tried to watch some television, but her mind was elsewhere tonight. Kate called and they talked about school and what they might do this weekend. Marisa heard Rufus in the background meowing and told her sister she better put him outside before management put her out. Finally, she said she was just drained and wanted to go to bed. She did have a headache, and she was tired of thinking about Wanda. She so much wanted to talk to someone else about this case, but she was too afraid what could happen if any of the information got leaked out. About ten o'clock she double-checked the locks on all the windows and doors, and went to her bedroom. In the darkness she looked out at the parking lot again. She watched the lot for any activity for about thirty minutes. When she was satisfied that no one was watching she went to bed.

About 4:30 in the morning the phone woke her from a sound sleep. Her heart was pounding. She hated calls in the middle of the night. Groggily she answered, "Hello. Who is this?"

A woman's voice she didn't recognize said, "You little bitch. I warned you not to mess with things. Now you're going to find out what can happen when you poke your nose in things that don't concern you. You have fucked with the wrong person!"

"Who is this, and what do you want?"

The next thing she heard was the receiver being slammed down on the other end of the line. Marisa jumped out of bed and ran to the window. She watched the lot for any movement. She sat up for about an hour, but nothing seemed amiss. She reached under the pillow. The gun was still there to protect her. She went back to bed, but all she did was toss and turn until her alarm went off about an hour and a half later.

She got up and looked out into the parking lot. Her car seemed fine. She looked outside from her peephole and saw nothing unusual. Rufus was not in his usual place, but then she remembered that Kate had taken him in last night. She decided to get ready for work, and act as if nothing had happened. After all, nothing had happened, she had just gotten a prank phone call. Today she needed to call the Unemployment office where those check stubs originated. She figured by now that Wanda was using her boyfriend's address as her permanent address, and collecting unemployment benefits there under her name and under her daughter's name. She hadn't quite decided how she was pulling this off, but she was certain to find out. She hurriedly ate some toast and grabbed a can of juice to drink on the way to work.

As she opened the door she saw what she thought was red paint on the floor of the common hallway. She stared at it for a minute and it registered that this was not paint. She started to step back into the apartment, and bumped into the door. As she felt the door behind her she realized something was different. She looked at the door, and shrieked at the top of her lungs. Hanging from the doorknocker was Rufus. The rope was tight around his neck.

Someone quite perverse had skinned the cat and broken all his limbs. His tail had been severed and was lying on the floor. Blood was everywhere. She could feel the bile rise in her throat, and she ran to the bathroom. She vomited and was crying so hard. She had to get a hold of herself, and take care of it before Kate saw what she had. Before she could do anything else she heard Kate scream. Marisa ran to the door that had closed behind her when she came back into the apartment. Kate was sobbing loudly in the hallway, and some other tenants came out to see what all the commotion was about. The man downstairs had his arms around Kate when Marisa came out into the hall. He told Marisa that he would take care of the mess, and she should take care of her sister.

"This is all your fault!" Kate yelled at Marisa. "You told me to put him out last night. If I had kept him in this would never have happened!"

"Sis, I'm sorry. I had no idea this would happen. Do you think I wanted something like this to happen?"

"Get away from me! I just want to be by myself now. Oh, I think I'm going to be sick!"

Marisa felt helpless. She went to the hallway and saw the man from downstairs taking care of the bloody mess. She told him, "I'm sorry for this. Thank you for being so nice." And she started to cry again.

"No problem Miss. We all liked that little cat. But you better call the authorities and make a report. This poor little thing didn't deserve this. And, you know management needs to be informed too, so they can get this cleaned up right away."

"Yeah, I know. I'll make the calls. Thanks again."

Marisa went inside. She wondered when this had happened, before or after the phone call. She took off her jacket. It was covered with blood on the sleeve. She knew she had to tell Charles of this new development. But she was not giving up this case. Maybe she would just keep this to herself for a little while longer. There was no way that anyone was going to find this out unless she told them about it. She called work and told them she was going to be a little late because she was having car trouble. She then called over to the apartment office and told them that someone had vandalized outside her apartment. She explained that she would take care of the police report, and a neighbor had tried to clean most of the mess up, but it might need professional cleaning. She told them she really had to go, but if they had more questions she would be home later this evening. She hung up before the manager could ask her anything else. She knew that the repairmen and cleaning people didn't come in for another hour, and she didn't really think that the manager would come over to find out what the damage was at this point.

She called over to Kate's but she didn't answer the phone. She grabbed the key to Kate's apartment and went out into the hallway, but decided she really need to clean up a little more. The sight sickened her. The neighbor had done a pretty good job of cleaning up the mess, but the blood was still smeared on her door. The rope was still tight around the doorknocker; apparently he couldn't get it off. Tears filled her eyes when she spotted Rufus' little food dish. She picked it up and took it back into her apartment. She grabbed an old towel and some abrasive cleanser. She took out a small pail of water and scrubbed the door until the paint was coming off on the towel. She could still smell the blood. It was making her sick. She heard someone downstairs, so she stopped scrubbing. It was the neighbor.

"Miss, I'll take care of that. I just went to get some bleach water and a knife to get that rope down. I know how hard this must be, so don't you worry with it. I'll get it taken care of."

"Thank you so much. I called the manager and told them about it. I imagine she'll send a cleaning crew over later. I'll make a police report when I get to work. I'm a probation officer. I think one of my clients had something to do with this."

"You really shouldn't tell them where you live, you know."

"No sir, I didn't. I think someone had me followed. They must have seen me with the cat. It was my sister's cat."

"Yes dear, I know. No one cared around here that she was taking care of it. You won't hear anything from management about that. If anyone asks we'll just say it was probably a stray. You better go on and take care of your sister and make that report. I'll take care of this, now go on really." Marisa thought to herself, there are still really nice people in the world. She knew this because she had just met one of them. But the irony was realizing that she was dealing with one of the worst in Wanda.

She took the cleaner and bucket back into the apartment then went back over to Kate's. She let herself in without knocking. Kate was curled up on the bed sobbing and holding onto a stuffed cat. She had always loved cats, and this was the first one she had ever really had. It would be a long time before she would get over this.

"Sis, I'm sorry this happened. I had no idea anyone could be so cruel. Whoever did this must think that the cat belonged to me. They must have been trying to get my attention, and in the process they hurt us both. I loved Rufus too."

Kate looked into her sister's eyes and said she didn't mean those things she had said earlier. "Do you know who did this?"

"I have a good idea, but I didn't see anything. I got a phone call in the middle of the night warning me not to be poking my nose into other people's business. I'm sure these things are connected. But please don't tell mom and dad. They would only worry needlessly. Tell them the cat ran away, or got hit by a car; just don't tell them that someone is trying to warn me. Okay sis?"

Kate just shook her head. Then she told her sister to be extremely careful, and make sure that her bosses knew about this. Marisa assured her that they would know all about it. She just neglected to mention when they would find out.

"Are you gonna be okay here today?" Again, Kate just shook her head yes.

There was really nothing Marisa could do for her, and she didn't think that Kate was in any danger. Wanda was warning her. Now things had heated up just like Marisa had expected. And now Wanda was going to realize that she, too, had fucked with the wrong person.

Marisa was about two hours late for work. She had thought long and hard about what her next move should be. She knew that she did need to tell someone what was going on at home, but she really didn't want interference. And, she certainly didn't want the case reassigned. She thought about telling Tom; he already knew she had been threatened and he hadn't said anything to anyone yet. He liked Marisa, and respected her judgment. Maybe he could provide someone to watch out for her, without getting anyone involved from her office. However, she didn't want Elliot finding out about this. He would then want to help, and she knew that would never work out because she still had feelings for him. She knew if she told Charles he would just go straight to the Chief.

When she finally got to her office and checked her voice-mail there was a call from Tom. He said he wanted to speak with her as soon as she got in. She was just about to dial his number when they buzzed from the front desk stating that Tom Roberts was there to see her. "Send him back please, and I'll meet him halfway."

Marisa was a bit puzzled by his unannounced visit, but she and Tom had always gotten along and helped each other out. As he approached her in the hall he said, "Damn Marisa, I called here twice already and asked that you call me back as soon as you got in. You need to be more diligent about checking your voice-mail."

"Tom, I did just get in, and was getting ready to call you when you popped in. What's so important that you stopped by and called twice?"

He glanced around to see who was within earshot and said, "Look, I was worried about you. Just wanted to make sure you were okay, after yesterday you know."

"Oh that, well we do need to talk, but not here. Can we go have coffee or something?"

"Sure, just let me call my secretary and tell her I'll be out of the building for a little while."

She led him back to her office and said she would be right back. She went to Charles' office to tell him she was going with the Newton D.A. to the coffee shop across the street, but that she would be back soon. He asked her if there were any new developments, but she lied and said no. When she got back to her office she grabbed the Newton file and they headed out to the coffee shop. Tom could sense that she was being more cautious than she usually was.

"Hey Marisa, what's up? Did something else happen?"

"Well, you could say something happened, but I don't want the prying ears of the building to hear it, so just walk with me now."

When they got over to the coffee shop, he grabbed two cafe lattes and a doughnut. She was looking everywhere like she thought they were being followed. If her luck was running the way it had been she knew somewhere, someone was watching her.

"Okay Tom, I'm going to tell you the whole deal, but please don't say anything until I'm finished. Okay?"

"Sure Marisa, whatever you say." Now he knew he had reason to be worried.

"A few weeks ago when I started with the violation proceedings I received a bunch of hang up phone calls at work, well I called her bluff and said I knew it was her. Well I knew it was her or her boyfriend, but I just took it as par for the course. This must have really pissed her off, because shortly thereafter my tires were slashed. They were slashed after the compliance hearing when she was ordered to do more service work, and almost thrown in jail by the Judge. Next came a threatening phone call to my home. I'm not listed in the book or in directory assistance, or in the criss-cross directory. But, the man called me by name and told me the tires were just an example of what could happen. Being the person I am, I decided to go out to her house and see if I could hear her boyfriend's voice. I took out one of our deputies and we sat on the house awhile until I saw a guy around the house that I was certain knew her. As I approached the man, I said hello to him and asked him if he was the landlord's husband. Well, he got really defensive, and told me it was none of my business. He uttered just enough of the same words from the phone call that I was able to determine he was in fact the same guy that had threatened me only the night before. It was at that home visit that she told me she was no longer going to report."

The story continued like a freight train, "After I returned to the office the landlord called me and told me some things that were very helpful. Then later that same day she came downtown with some papers she had scavenged from Wanda's room. That is how I got the bank documents, among other things. I made a few copies and took them home to study over the weekend.

Then on Saturday night I went out with some friends. Maybe this isn't related, but I felt like someone was watching me at this one bar we went to, and it was making me uncomfortable. All of a sudden a drink was sent over to the table and when the waitress tried to show me who had sent it, he was gone. We left the bar and went over to the place where I used to work. At least there someone would know if an outsider were watching me. Nothing happened."

Marisa's actions were getting more animated as she continued with her account of events. "The next evening there was a note on my car telling me to be careful what I look for because I could get hurt. I really thought it wouldn't get any worse, but then last night I got another call. It was about 4:30am actually, and it was a woman's voice I didn't recognize. She called me a little bitch, and said she had warned me not to mess with things. Then she said I was going to find out what could happen when I poke my nose into things that don't concern me. She then said I had fucked with the wrong person. Needless to say I didn't get much sleep after that. This morning when I started to leave for work I found my sister's cat gutted and hanging on my front door. There was blood everywhere. They must have thought the cat was mine. My sister lives across the hall and I had been caring for the cat this past weekend. So, that's everything. Now what do I do? And I will not back off, so don't even say that."

"Marisa have you told anyone else about this?"

"No Tom, just you. I don't really trust that many people and someone had to help them get my home phone number. I have a gun and I'm not afraid to use it, but what if they get me before I can get them?"

"Marisa we really need to protect you, and she needs to be charged."

"Tom we both know that at this point it's my word against hers. There are no witnesses to anything, and I don't have any of the conversations recorded. I know she is up to something more than just what we have already uncovered, and I'm not going to stop just because she thinks she can intimidate me. Oh and I also found out some other incriminating evidence. I checked out her social security numbers. I won't tell you how I did that, but suffice it to say that she is using several, and only one of them actually belongs to her. And, by the way, her real name is Velma Harris Reynolds."

"Marisa you really should be in another job. You're a great investigator, but if you keep this up you may end up dead. I don't think she's playing. Most people don't go around killing animals for the thrill of it. I think she is for real. We need to tell someone. Does anyone else know about this stuff, any of it?"

"Well the deputy that went out to the house with me witnessed that blow up, but I swore him to secrecy. I know he'll watch my back, but I don't think he would go to the bosses with that information."

"I need some time to think about this. Do you think you are going to be okay for now?"

"Well I think I'm safe as long as I'm in the building, but I know it's only a matter of time before she finds out just how much I know."

"Okay, let's get back to the office, and you stay in for lunch today. You meet me in my office for lunch and hopefully by then we will have thought of something to keep you safe. Promise me you won't do anything foolish."

"Fine, I promise. And, I would like tuna on wheat please with some chips and a soda." He laughed at her calm exterior.

He knew she was strong, but he could also tell she was worried. He didn't know if she was more worried about her safety, or that her superiors may take the case away from her and reassign it to someone else. They walked back to the office arm in arm, laughing like they didn't have a care in the world. If anyone was watching today, they would certainly be surprised to see how she was responding.

When she got back to her office, she finished looking through her mail and checked her voice-mail. Bill had left a message that indeed his legal department was working on his latest feat. Mrs. Snow called but said she really didn't have anything to report except that Wanda had come in really early this morning, around 3:30am. Marisa knew then that Rufus had been killed before the phone call, and someone had been to her apartment while she was sleeping. Then there were the two messages from Tom. While she still had some time this morning she decided to call the unemployment office and check things out. She called the office nearest her and asked for the number of the one where the checks had originated. She called the general information number and asked to speak to a supervisor. She identified herself as a probation officer, and told the operator that it was long distance. She was connected with Missy Birnbaum.

"This is Missy how can I help you?"

"Hello Missy, my name is Marisa Spencer and I'm a criminal probation officer about three hours from you. I have some questions about how a person receives benefits, etc. Do you think you have time to answer a few questions?"

"Sure, but why don't you call the regional office in your area?"

"Well, it seems that you have been issuing benefit checks to someone I have on probation here and I just wanted to see how your office operates. I think I may have caught her living out of town without permission."

"Oh sure then go ahead."

"Well, do your people have to come in personally to pick up their checks, or are they mailed out?"

"Well unless you are disabled, you have to come in to pick them up. Also you bring in with you some type of verification of your job search efforts."

"Hmm, I see. Well are people assigned to a caseload officer, or do they just come in and see different people each week?"

"No, we all have our own caseload. But if someone is out sick then we all pitch in and see their people as they come in."

"Could you tell me who is assigned to a specific person without being in any trouble?"

"Sure, that wouldn't be a problem. Who is it that you're trying to find?"

"Well actually I have two people I need to check on."

"That's odd, so far away from you and two of them are not living where they are supposed to, and they both are living here. But, okay, give me the names and I'll give you the caseworker's names."

Death Rides A Cold Horse

"He is ok personally, but I know what you mean about them dang dogs of his. I remember when he let farmer Lutz put them bee hives next to his catfish pond. I didn't say nothing but I was hoping that damn Akita looking male dog of his named Farley would have gotten an attitude adjustment from the bees for pissing on their box when they arrived. I told you once about that one damn time I tried to ride a bike over there? Damned dogs made me walk it half way up the road there and halfway back. That friggin Akita got a thing about bicycles and those other two dogs do whatever he does because he is the ornery Alpha male. Separated from him they are pretty sweet dogs on their own, but don't try riding a bicycle by them both without stopping and walking it." Mike said gruffly thinking he would of smacked one of them dogs if it had of kept up its barking charge that was hard to tell if it was all bluff, nervousness or naked aggression towards him and his bicycle.

"He feeds them catfish he raises in his ponds with regular pelletized fish food; I wonder what happens to that smaller catfish pond if he doesn't feed them at all? You reckon without that oxygen bubbler going and regular feeding those fish will just all up and die?" Mike asked thinking maybe tonight would be fish and forest food for the dinner plate.

"Damn good question Mike. What DOES happen to an overstocked pond if you don't feed the fish contained in it?" David said looking skeptical. He had not even considered that bit of info until Mike had brought it up for discussion.

"They eat each other and the big fish wins and chases the smaller fish around the pond at lunchtime?" Julie said not joking in the least and the group babbled questionably and vociferously about the future outcomes of the smaller fish in the ponds until Mike and David eventually rousted themselves and headed out of the house to go to Charlie's place and ask him the same question.

"Well it's the same old shit I see David. Those neighbors of yours got all their blinds closed up, front yard is full of weird junk and they are themselves nowhere to be seen. Hell the only way you know anything about them is to watch what type of junk disappears or appears in front of that rundown place." Mike said as he and David walked by the dubious structure.

"The first one is Wanda Newton, and the other is Cynthia Reynolds."

"Hold on a second while I look through the card files. Okay, can you give me a social on both just to verify that it is the correct person?"

"Well I can try. Let me see, on Wanda I have the number 506-52-6178."

"Sure, she is assigned to Debbie Meyers. Okay how about the other one?"

"Umm the name is Cynthia Reynolds, but I'm not sure about the social."

"Well we have her too. You don't have any numbers on her?"

"Well actually I have a few to choose from. You want to try this number? It is 501-66-4212."

"Yes that's the one we have. She is assigned to Dan Burris. Do you want me to connect you with either of them?"

"Sure, connect me to Debbie first. And thanks for all your help."

"No problem, hold while I transfer you. And, good luck!"

"Hi, this is Debbie. Can I help you?"

"Hi Debbie, my name is Marisa Spencer and I just have a few questions about one of your unemployed people. Her name is Wanda Newton."

"Oh, yes, poor Wanda has the worst luck. She is just so nice, but she was placed on permanent lay off and now she can't find something else. Luckily her boyfriend is taking care of her out on his estate."

"I see, and can I verify that address with you?"

"Sure, it's Box 4, Rt. 26 in Grenville. Is that what you have?"

"Yes and thanks. Oh one more question, how long has she been receiving unemployment benefits?"

"Oh just about eight months now. Do you need to verify anything else?"

"Well now that you mention it, could you give me a description?"

"Sure, she is in her late 40's and has black hair and brown eyes."

"Thanks again. Oh and don't tell her I was checking up on her if you don't mind. "

"Oh no I wouldn't do that. Might hurt her self-esteem."

"Can you connect me with Dan Burris?"

"Yeah sure. Hold on while I transfer you."

"Dan Burris."

"Hi Dan, my name is Marisa Spencer and I need to ask you a couple of questions about one of your clients. Her name is Cynthia Reynolds."

"Yes, that case is assigned to me. What do you need to know?"

"Well I was just wondering how long she has been receiving unemployment benefits, and does she come in or have them mailed to her?"

"Well she has been on our rolls for about five or six months, and her checks are mailed because she has no transportation presently."

"I see, but I thought that you had to come in unless you were disabled?"

"Well this is a small county and sometimes we bend the rules. She did come in initially, but it seems that every time she was scheduled something would come up with her car. She asked if she could mail in her verification efforts and if we could mail out her benefit checks."

"Oh okay, that sounds right. Can I just verify her address with you?"

"Sure, what address do you have?"

This caught Marisa off guard, because everyone else had given out the information rather than actually verifying what she had. Quickly she decided that Wanda was probably using the same address. So she said, "Let me see, is it Box 4, Rt. 26 in Grenville?"

"Yep, that's it."

"Oh, and just for my records can you give me a description?"

"Sure, she's middle aged and brown eyes, and dark hair. I think she dyes it, but don't tell her I said that," he laughed.

"I promise not to tell her about that, if you promise not to mention that I called to check up on her."

"Okay you have a deal."

"Thanks for all your help."

Marisa just shook her head as she hung up the phone. Wanda had done it again. She had wrapped these people around her finger and they didn't even know it. It must have taken her a few months to figure out their system, and then she decided to "double dip". She probably was submitting the same generic application forms to them that she submitted to probation, but they didn't think anything of it. Marisa wondered if Wanda even bothered to give the caseworkers different forms, or if she submitted the same paperwork to each one at her different visits. Either way she was committing another felony and she was stealing from the state this time. Marisa couldn't wait to tell Tom this new tidbit of information.

Marisa went to Dani's office to tell her that she was going to miss lunch again today. Dani said, "Marisa are you seeing someone and just don't want to tell me, or what's going on?"

"No, really I have been working a lot on a case and today I need to meet with the D.A. again to go over some things. I know I've been a bit preoccupied lately, but things are going to change shortly, I promise."

"Well what case have you been working on that is so important that you don't have time for your friends anymore? And why were you really late for work this morning?"

"Give a girl a break won't you? I had some car trouble, nothing real serious but I just had to wait for the road service. I get tired of bothering my dad to work on my car all the time. Since I do pay for the road service, I ought to use it when I need it. And, about the case I'm working on, you know I work hard on all my cases. This one is no different except that it may be a bit more involved. Listen I've got to get upstairs, but I'll talk to you later."

Marisa was out the door before Dani could ask any more questions. Marisa didn't like lying or even stretching the truth, but the less Dani knew the better off she'd be.

Marisa grabbed Wanda's file and ran upstairs to meet Tom. She just kept hoping that she didn't see Elliot again today, she didn't think she could handle it. She went back to Tom's office and on the table was a sack with her name on it. She smiled, and started to peek inside when Tom came through the door.

"Go on, lunch is served. I didn't know what kind of soda you wanted so I picked up a couple different cans. You can have your choice."

"Tom this is really sweet of you, you shouldn't have. I have the file, and more information."

"Marisa I don't think you're going to like what I have to say, but I want you to hear me out."

"Sure, I can listen, but no promises on anything else."

"Look, you're right at this point, the stuff she has done is probably not enough to charge her, but you have enough other stuff to get additional charges filed. I think that it would be a good time for you to take a vacation, lay low, and wait for things to cool down. Let the bank people work on the money. At this point it is out of our hands; that money is rightfully owed to their bank. But by going away, even if just for a few days, it will give us time to look into what you have found with the social security numbers and alias names. Do you think you could do that?"

"I have time to take, yes, but I don't want to just run away from this. Besides, who are you going to tell about all this?"

"Marisa I haven't told anyone yet. And we know you aren't running away from anything. You will just being buying some time and be out of harm's way. I will help you with a place to go. Please, just for a little bit?"

"Well, I can go back to the office now and request a few days off or I can just call in sick tomorrow and the next two days. Then I'll have the weekend too. Would that be enough time for you to get this stuff together?"

"Well, I don't know what we will accomplish, but we know that you'll be safe and out of danger for a little while longer. The calling in sick thing may just be the way to go. If Wanda tries to call you she will think you're at home. We can have someone watch your house in case she tries anything, but you will be somewhere else. Tonight I'm going to follow you home, and I want you to pack a bag and meet me in the parking lot. Pack light in case anyone is watching."

"What am I going to tell my parents, or anyone else that tries to reach me?"

"Well you better think of something before you leave, and make the calls from work. I won't get out of my car tonight when you go in. But I want you to meet me back in the lot as soon as it's dark. I'll be reading and watching the lot until you come out."

"You know I'm bringing my little *friend*, but will anyone else be on this trip?"

"Well, you'll be alone, but of course your *friend* is always welcome," he laughed.

"Hey, thanks for lunch, and thanks for taking care of me."

Back in her office, she decided to call her parents and leave a message on the machine. She would tell them she was going to be at a seminar out of town from mid-week until the weekend. She also lied and said she had forgotten to tell them earlier, but she would call them if she got the chance. She told them that she had only known about it for about a week and it had just slipped her mind to tell them when she found out. She then called Kate's machine and told her the same concocted story, but suggested that because of what happened to Rufus she might want to go home for a few days. Again she reminded her sister to tell them that a car had hit the cat, or that it ran away, so they wouldn't worry.

Now, she would have to tell Dani a story about leaving town. She decided that since she had neglected to tell her parents or sister where she would be and she knew Kate might get curious she would have to devise another plan to tell Dani. Marisa would again be lying to Dani about where she would be going and why she was lying to her parents. The only thing she could think of was to say that Elliot had called her and wanted to go away so they could talk and possibly work things out.

But, if Dani saw him in court she would know something was up. This plan wouldn't work.

She decided to tell Dani that she was meeting an old boyfriend from college that her parents didn't approve of, and they were going to spend a few days together in Chicago. She would explain that if Kate knew she might let it slip to her parents. That information would just cause turmoil, so she had to tell them both the same story. She would also tell Dani that she had plans for her accumulating vacation time so she was going to call in sick, but she would be back to work on Monday. With all the intrigue and romance she had woven into the story, she figured that Dani would accept it without question.

Just as she was about ready to tell Dani the story her phone rang. It was Seth. He was calling just to say hello and ask how she was doing. She told him she had been really preoccupied with a case, but other than that she was doing fine. He asked her if it was as intriguing as his case had been. She laughed and said nothing could compare to his life story. He asked if she could meet him tomorrow for a cappuccino on her break, but she told him she had to attend a seminar and wouldn't be back to work for a few days. But, she asked if they could get together for lunch or something when she got back next week.

"Sure Baby, I know you're busy. I'll call you on Monday or Tuesday. You be careful and learn a lot at your big meeting. I'll catch you later." Just before she hung up Dani was walking into her office. Marisa motioned for her to sit down. He hung up just as she was saying, "Bye Seth." He always knew just what to say, and just when to call. She wished that they had met under other circumstances, but they didn't and life goes on.

Now focusing on Dani, she said, "Hey woman I gotta talk to you about something important."

"Yeah Marisa what is it?"

"Well walk with me to court and I'll tell you."
She winked, and looked around the room. Dani knew
that this meant that she didn't want anyone eavesdropping
on the conversation. They got up and went out the back
door and headed to the law library instead. Once they
arrived they looked around to see if they knew anyone in
there. Satisfied that it was private, Marisa said, "Dani I
need to tell you that I'm going to be sick until Monday.
In case my sister or parents call you, I want you to tell
them that I went to a seminar out of town, say in
Chicago."

"Well okay, but why don't you just tell them that.
And, where are you really going, and with whom?"

"Well I just wanted to leave a brief message, and I
told them I would call them if I got the chance. I'm
really going to Chicago, but with an old college boyfriend
of whom they do not approve. I figure that if I just tell
them it is work related they won't think anymore about it.
Will you help me out here?"

"Sure Marisa, but behave. No, come to think of
it, have a great time!" As they were starting to laugh they
decide that they better leave, as the librarian didn't
tolerate any non-work related cavorting in her library.

Dani assumed that Marisa was meeting Seth in
Chicago, and just couldn't bring herself to admit it.
Marisa had confided to Dani about the odd relationship
she shared with Seth. Marisa had told her of the sexual
tension she feels when she's with him for coffee or just
talking on the phone. Of course both of them knew they
were just idle fantasies, nothing more. Dani knew that
Seth and Marisa continued to talk, but what harm was
there in that she often wondered. Dani knew that Marisa

115

would never cross the line with a probationer, but he was no longer on probation. What could anyone say? Of course it had been several years since he was discharged from probation, so who would even question the relationship. Dani wondered if she should say anything about her assumption, but by the time she thought about it they were re-entering the office. This conversation would have to wait for another time. She just hoped Marisa knew what she was doing.

Chapter Five

Marisa became close to a very small number of the people she supervised on her caseload over the years. Some of them, or their family members, continued to keep in touch with her. They always let her know the good, and the bad. They asked for her advice when they were in trouble, and they always told her she should come by to see them or have dinner. Seth Anthony was one of those people. He came into her life about four years ago, just after she started her career as a Probation Officer. He was on her caseload, a small time burglar with a heart of gold. He was on probation only a year but he had kept in touch with her as if he needed to check in even after she had closed his file. He called her at least once a week, more often if he was having trouble. He trusted no one but her. And, she knew she could trust him with her life.

After he was off probation he told her he really wasn't guilty of the crime for which he had been on probation. He did tell her he had stolen a thing or two in his youth, mostly shoplifting when he needed something and had no job, or money. He told her that because he had no means to fight the trumped up charges, no money, or family support he took the deal and made the best of it. Shyly he told Marisa that he had learned something in the process and had made a friend. She didn't know why, but she believed him. He didn't really have any reason to lie to her at that point. Seth was the most honest person she had ever met, but most people had a different image of him. Luckily for them both, Marisa had been able to break through the wall he had built around himself.

Once she got back to her office she started to feign a terrible headache. Charles happened to stop in and told her she should just go on home and get some rest. But she told him she only had another hour or so of work, and she thought she could make it. Her little plan was coming together. She did however, take some things with her out of Wanda's file. She took out all the new, incriminating paperwork and notes and made copies. She put both copies in her purse, she could mark one up if necessary, and the other would be untouched. She wasn't sure if she would be able to work on anything wherever Tom was putting her up, but she intended to if she got the chance.

Finally it was time to go home. She continued to play the part of becoming ill. She even went to Charles before she left and said, "I think I've been burning my candle at both ends and it has finally caught up with me. If I still feel this way in the morning I can tell you I won't be in."

"Sure Marisa, if you need to take some time off sick, just give me a call in the morning. I hope you get to feeling better, now go on home and get some rest."

She grabbed her briefcase and her purse and she was on her way. Tom was waiting for her on the first floor.

"Hey beautiful where are you going?" he smirked.

"Well, I really don't know, but I don't feel so good," she said sarcastically.

"Just remember what I told you, pack light and meet me in your parking lot after dark. I'll follow you home, but I won't be right behind you."

"Sure. We can do this, can't we?" Marisa was getting a little anxious. She had fooled Charles, but could she fool everyone else?

"We'll be fine, just act like you're not feeling well as you go to the car; make it look good."

She cautiously approached her car. No damage today she thought. She looked around to see if anyone was watching. She didn't see anything that looked out of place as she got in. But just for good measure she acted like she was testing her body temperature with her palm to her forehead. Then, she rested her head on the steering wheel for a few seconds, just for effect. If anyone was watching they would think something was wrong with her.

She watched the cars around her on the drive home. It did not appear that anyone was following her, not even Tom. As she parked, she noticed him pull in the lot a few minutes behind her. He drove slowly watching which building she entered then he went on and drove to another section of the lot. She went upstairs and was surprised to see that most of the bloodstains in the hall had disappeared. She knocked on Kate's door, but by the time she got her door unlocked Kate never answered. She went to the answering machine to see what had been left.

While she was listening to the messages she peered through the curtains to see where Tom was parked. He was parked with his trunk toward her, but he was adjusting his rear view mirror in an effort to watch her building. One call was from Kate stating she was going back home to be comforted by her parents over the loss of their grand-kitten, and to call her there when she got back from her trip. The next call was from her mother stating it would be nice to have at least the city in which her daughter would be in case of an emergency. The next call was a hang up call. The messages were over, and she rewound the tape.

She knew it would be dark soon, so she went into the bedroom and grabbed a rather large duffel bag. She threw in some magazines, a notebook and pencils, her address book in case she had time to write some letters to friends, and she threw in some casual clothes and lingerie. She figured she could just wear the same shoes all week long, so no need in taking any extra of those. She grabbed a small bag to put her toiletries and cosmetics in. She would have everything she needed in this bag and her purse. If anyone saw her leaving the building they would probably just assume she was going to the gym tonight. She then made sure she had her gun in her purse. She threw some extra ammunition into the bag. When she was finished she sat on the couch and waited for darkness to fall. She really hoped she wasn't going to hate being alone for the next few days. She also hoped there was a television and a telephone wherever it was that she was going.

She decided to call her parents and tell them that she was leaving now for Chicago. She would tell them that she was going to be staying with some relatives of another co-worker that was attending the same seminar. If she got a chance she would call them and give them a number. Her mother accepted this, but said the office should put out a little money and put her up in a motel. Marisa told her she worked for the government, not NASA. After speaking to Kate and her dad she said she really had to get going because her ride would be there soon. About forty-five minutes later, she grabbed her bags and looked out the window again. Tom was not in the same spot, but when he saw the curtains open he blinked the lights. She made sure the place was locked up and off she went to a place unknown with the only person she trusted right now.

"Well does it look like anyone else was watching me tonight?"

"No, actually, a few cars came and went, but they all got out and went in to the various buildings. If anyone were watching they would have to be in the complex somewhere I would imagine. Or, they may come back later in the evening to see what you're up to. So, did you already eat, or are you hungry?"

"Well I could eat, but I would rather get out of town and get to wherever it is that you are taking me. By the way, where are you taking me?"

"Don't laugh, but I'm taking you to my parent's place about an hour from here. Don't worry they aren't home. They are off visiting one of my aunts in Tucson. They won't be back for two more weeks. And yes, I called them to tell them that I had a friend that needed a place to stay for a few days. Mom just said to be careful with her cookie jar collection."

Marisa laughed and said, "The cookie jars and I will be safe."

About a half-hour outside town they stopped and picked up a bucket of chicken and a six pack of beer and some sodas. He told her that he had called a friend from back home and had arranged for his friend, Dave, to watch over her. The plan was to drop her off at the police station in his parent's hometown. It seems his buddy was a police officer in this idyllic small town and he would transport her to "the retreat". They ate the chicken and drank sodas the rest of the trip, and talked of his glory days in this little bitty "Podunk" town. Marisa said she had always wanted the conveniences of a big city, but the atmosphere of a small town. Tom told her the only thing he thought about while growing up there was when he would be old enough to leave. He said everyone knew all their neighbors' business, and although everyone helped each other out, it was a stifling feeling to live there. He told her that when they got to the police station he would drop her at the door and leave. His buddy would be there and ready to take her back to Tom's parent's house. Tom would already be there inside. They figured that anyone following them would be thrown off and probably stick around to see where Marisa was going. Of course, just in case, there was a decoy being taken to another location. A girlfriend of one of the officer's had agreed to come to the station and be taken to a friend's house as soon as Marisa arrived. Marisa knew Tom had called in a bunch of markers in order to protect her.

Tom dropped her at the police station and drove away. No one appeared to be following them. She went right inside and met Tom's buddy, Dave. Dave said they would wait a few minutes to leave, giving Tom some time to get inside and get some lights on. Dave showed her to the restroom in case she wanted to freshen up before they went over to the Roberts' house. When she came out Dave told her that Tom had called and said to come on over. She mentioned that it must not be far from the station if he got there so quickly.

Dave laughed and said, "Actually you can see one end of town from the other if you have good eyes."

Dave told the other officer to take his girlfriend out as the decoy and he would be about two minutes behind them. Marisa thought that if this was such a safe, small town they sure have more than enough police officers. She mentioned her thoughts to Dave, and he told her that was the reason the crime rate is so low, and people like living here. She smiled because she knew he was right. He went out first and looked around, then motioned for her to come out. He had carried her bag and put it in the trunk of the police cruiser.

About two miles down the road they arrived at the Roberts' house. She could see that Tom was scurrying around inside, probably tidying things up just for her.

Gallantly Dave let her out of the car, grabbed her bag and walked her to the door. As they walked up the sidewalk he told her that because the Roberts' were on an extended vacation the police department was patrolling it several times each day. He assured Marisa that she would be fine. Dave also said that he would check in on her periodically and make sure everything was okay, and to make sure she wasn't too lonely. Dave came in and talked to Tom for a few minutes, but said he had to get back on patrol. Before he left, Dave gave Marisa a business card with his home, cellular, and work phone numbers in case she needed to contact him. She was grateful to him and Tom for being so chivalrous.

After Dave left, Tom took her upstairs and showed her to his old room. It looked like the typical room of a sports fan. He said although he had been gone from home for about six years his mother left it just the way it was all those years in high school and college. He said his brother's room looked the way it did when he left for college too. He had told Marisa he would not be spending the night, but he knew she would be safe in here. If she had any problems he told her that Dave or any of the other officers would help her.

He told her that he had informed the neighbors that a distant cousin was staying there for a few days while her house was being painted. He also suggested that some of the neighbors would offer to cook for her or bring her something to eat, and she should graciously accept so as not to offend. She laughed at him; her parent's neighbors were friendly, but not to a total stranger. He told her that he was completely serious. He hugged her and gave her his home number and pager number. He instructed her to put in 911 if it was an emergency when she used the pager. As he left he told her he would be in contact with her, and would be back on Friday night to spend the weekend with her before taking her back home. She kissed him on the cheek as he left. She knew he wouldn't have gone to all this trouble if he wasn't really worried about her.

She decided to watch some television before unpacking. She turned on the television only to find that they didn't even have cable. She laughed and wondered what she would do without MTV. After flipping through six channels she decided she would go upstairs and unpack. She did now have a headache, so she maybe a nice hot bath would help her unwind. She made sure all the doors were locked and went upstairs. She turned on the radio in Tom's old room and listened to a country station.

She went across the hall and ran some bath water. His mother had several bath salts from which to choose, so she picked a lavender bouquet. The delicate scent filled the small room. She removed her clothes and stepped into the tub. She listened to the radio and soaked for nearly an hour. Finally, she got out of the tub and started to put on her pajamas, but she found she had failed to pack them. She rummaged through one of Tom's old drawers and found an old football jersey that was really big on her. This would do for the next few days. She then grabbed one of her books and curled up on his bed. Soon she drifted off to sleep. It was the first peaceful night's rest she had had in about two weeks.

She awoke to the sun streaming through the window. She had not remembered to close the curtains. She looked around the room to find a clock, but she couldn't see one. She got out of bed and looked at her watch. It was almost 7 o'clock in the morning. She decided to make her phone call to work now. She would call Charles' voice-mail and leave the message that she was still not feeling well. She used her long distance calling card to place the call, so Tom's parents wouldn't have a long distance charge on their phone. With that done, she went back upstairs, closed the curtains, and went back to sleep. It was near 11 o'clock when she finally got out of bed. She stretched lazily wondering what she would do today. It had been a long time since she had slept so soundly and so peacefully. She decided to see if there was anything to eat downstairs. Just as she reached the bottom of the stairs the doorbell rang. She could see that it was a little old lady at the door. She answered the door without even finding a robe.

"Hello dear. Tom called me last evening to tell me that his cousin would be spending a few days with us, so I thought I would bring you breakfast. I don't imagine that there is anything here to eat since his folks have been gone for a few weeks. My name is Mrs. Adelman. I live next door."

"How do you do Mrs. Adelman? Would you like to come in?"

"Well sure dear, would you like me to fix you some coffee?"

"Well, sure, I haven't been here in so long I don't know where Auntie keeps everything. Thank you so much for your thoughtfulness."

"Oh it's the least I can do. I used to take care of Tommy and Billy when he they were little, so I know just where everything is. Go ahead and eat those muffins while they're still warm."

"Oh these are wonderful. Thank you again."

Mrs. Adelman continued to putter in the kitchen while Marisa ate the muffins. Finally Mrs. Adelman told her that there was nothing fit for a nice young woman to eat in the cupboards, so she invited her for dinner that evening. Not wanting to offend her Marisa accepted this

most gracious invitation. Mrs. Adelman told her that
Tom had also called Claire from across the street, and she
knew that Claire would probably be bringing her famous
chicken salad over for lunch. Marisa couldn't believe the
hospitality that she was receiving.

"Thank you again so much. I hope I can
somehow repay your generosity someday."

"Marisa dear, just keeping old ladies company is
repayment enough. Now why don't you come over at
about six tonight?"

"That would be fine Mrs. Adelman. I'll see you
then. Thanks."

"I'll see myself out dear, you rest and enjoy the
coffee and muffins."

Marisa felt like she was being pampered in a fine
hotel. The decorations left a lot to the imagination, but
the treatment and the food here were divine. She lounged
around all morning and watched the talk shows, and
finally took a shower in the early afternoon. About 2
o'clock Claire arrived with her famous chicken salad and
fruit. She also brought over some sodas for them to
drink. Claire was not quite as old as Mrs. Adelman, but
she was just as nice. Marisa confided to her that she was
not used to all this attention. Claire said that many of the
neighbors felt a void in their lives after all their children
had grown up and moved away, so taking care of
someone in need was a great feeling for them. Claire
didn't stay long either, but she told Marisa that if she
needed anything she shouldn't hesitate to call, or come
over if she wanted to play cards. Marisa thanked her too.

"If I'm not being too presumptuous I was
planning to fix a spinach quiche tomorrow and would
love to share it over lunch?"

"Oh no, not presumptuous at all. I can hardly wait!"

The rest of the day flew by as Marisa read and watched television. She noticed that several patrol cars passed by the house about once an hour. She knew that the whole police force knew she was there. She did feel safe. Finally she decided to call her parents and let them know she was having a wonderful time at the seminar. Her father picked up and made the usual small talk, then called to Tina. Before her mother could get to the phone Kate grabbed it to say hello.

"Hi sis. How's the seminar?"

"Oh, it's okay, pretty boring though. How are you doing?"

"Well I'm doing okay, but still really sad. I told them that you found Rufus killed in the parking lot. The only part that isn't true is where you found him. You know how I hate lying to them."

"Yeah I know Kate. Get mom, this is costing me some money."

"Hello sweetheart, how is your seminar going so far?"

"Oh same old stuff, but they're taking really good care of us, so you don't need to worry about me."

"Well I'll let you go, and we will see you Sunday sometime right?"

"Yes mom, we are going to do some sightseeing after the seminar ends, but I should be home sometime in the afternoon. Tell everyone I love them and I'll talk to you on Sunday. Bye." She felt a little better having talked to them, but she really hated having to lie to them.

Dinner with Mrs. Adelman was nice, like eating with her grandmother. She thought Mrs. Adelman had probably been cooking and preparing dinner all day. She felt guilty when Mrs. Adelman wouldn't let her help with the dishes, but the old woman said it would give her something to do tomorrow. She told Marisa that she had some banana bread in the oven that she would send home with her and she could have it for breakfast. They looked at old family picture albums until almost nine o'clock. Marisa could see that Mrs. Adelman was getting tired so she said she needed to get back home and watch her favorite television program. Mrs. Adelman said she would watch and make sure she got in okay. Marisa gave her a hug and thanked her again for her generosity.

Dave was driving by just as Marisa was crossing the yard; he turned on his blue lights just to make sure she saw him. She waved and went on inside. She decided that she could really get to like this place; she wondered why Tom was so anxious to leave it. It would be a wonderful place to raise a family she thought. She flipped on the television, and found one of her favorite sitcoms. After watching the news she decided to go upstairs and read a magazine. She wondered what Wanda was doing now.

The next morning she awoke to the sun streaming through the curtains again. She was glad that she was getting this early wake up call from Mother Nature, as she needed to call into work again. Today she would leave a message that she had come down with the flu or something and definitely wouldn't be back to work until Monday. After she made the call she climbed back into bed and went back to sleep. She awoke to the phone ringing. She wasn't sure she should answer it, but then again it might be one of the neighbors. She ran downstairs just in time to catch it on the last ring.

"Roberts' residence," she answered.

"Hi Marisa, it's me, Tom. Just called to see how you were doing. I spoke to the neighbors, but I bet you already knew that. How was the food?"

"Tom these women have been so wonderful to me. I can't believe you didn't like living here."

"Marisa think about how they are doting on you. Now multiply that by all the houses on the block. It was like killing someone with kindness. At some point it just gets too much for a kid to take."

"Yes, but everyone watches out for you, and takes care of you."

"Marisa, think about what you just said. If you were a single woman living there, would you really want all that attention all the time? It won't stop as long as you're there. Those women are so lonely. It's great that we still have communities like that, but young people nowadays just don't mesh in that kind of society. Well listen I have to get off here, but just wanted to say things are fine here, and to see how you were doing."

"Tom, things are fine, I think I've finally gotten some rest, and I'm definitely eating well. Thanks for calling, I'll see you tomorrow evening."

Marisa started wondering how fine things really were at home. Had anything else happened and no one knew it yet? Would Wanda think that she was scared and things really would calm down? Thinking about this a moment she realized Wanda was just as stubborn as she was; neither of them would back down. It was now that

Marisa started contemplating her future. She also thought about how this whole ordeal had taken over her life. How could one person change things so drastically in such a short time? She decided that this case was just a catalyst in making her take stock of everything in her life.

Lunchtime brought Claire over with quiche and salad. Mrs. Adelman joined them for dessert that she brought over. They sat and chatted like old friends do; however, Marisa was just a bystander in this conversation. Mrs. Adelman then told her that dinner would be served at 6:30 p.m. tonight. She was fixing a pot roast and apple pie. Mrs. Adelman excused herself stating that "her story" would be on shortly and she just couldn't miss it. Claire laughed and said that Mrs. Adelman lived vicariously through the television set. She then cleared up the dishes and asked Marisa if she would like to play some cards and see her thimble collection. Marisa made an excuse about having to get a letter out before the postman came.

Claire told her she still had a few days left on her visit and maybe they could get together another time. Claire indicated she would be having french toast for breakfast if she cared to join her.

Marisa laughed and said, "Well Claire I'm pretty much what you would call a night owl, so when you're eating breakfast I'm just getting my deep sleep. Maybe we should just stick to lunch."

"Oh sure dear, I know how it is to be young and full of life. I'll fix something good for lunch tomorrow. Bye now, and if you get that letter out in time why don't you drop in?"

"I'll try Claire and thank you for the lunch."

Marisa was beginning to feel a little closed in; she was starting to understand what Tom meant earlier. She really just wanted to get out of the house, but she told Tom she would stay in. Besides, she didn't have anywhere to go. About that time she heard a knock at the door. She was a little afraid, but figured it must be another neighbor. As she approached the door, she could see a rather large man standing on the porch. She didn't open the door, but loudly asked who was there.

"Marisa, it's me, Dave." She gave a sigh of relief and opened the door.

"Hi there. I hope I'm not being too forward, but I thought that you might want to get out of here for awhile. I've noticed that the old mother hens have been taking care of you, but thought you might need a little younger company."

"Dave that would be great! I was just thinking that I'd like to get out, but don't have anywhere to go."

"Well your chariot awaits my lady."

She said, "Well let me grab my purse and get the keys, and I'll be right there." He waited outside for her.

"Where would you like to go?"

"Oh I have no idea, why don't you just show me around town. You know, show me what all the tourists like to do."

With a grin he replied, "Tourists, what are they?" He started the car and headed to Main Street.

Marisa thought to herself that every small town in America has a Main Street. As they cruised the cobblestone street he suggested that they grab a soda at the local drug store. She felt like she had been transported back in time as she walked in the drug store to see a real soda fountain. She asked him if they could go by the barbershop later and watch the old men play checkers. He told her that they probably did have a game going, and they could do that if it would make her happy. They both laughed. They talked about Tom for the better part of an hour. He and Dave were the star football players at the high school. He said that he tried to leave this town too, but when he became a Police Officer he knew he was right where he belonged. He asked her about her job. She told him that it wasn't all that it was cracked up to be.

He said, "Oh you don't like the glamour, the danger, the intrigue?"

"Well no Dave, I got into it for the money," she said facetiously.

He told her he would drive by the park to show her the new botanical gardens, but then he would have to drop her off because he had to be to work soon. When they got back to the house he left the car running, but he walked her to the door. He took the keys and unlocked the doors. Dave was so gallant she thought.

Just as he was about to leave, he whispered, "Look around I think someone is watching us."

She turned toward him and could see both Mrs. Adelman and Claire peering out Claire's front window. Marisa ever the one to get someone's attention reached up and kissed Dave on the cheek.

She said, "There, that should give them something to talk about for at least a week after I'm gone. I hope you don't mind."

Blushing, he said, "No it's fine. The only problem is, I will still be here when you leave."

"Oh Dave I'm sorry. I didn't even stop to think how that could affect you. Please forgive me."

"Well okay, but only if I can do it right?"

"Sure, I think I would like that." Dave then wrapped his arms around her and gave her the nicest kiss she had had in a long time.

When he finished, they were both blushing. He said he had a great time today, but he had to run or he would be late for work. As he ran down the walk she waved at the watching women across the street. She wasn't sure what would be said at dinner with Mrs. Adelman tonight, but she thought she just might receive a lecture.

The rest of the afternoon and early evening she lounged around the house, doing nothing in particular. She noticed now that there were cookie jars everywhere she looked. Mrs. Roberts had quite a collection. She then laughed to herself when she thought that perhaps she had really missed something when she turned down Claire and the viewing of the thimble collection. She pondered what Mrs. Adelman might be collecting.

Marisa thought long and hard about these women and their collections. She had never really collected anything, and to her best recollection no one in her family had any collections either. Maybe it was because in a small town that it was the way to stay connected to others; talking about your more recent piece and its value. Always thinking that you have a better collection than the next person does. If she was to start collecting something she thought about what it might be. Nothing really came to mind. The only thing she really liked a lot, probably more than anything else was watching the sun set, but you can only collect those in photographs that never do them justice.

It was nearly time to go to Mrs. Adelman's so she hurried to get ready. She could tell that Mrs. Adelman did not like to be kept waiting. Just as she was about to knock on the door Mrs. Adelman was right there already opening it.

"Hello dear, did you have a nice day with Dave?"

Although it came as no surprise that Mrs. Adelman might grill her, or even lecture her, she didn't think it would be the greeting as she came through the door. Marisa smiled and said they had had a lovely time.

"And how do you know Dave, only being here a short time and all?"

"Oh, we met the night I got in, and we hit it right off. I've heard so many stories about him from Tom that it seems like I've known him a long time."

"Oh I see. With the state of the world as it is I don't think I would be so familiar with anyone I had just met."

Marisa smiled, but decided not to argue or get into this discussion with Mrs. Adelman. They had only kissed, and they only did that for the amusement of Claire and Mrs. Adelman. Marisa didn't want to offend either woman, but she would have said something perhaps if they had not been so generous to her, or if she actually lived in their little world. For now, she would just take the lecture and try to change the subject.

Dinner was mostly eaten in silence but several times Marisa told her hostess how wonderful the meal was. She knew that Mrs. Adelman was disappointed in her "behavior" today, but she knew it would give them something to talk about for at least another week after she was gone. They may even share the story with Mrs. Roberts when she got back from Tucson. Maybe tomorrow she would find herself free of either woman since they both seemed so appalled with her actions this afternoon.

After helping clear the table, Mrs. Adelman asked Marisa if she had noticed Mrs. Roberts' cookie jar collection.

"Oh yes, Auntie really has some unusual pieces doesn't she?"

"Well I guess, if you like that sort of thing. Personally I think it is a bit garish to have such big objects sitting around. Oh dear, I hope I didn't put my foot in my big mouth, but she just has them everywhere. I'm sorry dear if I offended you."

"No, not at all. They do sort of overtake the place, but it's her hobby I guess. Who am I to judge? Claire asked me if wanted to see her thimble collection but I was busy at the time."

"Yes, isn't that pitiful? Collecting old sewing notions. I mean really, why would anyone want to paint a scene on a thimble, then again, why would anyone want to buy it?" Mrs. Adelman tickled herself with that last comment.

"Well then would I be correct in assuming that you don't collect anything Mrs. Adelman?"

"No dear I live in the here and now, and what good is a collection going to do someone? Just gives them something to show off I guess."

"Well, I don't have any collections either Mrs. Adelman. Looking around here though I've noticed that you have a lot of nice antiques."

"Oh those old things, just stuff I have had since I married. Would you like to see the rest of the house?"

"Sure, Mrs. Adelman that would be lovely."

She had seen the living room and dining room, and the kitchen, which was all on the first floor. Mrs. Adelman then led her upstairs where the bathroom and three bedrooms were located. As they ascended the stairs she noticed pictures of a bygone era lining the upper hall. Marisa loved looking at old pictures even if she didn't know the people staring back at her. She noticed that many of the places seemed familiar. When she asked where they were taken Mrs. Adelman told her most of them had been taken early in her marriage, and right here in town. She showed Marisa the small bathroom that looked like all ribbons and lace. Mrs. Adelman's bedroom was furnished with extremely old cherry wood furniture that Marisa assumed she had since she was a young bride all those many years ago. As they went down the hall Mrs. Adelman indicated that after the children left and had families of their own she had redecorated their rooms.

She opened the first door and said that she called it her angel room. When she flipped on the lights all Marisa could see from floor to ceiling were angels of all shapes and sizes.

Marisa said, "Wow this is beautiful. It just seems so peaceful in here."

"Well wait until you see the other room."

They moved across the hall, and Mrs. Adelman opened the door to the darkened room. When she flipped on the lights, music came on and lights appeared everywhere in the room. Elvis was singing a medley of his songs. All over the walls and on the shelves was Elvis memorabilia.

"This is really a nice room too," Marisa lied. Mrs. Adelman was just beaming. She believed that Marisa really liked her decor. "So, Mrs. Adelman you have two beautiful collections don't you?"

"Oh dear these aren't collections. These rooms are works of art. There is a difference you know," Mrs. Adelman said in a very matter of fact tone.

"Oh, yes I see. Well I guess I don't have any works of art either. I guess I would just not fit in up here with all of you."

"Oh dear, eventually you will find something that works for you; just be patient."

"Well Mrs. Adelman, I really need to get back over there. I have some things to do before Cousin Tom shows up tomorrow."

"Well dear should I bring over breakfast for both of you?"

"No, no. He'll be up in the afternoon, and I'm not sure what we'll be doing the rest of the weekend, but thank you so much for your hospitality. I've had a nice time visiting with you and Claire. Thank you again, in case I don't get to see you before I leave."

"Sure dear, it was our pleasure taking care of you. But a bit of advice, don't be so forward with the men in your life, nice girls don't do those things when they first meet a man."

"Yes Mrs. Adelman, I'm sorry that you had to witness that breach of conduct. Thanks again, and goodnight."

Marisa laughed all the way back across the yards thinking about the collections of this lonely old woman. She truly believed that what she collected were pieces of art. Of course, Mrs. Adelman most likely believed that the other women in town couldn't compete with her "artwork", Marisa theorized.

Just as she was closing the door she noticed a police cruiser passing by the house. It was Dave; he flashed his lights to let her know it was him. She waved to him from inside the door.

Marisa couldn't wait to get home. She was starting to feel like a caged animal. She knew she was safe here, but she was now tired of all the attention that the neighbor ladies were showering on her. She was tired of their opinions. She now fully understood what Tom meant earlier. She couldn't live here either. She thought that this was probably an ideal place to raise a family. The schools were good, there was plenty of police protection, and the community was close knit; however, it would be a bit stifling to live here and deal with all the gossip, and closed mindedness. Perhaps if you were retired and needed companionship this is where you might want to live too, but right now she knew Tom was right where he should be. Of course she was right where she should be, courtesy of Tom, but she couldn't wait to get home. She turned on the television as she was getting ready for bed. It had been a long few days. She was looking forward to seeing Tom tomorrow.

In the morning Marisa was a bit surprised that Mrs. Adelman didn't bring breakfast over, but for this she was thankful. She relished the fact that today she was truly alone with her thoughts. She sipped coffee and looked outside while thinking about how things would be when she got back to work.

She wondered if she was really safe if she kept delving into Wanda's life, or if Wanda was only capable of trying to intimidate her and nothing more. After thinking about all that had happened she decided to believe that Wanda was capable of almost anything. Wanda had been involved in too much to let someone get in her way. Marisa didn't know how to protect those around her except by keeping them in the dark about all that she had uncovered. Charles knew something was up, but he didn't have any details. Not yet anyway. Finally she decided that she didn't want to think about Wanda anymore, so she showered and applied her make-up. Afterwards, she did a load of laundry and picked up the magazines and papers that she had strewn around Tom's old bedroom.

Around lunchtime Claire came by with sandwiches but didn't stay long saying she had some errands to run before it got too late. Marisa was beginning to believe that the sidewalks get rolled up pretty early in town by the way these women acted. Marisa laughed to herself and felt fortunate that she had grown up in the big, wicked city. After lunch and looking at the last of the morning paper she started thinking about her future, or lack thereof, if Wanda followed through on her threats. She tried to get her mind off Wanda and immersed herself in one of Mrs. Roberts' women's magazines. She read several magazines cover to cover, even looking at the advertisements in the back.

She found she could mail away for kitchen hints, wallpaper, a business degree, and just about anything else. She also saw an ad for identification that caught her eye. She wondered how many kids in this small town had sent away for fake I.D. for underage drinking. She wondered just how easy it would be to obtain fake I.D., and she began filling out the form. She had taken her time filling out the information because she wanted a really pretty name. She settled on Sterling Summers, and she made up a phony social security number just like Wanda had done. In fact, she used the same unissued number that Wanda did: 506-52-6178. She had to pick a state for her new identification so she decided on a place she had never been: Wyoming.

In one of the other magazines she found a form to complete for a credit card. Before she realized what she was doing she had filled out the form using her new name and Social Security number. This was all done just for fun she kept telling herself, and just to see how easy it was to obtain false identification. Before she knew it she had put it in the mailbox for the postman to pick up.

It was nearly 4:00 p.m. when Tom finally arrived. She was a little surprised he had gotten there this early, but he said he had a relatively easy day in court so he slipped out about an hour early. He left straight from work to get a jump on the rush hour traffic. He told her he was going to freshen up and then they could go out for dinner. Before she could ask him anything about work he grabbed his bag and headed upstairs to his parent's room. His demeanor perplexed Marisa this afternoon, but she hoped she could put him in a better mood at dinner. He came down about a thirty minutes later looking like a new man. He had on a blue work shirt, faded jeans and work boots. He looked quite different from what Marisa always saw at work or at the bar where all the lawyers hung out after work. She liked this casual look on Mr.

GQ. He noticed her staring, and said, "Well this is the way I feel most comfortable. I hope you don't mind?"

"No way, I like it. Too bad you can't dress that way at work, maybe then you might have all the girls hanging on you."

He grinned and asked her if beer and pizza were appropriate for dinner. She replied, "I don't care where we eat as long as Claire and Mrs. Adelman won't be in attendance."

"Oh, so now you are tired of the little old neighborhood women, huh?"

"Well like you said, they mean well, but they are a bit intrusive. And, don't say I told you so unless you would like to eat dinner alone tonight."

"I won't say I told you so, but I'm sure they took good care of you and made sure you didn't starve to death."

"That they did, but I didn't have much time to myself as long as it was daylight."

"Oh well, we better hurry to the pizza place, the sidewalks get rolled up in less than two hours."

"Yeah! That I want to see, so let's go!"

They drank a pitcher of beer and ate a large, greasy pizza. They really didn't have a lot of time to catch up about work. All of Tom's old friends and former neighbors kept stopping by to say how long it had been since they had seen him. They would then play catch up and reminisce until the next person would stop by. This went on for several hours. Finally, he said, "We gotta get out of here. If this keeps up I won't have to attend my next high school reunion."

Marisa was ready to leave this little neighborhood hangout. As they got in the car he apologized for all the intrusions, but she told him she understood. He suggested that they rent some videos and just stay in the rest of the night. She agreed, but said she got to pick the movies. While they were driving, she asked him about work. She wondered if anything had happened that she should know about.

Just as he was about to answer her question he got a brief reprieve because he was pulling into the video store parking lot. Marisa was persistent and she knew by the way that he was acting that he had a lot to tell her. She realized, however, that this conversation would probably best be continued back at the house. Marisa knew that it didn't matter what movie they watched all she cared about now was what was happening at work, and how he was involved. They picked out a comedy/action picture and started toward home. Tom was chewing on the inside of his mouth and she could tell he had bad news for her, so she sat silently. She played over in her mind the questions she wanted to ask him, and how she thought he should answer.

They went inside and he went to the refrigerator and grabbed two bottles of beer. She said she had enough at the restaurant, and took one of the bottles back to the kitchen. He could tell by her tone that she was not going to react well to what he had to tell her about what had transpired in her absence.

As she came back into the room she said, "Tom I think we need to talk about what has been going on at work. I can tell that something has gone on by the way you're behaving, and I think I deserve at least an explanation."

"Marisa we do need to talk, but you have to promise to listen first, and ask questions later. And please try not to get mad."

"I don't make promises that I can't keep Tom, but I'll try to listen, and I'll try not to get mad."

"Well to start with I went to the deputies in your department and asked which one of them had accompanied you to Wanda's house on the home visit. You see, you never told me which deputy went with you. Frank finally spoke up and said he was the one that had gone out there with you. I asked him if we could talk privately about what went on. He told me he remembered exactly what happened then he pulled out a notebook and read to me his notes on the incident. He says he also made notes about the other things you had shared with him like the slashed tires and the first phone call. Frank told me that he was worried about you and had been watching you more closely than you had even realized. He also asked me if you had at least made the police reports he had asked you to. Now with this and the other stuff he doesn't even know about, you're in a mess of trouble, and you definitely aren't safe at home. So, I got to thinking, and I kept going back to what I should be doing, not only as your friend, but as a deputy D.A., so I called the Chief Probation Officer and asked her to meet with me." Marisa was quiet, but Tom knew it was just the calm before the storm.

Tom continued, "I didn't tell her why I needed to see her, but I told her it involved you and a client you were supervising. She then asked me who it was and I told her. Well at the meeting I was surprised to see your supervisor, Charles, in attendance too. They both wanted to know right away if you had done anything wrong that had gotten my department re-involved. I assured them you were doing a terrific job on this case, as you do on all your cases. Well it seems that the Chief was a bit bored by my little meeting until I told her I thought your life might be in jeopardy. Then she got mad that Charles had not told her of any of the things you had shared with him. Of course Charles was a bit surprised that anything was wrong because you always put on a happy face and trudge on as if nothing is out of place. Well I laid out the whole story including the dead cat incident and they both want to keep you safe, so there is a meeting on Monday morning."

"Great Tom, I trust you with my life and all my little secrets and you just can't keep anything to yourself? And you call yourself my friend? Shit, I'm glad you aren't one of my enemies!"

"Listen Marisa I'm trying to protect you until we can do something about Wanda. I'm not trying to undermine what you're doing. I'm your friend, but I'm also a deputy district attorney. She is continuing to break the law, and violating her probation at the same time. Someone needs to put a stop to both, and protect you from her and her goons in the process. I'm sorry if you can't see that right now, but I will not apologize for what I've done."

"Look, I understand what needs to be done, but that asshole that calls herself the Chief Probation Officer doesn't know her ass from a hole in the ground. She flies by the seat of her pants most often, and most often she is wrong! And now you think you and she can just fix everything. Well I will tell you what she'll suggest. She will suggest that we just cut her loose from probation and cut our losses. She doesn't like confrontation, and she doesn't know how to "fix" things. She was put in that position by a bunch of tired old men a very long time ago, and she hasn't seen the world change around her. She went through law school and finally passed the bar on her fifth try, but her daddy was well connected so she came here instead of to some giant law firm. She can't handle the pressure Tom. She likes to turn her head and sweep the problems under the rug. I'll tell you right now, no one, I repeat no one, is going to sweep Wanda and all she brings with her under the rug. If it is the last thing I do on this earth I will see that justice is done. She has wrecked too many lives already!"

"Marisa please be reasonable. What made you so down on Wanda in the first place? I mean why did you take an instant dislike for her?"

"Isn't it obvious Tom? She is a liar and a thief. Forgery is just a form of lying and cheating. You can never trust a liar or a cheat in my book. I can tolerate most things in this world, but lying and stealing for no good reason just really piss me off. Once someone has lied to me, I would never trust another thing they said to me. And someone that puts that much effort into his or her criminality is just evil in my opinion. Forgers just have to work too hard at being deceitful; it isn't a spur of the moment crime. I don't want you to think that I am okay with all the other types of criminals and crimes they commit, but I have never been able to deal with anyone that is a liar. I can deal with other types of criminals because I realize why they do what they do, but I do not tolerate people that lie or hurt people."

Marisa tried to explain her beliefs. "A murderer most often kills in the heat of passion; the burglar, robber and drug addicts are usually just feeding a habit. And in my most humble opinion the rapist and molester are just messed up psychologically. Something in their past made them be that way, but a forger is the worst of all that is bad in this world. And I guess that is why I also have such a problem that you involved the Chief. She too, is a liar. She lies about everything from statistics to how much time she spends at the office. And, she has a "boy's club" attitude and she doesn't deny it to those of us women that want to get ahead. You would think because she was a woman that she wouldn't want others of us to go through what she has had to get ahead, but she just doesn't give a damn. She got what she wanted, to hell with the rest of us!"

"Marisa, you're going to have to put your feelings about her aside. She is truly concerned about you."

"Bullshit! Please Tom, don't tell me you have fallen under her spell too! Her only concern will be how all this will play out on the evening news if something does happen to me. She doesn't want to besmirch her wonderful little department with news that one of our probationers wasn't rehabilitated."

"Okay Marisa, I understand that you don't like her, but I do believe she doesn't want anything to happen to you. And how could you sit here and say that she doesn't want her charged if she is continuing to break the law?"

"Tom I know her a bit better than you do. I have worked with her for four years. She is a snake, and if it looks like someone wasn't rehabilitated by her crack team of probation officers, it will make her look bad."

"Okay so answer me this, why wouldn't she want it on the news that one of her probation officers did a thorough job investigating a probationer and found out that the person was still committing crimes? That would make her department look good."

"Well that is what normal people would think, but she would get heat for making the Judge look bad and making your department and the police detectives look bad because they did not do a more thorough job. I am telling you she is politically connected and her job is very political. If she wants to keep it, she has to keep those people happy. She could give a shit about doing the right thing."

"Marisa look, what's done is done. I can't take it back, and I'm not sure I would if I could. This has gone way beyond the scope of your job, and it is putting you in danger. Let us handle it now. Put it out of your mind for now, things are fine now."

"Fine Tom, I will let it go tonight, but come Monday morning you may want to rethink your position. I think you might want to be on my side."

"Marisa I am on your side. Please believe that. Oh and by the way they know that you aren't sick."

"Great Tom, how did Charles take it?"

"Charles took it fine, he even said that you had been working a lot on this case and he could see that it was putting a strain on you. They asked where you were, but I told them that I had you somewhere safe. They pressed me for details, but I just told them I would have you here on Monday in one piece. There won't be a problem with your check if that is what you're concerned about."

"No Tom, I'm not concerned about the check. I have the time to take if I need to, I just don't like lying to people and this case has forced me to lie to everyone around me. I am becoming just like the people I detest, and I don't like what it's done to me. I hope you don't mind, but it has been a long day, and I'm really tired. I don't want to fight with you, I know you have only my best interest in mind, but I just wish you would have asked me before you involved the Chief. I hope you enjoy the movie. Good night Tom."

Tom just looked at her. He wished she could just see things from his perspective.

When she got upstairs she decided she was too angry to go right to bed. She grabbed his old shirt and a towel and went to take a long, hot bath. There were some candles under the sink so she got them out and lit them while the water was running. Once the tub was filled, she turned off the lights in the bathroom and stepped into the tub. The lighting and scent of the bath water were quite relaxing. She then tried to practice some relaxation techniques that she had learned at one of the annual probation officer's meetings. These annual meetings often taught them all about the newest ways to rehabilitate people, protect themselves on and off the job, and many other boring, but useful, topics.

She decided to use one of the techniques for stress reduction, positive imagery. In positive imagery the participant must relax the whole body and think positive thoughts, or of things that bring them peace. Right now Marisa was thinking of the beach, her favorite place. She was visualizing the vast, empty beach and the waves crashing on shore, and the sun was just about to set over the horizon. She imagined the gulls and sandpipers running along the beach in search of food. She could hear the calls of the birds as they mingled with the crashing waves. She was feeling more relaxed now, and was becoming very sleepy. She continued to think of nothing but the beach that she so wanted to be on just now. If only she could escape to paradise, and leave all the confusion in her life and troubles of Wanda behind she thought she might just be a happier person.

Finally, as the water started to cool she decided to get out of the tub and go to bed. She knew she shouldn't have yelled at Tom, but he just didn't understand how her office worked. She blew out the candles and replaced them under the sink, and went across the hall to Tom's old bedroom, her home for the past few days. She pulled the shade tonight and climbed into bed. She decided to think of the beach again as she started to drift off to sleep.

The movie was over about two hours later, and Tom was still upset about how the evening had turned out. He wasn't sure he wanted to get into the discussion again tomorrow, but he knew it was far from being over. He knew Marisa was right. He should have at least warned her that he was going to meet with her bosses. She had every right to be mad at him, but if she could only see he was trying to protect her. He climbed the stairs and went into his folk's room. He took off his clothes and put on a pair of gym shorts and a robe and went to the bathroom. He peeked in his old room to make sure she was okay before going to bed. He was a bit ashamed as he watched her sleeping. She had left the door open, and she was covered, but what would she think if she awoke to find him staring at her? He decided he better get to bed before she woke up.

As he lay there in bed waiting for sleep to take him away, he thought of Marisa and her predicament. He wondered if she was right about the Chief Probation Officer. He really hoped that he could protect her, and make them do the right thing. He then started thinking about his long friendship with Marisa, and wondered why he had never tried to ask her out on a date. He also wondered if she was truly finished with Elliot. He knew about their relationship, even though they were both very discreet. He was upset with her for dating Elliot, perhaps a bit jealous too, but he never told her this. He knew that Elliot would use her like he did all the other women he had ever dated, and somehow he knew that Elliot would go back to his wife. He just wondered why Marisa couldn't see that too.

Tom woke up kind of late. He wasn't used to sleeping in, but he was comfortable being back home, and he had nothing that he had to do today. On his way to the bathroom he realized that he had forgotten Marisa was right across the hall. He had forgotten to put on his robe, so he was very quiet and hoped that she wouldn't see him.

Just as he left the bathroom and started to pass by his old room she called out to him, "Hey stranger, come here."

"Uh wait Marisa, I need to put on a robe."

"Oh for goodness sakes Tom, I won't try anything. Come on in and sit down."

Sheepishly he came into the room. She was sitting up in bed with the covers hugged around her knees. She was a vision of beauty in the morning and in his old football jersey too. This was something he had always fantasized about as a kid: a beautiful woman in his bed, wearing one of his jersey's in his parent's house. Now, however, he was just sitting on the bed with an old friend. He caught himself smiling at the irony of the moment. She asked him why he was smiling and he told a little white lie. He told her he was just glad that he was able to be her protector, and glad she wasn't throwing things at him this morning. She laughed, and said she knew he only wanted what was best for her, but she just wished things had turned out differently.

"Oh well Tom, you know my motto. No regrets and never look back. We can't take back what has happened, but we can take care of what lay ahead. Will you still be by my side on Monday?"

"Marisa I wouldn't be anywhere else."

The rest of the weekend was a bit of a blur. They spent some time at Dave's house visiting, and of course he made the obligatory calls on Claire and Mrs. Adelman. He thanked everyone for taking such good care of Marisa in his absence. Before they left for home on Sunday evening they straightened up the house and you couldn't even tell that anyone had been there. On the drive home he told her he would not be taking her home tonight. He asked her if she wanted to stay at his place or go to a friend's house. She knew she would need change of work clothes and at this point had no transportation so she opted to go to Dani's house. She told him she would just call her parents and say she got in too late to come over, and she would see them tomorrow. He agreed that this would be a good idea.

When they got back to town she gave him directions to Dani's apartment. She only asked that he not go in with her because of the story she had concocted. He laughed but said her secret was safe with him but he said he would wait until she was safely inside the apartment. They arrived at Dani's apartment just after dark. She grabbed her bag and gave him a peck on the cheek. He told her he would be in her office at 8 o'clock in the morning. Their meeting was scheduled for 8:30 am. She knocked on Dani's door and glanced back at his car. He had the lights off so Dani wouldn't notice the car in the street. Dani opened the door a few seconds later and was a bit surprised to see her good friend with bag in hand.

"Hey can I crash here tonight and get a ride into work in the morning?"

"Yeah sure of course, but can I ask why you aren't at your place?"

"Well, I had my friend drop me there, and when we went in there were a bunch of ants in the kitchen and all over the bathroom, so I decided to come over here. Is that all right, or are you entertaining?"

"Oh yeah sure. Me the big entertainer, now get in here and tell me all about your trip."

"Well there isn't really much to tell. We had a good time, but my folks were right. He's not the guy for me. It had sort of lost its spark if you know what I mean. We just hung out mostly, watched television, and played catch up. Really I'm glad to be back, and glad he's gone."

"Well okay, I guess. But, you didn't really miss much here or at work." Dani decided now would not be the time to ask if she was really with Seth.

"Oh hey, can I use your phone to call my parents and let them know I got in safely." Dani handed her the phone and walked out of the room to give her some privacy.

As much as Marisa hated lying to anyone, least of all her parents, she wove yet another tale regarding her work related seminar in Chicago. Her mom was a bit put off that she didn't stop by, but she told her she was exhausted and just wanted to get some rest before going in to work in the morning. She then told her mother that she was unplugging the ringer, so she shouldn't bother to have Kate call when she got home. She told her she would stop by tomorrow around dinnertime to see them all.

Dani and Marisa sat up for a few hours talking about the recent happenings in court and the office, then Dani switched the subject to Marisa's weekend adventure. Marisa danced around the subject long enough for Dani to realize she really didn't want to talk about it, so she let it drop. Dani figured that it had all just been a big mistake and Marisa just wanted to pretend that it didn't happen. Finally Marisa said she really needed to get some sleep, so Dani gave her some blankets and a pillow and they fixed up the couch for her to sleep on. Before she fell asleep she thought about Elliot. She really missed him now. She wondered if he still thought about her too.

Marisa woke up when she heard the shower start and Dani getting ready. She climbed off the couch and started folding the blankets. She really hated these early mornings. Dani finally came into the living room and told her she had put fresh towels in the bathroom for her. She also told her she would start a pot of coffee while Marisa was getting ready. Marisa went on in silence. Dani was definitely a morning person, while Marisa was not. When she came out of the bathroom she asked Dani if she could borrow some work clothes.

"You know I thought you just came over here to raid my closet. Sure girlfriend, wear whatever you want."

Marisa then searched through the closet and settled on a long black skirt and a lavender blouse. She put on her tennis shoes and fixed her make-up before coming out to the kitchen.

"Nice shoes. They really make the outfit," laughed Dani.

"Yeah I know, I'm making a new fashion statement. No, not really I have some black heels and hose at work. I have a meeting as soon as I get in, so I'll have to hurry putting the rest of my ensemble together when I get there."

"A meeting huh? How do you know that? Or was it something that was planned before you left?"

"Yeah, of course it was already set up. I thought I told you about it. Well we better get moving or we'll both be late."

"No, you didn't mention anything about a meeting, but let's get going you can fill me in on the ride in."

On the car ride to work Marisa made sure the subject of the meeting never came up. They sang along with the radio, and talked about the various artists, and before long they were walking into the building. So far, so good Marisa thought.

"Hey, you never did tell me what your meeting was about Marisa. Is it a big secret, or what?"

"Or what I guess. Nothing major really, just some questions on a case I have, and I want to make sure I cover all my bases that's all."

"So, are you going to lunch, or should I make other arrangements?"

"Well I should be done by then I would think, so unless a better offer comes your way, we could eat together."

Chapter Six

Marisa went straight to her office and called Tom, and he agreed to come right down. She changed shoes and began checking her voice mail messages. Bill had called several times; most of the calls caught him cackling about how devious he had been with Wanda's accounts. There were several other calls regarding clients missing their appointments, or trying to reschedule. Then there was an anonymous phone call that was probably from Wanda's beau, Mr. Randolph.

The message said, "Well I guess you get the point that we aren't messing around. You can run, but you can't hide forever. Keep this shit up and someone is going to end up dead. Do what you need to do to get this straightened out to the way it was before you started snooping around, or else!"

She was never going to let them win she thought to herself. She knew that she needed to save this message, but she was not going to share it with anyone now.

Tom had arrived and with him he brought his boss, the District Attorney, Michael Redford. Marisa knew that Michael did not like to be backed into a corner, nor did he like people screwing around with "his" system. She figured that the first time Jansen mentioned discharging Wanda from probation Michael would ask her what she was doing in the Chief's position.

Michael waited in the hallway while Tom helped Marisa gather up her file and call Charles. The three then headed to Jansen's office. Jansen was there and a bit surprised to see the District Attorney walking into her office. She started moving about the room trying to gain the dominant position, but it wouldn't matter in which position she chose because when Michael spoke those around him knew exactly who was in control of the situation. Jansen couldn't hold a candle to Michael's intelligence, speaking ability, or ability to lead a conversation. Jansen would never be accused of being the brightest bulb in the pack. One of Jansen's big secrets was that it only took her five times to pass the bar exam, and then no large firm wanted her. Marisa reasoned that this would be an interesting meeting if nothing else.

Michael started the meeting by stating that he had several concerns, the primary concern being the safety of the probation officer. His next concern was that a probationer was continuing to break the law and was already in violation status. Jansen agreed with his statements, then made a stupid mistake by asking how the situation could resolve itself without a lot of trouble. During all of this Charles, Tom and Marisa had remained silent. Now they were all looking at each other wondering how Jansen had made it this far by being so stupid. It was apparent she had given this no more thought than from the first time she had heard about it. She didn't care about anyone but herself, and how she was going to look when all of this broke.

Michael stood and looked her square in the eyes and said, "I think we have more important things to be worried about than how much trouble this is going to cause you or this agency. I don't mind rocking the boat, and getting the message out that if you are a criminal in this county then you better be prepared to spend some time in jail!"

"Well, er, uh, I didn't mean that she shouldn't be in jail, but this is going to make a lot of people look bad. I don't think I need to remind you that it's an election year, and you and the Judge are running again."

"I don't give a damn about the election right now. I do care that some probationer is threatening one of your officers, is trying to pass herself off as someone else, and making money off the state at the same time. Maybe you better rethink your position, and what our mission is here."

Charles was shifting in his seat and tugging at his bow tie. It was clear he was not comfortable seeing his boss getting reamed.

Finally Marisa said, "Look, I'm the one she is pissed at. I'm the one she is threatening, and I'm the one that holds the key at this point. I have not updated the violation report yet. I can't until additional charges are filed against her. And, at this point there is not much more we can do to her until some other agencies get off their ass and do what needs to be done. I think it's time to start rattling some chains at the Social Security Administration, Department of Public Welfare, and at the banks that are involved."

Before she could say anything else Jansen said, "Marisa be quiet. Who do you think you are? You don't have any business telling people what should be done here. You got all this started and now you want to dump it in someone else's lap."

And before she could finish, Michael asked, "I didn't know she could file charges against someone, or file for subpoenas for all those agencies. She's right. We need to put a team on it, and get the ball moving. However, I don't think that she should be involved in doing any of those things. She has provided the information to investigate further, but anymore action on her part makes her a continued target."

Jansen's face was red, and everyone could see she was embarrassed by Michael's assessment of the situation. Jansen was out of her league. She knew it and realized that everyone in the room knew it now. Tom finally grasped that Marisa was indeed right about her boss. He wished now he hadn't involved Jansen initially. He gave Marisa a knowing glance; she responded with a smirk.

Charles was still pretending to be out of the room while the discussion on what Marisa had uncovered continued for another hour. At some point Charles asked to be excused and his wish was granted. Jansen then suggested that the case be reassigned to another officer. Marisa looked around at the other players and said she was totally opposed to this.

Michael then said, "Well, as I see it Marisa knows this case inside and out, and if we put someone else on it that puts two people in danger. Unless perhaps you were going to take the case yourself Jansen?"

"Well no, you have a point. Maybe Marisa should keep it. But when this thing breaks I want the department as a whole to get credit for the investigation."

"I think you're putting the cart before the horse, let's just get this thing worked out on paper."

Tom hesitantly asked how they planned to keep Marisa safe during all of this, or at least until they had Wanda locked up. Marisa was a bit taken aback by Tom's comment, but she knew she couldn't be mad at him. Jansen just looked at Michael and finally stated that the department didn't have any provisions for protecting their officers when they were away from the building unless they were on a home visit to a client. She said there was no money in the budget for something like this. Michael indicated that sometimes victims were put up in 'safe houses' until the culprit had been arrested, but they had never had to protect one of their own. Marisa then said she knew how to protect herself, she didn't need anyone's help. All of the men admired her spunk, but no one at this meeting, aside from Jansen perhaps, would let her go through this alone.

Michael then asked her if she had discussed this case with anyone else. She told him that she knew when to keep her mouth shut. She then explained that she had not even told her family the truth about the cat incident. Further, she told them that by keeping everyone else in the dark she believed that she was protecting them. Tom indicated that he had hidden her out of town for the past few days, but that place was not going to be available for much longer, and he wasn't sure if she was happy there.

"Look I don't care about her happiness at this point. I do, however, care that she stay alive and well," said Michael quite sternly.

She knew he meant this in a nice way, he was just a little upset with the situation at this point and the lack of concern by the Chief Probation Officer.

"Well Marisa I know you aren't going to like what I have to say, but I'm thinking of your best interest, and I think that Jansen will back me on this even though it will probably put a strain on the department."

Michael gave Jansen a look that said 'you will back me on this or it will be your ass'. Jansen acted as if she knew what was going on, and just nodded her head in agreement. Tom looked at Marisa to let her know that they all only wanted what was best for her. Marisa nodded at Michael. He had been kind to her in the past, and he probably wasn't trying to jam her up like Jansen would if she got the chance.

"Michael let me interject for a minute if you will. As I said earlier, and I want to reiterate now, I do not want this case reassigned. I'll back off and do what you think is best, but don't even suggest that I give it up."

"Marisa I don't have anything to do with assignments in this office, and as I said earlier, I see no reason to put this on anyone else at this time. It would be foolish in my opinion to give this case to another officer, or to let it just sit unattended until things actually blow up."

He had set the stage. If Jansen took this case from her now, Michael would be saying that she was foolish. Jansen was at least smart enough to know she wouldn't let Michael call her foolish. Also, Jansen wouldn't take the case herself and put her life in jeopardy. Jansen wasn't so sure that she wanted Marisa to keep the case, but what was she to do now?

"My suggestion would be for you to take a leave of absence, paid of course. Let some time get between you and Wanda and all that you have uncovered. Go away for awhile."

"Oh and let her think that I'm afraid of her, and that I run away from my problems? I don't think so."

Tom said, "Marisa you should be afraid of her. She has proven that she is unstable, that she will hurt you or something that you are close to. What does it matter what she thinks? You've always said that you don't care what others think of you. We all know that you're not running away, merely buying some time. Why can't that be all this is about? Think rationally Marisa, don't let your anger and frustration with things cloud your good judgment."

Marisa knew he was right. Reluctantly she agreed, but said she would only be gone for a week or so. Jansen asked her if she was going to use her vacation, and

Michael interrupted her and said that the department was pretty much making her take the leave, so they should just pay her and be done with it. Michael then indicated that no one in the department should be apprised of what was happening, and that if anyone asked they should just be told that she was taking some time off.

Jansen kept playing the 'what if' game, and Michael rather disgustedly said, "Jansen why don't you just be a department head and quit thinking about how this makes you look. Try thinking of someone else for a change!"

Marisa wanted so badly to laugh at the buffoon that was her boss, but she was able to maintain her composure.

Michael started to leave. He was angry that such an imbecile was the head of this department. Tom started to follow his boss out, but Marisa asked him to wait for her. Jansen stood just wringing her hands. She was wondering how all this could have gotten so out of control and thinking that Marisa had just continued to stir the pot of trouble she had uncovered. Jansen couldn't understand her drive, why she even cared about any of this when it didn't directly affect her. Marisa knew exactly what she was thinking, and she couldn't even stand to look at Jansen now. Marisa left the office without another word in her direction.

As they were walking down the hall Michael told her to call him if she needed anything and he gave her his card with all the personal numbers written on the back of it. She just smiled and told him she hoped she wouldn't need to bother him. Tom followed her back to her office. She had about another thirty minutes before lunch with Dani, but she wanted to talk to Tom privately.

"Do you think we can go grab a soda and talk for a minute?"

"Sure, or would you rather grab some lunch?"

"No, I already have lunch plans and I think I'll be on vacation after that."

"Let's go."

They walked outside the building and across the street to a little sidewalk hot dog cart. Tom paid for two cans of pop and they walked over to a bench and sat down.

"I believe what Michael says, and I completely trust you. But, I don't trust Jansen. Actually, you know that I don't trust that many people. She just won't be able to keep her mouth shut. She'll tell someone, and word gets around this building pretty quickly. Make sure that Michael knows that. I'm not even telling my family where I'm going. I'll call someone, when I'm ready, but I will not call into this office while I'm away, nor will I call you. But I just have an idea that Jansen will try something while I'm gone. Don't let her get to the Judge, and don't let this case get to court without me being there. Can you promise me that?"

"I know now your boss is a complete jerk, but I don't think she would really try to get it before the Judge without you there. She would have too much explaining to do."

"She may not be a smart woman, but she is underhanded and she'll do whatever she thinks she can get away with. Please don't let her get away with anything."

Tom assured her that he would keep a close eye out on this case and he would share her worries with Michael. She knew her friend wouldn't let her down.

She came back in time just to see Dani fretting about where her friend had run off to again.

"I thought you dumped me again for Tom. What's going on Marisa? Or, is this some big secret game of espionage that you can't share with your best friend?"

"Let's just go to lunch, we can talk some there, but not here."

Over lunch Marisa seemed a bit distracted. She wanted so badly to share what was going on with this case with Dani but she couldn't. Dani was a great friend but whatever happened Marisa knew that Dani just didn't have the willpower or wherewithal to deal with anyone in authority if they started asking questions. Also, Marisa figured that the first person anyone would go to would be Dani if something came up about this case. If Dani didn't know anything it may just save her from becoming sucked into this mess. Marisa told Dani that she was having some problems and she was going to get away for a little while, but it was nothing that wouldn't resolve itself in a few days.

Dani said she saw that Michael was in on the meeting and she wondered why the District Attorney was meeting with their Chief and Marisa. Marisa again lied to her friend. She told her that the relationship with Elliot had something to do with it, because they didn't believe that it was over. She told them she would take some time off and they could do what they wanted while she was away, but she just needed time to figure out what she was doing with her life. This seemed to make sense to gullible Dani, and she counseled Marisa not to make any rash decisions about her future or her job because of what the others were thinking about her now. Marisa said she really didn't care what they thought of her, or of her relationships, but she just needed to get away and think about a lot of things. They went back to the office in a rather somber mood. Of course both had different things on their mind right now, but it was best this way Marisa kept telling herself.

When she got back to her office there were two voice mail messages. The first was from Michael. He warned her to tell only her immediate family of her whereabouts. And, he promised that no one would get this case before the Judge without her being there to defend her actions. He then told her to be careful. The second message was from Jansen. She told her that she had a luncheon meeting, but that she should leave her phone numbers of where she would be just in case a question came up. She thought to herself that she would be gone before Jansen got back, and there was no way that she was telling her anything.

She still wondered how Wanda had gotten her home number. At this point she didn't put it past Jansen giving it to her. Wanda was quite the manipulator and in Marisa's opinion Jansen was a total idiot. She gathered up some papers and her Rolodex and put them in her briefcase. She decided to wait and slip out while Charles was at lunch. Anyone that would see her leave would just suppose that she was seeing clients or had a meeting to attend. She would leave it to Jansen to explain her absence.

She went home and called her friend, Julie, at work. Julie's family had a cabin that was rarely used this time of year. She told Julie that she needed some time to think and wondered if she could stay a week or so at the cabin. Julie said it would be fine and told her where they hid the key. Marisa asked that if her parents called to tell them that she was planning to join her the next day. Julie didn't ask any questions, she assumed that Marisa was going to the cabin with Elliot as sort of a last ditch effort to save the relationship. Marisa knew what she was thinking and she didn't let on any different. She knew that if Julie thought she had someone there, she wouldn't bother calling and checking on her. She said goodbye and thanked her friend for her generosity, and told her she would be in touch in a week or so.

Marisa then called her mother at work and explained that she and Julie were going on a vacation getaway that Julie had won on a radio station call in game. She explained that Julie was supposed to go with someone else but they had backed out at the last minute and since she had vacation time to take, she was going with her friend. Her mother said she was really turning into a traveler, but cautioned her daughter to not lose sight of her priorities with work and all the things she was doing presently. Marisa assured her mother that her job was one of her main priorities, but she was allowed to take vacations whenever she wanted to. Also, she said it wouldn't really cost her more than the food she ate because the airfare and room was included in the prize. She promised to call the moment she got back and asked them to tell Kate when she got in from school.

Now all she had to do was quickly pack and get out of town before dusk. Finding the cabin in the dark would not be any fun. She would also need to stop at the store on her way to the cabin, and it closed early during the week. Hurriedly she grabbed some jeans, T-shirts, sweatshirts and some books and threw them all in a bag. The cabin would have towels, blankets and pillows, so she left all that stuff behind. She really didn't know how long she would be gone, so she made a mental note to stop by the bank and get some cash. She pulled out her little cooler and filled it with some pop, lunchmeat and fruit. She could eat on the way. The cabin was about three hours away. She needed to get moving before anyone had the chance to call or see her leaving. No one would realize where she had gone. She was pretty good at covering her tracks.

Marisa got to the store just before it closed. She had been here several times before with Julie so she was familiar to the owner. She told the woman that she was staying a week or so up at the Grainger's cabin. The lady said, "Well it's pretty deserted around town right now, so you should have some peace and quiet."

Marisa thanked her for staying open a bit longer than she planned, and said she would probably be back later in the week for more supplies. Marisa wanted to get on her way before darkness set in, so she bid the woman goodbye and was on her way.

Marisa raced around the curving road and up and down the hills until the cabin was in sight. When she finally pulled onto their land she felt like a weight had been lifted from her shoulders. She breathed a sigh of relief and began to unpack the car. She had made pretty good time, and there was still a hint of daylight. From this vantage point she could see the valley all around her with no other cabins near her. The Grainger's owned about fifty acres here. They planned to retire here in a few years, but now the place was only used during long weekends, holidays, and for their family reunions. This place was idyllic to Marisa, a little piece of heaven on earth. Marisa knew that she would not be bothered by older ladies bringing her three meals a day, or stopping by just to check up on her. She could totally relax and unwind without any interruptions up here. She did have access to a phone down by the store, but she would only be calling home in a few days to tell her family what a good time she was having with Julie.

She planned to look over all the information she had gathered on Wanda or whomever she was this week. She decided to start by writing it all down in chronological order. By doing this it would be easier to present in court when the time came. Also, she would see if she had left any stones unturned. She wondered what Wanda was thinking about now. And, she wondered how Bill was doing with all that he had uncovered. Marisa looked at this time away as a working vacation.

All the while she was contemplating this information she kept wondering how Wanda had obtained her home telephone number. This was the only piece of the puzzle that really had Marisa stumped. Of course she then began thinking about how Jansen reacted when Michael got involved. She had always had a certain distrust of Jansen, but now she was beginning to worry that she could be bribed. Perhaps Wanda had applied her charms and told some wonderful story that she just had to have her officer's phone number and Jansen was stupid enough to give it to her, or finding that maybe that wouldn't work, Wanda paid her off in order to get the number.

Marisa had no reason to distrust Michael, Tom, or Dani. And, she was not really that close with any of her co-workers, aside from Dani, so they didn't have her home phone number. She knew that she could have easily been followed which would explain how they got to Rufus, but how did they get her phone number? She knew that her parents or sister would have never given out her number. When people had called them for it in the past, even old classmates, they had simply asked for the person's number and then passed it along to her. But this piece of the puzzle was perplexing to her.

The first night alone in the cabin was a bit unnerving for Marisa. She wasn't used to all the noises of the forest, and the creaking wood of the cabin. She drifted off to sleep, but with her gun under her pillow and a baseball bat by the front door. Once daybreak came she slept more soundly. The creatures of the night had quieted, and the shadows in which to hide were now gone.

When she awoke she stretched lazily and wandered about the big empty cabin, looking out all the windows. The scenery was amazing. She wished she could capture every image in her mind, never to forget it. She did bring along her camera. She grabbed it and went out on the wraparound porch and started snapping pictures. She stood and smelled the fresh clean air, and listened to the chirping birds. This place was a great stress reliever.

She started thinking about Seth. He had called early last week when she was getting ready to leave with Tom. He told her he would be calling her back this week on Monday or Tuesday to try to set up a lunch date. She decided she better call him before he called her at work today only to find out she was gone again. She pulled on some sweats and grabbed her purse and keys and drove down to the store. She used the pay phone outside to call him. It took about eight rings before he finally picked up. He said he was going to call her when he got up. Since it took so long for him to answer she realized she had awakened him.

He asked her to hold on a minute while he pulled on some clothes. She told him to hurry because it was long distance. When he got back on the phone he asked her if she was still at her meeting. She confessed that she had come back but then left abruptly on vacation.

He asked, "Vacation huh? I thought you were going somewhere later. What's really going on Marisa?"

"Seth if I tell you I'd have to kill you, and you're too good of a friend to have to kill. No, really it's more like a working vacation. I'm staying at a friend's place, but I'm alone. The department put me on vacation, but I'm fine with it. Don't worry about me. I'll be back in a week or so."

"Well Baby, I don't have anything real pressing now, maybe I could keep you company. Are you in trouble at work, I mean did they suspend you or something?"

"Or something. No, I really don't want any visitors and I don't think I'll be gone that long anyway. I'll call you when I get back. And don't worry about me Seth, I'm fine. I need to get off of here, but I just wanted to let you know I was thinking about you and I didn't want you to think I had forgotten that you called me last week. Take care, and I will call you when I get back I promise. Bye Seth."

"Bye Baby. Call me if you change your mind. Take care of you."

When she hung up she wished she could confide to someone. Seth would probably be the person to talk to since he was somewhat removed from her personal and professional life, and yet he knew just enough about her to want to protect her and help her. She knew she could always count on Seth. She just wished he could always count on her.

She made one more phone call before going back to the cabin. She was certain she would get voice-mail, but was surprised when the Elliot answered the phone.

"Green here."

"Elliot? You're answering your own phone these days?"

"Yes, I'm waiting on a call. How are you? I'm glad I didn't have to hold my breath too long."

"Well, I'm pretty good actually. Look, I need to just cut to the chase. I'm tired of walking on eggshells when I'm around you. I want to go back to being friends. I expect nothing more of you. I just want to be your friend again. I know you love your family, and I would never do anything to jeopardize that, but do you think we could have lunch a week from this Wednesday?"

"Wow! Lunch huh? You bet. I really miss you, and I want to talk to you about my family."

Marisa cut him off in mid thought and said, "Wait Elliot please. I'm not at work or home right now, can this wait 'til next week?"

"Sure Marisa. How about we meet at Tino's around noon?"

"Yeah Elliot, let's go to there. I'll see you then. Bye." She hung up before he could utter another word.

She drove back to the cabin singing along with the local radio station. It was a country station, but surprisingly she knew a lot of the songs. The radio would be her constant companion while she was away. When she got back to the cabin she went inside and grabbed a soda and headed back out to the porch. She would spend the majority of the week out here looking out into God's country. She read a lot, and just watched nature. Many nights she just sat on the porch swing and listened to the sounds of the night, and watched the twinkling sky.

Although she felt very peaceful here and certainly had caught up on her sleep, she was ready to go back and face the world. She just wondered if the world was ready for her to come back. Early Thursday afternoon she packed up all her belongings and cleaned up the cabin. Though it wasn't very messy, she dusted, swept the floor and cleaned the bedroom and bathroom. She also straightened up the kitchen and gathered up all the perishable items to take home with her. She decided to stop by the store to tell the owner that she would be leaving. After talking with her for a few minutes she was on her way back to reality.

She got home after dark, and cautiously went to her apartment. Nothing seemed out of the ordinary. When she got inside she could see the flashing light on the message machine. The first call was from her mother telling her to call as soon as she got back home. She had called the very day Marisa left on her trip. This made Marisa smile. There was a call from Dani telling her something was going on at work, just gossip, nothing important. Tom called to say he was thinking about her and wondering where she could be. He left his numbers and asked her to call him whenever she got in town. Then there were about ten hang up phone calls. On some of them you could hear breathing on the line, while the others just hung up as soon as the tone sounded. Marisa assumed these calls were from Wanda and her "gentleman caller."

She unpacked and called her mother. Kate answered the phone, and they spoke for some time before her mother finally got on the other extension to see how her older daughter was doing. Marisa could tell that her mother was worried about her, but she ignored it, not wanting her to know the truth. Her mother had good instincts too, but Marisa knew if she told her any of what she was going through Tina would insist on staying with her. Marisa said that she and Julie had had a great time.

She regaled them with all the fancy dinners they were able to afford since they didn't have to pay for airfare or accommodations. She wondered if her mother knew she was lying, but for now she just could not risk telling her family the truth. They finally hung up when she told her there were other calls she needed to make, and she had to get her stuff ready for work in the morning.

She called Tom and told him she was fine and that she felt like she could conquer the world now that she was rested and relaxed. He said he was glad she was back, and that Wanda still had not been in. By the way he said this she could tell something was going on with the case.

"Tom what's happened? Is something going on with Wanda's case?"

"Well when you left you didn't say when you would be back, and I have a feeling everyone, including me thought you would be gone longer. You were right though. Jansen filed a motion with the court, and it's set for hearing tomorrow at 9:00a.m. I don't know what she's planning to do, but I think you might want to be there. If I were you, I would just show up in court at nine, not stopping at your office. If you tell me where your notes are I can pick them up for you and have them in court when you arrive."

"That won't be necessary. I have a copy of my notes with me, and I'll be there before that bitch can do anything! Is the case still showing up under my name in the computer?"

"Yes it is. What are you going to do?"

"Well it's my case, so I guess I'll need to find out what her memo says, but you can bet your ass she won't be doing the hearing! Tom I need to go now, but I'll see

172

you in court just before nine. Thanks. See you in the morning."

Marisa was infuriated now. What was Jansen up too? She presumed that she was going to say that since the bank is going to get their money now, and she really isn't a threat to society maybe we should just go on and discharge her. This was her typical way of operating, and manipulating the system for her own good. Wouldn't she be surprised to see her subordinate in court right next to her as she started to speak; the Judge would probably find this amusing as well. The Judge would have to consider their opposing arguments, but Marisa was sure she could make the Judge see the truth and justice of keeping Wanda on probation.

Again she stood looking out into the darkness. Watching and waiting for something she could not see. Marisa went to bed sometime after midnight. Tonight the phone awakened her. She answered it on the third ring.

"Welcome back you little bitch! You keep running away, but you won't be able to hide from me forever. You better just watch your step!" Then the dial tone came on.

Marisa didn't go back to sleep but lay awake in bed contemplating this phone call. She also started wondering what would happen if she disappeared? Would anyone press forward with the Wanda situation, or is she the only one that cared? She thought back to the forms she completed at the Roberts'. Could she just walk away from everything? Would she really be safe if she left? How long would she have to stay away, or would she really ever want to return? So many questions to think about, so many other things going on in her mind.

Someone was still watching her, and she couldn't even see them. Did she dare tell anyone of this call? She was really getting scared. She wondered if the people closest to her noticed her nervousness. As she was getting ready for work today she decided she would tell Tom of the late night phone call. He would be worried, but she would assure him she could handle all of this. If only she could assure herself now. She so wanted to confide all this to someone, but she just didn't know whom to tell without alarming them as well. Before she left for work she called Tom and told him she would be sitting in a darkened corner of the courtroom waiting for Jansen to come in. She would not approach the bench until after the hearing had started. She also told him briefly that she needed to talk to him afterwards. He tried to ask her what she wanted to talk about, but she said she had to hurry now. She promised to talk to him later.

Marisa parked in another parking lot today, a lot opposite of the building where she usually parked. She went into the building through different doors and took the stairs to the courtroom. She did not go into the court office; she went in the main doors and chose a seat in the back of the room. It was very dark, and with what she had on she was very well camouflaged. A few minutes before 9:00 am, Jansen walked in through the court office doors and took a seat in the jury box with some other attorneys. They made small talk until the Judge took the bench. Wanda was nowhere around, nor was her public defender. Tom came in and looked around, but his eyes didn't see Marisa hiding in the shadows. Finally, the Judge called the case. Jansen and Tom took their respective seats. As the Judge asked why they were there, Marisa made her way to the seat next to her boss. She jumped nervously, and said she didn't realize Marisa would be back so soon.

She smiled and said, "No, I'm sure you didn't. But I'm here now, so I think I'll be taking over. Besides, you assured Michael, Tom and myself that you wouldn't be doing anything with this case. I wonder how you can sit here now and try to explain your actions. But don't bother."

"Marisa, I don't know what you mean. I believe I said that I would do whatever I could with this case to try to help you out. Why are you always so negative and distrusting of me?"

"Jansen don't try to act like the nice girl here, and don't patronize me. You know why I don't trust you, and if you don't, I certainly don't feel the need to explain it. Suffice it to say that I don't trust you or believe you now, I never have, and more importantly, I never will. My opinion of you will never change, so don't pretend to act hurt. We both know you don't care what others think. But, the thing I have always wondered about is how you can sleep at night knowing all the crappy things you do to people. Please don't bother to defend yourself or try to answer because I really don't give a damn."

Marisa then turned her attention to the Judge and indicated that there had been some misunderstanding on the chief's part about this case. She then explained that she had been out of the office for a few days and she thought she had intended to file this motion on this case, but it was an entirely different matter in another courtroom with another officer.

The Judge said, "Good, I was beginning to wonder. And, I would never let this probationer off early. By the way, why isn't she here?"

"Well Judge I believe that the chief would have to answer that as I just got into town last night after a few days off."

Jansen looked like a wounded animal now and started stuttering her words as she so often did when she was nervous. Finally it came to her, "Sir, Your Honor, uh, well she hasn't been reporting as she should, but I think Ms. Spencer is planning to file something to that effect shortly, isn't that right Ms. Spencer?"

"Yes Judge, I will be filing that by the end of the day. Thank you."

"Okay bailiff, call the next case."

As Marisa started to leave the table she turned to Jansen and got right in her face so she didn't miss a word. "If you ever try that again with one of my cases I will report it to the panel of Judges that oversee our department before you can blink. Now stay out of my cases, and let me do my job. And if you want to write me up for insubordination that would be fine, but don't even try anything else because too many people are watching for you to fail right now. Believe me everyone knows how stupid you really are and how you got this job. Oh, and one more thing, everyone knows your secret about the bar exam!" Marisa then looked at Tom and headed out of the courtroom.

"Good save in there Marisa. What were you saying to her before you left the table? She didn't look like she was the boss at that point."

"Listen to the court reporter's tapes, I'm sure the microphones were still on and captured every breath."

Tom just shook his head. He knew that Marisa was one tough cookie and the chief better stay out of her way this time. There were several people in important places watching this case.

"Hey what did you want to talk to me about?"

"Oh just a lovely little phone call I got last night."

"Okay Marisa, was it her again or is that a stupid question? And, what did she say this time?"

"Well she knew I had been gone and welcomed me home. Then she said I better watch myself because I could run but I couldn't hide. That was the gist of the conversation, then she hung up."

"Damn, she is good at being bad isn't she?"

"I know that no one followed me to my retreat, but apparently they had been looking for me if she knew I wasn't at home. And there were several hang up phone calls on my message machine when I got in last night. I assume those were from her too."

"Well I wish you would let me stay with you or you with me, because I think she means what she says."

"Yeah, somehow I knew that you just wanted to get me in the sack," Marisa said as she tried to laugh it off. He knew though that she was worried.

He would indeed be watching the parking lot without her even knowing it just to put his mind at ease. Of course he wouldn't be sharing this information with her. She finished out the day as any other. Dani was full of gossip from the previous week. She indicated that Monika had been in and out of Jansen's office a lot this week. In fact she even mentioned that Monika had been in Marisa's office several times. Every time Dani asked Monika what she was doing she indicated that she didn't want to walk all the way back to her office to get a piece of paper, or use the phone, so she just borrowed from another officer. Although Dani didn't like that answer, there was little she could do about it. She never saw anything out of the ordinary while she was in there, but she knew that Marisa wouldn't like it. She was right.

Marisa had never liked Monika. She was sneaky and underhanded just like Jansen. They made quite a pair. Everyone suspected that they were having an illicit lesbian affair, but they claimed they just shared a mutual respect for one another. It seems what one of them didn't think of the other one did-much like evil twins.

Marisa didn't trust many people and she certainly didn't trust Monika or Jansen. Now she started wondering if Monika could have leaked her phone number to Wanda. Or perhaps she was the voice that Marisa didn't recognize when she was so rudely awakened a few weeks ago. Things were starting to gel about the culprit. Marisa told Dani to watch herself too. She indicated that Monika should never be trusted with information, and if she saw her in her office again she should say something to Charles. Dani started questioning again what was going on, and why was everything such a big mystery. Marisa cut off the questions and just told her it was better not to know anything, at least for the moment. She also told her that she was forced to go on leave because of what was going on in the office, but she was back now and things would be fine.

Dani was more worried now. She knew that Marisa could take care of herself, but she still worried about her friend. She wished that Marisa would confide in her, but she also realized Marisa was just trying to protect her from something, yet she didn't know what.

Marisa called Seth's number when she got back to her office. They talked about her trip for a few minutes and he asked if she could meet him for a coffee on her break this afternoon. She told him to meet her across the street at the usual place, but cautioned that she couldn't stay long. He knew she was busy, but he was thankful for any time she would give him. Besides he wanted to tell her he might take a temporary job hanging drywall with a friend. He knew she would encourage him on this point.

Marisa and Dani left work at the same time and decided to go out to dinner directly after work. Marisa left her car in the lot and planned to pick it up later. They called Kate and asked her to join them. After dinner they grabbed some movies and headed for Marisa's car. Dani followed Marisa home. When they pulled into the parking lot Tom was there watching. He wondered where they had been, but he was glad that she was now home. He sat in the parking lot watching and waiting, and hoping that no one would be there. The trio went to Marisa's apartment to watch the movies. Afterwards, Dani said she would take the movies back since she had to leave anyway. After Dani left, Kate went back to her apartment. She hadn't been back in there since Rufus was killed. Marisa asked her if she wanted her to stay with her tonight, but Kate said she could handle it by herself. The girls hugged and said they would see each other in the morning.

Marisa went to check all the windows and door locks. Once they were secure she turned out the lights and changed clothes. Instead of going to bed she went to the window to watch the darkened lot. She watched it about thirty minutes when she noticed movement in one of the cars. She could only make out one figure. She slipped on some shoes and grabbed her gun. She slipped down the back stairway and went around the side of the building. She crouched down low and moved through the cars quietly. When she came to the row where she saw the figure she crept slowly between the cars. No one was in the car, but a man was standing near the trunk.

She stood up quickly and pointed the gun at him and said, "FREEZE!"

179

"Uh, hold it lady. It isn't what you think. May I turn around please?"

"Tom? Is that you?"

As he turned around she could see him zipping up his pants. She was still pointing the gun at him.

"Marisa it's me, do you think you could put that down please?"

"What in the hell are you doing out here? Are you trying to get yourself killed? I told you I can take care of myself."

"Damn Marisa how did you get out here without me seeing you? I'm glad you didn't shoot first and ask questions later."

"Well Tom I got out here without you seeing me because I'm good and because you let your guard down when you decided to take a leak," she laughed. "Look, I'm glad you care enough about me to watch me, but what happens if they get you first? Please go home, and stop worrying about me. I'll be fine, really."

"Can I come in first and make sure that everything is okay since you have been out here with me?"

"Yes, sure come on in and have a drink to calm your nerves."

He didn't stay long. He walked through the apartment looking in the closets and shower. He then re-checked the locks. When he was satisfied that she was secure he gave her a peck on the cheek and told her to call him if she needed to talk or anything. She thanked him again for being so chivalrous, and he was on his way. She grinned to herself as she locked the door behind him.

Why hadn't someone scooped him up already and made an honest man of him?

After he left she went through the day's mail. The fake identification she ordered a few weeks ago had arrived. She was astonished to see how real it looked. It could probably fool a lot of people if necessary.

Marisa and Kate spent the majority of the weekend at their parents painting and tearing down wallpaper. The weekend flew by, and by Sunday night everyone was too tired to eat. Tina made them promise to come back for a family dinner on Tuesday night. Both girls agreed. When Marisa got home there were several messages on the machine. All of them were hang up calls.

Before going to bed she decided to glance at the Sunday paper. While looking for nothing in particular in the classifieds, she noticed an ad for a company that will transport your car to another location for a fee. The company was called Auto Movers Inc., and it listed a number to call if you needed their services. Marisa figured they probably had regular full time employees, but they may have temporary drivers too. She called the number listed and spoke to the manager, Bud Lewis. She concocted a story that she was a college student trying to earn some extra money, but didn't want to be confined to an office setting. She said she wanted to see different parts of the country, and since she was about to complete a semester so this might be the right time for a break. He agreed to meet her for an interview. She told him her classes would be over in a few more days and she would call him back. He told her she would need to provide two pieces of identification and a clean driving record.

Since she already had the fake I.D. all she needed was one other piece of identification. She decided to get a new driver's license with her new name on Monday. Perhaps Monday's mail would bring her the previously requested credit card. The form she had filled out indicated that most requests were filled within in two to four weeks.

Before drifting off to sleep tonight she again thought of leaving all of her troubles here behind and starting over somewhere else. A new face, a new name, and no one from this life to share it with. Where on earth could she go and be happy, and safe?

On Monday, Marisa received a phone call at work from Wanda. "Well entertaining your boyfriend again on Friday I see. He must have some sort of a sexual problem, since he didn't stay long enough to make it worthwhile. Or maybe you're the frigid sort," Wanda cackled.

"What do you want? If you think I am afraid of you, think again. If you want to hurt me, go on and get it over with, but stop calling me and wasting my time." With that, she hung up on Wanda. A few minutes later the phone rang again.

This time Marisa answered with, "WHAT?" Tom was on the other end.

"What, what? Marisa, is everything okay?"

"Oh, sorry Tom. Wanda is up to her old, boring tricks again and she is really starting to piss me off," Marisa said angrily.

"Well, I was just calling to see how the rest of your weekend was."

"Oh it was just great. Wanda just informed me that you or I must have sexual problems since you didn't stay long on Friday night."

"What? You mean she was watching all along?"

"Well someone must have been!"

"This has got to stop Marisa! I want you to request a warrant for her now. Did you already file that violation with the non-reporting issue included?"

"Yes, but Jansen wouldn't authorize a warrant request. It hasn't come back from court yet, but I'm working on it." Tom told her he would see the Judge about it, and let her know something soon.

Marisa left work early on Monday without hearing from Tom again. She suspected that he had gotten busy, or couldn't get through to the court clerk to see what the hang up was. She told Charles she had a doctor's appointment, but she really had a job interview. Before leaving the building Marisa went into the bathroom to fix her hair into a ponytail, wash off her make-up and put in her new contacts. A few weeks earlier Marisa had her eyes checked and ordered new contacts. The optometrist was offering two sets of contact lenses for the price of one set, so she ordered two sets. One pair was the color of her own eyes, green, and the other she ordered in brown. The brown set was just to have for fun. Now, however, they would definitely come in handy because they really changed her appearance.

After checking her new look in the mirror she left the building and headed home to check her mailbox. Afterwards she would go straight to the license branch. She had something important to take care of. She was pleasantly surprised to find her new credit card in her stack of mail. She swore to herself that she would never use it for anything except identification.

Getting the driver's license was harder than she expected, but after she told them her hard luck story they issued her a new license for ten dollars. She made up a story of being brutalized in her own home and everything stolen by two thieves that the police never caught. She told them the only thing she still had was her old identification card from where she lived before, Wyoming, and a credit card that was hidden in a drawer when the thieves broke in. By now she had told just a few little innocuous lies. She rationalized it all by believing that she wasn't hurting anyone.

Once she obtained the driver's license she called back to the manager at Auto Mover's and set up a time for the interview later that afternoon. He told her at this time he didn't have any cars scheduled to leave, but he would call her back after he checked her driving record with the DMV. Hopefully he could line something up for her in the next few weeks. She told him she didn't have anywhere particular she wanted to travel, so she would take anything available. He explained that her return trip would be up to her to figure out, but she could usually count on at least $50.00 for a two-day trip. She decided this would be the perfect way to leave the city. No one would be able to track her movements because she would be traveling in another person's car, and under an assumed name. After talking with Mr. Lewis for about an hour she went directly home, and contemplated what would happen next. She didn't quite look the same when she got home. She wasn't sure if she should let her sister see her in her "disguise". She knew there would be an onslaught of questions, and she was already tired of lying to everyone.

She took out the contacts and took down her hair. She turned on the stereo and ran some bath water. Tonight she needed to relax. She could sense that there were a lot of changes in store for her in the next few weeks. The phone rang a few times while she was in the tub, but she let the machine pick up. All but one call was a hang up. The only person that started to leave a message was her mother. She picked up the phone while sitting in the tub. She didn't say a lot. Tina was just wondering if she was okay. Marisa told her she was just tired and was trying to relax because she had a busy day. She told her that she would be over for dinner tomorrow night.

Later that night Marisa got a call from Mr. Lewis stating that he had a car that needed to be transported to Kingsport, Tennessee. He apologized for calling so late, and to say that it wasn't a real glamorous getaway spot, but he assured her it would be very scenic along the way. Marisa said her classes wouldn't be over until Tuesday afternoon, but she could leave right after her last class at 3:30 p.m. He told her that the customers had used his service before and never gave him much time, but they didn't need the car to their destination until Friday morning. He told her the trip itself would take only about eight or nine hours, so she could wait and leave on Thursday if she wanted. She told him she would rather leave on Wednesday and stay overnight somewhere along the way.

They agreed to meet at 8:00 a.m. on Wednesday morning at the airport. She then lied and said ironically her girlfriend was flying in from Denver and she was supposed to give her a lift home, now however, she would just let her girlfriend take her car home. She told him that she would leave her car in the long term parking lot at the airport and her friend could pick it up. Mr. Lewis agreed to meet her at the airport if she would take him back to the shop before she left town. This plan was really starting to come together, but a bit faster than she had expected. It was set; she would be leaving her life behind on Wednesday morning. She was tired, but she couldn't sleep. She watched television until it went off the air. Her whole life was about to change. Even though it seemed that her life was spinning out of control, she felt like she had a grip on what she needed to take care of in the next thirty-six hours. She just hoped Wanda wouldn't mess up any plans.

She didn't sleep at all, but she drank a lot of coffee and took a cold shower before going into work. She was wired. At any point she felt like she was going to have a meltdown. She had to stay focused. She had to just get through this day, and night.

On Tuesday she muddled through the day. Charles stopped by and told her she looked like she could use some sleep. She told him she was fine. Dani told her she looked like hell. What are friends for if you can't count on their honesty? Marisa told her she would perk up after she ate lunch. Dani could tell that something was wrong, but Marisa insisted on keeping whatever was bothering her to herself. Lunch was miserable. Dani did all the talking today, and all she could talk about was one of her cases. Marisa just wanted to go home and crawl into bed. She couldn't even take a nap today, because she was going to her parent's house for dinner. This was a dinner she would not miss for anything in the world. She decided to slip out of work a few minutes early today, she just wanted to be alone with her thoughts.

A court clerk called just before she left and said the warrant for Wanda was on the system. Marisa called Bill and informed him that there was an active warrant for Wanda if he happened to see her he should have her arrested. He laughed and said Wanda wasn't foolish enough to attend the court hearings, she was only sending her attorney to them.

Marisa made one more call before leaving. She called Mrs. Snow. Mrs. Snow indicated that Wanda had not been home or called in a few weeks, but she had left behind a lot of her personal effects. Marisa told her to be careful because there was now a warrant for Wanda's arrest. Marisa suggested that she should have the locks changed and if Wanda returned she should call the police. It was a slim chance that Wanda would be stupid enough to return to Mrs. Snow's house, but Marisa felt better for warning her. She then lied and said she had another incoming call that she had to take. Mrs. Snow said she would stay in touch. Marisa didn't know if she would ever get to talk to Mrs. Snow again, but she said she would look forward to her phone calls.

While she sat in the parking lot, she took out all of her own identification from her wallet and put it in an envelope to take to her safe deposit box. She didn't want to have her real I.D. with her, nor did she want to leave it behind in the apartment when she left. This way the police and everyone else would assume it was gone right along with her. It was in this same safe deposit box that she had placed duplicates of all the incriminating evidence against Wanda just a short time ago with Dani.

She had told no one of this safe deposit box. It was just part of the service the bank had offered free of charge when she opened her accounts. Dani had been with her once to put some papers in it, but she had told her it was her parent's safety deposit box. She did not give the second key to anyone for a long time. But, after her relationship with Elliot began she told him she wanted him to hold the key to her heart. She put the key on his key chain. He had asked her what the key went to, but she just told him it was the key to her heart, and everything important. Right after that she notified the bank that he was the only other person allowed in the box. She wasn't aware then that the box would ever hold anything significant.

Chapter Seven

Once her investigation of Wanda had intensified,
she knew without a doubt that she would have problems
with her safety. It was at that time she started planning
for her getaway. She knew she could tell no one of her
plan, or they too would be in jeopardy. Marisa thought of
the money she had been saving at home. She knew there
was at least enough money there to get her out of town
and somewhere safe for at least a few weeks. Before the
money ran out, however, she would need to find a job if
she was not planning to return home. Marisa wondered
how long she would have before everyone realized she
was missing. She figured her family would know within
twenty-four hours because of her close proximity to
Kate's apartment. Kate would know immediately that
something was wrong. Hopefully Kate would contact
Dani for information of what was going on at work.
Marisa didn't have any enemies, or old jealous
boyfriends.

She had always been wise and frugal with her
money. Her spending was planned, and done cautiously.
She bought expensive furnishings for her home, but they
were well-made items that would last a lifetime. She
didn't spend a lot of money on clothes, but she took care
of what she had. She worked hard and saved a lot of
money. She didn't put all of her money in the bank,
however. She always had a lot of cash at home. For
some unknown reason she always put a certain amount of
her paycheck in her lingerie drawer. Marisa thought this
was an eerie coincidence the day she decided to leave.

Elliot once ran across her "mad money" and told
her she really should put it in the bank. She promised she
would the very next day. She explained that her sister
had just repaid a loan a few days earlier and she hadn't

had a chance to get to the bank. She never took it to the bank; she just put it in a place he would be unlikely to find it again.

Marisa's "mad money" would prove invaluable in the long run because no one would be able to track her movements if she paid cash for everything. The day she left she counted the money for the first time in four years. She had accumulated $5200.00! She had been putting fifty dollars from every paycheck in this drawer since she had gotten her job in the probation department, and she never withdrew from it. The amount she had accumulated completely shocked her. No wonder Elliot had really yelled at her to put it in the bank. She didn't know how long she would be gone, or how much money it would take to start over, but she thought she had a pretty good start.

Marisa realized she would have to get out of town quickly, and because she didn't want to tip anyone off, she would need to take as little as possible with her. She figured that once the police were involved they would search her apartment, since she didn't want them to know anything, she left the place exactly as it was the morning she left for work. She knew that her parents or her sister might recognize the personal items she had taken, but hopefully they wouldn't say anything to the police.

Marisa knew she would have to go somewhere warm because she hated the cold, so she took with her mostly summer clothing. And, planning for a good time on her little adventure, she took her favorite bikini, and cover-up. Those items and her lingerie had been packed for about two weeks and put in the back of her closet, just waiting for the right time to leave. All of her toiletries, cosmetics and contact supplies had been sitting in their own little piece of luggage for a few weeks too. One evening Kate asked why all of her cosmetics were stored like that. Marisa just told her it makes it easier to use when she wants to sleep in a little bit and put on her make-up in the car on the way to work. Kate said that was a good idea and went out and bought herself a make-up organizer just like Marisa's.

When Marisa left work on Tuesday afternoon, no one knew she wouldn't be coming back. The only thing she took from her desk was the information that had gotten her in all this trouble and Seth's personal information she had always kept. She last talked to Seth on the Friday before; she didn't know then that she would be leaving so abruptly, therefore she couldn't tell him. Marisa never discussed cases with Seth, but he knew something was troubling her.

After running to the bank she went to her parent's house for dinner. She had called Kate and reminded her to join them. It would be the last time that she would see her family for quite a while; a fact they did not know. During dinner Marisa could feel she was getting in a melancholy mood, and when her mother asked her about it she lied and said it was a headache and work related stress; nothing that she couldn't handle, or wasn't used to dealing with. She knew she had to leave them a clue that she would be okay. But she couldn't risk them finding it before she left town. She decided the best thing was to concoct a story about her headache and lock herself in the bathroom for awhile. Her mother told her that sometimes the best thing for a headache was steam. Marisa went to the master bathroom where she could sit in peace and quiet and let the room fill up with steam. After a few minutes the mirror was foggy. She wrote with her finger the following message:

I HAD TO DO THIS-TRUST NO ONE
I'LL BE FINE-I LOVE U ALL
PLEASE UNDERSTAND

Afterwards, she let the steam dissipate and left the bathroom. They watched some old home movies and played a game of Monopoly. Finally one of the girls said they needed to go home and get some rest; it was a weeknight and everyone had to work in the morning. On her drive home, she knew that they would not find the message until at least the next morning, she hoped they wouldn't find it until Thursday. She just needed to buy herself some time, but she had to let her parents know that no one could be trusted and she would be safe. At least she hoped she would be safe, eventually.

After getting back to the apartment complex that was only a few miles from their parent's home, both girls hugged each other and said they would see each other the next afternoon. Marisa waited for an hour or so with the lights out and the television on very low. She didn't want Kate to see her taking her bag out to the trunk of the car. In the morning she would have to get up and act as if she was leaving for work, in order not to let anyone in on her little plan. Then she remembered she was supposed to meet Elliot for lunch on Wednesday. If she called and canceled he would ask her too many questions. Although she didn't want to stand him up, she was sure he would understand in time. Anyway, they were just going to lunch as two old friends weren't they?

On Wednesday morning she called Mr. Lewis and asked him to meet her at the long term parking gate, although her car was actually parked at a one-hour meter across from the long term lot. With any luck it would be towed soon. By doing this Mr. Lewis wouldn't know what kind of car she drove, just in case he heard anything on the news about her disappearance after she left. It probably wouldn't have mattered anyway, because she wasn't planning to stay in Tennessee.

Mr. Lewis got there a few minutes after she got out of the car and unpacked her bag. He said that she must not be planning to be away a long time, because she was definitely traveling light. She told him she wasn't sure where she would be going after dropping the car off but she knew it would be somewhere warm, so all she needed was her bikini and her make-up. He laughed, and told her he had some coffee and doughnuts in the car. After helping her load the car he offered her the keys. She asked if he would mind driving so she could look at the map she had brought along. He agreed, and even offered some road tips for her journey.

Mr. Lewis had grown up in Tennessee and began telling her about interesting points she might want to see if she had the time. Several times he spoke of how he missed "home" and what a beautiful part of the country it was. During the conversation, which was minimal on her part, she was thinking what might be going on at the probation department. Mr. Lewis didn't even seem to realize she wasn't an active participant in the conversation. Within a few minutes they were finally back at the shop. He told her to keep the rest of the doughnuts because his wife had him on a diet. Then he told her to be careful on the road. Lastly, he went over the map for the best route to Kingsport, Tennessee and instructions on what to do once she arrived. He then issued her a check for $50.00. She would need to cash the check before she left the city.

He said, "Well since you want to get on your way little missy, I'll cash it for you. Shoot, I do that for all the pretty girls, just don't tell my wife."

Marisa thought this was great because she wouldn't have to mess around at the bank with her new fake identification. Of course, she was all decked out in a baseball cap that covered a lot of her hair, and she was wearing her brown contacts. Mr. Lewis never seemed to give her looks a second glance. Her plan was working so far. She told Mr. Lewis that she was planning to stay in

Kingsport or the surrounding area for a few days and wondered if he knew anything about the area. He told her that if she was a NASCAR fan she should drive over to Bristol, Tennessee and take a look around the track. He also told her she is going to be near several different mountain ranges, like the Appalachian Mountains, the Blue Ridge Mountains, The Great Smoky Mountains, and also near the Cumberland Gap. She told him she would visit some of those places just for him as she bid him farewell. As she pulled onto the highway she realized her life was about to drastically change. She woke up today being Marisa, but by this evening Sterling, her alter ego, would start to emerge.

When she pulled out of town on Wednesday morning she knew it would be a long time before she would see this city again. She was exhilarated to be getting away, but there was some sadness too. She knew her family and friends would be heartbroken, some might even think she was dead. She wondered what Wanda would think about her disappearance. Marisa knew that many people believed that Wanda was to blame. She was, but not in the way they thought. When Marisa left she truly believed that she was doing so to save her own life and to protect those around her. What she wouldn't admit was that she needed to get away from all the pretending that was going on in her life. She pretended she still loved her job, she pretended that her break-up with Elliot didn't really upset her and she pretended that in general her life was not boring. She also pretended that she wasn't affected by Ian's death.

Ian was Marisa's best friend and soul mate, and he had died only the year before. Marisa had never really gotten over his death; she didn't think she would ever recover from his absence. Ian knew her inside and out, but although people always assumed they were lovers, they were never more than best friends. Only Dani knew how unhappy she was about Elliot, and how much she mourned for Ian, but they never spoke about it while at work. No one else could ever know how sad she really was. She never wanted anyone to know she had feelings. She really had people fooled too. She always presented a calm, cool exterior. An over confidant young woman that had to put a mask on her true feelings every day. No one really knew how insecure she really was, and if they ever found out, especially her probationers, she would lose all credibility and control.

Marisa left more than her friends and family when she left. She left her peace of mind, the love of her life, a job, an apartment with all of her personal possessions, her car, and most importantly, a piece of herself. The only things she took with her were her memories, two teddy bears, a family picture, a military duffel bag, a packet of information, and a plan so vague she wasn't sure if it even existed.

Marisa had never driven on such a long trip by herself before, so this too would be a new challenge. Luckily, the car had a tape deck and she had brought along a lot of the music she liked. She figured she would listen to the radio until she ran out of stations, then she would switch over to the tapes. She liked the changing scenery. She had never been on any of these highways. Marisa was fine the first few hours of her trip, but something in a song reminded her of what she was leaving. Sadly, she drove on until hunger told her she needed to stop and get something to eat and take a break from the road. She pulled into a roadside diner about 1:00 p.m., and the place was still pretty full from the lunch time crowd. She sat alone at the counter, and ordered a grilled cheese, fries and a strawberry shake.

A few minutes later one of the local policemen sat down beside her. "Do you want some company, miss?" Sterling just smiled sweetly, and said she didn't mind.

He asked her where she was from, she lied and told him she wasn't really from anywhere, because she had been raised in the military and her family had moved often. She told him she was on her way to Kingsport, Tennessee to drop a car off, and then she was going to try to hike some of the Appalachian Trail. He told her to be careful, that it was no ordinary hiking trail. And, he added a young woman shouldn't be going by herself. She informed him that her fiancé was meeting her there in a day or so. When she finished her lunch the waitress asked her if she wanted some peach pie, the specialty of the diner. Sterling declined and left a $5.00 bill to cover her $2.95 lunch. The waitress thanked her for such a large tip. As she left the restaurant she turned and winked at the officer; she knew he was watching her leave. All the men had always noticed her walk away.

Back in the car, she gave a sigh of relief. She really had no reason to be nervous at this point but she knew she would have to start worrying soon enough. She made a conscious effort to maintain the speed limit, use her turn signals to make a lane change, and wear her seatbelt. Of course she knew once she got settled somewhere, someday, she wouldn't be as nervous as she was right now. She drove in silence for another hour or so, contemplating her next move. She stopped several times at scenic overlook spots. She didn't know if she would ever pass by this way again. Mr. Lewis was right; this was beautiful country. She wanted so badly to call home, call Dani, to call anyone at this point.

Loneliness was setting in as the sun was going down behind her. She decided to drive until dinnertime then she would find a motel and stop for the night. She stopped just north of Knoxville, on the outskirts of the city limits. Although dusk had not yet started to settle into the mountains she decided to pull off the road for the night. She had time on her hands and she was really tired of driving. She took a room at the Holiday Inn. When she checked in she asked for a 10:30 a.m. wake-up call, which only gave her a half an hour before check-out time. All she had to do was shower, fix her hair and put in her contacts. She wasn't putting on any make-up for at least the next few days. She grabbed her bags and headed for her room. When she got there, she called the front desk and had them turn on the movie channel. She didn't even know what was playing. She just knew she had to put her mind on something else. Around midnight she finally dozed off. It was not a restful night.

The phone rang and startled Sterling awake. She looked at the phone, anxiously wondering who was at the other end. After several rings it stopped. She looked at her watch, it was 10:33 a.m.; she knew she needed to get up and get out quickly. When she went to return her key, the front desk clerk informed her that he had attempted to give her a wake-up call, but no one answered so he assumed she had already left.

She said, "I woke up a little early, I must have been in the shower. But, thanks."

"No problem, well doesn't look like you made any telephone calls so you only owe me three bucks for the movies." Sterling paid him and told him he could throw away her receipt.

Before getting back on the road she stopped at the local pancake house and had a big breakfast. Only the waitress talked to her today. Maybe she looked as bad as she felt. Although there was nothing physically wrong with her, she was in a very bleak mood. She decided by now somebody should be missing her. She knew Dani must have called her at home and got only the message machine. Dani had Kate's number but she probably wouldn't call until after work today. Marisa then realized not only was she standing Elliot up for lunch today, she had also forgotten about Dani last night. During this whole frenzy she had been thinking only of herself. Marisa started to wonder for a moment what she was going to do after she turned the car over to the drop site this afternoon. "Oh well, I guess I'll just cross that bridge when I come to it," she said to herself.

On the drive she started thinking about the relationship she had shared with Elliot. She wondered if he missed her, and did he even realize that she was missing. Marisa hoped that he wasn't angry with her for missing their lunch date. Surely, Dani would have gone to him and told him of her disappearance so that he wouldn't believe he had been stood up.

When she called to ask him to lunch she had no expectations. And, she wasn't trying to lure him away from his wife. Marisa just wanted to go back to being friends, the relationship they had shared before they became lovers. She was certain he knew this. He sounded like he truly missed her. She knew he couldn't have been the one to call. How would that have looked? His wife, Tess, knew he had been in a relationship, but she too had had a boyfriend during their separation, and even before that. She certainly didn't want him to question her about her affairs while they were apart, so she had never questioned him when he came to visit the children.

Marisa never accompanied him to Meg's piano recitals, or to Ben's little league games. She knew it wouldn't be good for the children to see their dad with another woman. A woman they knew from office parties and court staff cookouts. Of course, if Elliot had ever left Tess and committed himself to her, she would have no problem becoming a stepmother to his children. But as long as she was just the other woman she didn't want to confuse them or place any undue pressure on them. Elliot understood how she felt, and he agreed with her decision.

Although they went out as a couple everywhere, they were very discreet at work. Neither of them wanted to be scrutinized by Judge's, or their superiors. Other staff members dated, but how they were talked about if the relationship ended. Only Elliot and Marisa's closest friends at work knew of their relationship. Since they were rarely together at work most people suspected nothing. When the relationship ended it was not fodder for the rumor mill. And although she was devastated by his absence in her life, no one at work, aside from Dani, would ever know how she felt.

She finally arrived at the drop site and looked for a guy named Louie, apparently he was a relative of Mr. Lewis. Louie took the keys, inspected the car for any damage and helped Sterling unloaded her belongings. He told her there wasn't much to do in Kingsport, but he would be happy to show her around.

"Well hon, if I wasn't already engaged I might just take you up on that offer, but I'm heading over to Bristol to see a friend of a friend," Sterling lied.

Louie blushed and offered to give her a lift after he got off work in a few hours, but again she declined opting instead for a cab. He told her that ride would be an expensive trip, but if that's how she wanted to spend her money he would call the cab company. She thanked him and went to use the restroom.

The ride to Bristol was very scenic and quite hilly. She asked to be dropped off in downtown Bristol. She had no idea where she was going, but she figured there must be someplace near town to eat and sleep. The cab driver pointed out some of the sights along the way. Bristol was about the size of her hometown, but because of the racetrack it did have a few motels from which to choose. She settled on the Mountain View Lodge, which was nestled right at the base of the Cherokee National

Forest. When she checked in, she indicated she would probably be staying at least a week. She decided to treat the next few weeks as if she was vacationing alone. She bought some magazines and some paperbacks and sat on the front porch and read for the next three days.

Two days earlier when she didn't show up for work Charles had waited before calling her. He knew she was under a lot of pressure now, and thought that maybe she just overslept. Finally at lunchtime Dani went to him and asked if Marisa had called in sick. He said she hadn't and he was just getting ready to call her. Dani sat down while he dialed the numbers. Charles got a busy signal, not the answering machine. When he hung up the phone Dani indicated that Marisa missed their regular girl's night out the night before. She told him that she knew Marisa was supposed to have dinner with her parents last night, but she was still planning to go out afterwards. She told him that Kate, Marisa's sister, usually went too, but she didn't make it either. Charles told her that maybe there was some family emergency, and they just didn't have a chance to call her about missing the night out. Dani knew that this wasn't likely, but she let it go for now.

After lunch and still no one had heard from Marisa, Dani called Kate's apartment. There was no answer there either, so she left a message for Kate to call her. Something still wasn't right in her mind. She knew Marisa had been really troubled these last few weeks. Dani decided to call Tom. His secretary said he was in court until late this afternoon. Dani didn't leave a message, indicating that she would call back later. She thought of the lunch date that Marisa had made with Elliot. Taking a chance she called his number.

He answered but sounded really depressed. "Elliot Green here."

"Elliot this is Dani. Are you okay?"

"No, not really. What do you need Dani?"

"Well, I don't mean to pry, but I know you were supposed to have a lunch date with Marisa today. Have you talked to her?"

"No, no I haven't. She stood me up. I waited and waited, then I called her office and her apartment, but she never answered. She must have changed her mind, I guess."

"Well I don't know about that, but she didn't show up to work either. In fact, she stood me up last night too."

"This is odd behavior for her. Has anyone been out to her place to check on her?"

"No, I don't think so, but I'm going to call her family now. If I learn anything I'll call you back. Don't take it personally Elliot. Marisa has a lot going on right now. See you later."

Dani tried Kate's number again, and just after the machine came on Kate picked up and said, "Hang on, let me shut the machine off."

"Kate, it's Dani. Have you talked to Marisa today?"

"Well no, not today, but we were together at mom's last night. Oh my gosh! We forgot all about you last night didn't we?"

"Well that isn't exactly the problem, but yes you did forget about me. Was anything wrong?"

"No, mom and dad just had us over for dinner since we didn't eat there on Sunday after we finished painting. Marisa was in an odd mood though. She complained of a headache and said she was going to bed when we got back to the apartment. Why, what's going on?"

"Well she hasn't shown up for work today, and no one has heard from her. I called but got a busy signal. I was just wondering if you knew where she might be?"

"No, and I'm sure if she stayed home today she would have called me, or mom. I was just at mom's house and she didn't mention anything. Can you hold on a minute and I'll go over to her apartment and see if she's there. Hold on, I'll be right back."

Kate left her apartment and went across the hall. She knocked as she was starting to unlock the door. Still no answer, but it was odd that the door was already unlocked. Kate yelled to her sister, but there was no response. The radio was on, and the light was on in the kitchen. Cautiously she walked through the apartment looking for her sister. When she reached the bedroom she noticed that the covers were in disarray, which was very unlike her sister. Marisa always made the bed before she did anything else. Kate looked in the bathroom, but it too was empty. She even looked in the closet, but all her searching was in vain.

As she started to leave, she noticed the phone was off the hook. She ran back across the hall and told Dani that Marisa wasn't there, then explained all that she noticed. Dani told her that she should call her parents and see if they had heard from Marisa. Dani told her to make the call, and that she would call her right back. Dani said she had another call to make. Dani was troubled by what Kate found. Hurriedly she dialed Tom's number again.

Tom's secretary picked up immediately. She informed Dani that he was in an important meeting. Dani told Estelle to tell him it was urgent and that she was on her way down. Dani called the front desk and told them she had to go to the D.A.'s office for a minute, so if any of her clients came in they could fill out a report form and call for their next appointment. She went to the elevators, but there were already so many people waiting that she decided to take the stairs. Dani flew up the three flights of stairs, and was pretty much breathless when she went into the hallway. She stopped a minute to catch her breath and get a drink of water. Something inside her told her that Marisa needed her help right now. She went into the main office and was surprised to see Tom coming down the hall toward her. He had a determined look on his face, but he knew that she wouldn't just pull him out of a meeting unless she felt it was really important.

"Dani, what's the matter?"

"No one else knows I'm here, but I think Marisa is missing. She didn't report for work today, and none of her family has seen her since last night. Her sister went into the apartment and found a few things out of place, and the door wasn't locked when she went in." Dani was talking about a mile a minute but she could see that Tom was very worried.

"Okay, I need to get these people out of my office, and find Michael. Go back to your office, and wait for me. I'll be there shortly. And, don't tell anyone what you've told me, not yet anyway."

Dani went to the elevators slowly. She would have a hard time hiding her feelings and emotions from everyone. She decided to ride all the way up to the top floor and then back down, just to waste some time. It would be a long ride. By the time she was got back to her office, Michael and Tom were at the reception desk having her paged.

"Is the chief available?"

Dani said, "Let's just go on back this way and look her up. She's here somewhere."

On the way down the hall, the trio ran into Charles. "Dani could you call Marisa's parents and see if they have seen her today?"

Before Dani could answer, Michael said, "I think we all need to sit down and talk about Marisa. Can you locate Jansen for us, or we can start without her?" Charles looked a little nervous, but said that Jansen was near the fax machine, so they all moved in that direction.

As they all approached, Michael said, "Jansen we need to talk now. Can we go to your office so that we can discuss something of the utmost importance?"

By the tone of his voice he was not giving Jansen a choice. Jansen motioned to her office, but she wasn't sure that she really wanted to hear what they had to say. And, she was thinking to herself what part Dani played in all of this. All of them went into her office and she closed the door. Michael remained standing as the others took seats around the large conference table.

"Jansen we have a problem. Tom has just told me briefly about Ms. Spencer's disappearance. What can you tell me?"

Jansen looked first at Charles and then at Dani. "Well, it would seem you know more about my staff than

I do. Are you sure she's missing, or just decided to take another little holiday?"

"Be reasonable Jansen! One of your officers has been receiving threats, and now she hasn't reported to work, not even her family has heard from her and you want to ask me if she is on holiday?"

Charles spoke up first. "Who called her family?"

Dani responded that she is a family friend with the Spencer's, so she called Kate to check on Marisa. When Kate went to check on her there were several things out of order in the apartment. Tom had a grim look on his face. They were all on the same team here, yet he felt like Jansen wanted to sit this one out.

"Okay, one thing at a time. Charles, she did not report for work, and you called her right?"

"Well I called before lunch, but all I got was a busy signal. I was just about to call her again when everyone showed up here just now."

Dani interjected that she told Kate to call their parents and see if they had any idea where she was. As they all looked to her for an answer she said she was supposed to call Kate back.

Jansen pushed the phone in her direction.

She dialed Kate's number. "Hello Dani is that you? Mom and Dad are on their way over here. They haven't heard a word from her. I'm scared. What's going on?"

"Kate hang tight just a minute."

Dani then covered the receiver and asked what she should tell her. Michael said to tell them not to enter the apartment until the police arrive.

"Police! Who in the hell called the police Michael?" Jansen yelled.

"Dani just tell her what I said and make sure no one enters that apartment, and be quick about it! Jansen you're going to call the police and tell them what we know. I'm going out to her apartment now, and you should stay here I think, but have 'no comment' for any of the media just in case they are monitoring the police channels. I think you should be pretty good at those two little words."

Dani was trying to listen to the two shout at each other, but she was also trying to calm Kate down. She said she would be there as soon as she could. She hung up the phone but reminded Kate not to go back into the apartment.

As soon as she hung up the phone, Michael asked where Marisa lived. Dani gave him the address and he called the chief of police himself. The police chief said he would put his best people on it, but someone that had any idea of what is going on should try to get out to the scene. Michael said he and one of his men would be there shortly. He looked at Tom and motioned that he was about ready to leave. Tom excused himself and went to another phone in the outer office. Michael was still giving all the details to the police chief, and Tom was lining up a car and driver for his boss. Charles decided to talk to Dani about the need for privacy and security of this matter until they knew more of what was going on. Jansen busied herself with Marisa's personnel file.

Michael hung up and told Jansen he would be in touch. He then informed her that the less said to the media and the staff the better it would be for the investigation. Jansen said she knew that and to remember to keep her in the loop. Charles and Dani went back to their offices while Jansen went to Marisa's office and started looking around.

Tina and Cliff arrived at the apartment just as the police cruisers were pulling in. Tina was nearly hysterical. They went up the steps to Kate's apartment, but when they attempted to go into Marisa's apartment they were told that it was being looked at as a crime scene and they could not enter. Tina nearly collapsed in Cliff's arms. Kate hated seeing her mother cry and she too began to sob. Cliff took them both into Kate's apartment and told them that they had to remain strong and be able to answer questions. They needed to put on a brave face for Marisa in case she was okay and watching all of this. Although he didn't believe she was okay, he wanted his wife and daughter to believe it now, and he wanted what he told them to be true.

When Tom and Michael first went out to Marisa's apartment on Wednesday, police were involved taking pictures of the apartment and looking for clues. Michael indicated to the detectives that her disappearance might be related to a client she had been having problems with, or perhaps she left on her own accord. There was little to help the police in this odd investigation. Michael told them that her boss, Jansen Oliver, might be able to help them further with this information. He also told them if they didn't have any luck with Ms. Oliver they should contact him and he would see that they would get the information they needed. With this statement, the detectives knew that Oliver would be less than cooperative. Michael wanted the information to come from her boss rather than him. He would give Jansen just one chance.

The detectives were finished talking with the immediate family members by late Wednesday evening. All along detectives were trying to speak to the Chief Probation Officer, but she was being difficult, and uncooperative. She decided to get the legal department involved, which really slowed down the process. Of course everyone wondered why she was being such a jerk, but she just said she didn't want to violate client's rights in the process of tracking down one of her officers that may just be taking a little vacation. She apparently did not realize the severity of the situation, or she just didn't care.

The rest of the night lingered on, and still no word from Marisa. Her mother was frantic and couldn't sleep. The whole family had stayed at Kate's apartment thinking that if she called in she would probably call Kate first. Dani stopped by after work, bringing them dinner that no one could eat. They all cried together. Dani went home lonely and alone tonight. Her best friend was somewhere out there, and she felt helpless. She wondered if Marisa had left voluntarily or if someone kidnapped her.

The story didn't make the six o'clock news, but there was a short piece on at eleven. Jansen just said no comment to all the reporters' questions. She indicated that sometimes people need a break from their lives, and she was certainly hoping that Ms. Spencer was watching and was coming back to work soon. She indicated that Marisa had taken a brief leave of absence a week ago due to stress and personal problems, but she had hoped she had worked everything out. Her parents were livid, as were Michael and Tom, when they saw how she was placing blame and manipulating the media. Jansen was being more open with the media than she was with the people assigned to find Marisa.

Michael called Jansen and told her to answer the detective's questions and stop posturing, but he did advise her to continue with 'no comment' for the media. He then reminded Jansen that it would look better if she gave them the information about her employee rather than if the District Attorney's office gave it to them. He said questions would really start to fly and it would not look good to the Judges if another department became involved. Jansen was still a little reluctant to talk to the police the next time they called, but she did answer their questions. It would be over twenty-four hours before she would actually provide them with something to really go on and investigate. By then, the trail of Marisa would start to go cold, as would the trail of the person that caused all this turmoil: Wanda.

On Thursday morning Tina decided to go home and check the messages to see if they had missed her call. She said she would take a quick shower and return in an hour or so. Cliff stayed there with Kate, waiting. Tina drove home looking at every car that passed her and looking into every parking lot hoping to catch a glimpse of Marisa. She got home to find three messages on the machine. All of them were from friends who had seen the piece on the eleven o'clock news. She went into the bathroom and cried as she showered. She took a very long shower today. When she got out and was toweling off something caught her eye.

She glanced around but didn't know what it was that got her attention. Just as she started to hang the towel up she noticed something drawn in the steam on the mirror, but whatever it was had started to fade. The steam in the room had dissipated so she turned the hot water on again and let the room fill up with steam again. She was startled to see words forming on the mirror. This is when she saw the message. She realized this was a message from her daughter. She remembered that Marisa had a headache on Tuesday night and went into the bathroom to get some steam. The message said; *I had to do this-trust no one, I'll be fine, I love you all, and please understand.* Although this was a troubling message, it helped to ease her worries. She knew that Marisa had gone somewhere voluntarily and not been kidnapped like the police thought. Now though, she wondered why.

Tina returned to the apartment and told Cliff she needed to speak to him privately. She whispered to him that she thought Marisa was fine. She told him she saw a message on the bathroom mirror and it said she hoped they understood and to trust no one. They discussed it for several minutes and decided that they would not let anyone in on this message. Apparently Marisa knew what she was doing and they would just have to trust her instincts. They decided not to tell Kate just yet. Although they didn't like seeing her in pain, they knew she wouldn't be able to keep it to herself and that might put Marisa in jeopardy. The police still had the apartment cordoned off, and would not let the family in. Detectives were questioning them, but Cliff and Tina just said they had no answers, that she never shared her work with them. Kate said the same thing, though she added that her sister had been under a great deal of stress for the past few months.

The detectives questioned Kate further about why she felt that her sister was under a great deal of stress lately. She told them that she didn't have any real answers, only that Marisa had been distracted a lot recently. She also mentioned that Marisa had told her that she was having particular difficulty with one client. She also told them about Rufus being killed and the note on the car before that. Kate suggested that Dani might be able to provide more insight. Kate told them that Dani was really close to Marisa at work, as well as socially. They took Dani's information down from Kate and said that they would be in contact with her. The questioning emotionally drained Kate. She just wished she had pressed her sister to be more open with her about her job, the clients and the cases she was working on. Her parents told her that she was not at fault here, and that with any luck the police would find who was behind Marisa's disappearance when they talked with her co-workers and bosses.

The detectives assigned to the case knew Marisa only casually. She sometimes frequented the bar where a number of the cops hung out. They remembered her by the reputation she had around the courthouse. Marisa's reputation was that she was pretty tough on her clients. Tough, but fair. They liked that she did not perform her job like a social worker, but rather like a cop. She was what the street toughs referred to as "straight up". She didn't pull any punches, and she always meant what she said.

It was tough on cops to be looking for one of their own. No one wanted to find her dead, but this was one possibility. Although there had been no demand calls, or anyone coming forward with information they had to presume initially that she had left involuntarily. Her family told the detectives that Marisa would never leave without telling them. Initially this was true, but as time progressed they didn't feel the need to tell them the truth.

After Tina found the cryptic note she realized Marisa must have been in grave danger to leave the way she did. Because of what the note said she wanted to honor her daughter's wishes and keep it to herself. Marisa had always had good instincts; it was no time to be questioning them now. In some of their past conversations Tina and Marisa had spoken of these detectives; however, now she couldn't remember the ones that Marisa really trusted. Even if she shared this information with one that Marisa trusted, he would have to act on it and involve others. For the time being Mr. and Mrs. Spencer decided to let the police figure it out on their own. They knew that Marisa was strong, and could take care of herself. They only hoped this wouldn't go on very long.

Thursday was a long day for everyone involved. Her parents couldn't figure out Jansen's behavior. She seemed more concerned with the media attention being focused on her department rather than trying to assist the detectives in locating one of her officers. Tina and Cliff could only sit by and watch the circus around them. They tried to console Kate, but she wanted only to hear that her sister was safe. No one could really tell her that, not even her parents. Dani went to work, but had a tough time concentrating. The detectives had called her and asked her to come down to be interviewed. When she told Charles, he said he would need to discuss it with Jansen and see how they should proceed.

Dani was confused, but she agreed to talk to Jansen herself. Charles seemed to want to bury his head in the sand and deny that there were any problems. When Dani approached Jansen she accused her of sticking her nose in where it didn't belong. She told Jansen that the detectives had called her. She informed her that she and Marisa were not only co-workers, but also best friends. She guessed that the police had obtained her name from Marisa's family. Although she wasn't sure she would be of much help, she told Jansen she was talking to the detectives whether she liked it or not. She decided to use some of her personal time just in case Jansen tried to say she was being paid to work and not consort with the police on this case. Dani was now starting to see why Marisa could never stand to be around Jansen. She was an odd woman, and only cared how this whole thing was going to affect her, not the department, or Marisa.

Dani met with the two detectives working the case. She could only tell them virtually the same thing that Kate had told them. Marisa was not one to share case information, but she had really been preoccupied with one case for the past few months. She told them that Marisa had never been afraid of her clients, but she was more cautious lately. When pressed for a name, Dani drew a blank. She told them that she and Charles had even helped with some tedious phone calling on the woman, but she could not recall her name. She became quite frustrated with herself, and as the pressure mounted for her to remember the name, she cried. Finally she said it was a fairly new case and she asked to call Charles. They gave her a phone. Charles hemmed and hawed around finally stating the name was Newton, Wanda Newton. Dani was excited. She told the officers that perhaps Charles could give them more details, or perhaps they should call Tom. She indicated that Wanda was in violation and Tom Roberts was the D.A. assigned to the case. The police now had more to work with. They, too, wondered why Jansen had not divulged this information.

Dani called Tom to tell him that she had spoken with the detectives about Marisa. She said that she had given them his name because she knew that he was somehow involved in the Newton case. She didn't realize that he was aware of Marisa's state of mind surrounding this case. He played dumb with her, but when the detectives called him he would give them anything they wanted to know. After hanging up he ran down to Michael's office and told him that their office had now been thrown into the mix. Michael was pleased. Now maybe the police could set out to find Marisa and get on with the investigation. Tom went back to his office and found the note that he had made to himself regarding the Newton case: *call court and call M, regarding Newton warrant*. He realized he had never called her back. He now tried to remember their last conversation.

When Tom got back to his office Estelle gave him the message that Detective Konjesky wanted to speak to him as soon as possible. Tom dialed the number quickly. The detective asked him if they could speak privately in the detective's office. Tom agreed and left immediately. He grabbed Wanda's file and told Estelle he didn't know when he would be back. He also told her that Michael would know where to find him. Estelle never asked questions, she just shook her head and told him to be careful.

Tom greeted Detective Konjesky with a handshake, and indicated he knew why he called. Detective Konjesky asked Tom if he was involved with Marisa outside work, or if they were just professional acquaintances. Tom indicated they were good friends, but they had never dated. He also indicated that he and Marisa shared several cases as well. The detective was taking notes.

Tom indicated that he knew Marisa had received threats several times in the last few weeks or month and he believed her disappearance was tied to that. He gave the detective the client's name, Wanda Newton. Tom told the detective all about the threats Marisa had been dealing with. He told him other phone calls and how Wanda had acted toward Marisa during home and office visits and that someone had killed her sister's cat thinking that it belonged to her. The detective was surprised by the wealth of information that Tom was providing; he didn't understand why the Chief Probation Officer hadn't told him of all of this.

Tom filled him in on what Marisa had shared with him about her own little investigation of Wanda. He told him that a few weeks earlier he had taken Marisa to his parent's house for a few days until they could think things through and thought it might calm down. Her boss and co-workers were given the impression that she was ill, but Tom was really just protecting her. He had told his boss everything while she was away. And, when she returned home she learned he had scheduled a meeting between their department heads. It was at this meeting that it was decided she should take a leave of absence. She left, but didn't tell him or anyone else where she was going. He explained that he had received a call from her and she asked about the case and learned that her boss lied and had filed a motion with the court. She returned home immediately, returning to town as quickly as she left.

He continued with his information that on her first night back from her brief leave of absence she received another frightening phone call, presumably from Wanda. But, she didn't let it stop her; she showed up in court to her boss' great dismay. Then he said that he called her on Monday to see how her weekend went, but she answered the phone by screaming something he couldn't remember into the receiver. When he questioned her further why she was yelling into her caller's ear, she explained that Wanda had called again. It was obvious by what she said to Marisa that someone had been watching her at the apartment. He told the detective that he was supposed to check with the court clerk about a warrant that had been requested for Wanda, but he just realized today that he had never called Marisa back to tell her. Tom seemed very sad and concerned. The detective knew that Tom was trying to remember anything and everything about the last few conversations he had with Marisa in case it would be of any use to the investigation. Detective Konjesky thanked him and told Tom he would be in touch if he had any questions, or any updates. Tom shook his hand as he left.

Detective Konjesky decided now would be a good time to start looking for Wanda. There was already an active warrant out for her, but it was rare that anyone besides the probation officer looked for a probationer that had violated probation. And, from what Marisa had already uncovered, it proved Wanda was good at being a chameleon. It had been a long day, Konjesky was going home, but he wouldn't be sleeping well tonight.

Friday morning the detective called Mr. and Mrs. Spencer. He asked if one or both of them could accompany him to Marisa's apartment and see if anything looked out of place to them or if they noticed anything missing. Both of them were anxious to look inside, and told him that they would meet him there. They asked if Marisa's car had been located yet, but he told them it was still missing.

Tina was at the door when the detective arrived. She had waited only because the place was still sealed off with yellow crime scene tape. She had her key with her and was opening the door as he came down the corridor. He nodded his approval. As they entered the cozy apartment the phone was still off the hook. Tina replaced the receiver. She pulled her sweater around her tightly as she looked all around. Immediately she noticed that a family picture that was usually atop an end table was nowhere in sight. She moved silently into the bedroom and noticed that both of Marisa's prized teddy bears were missing from their perch on the bedside table. Still Tina said nothing. He asked her to look through the closet and bureau drawers to see if she could tell what was missing, if anything. Marisa's luggage was sitting on the floor of her closet. Tina looked through the clothes, but said she couldn't tell if anything was missing. She was trembling. Detective Konjesky noticed her demeanor and asked if she was all right. She was nervous because she knew she was lying; he thought she was just upset because her daughter was missing.

Detective Konjesky asked where the answering machine was, and Cliff pointed it out and offered to rewind and play any messages on it. As the tape started to play a woman's voice came on and Marisa answered as if she had been asleep.

The caller said, "Welcome back you little bitch! You keep running away, but you won't be able to hide from me forever. You better just watch yourself." The dial tone then came on, and Marisa hung up.

There were several more hang up phone calls on the machine. The detective removed the tape and wrote a note about it. Tina was crying quietly and Cliff had his arms around her with his head down. The detective apologized for making them be a part of all of this, but told them he would do everything he could to find their daughter. They told them that they would be at home waiting for any news he had.

Once inside the car Tina told Cliff that she truly believed that Marisa was safe and had left voluntarily. He asked her why she was so sure of this. She told him the items that were missing, and said quite a few of Marisa's favorite clothes were missing, but her luggage was still in the closet.

Cliff said, "Did you see my old army duffel bag in the closet, or anywhere?"

Tina remembered that he had given that to Marisa when she moved out. She had not seen it anywhere in the apartment. Now they just wondered where she was, and if she was okay. And they wondered why she couldn't have confided in them about her desire to leave.

Back at the office, Detective Konjesky asked his partner, Detective Matheson, if there had been any luck at the bus station, airport, or train station. Matheson informed him that no one matching Marisa's description had boarded a plane, train, or bus. He also said he had squad cars out looking in the airport parking lots searching for her car, but they were nearly done and it had not yet been located. He had also called all of the city cab companies and asked if anyone matching her description had booked a cab from late Tuesday night to mid afternoon Wednesday, and still no luck. He was about half way through calling the rental car companies, but he was coming up empty there too. He had an assistant helping him with the calls, he said. They had already notified the State Highway Patrol and put out a computer message to all the other police agencies in the state to be on the lookout for her car. Konjesky stated that if she had left on her own, when they found her they better ask her to share her secret of disappearing. He also indicated that if anyone had kidnapped her it must have been like a carjacking, but they were taking a huge risk if they were still driving her car.

The day went by slowly, and still no word about her car. Konjesky and Matheson would think of little else the next few days. A break would never come their way. About three weeks after Marisa was reported missing Konjesky received a call from Mrs. Snow. She told them that she had been a friend of sorts with Marisa and she was Wanda's landlord. He could tell that Mrs. Snow was worried about Marisa, but she was the nosy sort too. After a few questions he learned that Marisa had been in contact with Mrs. Snow on Tuesday afternoon before she disappeared. Marisa had told her to be careful if Wanda showed up because there was an active warrant for her. Nothing in this conversation was very useful in finding Marisa, but she may call them if Wanda made an appearance. At this point they were beginning to believe that Wanda really did have something to do with Marisa's disappearance.

On Friday morning Seth called Marisa's office, two days after she left town, and was met with a barrage of questions; he hung up immediately. Luckily he had called from a pay phone in the building; he was calling to ask her to meet him for a cappuccino on her break. He knew then that she was in trouble. He went to another pay phone across the street and called Dani. He had heard Marisa mention her name periodically, so he figured they must be close. Whispering, Dani told him that Marisa was missing and something was going on with one of her cases and the only thing she knew for sure was that Marisa was definitely in danger.

"She didn't meet me for our regular "girl's night out" on Tuesday after work, and she didn't show up for work on Wednesday or Thursday. Have you heard anything?"

"All I know is what I have heard on the TV. and read in the paper. Don't worry, she knows how to take care of herself."

"Management has been through everything in her office. And, they keep asking me stuff I know nothing about. I can't talk now, how can I get in touch with you in case I find something out?"

"Umm, well I'm staying with some friends," he lied, "so I don't really have a permanent address."

"Well will you please keep in contact with me?"

Seth could sense the desperation in Dani's voice, but he told her to tell no one of his call. He promised to call her again soon. "Yeah, sure. I'll call you again when I know something."

After he hung up, he sensed that he would hear from Marisa. He only hoped that he would be able to help her. He knew that she had been in a previous relationship with a D.A. by the name of Elliot Green. He thought that maybe she had gone to him for help.

Just after hanging up, reality struck Dani and she knew she had no idea how to contact Seth. She quietly went to Marisa's office and looked through her address book. Seth's name was not there. Dani wondered if it had ever been there. Dani then went to the front office

219

and looked up Seth's file number. She would let some time pass before she started looking in his file for information. As she went back to work on her own cases she wondered if Marisa was going to be okay. She also wondered if Seth could help Marisa; she knew he would try.

After she had returned from lunch she went to the file room and retrieved Seth's file. She hid it in a file she had with her so as not to arouse suspicion. She could find nothing in the file that would be of any use to her. She knew too that Marisa had probably taken everything out of the file that would lead anyone to Seth. At that point Dani wondered if Marisa had been kidnapped or had she left voluntarily. If she had left on her own, Dani wondered, how long she had been planning this, and was Seth ever a part of the plan?

The newspaper had stated that Marisa had been investigating an unnamed person on her caseload, but it gave no further details. The Chief Probation Officer was quoted as saying, "Ms. Spencer is a cautious, hardworking professional, and we are hopeful of a safe return." She did not indicate whether she left voluntarily, or if anyone had heard from her.

Seth decided to look up Mr. Green in the phone book. After he found the address he drove over there. Figuring Green was at work, Seth decided to have a look around. The house had an alarm, but it looked pretty well deserted. Most of the furniture was gone, but he could see a cup and bowl was still on the table. He assumed that someone had eaten breakfast there, probably this morning.

Dani had only heard from Seth once more after his initial call. He was trying to piece information together; he still had not heard from Marisa. Dani assumed he knew about Marisa's personal life, and where she lived, so when he asked for Marisa's address Dani laughed but didn't give it to him. She thought he was just trying to hide Marisa's relationship with him or help salvage her reputation. Little did Dani know that Marisa had never allowed Seth to become involved in her private life.

As much as Seth always wanted to be a part of her life, he understood her reluctance. They were from different worlds. She had a college degree; he graduated from the school of hard knocks. She was a professional; he worked odd jobs, but always with a pocketful of money. She had a close-knit family; he had no family. They would always be too far apart to ever be together, but he trusted her, and would settle for whatever time she would give him. Dani, of course, never knew this. She truly believed that Marisa was secretly dating Seth whom she thought of as a diamond in the rough.

On the evening news the reporter had interviewed Marisa's family. They indicated that they believed their daughter had been kidnapped. Her mother seemed pretty distraught, so her father had done all the speaking. He pleaded to his daughter's "captors" to let his little girl go unharmed. Seth didn't have much use for religion, but tonight he prayed for Marisa. And, he cried. Seth realized that he was out of ideas so he decided to sit by the phone and hope that she called.

It was going to be a long weekend. Some of Seth's friends dropped by, but he wasn't in any kind of mood to be with them. They kept insisting that he go out to the bars with them, but he declined. They didn't know of his ongoing relationship with his former P.O. because they would never let him live that down. He told them he just wasn't feeling well, but he would catch up with them later. Finally on Sunday evening the phone rang. Seth looked at it as it rang; he picked it up on the fourth ring.

"Seth, I'm in trouble, please help me." He knew her voice. She was crying. God had answered his prayers.

"Where are you baby?" he asked.

"I can't tell you that, will you help me?"

Seth asked her if she is okay. She said she misses everyone terribly, but she is fine. In a voice that is now calmer, Marisa tells him there is a bus ticket in the city waiting for him. All he has to do is pack and leave town. She says the bus ride will take about nine hours, and the bus is leaving the city at 9:45 p.m. tonight. He should arrive no later than 7:30 a.m. on Monday morning. When he arrives he should take a cab to the Mountain View Lodge, and go to room 13.

He tells her that all the news outlets are indicating that she's been kidnapped. She is still crying, but assures him she's fine. She tells him that he is the only person she has contacted. She implores him to tell no one of the call, and to tell no one where he is going if he decides to help her. He again asks her where she is; she tells him he'll know when he picks up the ticket. She reminds him that if he isn't there by the time she checks out at 9:00 a.m. he won't see her again. Just before she hangs up she tells him he is the only one that can help her now. Before he can ask her anything else the dial tone clicks on. He looks at the clock, he has an hour and a half to make a decision and get to the bus terminal.

Seth packed what little he had in a beat up, old suitcase. He went to his landlord and paid for the previous week's rent. He told the old man that he has a new job across town that starts tonight, and he would be staying with friends. He had taken the phone from the apartment and given it to his landlord. He asked the old man to disconnect his service in the morning. He handed back his keys and shook the old man's hand. Seth promised to come back and visit soon. He told the old man if he took him to the other side of town, he could keep his car. The landlord questioned him about such an extravagant gift, but Seth told him he was the only person to treat him like family and he wanted to repay him somehow. The old man agreed, and Seth signed over the title to him. Seth asked him to drop him off at a strip bar that happened to be across the street from the bus terminal. The old man laughed and said that if Seth ever needed a replacement at work all he needed to do was call. Seth laughed and told him he would keep him in mind.

After the old man drove away in the beat -up Malibu, Seth ran across the street. It was 9:36 p.m. He went to the ticket window and said he was Seth Anthony. She issued him the one way ticket and told him to hurry because the bus would be pulling out in nine minutes. When he finally got settled in on the bus, he looked at the destination, Bristol, Tennessee. What was Marisa doing there? Realizing he had not eaten in quite some time, he asked the driver not to leave without him. He ran in and grabbed a can of soda, a hot dog, some popcorn, a candy bar, and a magazine. He was in such a hurry he threw a $20.00 bill on the counter and ran out. The bus doors had just closed and it started to pull away. Seth ran alongside it, banging on the doors. The driver, shaking his head, let him back on. Seth hoped his luck would soon be changing.

After he finished the food, he put the candy bar and magazine in his backpack. He decided to get some sleep; he had a long trip ahead of him. The bus made several stops but Seth decided he wasn't taking anymore chances. He stayed on the bus each time and continued to sleep. When the bus pulled into Knoxville, Tennessee he asked the driver how much time before they reached

Bristol. The driver indicated it was about another ninety minutes, give or take. By now Seth was wide awake, and anxious to see Marisa. He got out his candy bar and looked at his magazine. He just wished time would pass a little faster.

Many of the passengers were starting to stir around, but he didn't want to talk to any of them. He didn't like strangers, and everyone always had so many questions. Since he really didn't have any answers he just sat in silence. He had packed his personal stereo in the suitcase, so he didn't even have his music to keep him company. Seth did enjoy the scenery though. He had never given much thought to the things around him. He lived in a poor section of town, so all he ever saw was poverty. He had never been out of state either, so this would be a great adventure. At least he hoped it would be.

The bus pulled up near the town square of Bristol, Tennessee about 7:00 a.m. on Monday morning. After grabbing his luggage and his backpack he headed toward the restaurant on the corner. He smiled at the waitress and asked her if she could help him with directions. "Sure, hon'. I could probably help you with a lot of things."

Shyly he put his head down and asked how far the Mountain View Lodge was from the restaurant. She told him to go outside and look around for the tallest mountain and head in that direction. Her tart comment made one of the local boys' start laughing at the "Yankee". He thanked her for her lovely assistance and headed out the door. He spun around to see that mountains surrounded him, but if she was right he needed to walk straight out of the door and keep walking. He walked about a block, and stopped a man on the street. Again he asked if he was going in the right direction. The man said yes and told him he would see the Lodge if he went about another half block. His suitcase was getting heavy, so he hoped to get there soon.

The lodge came into sight, but he became nervous about what the future might have in store for him. He started thinking about Marisa and realized she could be injured. He better get to her soon. He sprinted the rest of the way to the Lodge. When he reached the Lodge he was out of breath. He glanced up and down the front of the place and could see that room 13 was at the top of the stairs. Nervously he climbed the stairs.

He knocked lightly on the door and said, "Housekeeping."

Marisa came to the door, but without opening it said she needed another hour, and for him to come back later.

"I'm sorry ma'am, but we need in the room, we have a leak downstairs."

Marisa said, "Hold on a second while I get dressed."

Seth couldn't stand it; he could hardly hold back the laughter when he said, "Ma'am I really need to get in there, I promise I won't look, I'm a married man."

Marisa exclaimed, "Mister, you better just wait a second, or I'll shoot you right between the eyes!"

By this time Seth was doubled over in laughter. She pulled open the door to find the only man who could help her.

"You big jerk, get in here!" She playfully hit him; then she hugged him so tightly and said, "You don't know how glad I am to see a familiar face."

She asked him if his trip was okay, and he said it was. She told him she didn't get much sleep last night, or for that matter she couldn't remember the last time she had a good night's rest. He told her he was a little tired, and if she wanted to lie back down he would take a nap too. She said she really appreciated it as she climbed back into bed. He put the do not disturb sign out, sat down in the chair and tried to get comfortable. She sat for a moment and watched him with tears in her eyes. He didn't know what to say, but he smiled at her.

Finally she said, "I think I can trust you this far, so come on and get in the bed. Just remember though, any funny stuff and I'll shoot you right between the eyes!" They both laughed.

Seth woke up around noon, but he didn't want to wake Marisa, so he just stayed still on the bed. She finally woke up about 1:15 p.m. and said she was famished.

He offered to run out and get something, but she said, "I want to get out of here, just let me shower."

He grabbed his toothbrush and went to the sink to brush his teeth. He noticed her open wallet was on the countertop. He saw a picture of a girl that looked very much like Marisa, but the I.D. indicated the person's name was Sterling Summers. He didn't know what to think or say to her, so he decided to let her tell him at her own pace.

They both were ready to go about the same time. He asked her where they should go and she suggested the diner on the square. He laughed and said, "This Yankee boy has already experienced their hospitality, maybe we should try someplace else."

After they ate, she asked him if he would like to go over to the racetrack and look around. He has always been a huge NASCAR fan so he said he would love to go. They watched some cars out on the track, but he didn't recognize any of the drivers. As they headed back to the Lodge, he asked her what she has planned.

"Gee, I don't know, I was kinda waitin' for you to get here and see if you had any ideas."

He started laughing so hard and said, "You mean to tell me if I hadn't shown up you were just gonna wait things out here?"

"Look, dammit, I have been really upset for nearly two weeks, planning the rest of my life just hasn't been my priority."

"Baby, it's okay, I'm here now, we'll figure something out together," he said as he put his arm around her waist. They walked back to the Lodge in silence. They both were contemplating their next move.

She told him she felt really close to him, but she didn't want to give him the wrong idea. She said no one else could, or would, just drop everything for her. She knew everyone would just want her to hide in the city until things had cooled down, but she knew she would never feel safe. She told him she had always known she could trust him with her life, and she really appreciated what he was giving up to be with her now. He told her that she meant the world to him, and he would do anything for her. He told her he really didn't have anything to give up, and perhaps he could get a fresh start in a new place with her by his side. He told her he would never push himself on her, and he would never intentionally hurt her.

They talked late into the evening about what she

had been doing for the past ten days which was when he last talked to her. They sent out for pizza and discussed late into the evening what their next move should be. They both agreed they should not stay anywhere for more than a couple of nights until they were sure they had not been followed. He decided that after they left someplace they should call back about two days later pretending they had left something behind. Then he could also ask if any calls had come in for them since they left.

In the evening she told him, "Seth, you need to realize that Marisa got left at home. I've done some things for my protection, and one of those things is using another name. If this plan is going to work, you need to start calling by my new name, Sterling Summers."

She told him how she had always liked unusual names. "You know how much I like sterling silver jewelry, so I picked Sterling as my first name. And, summer as you know is my favorite time of year, so that sounded like a perfect surname for now. He laughed and said his new name would be Hugh Dick. She laughed with him but said since no one was looking for him he should just stick with his given name. She told him again how she hated lying, and that one person lying is too many, but it was something that she considered necessary for the time being. He was laughing pretty hard at himself; and said that maybe he could be a stand-up comic whenever they got where they were going. Sterling just laughed and shook her head. She was really glad she had called him. He could make her laugh.

After they woke up on Tuesday they decided that since neither of them was in a hurry to be anywhere they would just take things one day at a time. They had the rest of their lives in front of them, why hurry? There was one major problem. They had no transportation, and as much as Seth had seen a lot of beautiful scenery, he didn't want to get back on another bus. He told Sterling of his luck before leaving town.

She just laughed and said, "Only you!"

She told him she had plenty of money, but they had to be frugal since eventually the money would run out. He said they could probably buy a decent car for $1500.00. She said that would take a big chunk of change from her cash, but they needed dependable transportation. They asked at the Lodge if anyone knew of a decent car lot. The desk clerk said his brother-in-law buys and sells cars as a hobby. He fixes them up and sells them for reasonable prices, but he doesn't have a real big selection. Seth asked him to call his brother-in-law and find out what he had available. They went back to their room and started to pack.

The phone rang a few minutes later with news that he had a $500.00 purple '73 Volkswagen that was not in any shape to drive, a $900.00 green '71 El Camino, a $1995 brown '53 Biscayne, and an $1800 black '63 Chevy II. The brother-in-law, Ed, came over in the Biscayne and took them back to his house to let them drive the Chevy II. Those were the only two cars that interested them. After driving both, they chose the Chevy II. Sterling gave him $1800.00 and Ed had his wife, the local notary, handle the legal paperwork with the title and license plates. They decided to put the car in Seth's name just to keep things simple. They had thirty days to plate the car. They decided to do that after they had found a place to live. Driving back to the Lodge, Seth asked if she had ever been to Myrtle Beach, South Carolina. He said that was a place he always wanted to go. The next destination was chosen; that was a place she had always wanted to visit too.

They decided to check out today, and drive to Myrtle Beach. The trip should take about six or seven hours, which would put them there after dark. Seth

229

thought they should buy a road atlas, but Sterling already had one packed away in her bags. He loaded the car and bought them a couple of sodas to take along, while she found the atlas. She asked him if he would do the man's job and drive. He thought that was great, and told her he would. He didn't care for women driving his car. He chuckled to himself because he was now a "kept man".

They checked into the Sea Mist Motel in the heart of Myrtle Beach. The place was booming with activity. They went to the beach; it was Seth's first time to see the ocean. He was now truly in love. He wanted to go for a swim, but Sterling told him he would be swimming alone. "Well Seth, you need to take this swim alone. I never swim after dark. Don't you know that the big fish are just waiting to gobble you up?"

He laughed at her and asked, "What do you suppose those big fish do in the daylight?"

She curtly replied, "They sleep in the really deep water smarty pants!"

He was roaring with laughter. He pulled off his clothes and went running into the waves. "Seth you're going to get arrested! Please Seth it isn't safe to swim now."

He was romping around all by himself, acting like a little kid. Pretty soon, he yelled, "Help me Sterling, a big fish has my leg! Oh, Sterling baby you gotta help me!"

An older couple walking by asked if her friend needed any assistance. Sterling laughingly replied, "Only if either of you are a psychiatrist." She told them he had never seen the ocean before. They just shook their heads knowingly and kept walking.

"Seth, would you please come out now?"

"Yeah baby, but promise to swim with me tomorrow, okay?"

"I will tomorrow in the daylight, now come on." Quickly he ran out of the water and without a towel, he simply tugged his jeans back on. She noticed then that he didn't have on underwear.

"Seth, where are your underwear?"

"Lighten up baby, I go commando. You should try it." She could see now that she was in for a steamy adventure.

Sterling counted the money she had left. She was down to just over $2800.00. She told Seth that they should get to their next destination in a few days. And they should start thinking of a permanent destination. When he asked her what the hurry was she informed him of her financial situation. He told her he had some cash, maybe $200.00. She told him not to worry that they would be fine. She hoped. She asked him if he would mind dropping her off at a beauty salon they passed last night as they drove into town.

He laughed and said, "Well we may get low on money, but Sterling can't forego the beauty shop."

As she stepped out of the car, Seth asked her how long she would be. She told him she shouldn't be more than an hour and a half, two at the most. He told her he was just going to look around town, and try to find some action. She told him just not to forget to pick her up in an hour or so.

Sterling entered the shop and asked if she needed an appointment to have a cut and dye job. The receptionist told her she didn't, but it would be a few minutes before someone could get to her. A short time later, a heavy set, young woman asked what she was thinking of doing to her hair. She said she wanted a whole new look. She wanted to have her shoulder length, naturally blonde hair cut short, and a new color. Perhaps she would try a red, or maybe an auburn color to go with her brown eyes. The stylist showed her some short styles, and Sterling settled on a short, shag style. All she would have to do after shampooing was to blow it dry. The color she decided on was a dark, golden red. It was almost bronze in color. She thought Seth would hate it. She didn't even tell him what she had planned to do. When she was ready to leave, all the women in the shop told her she should be a model. She was quite happy with what she saw in the mirror. She gave the woman a great tip, paid her bill and left the shop.

It had been an hour and forty-five minutes. Where was Seth? She called the motel, but the clerk said no one answered the phone in the room. She sat at the curb and waited. She had waited thirty more minutes. Where was he? She decided to walk towards the beach, his new favorite place. Along the way she spotted their car parked outside a seedy looking pool hall. Seth loved playing pool, and he was quite a hustler. She was glad he had some of his own money at this point. She walked in, but no one gave her a second look. Everyone was too intent on the game in the back. She pulled up a stool, and just stared through the crowd. She was looking directly at Seth. He didn't notice her, yet. She wasn't mad at him; she loved watching him play. Some of the other bystanders started looking at Sterling and talking among themselves. One guy came up to her and offered to buy her a drink.

She said, "There's only one guy I'm leaving here

with today, and it isn't you."

He said, "Do you know anyone here?"

"Not yet, but I'm looking at the man who's going to leave with me," Sterling said slyly. The man walked back to the action in the back of the room. Sterling just laughed at herself.

Back at the pool table, the man told some of his buddies about the "little flirt" at the bar. "Says she's leaving with the shark at the table, and get this, she doesn't even know the lucky bastard."

Seth told them all to, "shut up or get out!"

One of the other men told him, "Little Miss Thang at the bar says she's with you."

Seth looked up and said she was nice, but his lady was at the beauty shop. "Shit, I gotta get this game over with and pick her up, come on man shoot!"

The other man corrected his friends comment. "No man, that ain't what the lady said. She said she don't know anyone here, but she planned to leave with Sharkie here."

Seth looked up from the table and looked at the cutie across the room. *Sterling would kill me if I brought this girl back to the room*, Seth thought to himself. As soon as he won the last game, and collected his winnings he sauntered over toward the red headed woman. He winked at her, she winked back and pointed to him and motioned for him to keep coming toward her.

Once he was close to her, he said, "Sterling is that you? Hell those guys had me thinkin' I was gonna get lucky!" They both laughed.

He apologized for making her wait, but once they got in the car he told her he just took $600.00 off those guys while he was waiting for her. He never said anything about her new look.

Finally, she said, "Well, are you blind or don't you like the new me?"

"Baby you look hot! I noticed, and so did every other guy in there. Why did you wait so long to do this?"

"You really like?" she questioned.

"Baby, I love it, and if you want I'll show you how much."

"No, I think I got the idea, but thanks, a girl can never get too many compliments."

"While I was getting my hair done I started thinking of a place we could go and settle down for awhile. Maybe not take our time after all, just get to where we're going and watch our backs?"

"Baby, wherever you want to go, just name it and I'll take you there. You know though, I think we both agree that it has to be somewhere warm."

She told him that she had always liked Florida. She told him that going to Daytona Beach, as a kid, on family vacations were the best memories she had. The natives say once you get sand in your shoes you just keep coming back. He said if she would be happy there, he would be too. So, deciding to go back to the beach was the best vacation from reality she could think of but probably not the smartest idea she ever had. She wondered if her family would remember that Daytona was her favorite place on the planet and would try to find her. If they did, of course she had made it nearly impossible; she had done everything under an assumed name, and changed her appearance. She now knew why so many runaways go to Daytona. If they couldn't find the runaways, how were they going to find someone that had her experience and a plan? Although Daytona was not like New York or Los Angeles, a person could become lost if they so desired.

Chapter Eight

As the weeks turned into a month the investigation was going nowhere. There were no new leads, Marisa's car, and Wanda, were both still missing. The trail, what little trail there had been, was now cold. This case had been moved to the back burner. Cliff and Tina still called weekly and inquired about any updates and each time were disappointed when they hung up. And although they did believe that Marisa left on her own, they still wanted word of her whereabouts. To the police and Probation staff Cliff and Tina continued to play the role of distraught parents. They were truly distraught because they didn't know why she left, where she was going, or if she was coming back.

After she had been gone about a month, Marisa made a call to her parents. She knew that the phones, both at home and their jobs, could possibly have been tapped, so she didn't risk calling them there. She also figured that if they had bothered to tap her parent's phones they would also tap Kate and Dani's phones too, so she couldn't call them either. However, she knew they couldn't tap every phone in the city, so she waited until she knew her parents would be away for an evening and she would call them then. She knew that they regularly ate at the Nagasaki Inn, so she would just call them there. What a surprise that would be. She never left her name and if they didn't answer the page she just hung up and would try again later over a period of several hours.

She called the restaurant every night for four nights before she finally caught them. On the fourth night they were in the middle of their dinner when the manager paged them for the call. When her mother answered she was so shocked she couldn't speak. That was unbelievable because her mother was never at a loss for words.

Marisa told her mother she had no choice in the manner in which she left, and that she was perfectly safe. She refused to tell her mother where she was, but indicated that it was paradise. Tina told her that people from Marisa's office had continued to come around to see if anyone had news of her whereabouts. Of course Marisa made her mother and father promise to keep her secret, for their safety, as well as hers. They agreed to do so, but they wanted her to call them like this regularly. Marisa told them she couldn't do that because if they were being followed people would eventually catch on. She told them that the people who were looking for her were ruthless and would stop at nothing to have her or her family killed for the information she had uncovered. Marisa asked them about Kate, but told them that they should probably keep her in the dark about this phone call. She believed that because Kate was a very emotional and dramatic person she probably would be unable to keep the news to herself.

Briefly her mother told her that when she accompanied the police to the apartment that Friday morning she knew immediately that Marisa was okay, just by what she noticed missing. Marisa laughed because she knew that her mother had always been very observant. Tina told Marisa that she told the police that nothing appeared to be missing. She said she now understood the importance of the cryptic message on the bathroom mirror she had found only the day before being allowed to enter the apartment with the detective. She went on to say that she didn't notice initially that Cliff's duffel bag was missing, but she knew several of her favorite clothes were missing. She told her daughter that because of the cryptic note and the things that were missing she decided to keep her mouth shut. At that point she believed no one could be trusted and therefore did not tell the police or anyone else that asked.

Tina explained that when she told Cliff about the note, they both knew she had to have a good reason for leaving so abruptly, but they were still worried. Again, she told them she was fine, and that she loved them. She instructed them to go back to dinner and act as if it were a call about a sick relative. She was adamant that they not discuss the phone call or her in front of anyone. Again they agreed. They wanted only a quick and safe return for their daughter. She told them both she loved them, and again she apologized about her departure. She also told them she wasn't sure when she would call them again. They should just assume she was fine, and not worry about her.

After Marisa hung up she was certainly glad she had called. She knew this would be difficult for any parent to endure, but it was hard for her too. She was glad that they didn't ask her any questions about her financial situation, or if she was with anyone. Did they assume she had a job and a significant other, or were they afraid of the answer she might have given them? She knew she couldn't tell Seth of the phone call. He wouldn't understand. He had no real family, and he would worry needlessly for the next few weeks that they would be found. Why waste time worrying? They were both fine now, why mess that up.

The months went by and no one was even working the case at this point. Konjesky and Matheson still looked at any and all leads, but it was as if Marisa had just vanished into thin air. Marisa's family and friends were understandably upset that no one was actively looking for her, but they understood too, that there wasn't enough manpower to put these two officers on the case full time. Because the Spencer's knew their daughter had left voluntarily they did not hire a private detective. Several of their friends offered to help them finance it, but when they refused their friends worried about what a detective might find. Most everyone now believed that Marisa was dead. And, in a way, she was.

Chapter Nine

For the first month and a half Sterling lived at the beach or the pool. She worked on relaxing and forgetting her past, and of course she worked on her tan. Seth was content to take care of her, and she was content to let him. She knew she had enough money to take care of them for awhile, so working didn't seem that important to her. Seth, however, knew one of them should be employed. He wasn't interested in working in construction or roofing like he did back home. And, he didn't have an education to do much else, so he started looking for jobs at the various bars on the strip. After several interviews he finally landed a job at an exotic nightclub.

When Sterling decided she needed a job she asked Seth if he would mind her working with him at the bar. Seth was furious! He said no woman he was with was going to work as a dancer. Sterling laughed and told him, "Number one, I am not your woman. We are fantastic friends, not lovers. And, number two I was not planning to be a dancer. They do employ bartenders and waitresses you know!"

Although Seth wasn't thrilled with the idea of her working in this low class bar, or dump as he referred to it, he knew he could always be there to watch over her. He worked as a bouncer initially, but then worked his way up to assistant manager. Now he only worked as a bouncer on an as needed basis.

He was picking up a lot of management experience, but he knew most people wouldn't consider this place a real good place to put on a resume when he decided to change careers. He and Sterling had discussed that, but he said he liked beautiful woman, music and liquor so why not give it a shot. Sterling was unimpressed, but after she met some of the people he worked with, she changed her mind. She thought any woman that would strip for money had to be a whore. She found out that a lot of the girls were dancing their way through college, and had steady boyfriends. Their boyfriends were never customers, and their customers were never boyfriends; Seth made sure of that.

Seth was in charge of ordering the liquor, hiring and scheduling of bartenders, and security if necessary. He also made sure the girls were not involved with the customers. Seth used to tell Sterling the only thing the manager did was the hiring and scheduling of dancers. The girls did have guys that showed up regularly, but if Seth thought things were starting to heat up, he would tell the girls her days of dancing there were numbered. He would also take the guy aside and tell him she had three kids to support and she would be fired if they started dating. After hearing that the girl had three kids, the guy didn't want anything to do with her anyway.

When the girls would ask Seth what he had told the guy, Seth would always say with a very straight face, "I told him you had herpes." Seth cracked himself up most of the time.

Once Sterling started working at the bar she became friendly with some of the dancers. She realized she had been wrong about most of them, and she often said she thought she might even like to try dancing one day. Seth just said, "That won't happen in my lifetime!"

After Sterling started working full-time at the Buff Bunny Lounge she too had a following. Her outfit was a rather skimpy bikini, but she sometimes wore less on the beach. One of the men that became Sterling's regular customers never seemed to watch the dancers after he noticed her. His name was Ahmir and he was constantly asking Sterling if she would dance for him.

She always laughed as if he was joking, and told him no.

She had described Ahmir to Seth as a swarthy businessman. Seth told her never to go out with this guy because he thought he was a pervert. Seth would go out to the parking lot every time Ahmir was there to try see what car he was driving. He couldn't find anything that looked like Ahmir would own. He once asked Sterling about it, but she said, "Since I've never gone out with him how would I know?" By now Seth had his own Harley, and Sterling got around town driving the car she had purchased for them in Bristol. He assumed by the looks of Ahmir that he probably drove a BMW or Mercedes.

One evening Seth was not working and Ahmir was there talking to Sterling. He had finally convinced her she should go out with him. She agreed to meet him for breakfast after she got off work at 4:00 a.m., but she told him she would meet him at the restaurant. They had a great time, and he asked her out for another date, but she declined stating she could be fired for dating customers. He told her that rule only applied to the dancers. Sterling stood her ground and said she really couldn't go out with him. When she got home Seth was furious; he knew she didn't come home at the regular time. When he called the bar, the clean-up guy told him she had left with a dark complexioned man. Seth told her she could not date customers!

Angrily, she said, "I didn't have a date. I didn't fuck him! I ate breakfast and I met him at the restaurant! Besides, what if I did? You date the girls, hell you fuck them and don't deny it!"

Seth told her, "I am not a woman, I can't be raped! I can take care of myself in any situation. I don't want you to get hurt. I love you and I'm just trying to protect you. Why can't you see that?" Seth stormed out,

242

and as the door was closing Sterling threw the remote control at him.

Several nights later Ahmir came in again. He asked her if she would accompany him to a dinner meeting for some of his out of town clients. She agreed, but knew she would not be telling Seth. She told him she really didn't have anything appropriate to wear, and maybe another time she could go with him. He told her that he had already thought of that. He said he saw a beautiful dress and he knew she had to be the one to own it. So he bought the dress and matching accessories for her. Although she had not even seen it she told him that it was much too extravagant.

"Nothing my pet is too extravagant for you. You are like a queen and should be showered with beautiful gifts. Please go with me. It's only dinner, and maybe one dance."

"Ahmir, you're so sweet. I would love to go, but we must not let anyone here know of it."

"Of course my pet. I'll pick you up at your house at 6:30 p.m. The meeting with my clients is at 7 p.m."

"I'm sorry, but I'll have to meet you at the restaurant. I can't risk my roommate finding out about this. I hope you understand."

Although he was slightly insulted he agreed. She told him she would just change clothes in the restroom before dinner. He gave her the directions to the restaurant and she told him to tell his clients that she was meeting him after she got off work. He agreed reluctantly and went to the parking lot to get the clothes to give to her. The outfit was beautiful and she could tell it would fit her nicely.

Dinner couldn't have been lovelier. The clients, two foreign men that spoke no English, came late and left early. Sterling didn't have a problem with that as she and Ahmir had a chance to get to know each other. She excused herself to the restroom, and when she returned he had another 7 and 7 waiting for her. They danced several times, but as the evening progressed Sterling started to feel ill. She finally told Ahmir she wasn't feeling well, and she needed to leave. She stumbled as she got up, and she told him she was very dizzy. Ahmir told her would drive her home, and she could pick up her car later. Reluctantly she accepted his offer. In the car she started to pass out, but Ahmir kept telling her she "should be awake for this." The last thing she remembered was Ahmir laying her on the bed. She couldn't remember telling him where she lived.

Sterling awakened with the sun shining brightly in her eyes. She was still very dizzy and rather nauseous. She started to get out of bed when she realized she wasn't at home. Where was she? Where were her clothes? What had happened to her? She started to get up, but she fell onto the floor.

Sterling yelled, "Seth! Somebody please help me!"

She couldn't stand up without stumbling around, so she stayed on the floor and started to sob. She made her way over to the phone and she called work and asked for Seth. They told her that Seth didn't report to work today, but he had called several times looking for her. She called home immediately.

Seth answered, "Sterling is that you baby? Where are you?" Sterling was crying so hard that she couldn't speak. "Baby, calm down. I can't help you if you don't stop crying."

244

He told her he would make things okay if she just told him where she was. Sterling said she didn't know; she couldn't see things very well, and she was sick. Seth told her to go to the door and open it, look around and tell him what things were around her. She pulled the phone along the floor with her as she crawled to the door. Finally, she told him that she had never been here before. Across the street was what looked like a boarded up motel that had a sign that indicated it was the Stop Inn Motor Lodge.

"Seth, I'm scared."

"Baby, I'll be there soon, now look at the door and tell me what room you're in."

"The numbers are moving, Seth, but it looks like 156, and the walls are orange and red."

"Baby, I'll be right there. Hang up the phone and don't try to leave, go back to the bed and lie down." Sterling did as he told her.

Seth immediately got out the phone book and looked up the address for the Stop Inn Motor Lodge. She was in north Ormond Beach, and it would take him at least thirty minutes to get to her. He prayed to God again, *"Please Lord, help us both. Let her be okay."*

When he got to the Stop Inn Motor Lodge he looked across the street. Sterling was in a "dump", a place that should have been condemned. The place had trash everywhere. The clerk was asleep, or passed out on the front counter. He ran around and finally located room 156. He opened the door and walked slowly to the bed. Sterling was naked, and still asleep when he rolled her over. Tears filled his eyes when he saw her. Her lip was split, she had bruises on her arms and legs, and her hair was all tangled. Either she had put up a hell of a fight, or someone, Ahmir most likely, really liked having rough sex. When she opened her eyes she became filled with emotion and she started sobbing again.

"I'm sorry Seth, I'm sorry." Seth just held her.

She finally calmed down a little bit and he said, "Let's get out of here, where's your clothes?"

"My clothes, I, I had on this beautiful dress. It's gotta be somewhere around here."

Seth looked in all the drawers and the bathroom, but finally said "Babe, I think the jerk took everything."

"That sonofabitch! He said I should own that dress! Seth I don't have anything to wear. My clothes are in my car."

Her head was pounding, and her heart was racing. She felt horrible. She had never been this sick. Seth was wearing a denim work shirt, leather vest, jeans, and his boots. He took off his shirt and gave it to her. She wrapped herself in the sheet and went into the bathroom. She yelled from the bathroom, "What about pants, I don't have underwear or pants!"

Seth replied, "I guess you'll go commando just like me!" Seth could find humor in any situation.

There appeared to be no one roaming around outside. Seth's Harley was going to be her transportation home. Seth climbed on and started it up. Gingerly, Sterling climbed on behind him, and held him tight. As they started to leave the motel, she asked him to get on the beach as soon as possible. She never wanted to see this place again. As they drove Sterling never let go of him. He could feel her place her head against his back.

Seth decided on the way back home that he would wait a while to ask her about her "date". He did ask her if she wanted to call the police or go to the hospital, but she declined. She knew she should report what happened to her but she was not ready for that. She knew she did a dumb thing, and she knew she had been raped. She also knew that Ahmir had probably drugged her, but she would leave the police out of it. They wouldn't be able to find Ahmir, and what if they did? She couldn't stand facing him again. Seth told her she was in no shape to go back to work for a while. They would just tell everyone she was on a little vacation. Once again she was being forced to take a vacation and run from her problems.

After they got home she realized her car was not in her parking spot. When she started to question Seth about it, he gave her a perplexing glance. She told him they really needed to find the car. He told her they would find it, but first they needed to take care of her. She told him the restaurant was over the bridge, in Port Orange. She couldn't remember the name of the place, but said it was really fancy, and it had a dance floor with potted palms. He told her she just described ninety per cent of the ritzy restaurants in Florida. Tears were streaming down her face as she tried to smile. She apologized again, and told him she wished she had listened to him. Sterling said she had a migraine and she was still a little light-headed. Seth carried her from the cycle up to the condo. She held onto him tightly and placed her head on his shoulder.

"Would you please stay with me tonight? I know you're really mad at me and I look a mess, but Seth I'm really afraid to be alone."

"Baby, I'm not going anywhere. I'm going to take care of you. And, yes I'm really upset with you, but if I can find Ahmir I'm going to kill him."

The mere mention of that name sent Sterling to a place inside herself that was filled with rage. She started weeping again. She was worried too, that Seth would do exactly as he said.

When they got inside, Seth took her to the bedroom. He suggested that she might want to take a bath. She told him she wanted to take a shower, a long, hot shower with plenty of soap. Sterling had not seen her reflection in the mirror yet. When she passed by the vanity mirror she gasped at the sight. She couldn't stand to look at herself.

While she was running the water, Seth got out one of her nightshirts, but she said she was cold and wanted to wear a sweatshirt. He gave her some clean panties and asked her if she needed anything else. Seth told her he would be in the living room listening to the stereo, just to yell if she needed anything.

The shower was on for over forty minutes. He thought she was probably out of hot water by now, and he went to check on her. He called her name, but she didn't answer. When he pushed open the door, he couldn't see her through the shower doors, but the water was still running. Still calling her name, he walked closer. She was sitting on the floor of the tub, hugging her knees to her chest with her head down and crying very quietly.

Seth grabbed a big towel, and turned off the water. She didn't seem to notice he was there. She was holding just a little piece of the soap. Her skin was red, irritated, from the force she must have used. As he put the towel around her, and lifted her from the tub, he too, was crying. What had that bastard done to his baby? He knew that Ahmir had probably used that new "date rape" pill on her without her knowledge. He also knew that even though it would be scary and sad for her to think about, remembering what happened would help her recover. Not knowing what was done to her would probably torment her for the rest of her life. Even though she was obviously raped, many questions were going through Seth's mind. How many men had been involved? Were there any pictures or movies that could come back to haunt her? And had they done anything physically damaging to her?

Seth dried her off and helped her put her clothes on, and then he dried her hair. She still had not spoken to him and she had a vacant look in her eyes. He didn't know what to do. When he spoke to her she just looked at him, as if she could see through him. She was no longer crying. It was now late in the afternoon and he knew she hadn't eaten. He tried to get her to eat a sandwich and an orange, but she said she wasn't hungry. She asked him to fix her a strong drink. He fixed her a 7 and 7, her favorite. She drank it fast and asked for another. Seth fixed her another, but told her that the bar was now closed.

"Damn you, if I want another drink, just fix it!" she shrieked.

He stood his ground and told her she was not having another drink. She drank this one quickly, knowing the quicker the liquor was down her throat, and the faster she would feel its effect.

As she was going to the bathroom she yelled to Seth, "You know you can't be here forever guarding the liquor! And, you can't be here forever guarding me!"

Somehow, she had turned this on him. Not only was he hurt, but he didn't know what to do. Was she mad at him because he was a man, or was she mad at him because he wouldn't let her get drunk, or both? He knew she was at least a little tipsy, so reasoning with her would not be appropriate. He would just have to wait and see how things went when she came back into the room.

Sterling was in the bathroom a long time. After a while he thought she might try to harm herself, so he ran into the hall and asked her if she was okay. He could hear her vomiting, and crying. He opened the door and asked if she was going to be okay.

She turned to him and said, "Throw out that shit! Please?"

He didn't think that liquor could go bad, but he poured it down the drain and took the bottles to the trash chute as she requested. When he came back she told him that she remembered drinking two 7 and 7's at dinner, and when she remembered this she could feel herself getting sick. She knew it was psychosomatic. She also apologized for berating him earlier when she knew he was only trying to help her. She told him she was really scared and lonely. They sat on the couch, listening to the stereo until she finally fell asleep. He carried her to bed and got in beside her. She snuggled close to him. He had wanted her so badly over the last few months, but he knew she wouldn't be ready for a long time now. If it ever was going to happen he knew their lovemaking would have to be on her terms.

Chapter Ten

Several weeks passed after the attack and Sterling missed her period. She had told Seth, but he believed that the trauma she experienced was the culprit. She decided he had to be right. She didn't even want to think about the other possibility. Although Sterling didn't go back to work for a few weeks, she had been thinking about everything going on around her. She realized that Seth didn't want her to return to work at the Buff Bunny Lounge. She had worked at the lounge only three months prior to the attack, and because of it she was suffering a lifetime of anguish. He repeatedly told her that it would bring back too many memories, and there was also the possibility that Ahmir would return. Seth really didn't believe either of them would ever see Ahmir again, but he had to convince Sterling not to return to her old job. He constantly scanned the want ads for her because he knew she wasn't content to stay at home forever. He wanted her to work somewhere safe, a motel, a souvenir shop, or even a restaurant. Sterling didn't seem interested in any of the jobs he mentioned.

Seth had moved back in the night after the attack on Sterling. He still came and went as he pleased, but his home was with Sterling. About a month after the attack and her period was still absent she decided to take a home pregnancy test. She was alone when she read the results. She stared at the positive indicator with tears in her eyes. How could this have happened to her? They had been gone only four months; it was beginning to seem much longer. She called Seth at work and told him she needed him now. She was hysterical on the phone, so he left immediately.

When he walked in she was sitting on the balcony holding something. He walked out to her and she handed him the test results. He didn't know immediately what it was, but then he realized why she was crying. He told her he would marry her and accept the child as his own, that no one had to know any different. She told him she couldn't carry this child, and everyone would know it wasn't his when it was born. Its father was Ahmir, a Middle Eastern man. Everyone would know, and we would too. She told him she had no other options but to have an abortion. He knew he couldn't talk her out of this, and he was certain he didn't want to try.

Seth went to the phone book and looked up a number for abortion clinics. He couldn't judge her, or try to talk about other options, the people at the clinic would do that and she would have to listen. But, she knew what she had to do and he would do whatever she asked of him. An appointment was made for the next afternoon. He called work and told them he needed some time off, a few days or possibly a week.

They drove to the clinic in silence. There was a waiting period of twenty-four hours, so an appointment was made for the very next day. The rest of the day, and most of the night, Sterling kept to herself and cried. The next morning he drove her to the clinic. She told him he didn't have to stay, but she knew he wouldn't leave her. Two hours later Sterling came out looking kind of groggy. The nurse assumed that this had been his child, and she gave him all the information about aftercare and what to do in case of heavy bleeding or other emergencies. She suggested that Sterling take it easy for a few days. Seth told the nurse he would take excellent care of her. The nurse said, "Perhaps next time young man you'll make sure you have protection so something like this doesn't happen again."

Seth said nothing in response. There was no way he could tell the nurse how much he loved Sterling and didn't want this to happen to her, and that it wasn't his fault. Instead, he just nodded. The drive home was hard for both of them. He didn't know what to say to her, and she was devastated at the turn of events in her life.

Although they didn't speak, Sterling sobbed quietly. She knew this was not the way things were supposed to be.

After three days of being miserable and depressed she told Seth she could not dwell on this part of her life. She said she had begged God for forgiveness and had made her own peace with it. But, she never wanted to speak of it again. He told her he would do whatever she wanted.

Two months after the attack Seth came home earlier than usual; he was quite surprised at what he found. There were all sorts of evening dresses and shoes scattered on the furniture. He walked into the bedroom and found Sterling all dressed up, her hair was piled on top of her head and she was dripping in jewels. The scent in the air was new as well. He asked her what was going on. She looked at him and told him she was going into business.

Seth replied, "What kind of business are you in, modeling?"

She looked at him demurely, and said, "If that's what they want, I can model, I can talk with them, and I can have dinner and cocktails, pretty much whatever I'm paid to do."

Seth couldn't believe what he was hearing. He started yelling at her, telling her that she was making another huge mistake. She didn't listen. She continued looking at herself in the mirror. Seth asked her how she had paid for all these dresses and accessories. Sterling told him the escort service that she was now working for had provided them. She also told him she had an important "date" that evening and her limousine would be here any time. Seth was furious. He told her he was going to go with her and wait in the limo. Sterling told him he was crazy.

"Oh, now I'm the crazy one huh? Have you even thought of what you're doing? Have you lost your ever-lovin' mind? Jesus! Marisa, you're a probation officer; you can't work as a hooker!

"Don't you call me that!"

"What? Call you by your given name?"

"That's not who I am anymore Seth! Don't you ever call me that again! And, I am not working as a hooker!"

"Baby, just because you changed your look, and changed your name, doesn't mean that you can change who you are and what you believe. You are Marisa. Sterling is just a figment of your imagination."

"NO! I'm Sterling. Just because you think of that other person, doesn't mean that's who I am!"

"Marisa, listen to me. You need some help now if you have completely lost yourself in this character you've created. Maybe I can't help you, but you need to think about what it is you're doing, and why we're here."

"I don't want to talk about this anymore. I don't need one more person judging me. I do that everyday on my own. I don't answer to you. I don't answer to anyone! Now leave me alone!"

"Don't you even remember what just happened to you and how you had to take care of that?

She shook her head and said, "Look, what's done is done. You don't want me working for the lounge anymore, so I'm not. I want to make good money and work my own hours, and I'm not gonna sell Tupperware. Since I can't work just anywhere I figured I might as well try this. Besides, I might as well get paid for what Ahmir did to me, no one's getting it for free. The first and last guy I was in love with went back to his wife remember?"

"Oh I get it. So instead of selling Tupperware, you would rather sell yourself?"

"Shut the fuck up! I don't need your lectures!"

Seth could only assume she had some kind of mental breakdown. There could be no other explanation. What could he do or say to make her see what she was doing was wrong and against everything she had ever stood for?

Seth couldn't believe she was going this far. He tried to reason with her, but the buzzer rang and she flew out the door. At the elevator she yelled to him not to wait up. Seth ran down the stairs trying to catch a glimpse of the limo, but he knew he would never be able to catch them, his cycle was downstairs and she was already pulling out of the drive.

In the limo the driver told her they would be going to meet her date, Mr. Taglio, at the convention center. He also told her that Mr. Taglio was only in town for two nights and he should just about be finished with one of his presentations when they arrive. The driver didn't know of their plans, just that he was on stand-by for the rest of the evening. On the drive over, Sterling was nervous about her first "date" and was thinking about her new job.

She had not completed any paperwork at the

Beachside Escort Service. This service catered to upscale tourists and out of town businessmen. Sterling had heard of this escort service from one of the dancers at the Buff Bunny Lounge. The dancer had given them high marks, but said they wouldn't allow her to work as a dancer and an escort too, so she quit the escort service. It seems that she liked regular hours, and more importantly, she didn't like being told what she could or couldn't do on her own time. She told Sterling that they paid well, they arranged everything and only took forty percent of the fee. They also didn't serve area businessmen, which made it seem less seedy. The dancer had told her she usually was home by midnight and most of the men just wanted a dinner companion, nothing more. She said for a fee of a thousand dollars or more and tips, she wouldn't complain.

Sterling thought being an escort would be the perfect job, and she didn't understand why Seth was so upset. Sterling decided on using another assumed name. This time she chose Eden Elliot. Eden was a classy character on one of the soap operas she watched, and Elliot was her one true love. She also knew that if she ever returned home she didn't want anyone to know about her new "job".

Mr. Taglio was a perfect gentleman. He had an aide meet her at the door. The aide explained that she would act as if she were the daughter of Mr. Taglio's business partner, and that they were meeting for dinner after his presentation. It appeared that Mr. Taglio was very wealthy, and very well connected. The presentation had just concluded when Mr. Taglio's aide escorted her to the dais. Mr. Taglio kissed her on the cheek and gave her a hug like he had truly missed her. He told her loud enough for those around him to hear that her father is so proud of her and was happy to set dinner up for them after the presentation. He commented that he was thankful that she had time for him in her busy schedule.

Sterling played the part of Eden and said, "Daddy just goes on and on about you and when he told me you would be in town for just two nights I told him that you better stop in and see me."

Eden and Mr. Taglio mingled for about thirty minutes, and then he told the aide to call the limo because he was starving. A few minutes passed and the aide motioned for them to come to the door. Mr. Taglio shook hands as he left the room, and Eden just kept heading toward the limo. Once they were safely inside the car Mr. Taglio told her she sounded like she knew his business partner, but he laughed because his partner had never married, and didn't have any children. He told her that his own wife didn't like to attend his seminars, so she usually stayed at home on the short trips. If the seminars were abroad, or in exotic locales, Mrs. Taglio would accompany him.

Mr. Taglio appeared to be in his late 40's, he was graying at the temples and seemed quite physically fit. He reminded her of Elliot. He wore an Armani suit and expensive smelling cologne. Sterling had definitely had worse blind dates. The limo came to a stop at a condominium complex. She looked puzzled and he told her he had the penthouse clubroom reserved for just the two of them. Dinner was being catered by one of the finest restaurants in the area. He told her that the champagne was chilling and dinner was to be ready when they arrived. He told her he had a friend that owned one of the penthouse suites, so he usually stayed there when he was in town. He also informed her that his friend was in Orlando for a week on business, so they wouldn't be bothered.

As she rode up in the elevator he put his arm around her waist and told her that she smelled heavenly. She was a little uneasy, but she continued to play her part.

257

She let him make all the moves. She wasn't sure how the night would end, but she was fine so far. When they arrived at the penthouse level, he unlocked the clubroom. Soft music was playing on the stereo, and she could see the last of the sunset out the west windows. The balcony doors were open and she could hear the crash of the tide coming in. A gentle breeze blew through the sheer curtains. The clubroom had everything: a fully stocked bar, a full kitchen, a grand piano, beautiful furnishings, lush tropical plants and elegant lighting. It was better than a fine restaurant because there was no one else around but a few of the caterers.

About half way through their meal of steamed lobster, filet mignon, baked potatoes and an array of steamed vegetables, Mr. Taglio excused everyone. He told them they could return in the morning to retrieve the items they brought. He tipped all of them generously and no one complained. After they were alone and they had finished their chocolate mousse for dessert, Mr. Taglio requested that she dance with him. Eden couldn't resist. She actually started to feel like she was really on a romantic date.

They danced for a long time, until it was so dark outside that she began to wonder how she was going to get home. As Mr. Taglio started to pour himself some more champagne he asked her to come and sit with him on the very small couch. He was beginning to get more comfortable with her and began kissing her quite passionately. She kissed him back and felt like she was about to melt. He then started talking about his wife, and how the passion had seemed to fade from their marriage.

Eden told him that he seemed like a very romantic man, and maybe he should try the same things with his wife. She also told him that he should insist that his wife travel with him, possibly getting her more involved in his business. He confided to Eden that he thought his wife was having an affair with one of his colleagues. At that point Eden started to wonder when he was really going to come onto her. She found she couldn't really concentrate on what he was saying, so she excused herself to the ladies' room. When she returned Mr. Taglio was gone. She heard a knock at the door and when she opened it she found the limo driver. He told her that Mr. Taglio had asked him to return her home.

On the way down the elevator she asked if Mr. Taglio was okay or had she done something to offend him. He told her that nothing was wrong as far as he knew; he was only doing as his boss had requested. Sterling was in shock at first, but then realized she hadn't been paid. She wasn't really too upset. She did have a lovely dinner and a very romantic evening and all she had to do was keep a lonely man company. When she got into the car she found an envelope addressed to Eden. Inside she found two five hundred-dollar bills, and a note that said, *"Thanks for listening and for a wonderful evening."* Sterling was astonished. The service always collected their fee up front, and whatever the girls were paid at the end of their "date" was theirs to keep. Now what would Seth say?

When she arrived home, Seth was asleep on the couch and a movie was on the television. Quietly she went into the bedroom and changed into her pajamas. She put the money inside an empty purse in the closet.

She was washing her face when Seth walked in. "So how does it feel being a prostitute?"

She was livid! She spun around and said, "Look, all I did was have a wonderful dinner with a very romantic man. Nothing more happened. Why can't you just let me be?"

Seth just smirked, and said, "Oh please Marisa, you and I both know more than that happened. And besides, even if you are telling the truth there will come a day when you have to have more than dinner with some creep!"

"I told you before, and I'll remind you once more: Don't call me that again! Why don't you just leave? If I disgust you so much, why do you stay here? No one is looking for me here, and everyone is safe at home. Just leave! One more thing, I don't know how you can be so hypocritical. You work in a strip club, and go out with some of the dancers, and many of them hook on the side, you just don't know about it. And I'm quite sure that you fuck the ones you date!"

"Look, I manage a bar, and I date women. I don't pay women to fuck me!"

She decided she couldn't keep arguing with him about this. He stormed out past her and a few minutes later she heard the front door slam shut as she was crawling into bed, alone. She decided not to let his leaving bother her.

She awoke the next morning to the smell of coffee and bacon. Seth had either returned in the middle of the night or come back this morning. He was in the kitchen fixing breakfast for them. She was very surprised to even see him back. As she entered the kitchen he said, "Baby, I don't want to fight with you. I'm just worried about you. I'll always worry about you because I love you. Please think about what it is that you're doing, and reconsider this new line of work? And try to think about the future and what you will tell your parents and friends if they ever ask you what you did for a job while you were away."

"You know, I've already thought of that. My plan is just to tell them I worked as a bartender. I know they'll buy that story since I did that before I started work as a P.O."

"Please Baby, don't go back."

"Seth I respect your opinion. I really do, but I have to live my own life and I'm not hurting anyone." She had no idea how hurt Seth was inside. He loved her, and he wanted her to love him too.

As the weeks passed Eden had several more "dates" but nothing compared to her first "date" with Mr. Taglio. Most of the men were much older, and most just wanted to talk or show her off to their friends. Probably telling their friends afterwards what a stud they had been in bed. She laughed about this to herself because she really had to play the part of the doting, frisky girlfriend. Most of the men just wanted to look at her or touch her backside. Occasionally one of the older men would playfully grab at her breasts. She would act coy and slap their hands. They acted like naughty little boys. When she would return home she would just roll on the money and be thankful that nothing more had ever happened. After her first "date" she and Seth had never discussed her "dates" again, though he made sure she was painfully aware of his opinion.

About two months had gone by and the most she ever had to do was let some old man paw at her, and a few times she had to watch them "perform" for her. Most of these old men disgusted her, but as long as they left her alone she felt lucky. She knew her luck wouldn't last forever, but she was looking for a little excitement when she took this job. She had been averaging about four "dates" per week, and most of the time she came home with approximately eight hundred dollars! She splurged on furniture, clothing, expensive perfumes and a lot of fun; however, she was also paying all the bills and putting away a little money for emergencies.

One afternoon she received a call from the service that she had a date with a repeat customer, Mr. Taglio. Sterling was truly excited. Mr. Taglio had requested her by name and reported to the service that it would be the same sort of affair, but he booked her for two separate "dates". Sterling picked out two beautiful cocktail dresses and her matching accessories. She got ready quickly because the limo was going to be at her apartment in one hour. She was acting like a nervous schoolgirl. She left a note for Seth indicating that she had just received short notice for a "date".

The limo arrived with the same driver. He remembered her and told her that Mr. Taglio would be making another presentation at the convention center. He told her he didn't know any other details. Once they arrived she could see that it was the same scenario as the time before. Mr. Taglio whispered in her ear that she looked ravishing. Eden blushed and told him she was glad he had called her again. Again dinner was in the same penthouse clubroom, only the menu and caterers were different.

During dinner Mr. Taglio again excused the caterers. As they finished dinner, Eden asked him what he had planned for them the next evening. He told her it was a surprise, but she should bring her bathing suit. After dessert, Eden asked him if he was going to leave abruptly tonight or if he would tell her goodbye. He told her he was about to go over the line with her and he hadn't planned for that so he thought he should just let the evening end. He apologized for not telling her himself, but he didn't want to offend her with unwanted advances from a married man. She told him she appreciated his honesty.

They began to dance and Mr. Taglio pulled her closer than he had before. He started kissing her on the neck and she could feel his hands up and down her back. He then started to unzip her dress. Eden didn't refuse. The dress, a purple strapless Versace, started to move down her body. They continued to dance slowly. She pulled back so that he dress could fall to the floor. Her lingerie was light lavender and she had on a garter belt and heels. Mr. Taglio held her hands and just looked at her. He pulled her close to him again and they danced slowly, silently, for what seemed like forever. Mr. Taglio took off his suit jacket and asked her to come out on the balcony that overlooked the beach. The beach was deserted and it was eerily dark outside.

They stood on the balcony, one in front of the other. He had his arms draped around Eden's shoulders as they swayed to the music playing softly inside. Sterling was confused, she knew what might come next, and she wasn't sure if she was ready. She could feel that Mr. Taglio was excited but she didn't know what to say or do. She just decided to stay in character as Eden, and let him decide what was going to happen. Mr. Taglio had never told her his first name until now. He spun her around toward him and told her he wanted to hear her whisper his name. Innocently she said she didn't even know his first name. He told her it was Roger. She leaned into his chest and whispered, "Roger, Roger." He started kissing her passionately and he unbuttoned his shirt. Eden was a little scared, but she knew that this day was coming. She was grateful he was such a gentle, handsome man.

Roger then asked her if she would dance for him. She agreed and moved back inside. He sat on a chaise lounge and watched her intently. She was a little embarrassed, but she had seen a number of dancers in her day, so she let the music enter her body and moved with it. She didn't take off any of the remainder of her clothes, but she did give him a little peek a few times. The music finally stopped and he brought her dress to her and thanked her for the little "show". Eden was now more than a little confused but said nothing. He told her his driver would be there in five minutes to take her home. He gave her an envelope and asked her to wait to open it until she was in the car.

On her way home, she opened the envelope and was startled to see three five hundred-dollar bills. She believed that he might be paying her in advance for their trip tomorrow. It was one o'clock in the morning and she was exhausted. Once back at the condo she took a shower and crawled into bed next to Seth.

The next day she was picked up at 4:00 p.m. and taken to a chartered boat business at Ponce Inlet. She was dressed elegantly, so she was hoping that they weren't going fishing. She had brought with her a bathing suit like Mr. Taglio had requested. As the driver pulled out of the lot she heard a man calling for Miss Eden Elliot. She looked around to see one of the finest looking yachts she had ever seen in that area. Mr. Taglio was on the upper deck waving to her. The captain helped her aboard and told her to watch her step. She started up the steps to the upper deck. Mr. Taglio told her they would be taking a dinner cruise and later could go into the Jacuzzi. He told that it was just the three of them on the boat. He had picked up the dinner at an area restaurant.

The boat went out of the cut into the open sea. She was glad the sea was so calm. She loved the water, but not everyone could handle it if the ocean gets rough. The sky was turning a beautiful shade of orange and pink. It had been a cloudy day, so she was sure that the sunset would be spectacular. They started eating their dinner of cracked crab, hush puppies, and salad. She felt a little overdressed but she knew she looked good. Roger had repeatedly told her how nice she looked. After they finished eating he cleared up the mess they had made. She sat and watched the sun sink lower in the sky. He sat down beside her and asked if she needed anything. She told him she was fine and just liked to sit and watch the water and the sunset.

They had gone so far out now that the shore was difficult to see. She heard another boat approaching. Roger told her that he owned this boat and he was dismissing the captain for the evening. The boat she saw approaching was the captain's pick up boat. He explained that he couldn't very well drive the boat and have dinner, so he arranged to be chartered out to sea. Eden was a bit concerned that he might hurt her and throw her overboard, but really he had never done anything to scare her before so she decided to let the evening progress.

The captain bid them both farewell as they drifted without the engine on. Roger assured her that he knew how to get them home. He then asked her if she would like to get into the Jacuzzi. He showed her to the cabin where she could change clothes and told her to meet him on deck when she finished.

Sterling took her time and looked around. Nothing seemed out of the ordinary, and she did find some pictures of Roger and his wife on a bedside table. She went up on deck and found that he was already in the Jacuzzi with a split of champagne alongside. She got in next to him and he put his arm around her shoulders. He was telling her how long it had been since he had been out on the boat with his wife. He laughed and said, "Phyllis is afraid of the ocean, and everything contained therein. She wants no part of this boat, or me, if I'm on it."

The sun was setting in the sky behind them. It

was as magnificent as she had thought it would be. Roger started kissing her and pulled her onto his lap. As they were kissing she could feel him untying her bikini top. The bubbling water whisked her top off. Roger began kissing her neck, and his head continued to move down to her breasts. She felt so different, but she was also having a hard time remembering that this was all just an act in a very bizarre play.

Roger started caressing her breasts. As his hand moved down her stomach she knew that this evening would end quite differently than all the others. He then removed her bikini bottoms. She could tell that he was still wearing his swim trunks. She wondered when they too would come off. After an eternity of foreplay, he asked her to come up to the upper deck. She got out of the Jacuzzi and walked in front of him completely nude and dripping wet.

Once on the upper deck he asked her to lie down on one of the chaise lounge chairs. He then stood over her and looked at her like he had never seen a naked woman before. He removed his trunks and continued to stare at her. She could see the desire in his eyes, but suddenly he walked away. He disappeared from the upper deck and left her sitting there totally alone and exposed.

After a few bewildering moments Sterling went to the Jacuzzi on the main deck. Roger was nowhere in sight, but she grabbed her wet suit and wrapped herself in a towel. She walked around the boat calling for him, but she couldn't find him. Sterling was becoming a bit concerned, and apprehensive, and decided to go back to the lower deck and get dressed. As she went down the lower hall she could hear noises. She realized it was Roger, alone in the cabin where she had changed. She heard the bathroom door close, so she decided to return to the upper deck and wait. However, as she began to climb the steps the door swung open and Roger saw her. He seemed to be out of breath and a little startled to see her. Sterling didn't know what to say. She just looked at him.

"I, uh, Eden, I'm so sorry."

"Roger, what's going on? Or do I want to know?"

"I, well, I, umm, I just can't be with you. Not completely." He continued to stammer, "I just can't be with you totally. If I allow myself to make love to you then I'm no different than her. I just can't be unfaithful to Phyllis. I still love her, and I can't cheat on her."

Although she was still a little confused, she wondered what his wife would think of what had been occurring these last few weeks. Sterling finally realized that she had gotten involved in a very bizarre scene, and she was only being used. She was merely a toy for the men that paid her. Not one of them loved her, or cared anything about her. How could she have been so blind? She had to get out at all costs. Seth had been right all along. She was so stubborn, and naïve. She wondered now, if this situation was just her own bad judgment, or something psychological related to the attack by Ahmir, and all the other turmoil in her life? Sterling felt sick and terribly tormented now.

She went downstairs and took a shower. She got dressed and went to the bar to get a drink when she heard another boat approaching. Roger was helping the captain back aboard. He then explained that he was unsure of the channels in the dark, so he called for the captain to return. Of course she didn't believe him. She knew it would take longer for the captain to return than the time that it took her to shower and re-dress. She figured that the captain was probably told to be back at a certain time, or the boat was anchored just out of sight and watching the whole sordid episode with binoculars.

On the boat ride home Roger seemed distant. When they arrived back onshore he told her he was leaving the country for at least a year and then he handed her an envelope. Inside was a note stating that he and his wife had not been intimate in over a year. They had gone into counseling and she admitted to an affair. He told Eden that he admitted nothing and was heartsick when she told him of the affair. He said that they were moving overseas to take a new post within his company, but he had hoped they could mend their marriage and get past her infidelities. In the envelope along with the note was five thousand dollars. The limo was waiting for her when they docked the boat.

Even though the money was incredible, Sterling felt used. Not the way she felt when she was attacked, but used emotionally. She cried on the way home in the limo. The driver tried to console her, but she told him she didn't feel like talking. He dropped her at the condo and left. She left the money and the letter in the limo. When she got inside, she was hoping Seth wouldn't be there. She just wanted to be alone now. Inside the place was dark, and silent. Seth had left a message on the machine. He wouldn't be home tonight. She took a long shower and sat on the balcony until the sun came up.

The phone was ringing, but she let the machine pick up. It was the service. She waited until they hung up, then she erased the message. She left the balcony doors open, but she closed the curtains and went to bed. She slept until the late afternoon. When she got up, she called a messenger service and requested that they come over immediately. She then called down to the manager and asked if they had a very large box. The manager told her someone had moved in recently and there were still some boxes in the storage area downstairs. Sterling went down to the underground garage and picked out the

268

largest box she could find. Hurriedly she went back upstairs to pack.

She took out all of her evening dresses, matching shoes, and accessories. The lingerie was hers to keep she had been told, but she put it in the box too. Just as she was finishing, the buzzer sounded from downstairs. Quickly she turned on the television so she could look at the closed circuit camera downstairs. She could see the messenger. She told him to pull open the door when he heard the click and to wait in the lobby. She keyed in the pass code and the messenger entered the building. She struggled to pick up the box, but she was on a mission.

As she entered the lobby, the messenger could see how she was struggling and he took the box from her. He took out his invoice paperwork and had her complete it. She was sending all of her clothes back to the Beachside Escort Service. She signed the paperwork in the phony name she used: Eden Elliot. She told him to make sure that they realized the package had come from her. He told her they would get a copy of the invoice. She gave him a hundred-dollar bill and told him to keep the change. She hoped and prayed that no one would call from the service and ask her why.

When she came back upstairs, leaving nothing to chance, she called the phone company and requested a temporary disconnect on her line. She told them to leave it disconnected for two weeks. She figured that the service wouldn't try more than a few days and when they realized her phone had been disconnected they wouldn't bother her anymore. She wanted her old life back. She needed to contact Seth. She went to the bait shop across the street and called his beeper number. About ten minutes went by and the phone finally rang. Of course he didn't recognize the number to know who had paged him, so he was quite surprised when he called back to hear her voice.

"Seth, will you be home for dinner tonight? We need to talk."

First, he asked if she was okay. She told him everything was fine, she just wanted him home tonight. He told her he would be home around 6:30p.m. He then asked why she didn't call from home. She told him there was a problem with the line and the phone company was checking on it. He told her he would see her later and hung up. Sterling went out to the beach and took a long walk. She had at least an hour until Seth got home.

While walking in the sand she wondered how her life could get so screwed up. Her mind was racing. She questioned if she should stay here in Daytona. She knew that she wasn't safe at home, but she often wondered if she was safe here. Seth did his best to protect her, but he couldn't protect her from herself. She had always made pretty reasonable decisions, but since arriving in Daytona she had made one disastrous decision after another. She decided that from now on she would truly listen to Seth. He always seemed to know what was best for her. She knew he really cared about her; she cared about him too. She hated to think about what he might have left behind. If he left a woman behind, she would never forgive herself.

Marisa had always kept up with his jobs, where he was living, but she never pried into his relationships. Occasionally he would mention a new girlfriend, but his relationships never lasted more than a few weeks or a month at most. He didn't seem to be the marrying kind. He had a child with a girl, but they had broken up before his daughter was born. She recalled the story that Seth told her about his daughter that was born about three years earlier. The girl's parents hated him, and forced her to move away with them with no forwarding information

270

he could ever find. The last time he saw his daughter, Paige, he handed over every penny to his ex-girlfriend and she gave him a handful of pictures. He prayed one day he'd see them both again.

Now she wondered if Seth would go away with her for a little while. She just wanted to clear her head, and think about something other than how she had messed up both of their lives. She would ask him at dinner if they could take a trip. *"Dinner? Oh no!"* she thought, as she raced back to the condo. She hadn't even started dinner and he would be there any minute. Just as she reached the security gate, Seth was coming out to get her. She was embarrassed, and he thought it was cute.

"Lost in your thoughts again Baby?"

She replied, "Well actually I was thinking about you. How I've screwed up not only my life, but yours too."

"Don't worry about me, I'll be fine. I'm like a cat with nine lives. Let's forget about cooking dinner and walk down to that reggae place that serves on the beach."

Sterling liked that idea, but she knew that they wouldn't really talk about any important things there. Oh well, she knew she had plenty of time. And, Seth didn't appear to be going anywhere. Off they went hand in hand, Sterling in her bikini and his work shirt and Seth in his jeans and leather vest. Neither of them had on shoes-typical attire for an evening at a beachside bar.

Once they reached the restaurant, Sterling realized she always had a good time when Seth was around. She just couldn't understand how he could be so forgiving. They ate swamp chicken and rice, and drank a pitcher of beer. After they ate they went out on the dance floor and had a great time. She told him they better save some strength because they had a long way back on the darkened beach. They sat at the bar for a few minutes to catch their breath, and then they started home.

On the way back Seth asked her what she had wanted to talk about at dinner. She stopped and took his hands and said, "Seth you have been with me through thick and thin. You have cared for me when I couldn't care for myself and you've done your best to protect me. I just want you to know that I'm very sorry for the last few months and the way I've behaved."

Seth hugged her and looked into her beautiful eyes, and said, "Baby, we all make mistakes, but if you can learn from them you won't make the same mistake again. Do you remember telling me that a long time ago?"

She had told him the very same thing when he was on probation with her. She had always believed mistakes were a good thing if you could learn from them. Somehow she felt a little better. She was also happy because he had remembered something she had told him.

She said, "Well I made a decision today, and I think you'll be pleased."

He was looking into her eyes when she told him that she was no longer working as an escort. "Seth, I should have listened to you a long time ago, and now I wonder how I'm going to get out of this without anyone but you finding out about it. I just kept rationalizing it as a job, and I never thought I would go over the line I drew for myself, but things got out of hand."

As her voice was beginning to crack Seth took her in his arms and tried to comfort her, and finally she just started to sob. Still holding her close to him, they sat down in the sand. She had been holding in so many emotions for so long, and he knew she wasn't going to get over this as easily as she thought. As much as she wanted to look at it as just another job, it really wasn't, and they both knew it. Not only would she have to deal with the present, but probably with her continued repression of the Ahmir incident. It was going to be a long, bumpy road, but Seth knew he could get her through it.

Finally, she calmed down and told him she needed to talk about everything that had happened on the job. He told her that it wasn't really necessary to do that for his sake; he knew he would just be angry with all the men she had been with. She told him she needed to make him understand why she had done the things she had. He listened attentively while she told him that her first "date" was with a wonderful man that just needed some romance because his marriage had lost the passion it had once had. She told him how Mr. Taglio disappeared toward the end of the evening and how much money she received as a tip. She explained that he had been a perfect gentleman the whole evening, so she was completely taken by surprise at how the evening ended.

She then mistakenly or foolishly believed that the rest of her "dates" would also be this nice. After that she seemed to be on "dates" with silly old men that couldn't do anything sexually if they tried. Again, she was making so much money that she couldn't just walk away from this job. She would try to make the degrading thoughts disappear by focusing on the money she was making, but it wasn't always enough. She told him that most of her older "dates" would paw at her breasts, but it never went much further than that. She told him of the disgusting old men that only wanted her to be their audience. Most of the older men just tried to impress their friends that they could have a frisky girlfriend, even if everyone around them knew she was a hired escort. She told Seth that she usually laughed at the end of the evening because she believed the men would go back and tell their friends of their sexual prowess with her, and truthfully, it never happened. Seth agreed and chuckled at that remark.

Ultimately, she told him of her last tryst with Mr. Taglio beginning with her little strip tease dance number, and that she never removed her lingerie. She told him that she kept thinking about someone from her past while she performed for Roger, but then she would be jolted back to reality by something and wonder what in the hell she was doing with her life. She said he had made her feel special by the way he treated her on their "dates" and she would get caught up in the ambiance of the evening.

She concluded the story with her surprise boat trip the very next day. She said she was a little apprehensive after he dismissed the boat captain, but he had put her fears to rest by continuing to be a gentleman. She continued with the details of the Jacuzzi and how that escalated and moved to the upper deck. She only told Seth that they didn't make love, but that afterwards she felt used and very cheap. She told him of the captain's return and how that really degraded her. However, when she was delivered home she was five thousand dollars richer, but she left the money in the limo on purpose because she just wanted out of this situation, and the money only made it worse.

She told him of the money she had been squirreling away, and he was aghast to learn that she had over $10,000.00 in cash hidden at home. She reminded him she really couldn't open a bank account and she needed it to be easily accessible in case of an emergency, so she had just hidden it at home. He knew she was right, but that much money in cash scared him a little. It would be very easy to get into it and spend it foolishly he thought. She told him she knew they weren't returning to their real home any time soon, so she was planning to pay for a few more months at the condo in advance.

She also told him she really wanted to get away for a little while and clear her head, and this too would take money. He agreed that a getaway would be a good idea, but he had no idea where to go. She told him she had always wanted to go out west, but she never had the courage to go alone. He told her it was her money and she should go wherever she wanted. She told him she also wanted to go to the Bahamas, but was worried about the legalities of going out of the country. Seth told her she better stay in the United States because it may be a little safer. They started walking home along the blackness of the beach. The tide was coming in, and it the air was getting a little cooler. A storm was coming in according to the local forecast, and they both hoped they would make it back before the rain started.

Just before they reached the condo a light rain was coming down. They ran the rest of the way home. By the time they got upstairs they were soaked. Sterling said she wanted to sit on the patio and watch the rain. They both changed their clothes and grabbed blankets and headed to the patio. They sat in silence a long time just listening to the rain and the crash of the surf.

Finally, Sterling broke the silence by asking, "Seth, do you think less of me for what I've done?"

There was a long pause before he answered, but he told her "The way I see it is you just got caught up in something that was bigger than you were and you didn't know how to get out of it with respect for yourself intact."

"Seth, that isn't what I asked you. Please tell me how you feel about me and what I've done."

Seth responded by saying only three small words,

"I'm still here."

He knew he couldn't tell her how hurt he was, it would only make her more miserable. He knew he could get over it and he had forgiven her a long time ago.

"Seth what do you think my family will say about this if we ever get home?"

"Baby, why would you ever tell anyone about this little episode in your life? You will just rehash all the feelings you have now; and for what? Your parents love you and want the best for you. I'm sure they would be more than a little shocked to learn you had to run for your life only to be degraded while you were gone and there was nothing they could do to help you."

She knew he was right, but she didn't know if she could always keep this secret to herself. Talking about the bad things has always helped her to get on with her life. Seth told her that must be another reason he was with her now, not only to protect her, but to listen to her too.

"But what if someone finds out?" she said.

"Baby, how is anyone going to find out, I'm not telling anyone."

"Seth, you know when I return, if I return, someone will start looking into things and find out what I did to survive."

"Remember, you told me that you would tell people that you had worked as a bartender, which you did."

"Seth, they do have record of me working at the bar, but remember I quit. Then what?"

"So you tell people about me, that I was your sugar daddy."

Seth made it all sound so reasonable, so easy. He also reminded her that she had used an assumed name, she didn't sign any papers at the escort service, and she was paid in cash. There was no paper trail. She kept thinking of the "what ifs", and he kept giving her the answers. She asked him if they had not yet met and he came into her future, would he want to know of her past.

"Baby, the past is the past. We've all got 'em. You've got to move on, besides weren't you the person that always said you don't care what others think of you?" She knew he was right, but she was in a mood to keep beating up on herself.

"I just wonder what my friends would think of me now, would they still be my friends if they knew about my 'job'. That's what I can't get out of my head. How can they like me if I don't even like myself right now? Seth, I hate what I've done. I didn't need the money that badly. We were doing okay. I got so caught up in the control aspect I had, and I was making a lot of money doing it. It just seemed like an act. I kept thinking I was just playing a part, like an actor. Then when I would get home and think of what I had just done, I felt so cheap and nasty."

"Baby, one day, hopefully soon, you'll get past all those feelings, but you can't keep beating yourself up about something you can't change."

She knew he was right. She just wished she had listened to him more often, especially two months ago when she took on her new 'job'. If only she could go back in time. Now she began to think about Elliot and what he would do if he knew he had been dating a future hooker. He used to lock people up for the very same thing she had done to support herself. Oh well, Elliot was back with his wife and he would never have to know about any of her life's details. She wondered silently if she would tell him about it if they were still together when and if she returned home after this disastrous ordeal.

The storm grew stronger and they decided to go in and go to bed. They climbed into bed like an old married couple. They cuddled together, but both thinking of different things. Seth wishing she were his, and she still hating herself for the person she had become. It was a restless night for both.

Chapter Eleven

When the sun drifted through the curtains, Sterling awoke to an empty bed. She wondered when Seth left, and how he felt about all they had discussed the night before. Sterling decided that she was going to a travel agency and look into a trip out west after she took her shower. Seth left a note stuck on the bathroom mirror. *"Baby, I had some things to do at work, I'll probably work late tonight. Please don't leave without letting me know where you'll be. Love, me"*. She wondered what he meant about leaving and not telling him. Didn't he understand that she wanted him to go with her? He had to go with her. She didn't know how to take care of herself. She ran across the street and called the bar. It wasn't open yet, but he said he would be there. No one answered the phone. She decided to drive over there; maybe he just didn't want to be bothered with the phone.

First, she stopped at the travel agency down the street and picked up some literature on Montana and Wyoming. Those seemed like far off destinations, not heavily populated and lots of open land to clear her head and get away. She sat in the parking lot for a long time and just looked at all the literature.

When she got to the bar there were two cars in the lot and Seth's Harley. She didn't recognize either of the cars, but she hadn't been there for quite some time. The front door was locked, so she went around back. She walked in and the room was dark. She could see a repairman working on an ice machine in the back of the bar area. She could hear voices coming from the dressing rooms. Casually, she went back there wondering what she might find. As she stepped into the back hallway she could hear a female voice and Seth. What was he doing back with one of the dancers she wondered? She was beginning to get a little angry because he had told her long ago that he never went back there if he didn't have to. She tried to stop herself from taking another step, but her curiosity was getting the better of her. She knew what she found might be embarrassing, and it might make them both angry, but she just couldn't stop herself.

As she stepped through the door she saw Seth kissing a half-naked girl she had never seen before. The girl looked right at her but Seth's back was to the door and he didn't notice her. The girl didn't even act surprised. Sterling spun around and ran down the hall as fast as she could. When she got to the exit she hit the door so hard it clanged against the back wall.

The noise startled Seth, and he jumped up saying, "Did you hear that? What was that noise?"

The girl looked at him with a grin and said, "I think someone just caught us, must have been your girlfriend or wife."

Seth asked her to describe who caught them as he was running down the hall to see if it was Sterling. As he hit the exit, he saw her careening out of the lot. He yelled for her to come back, but she didn't hear or see him.

In the car, Sterling was crying hysterically. She didn't want to go back to the condo, so she drove to the pier. Angrily she questioned herself about why she was so mad. She didn't have any rights to Seth. They were just friends. No, he was her protector, and he had told her he loved her. How could he betray her like this, and with some cheap whore? She knew he didn't always come home, but she envisioned a better class of woman than she had just seen with him. How was she ever going to get over this betrayal? Or, she wondered, was it a betrayal?

Seth went to his office and dialed their number.

The recorded message about the phone being disconnected was too much. He went in the dressing room where Michelle was trying to entice him back to where they had left off. He told her he had to leave, and to let herself out. He ran to the bar and told Stan, the repairman, he had to leave and he didn't know when he'd be back. Stan said he'd only be another two minutes if Seth could just wait. Seth told him to hurry as he poured Stan a beer to go. Seth was putting the tools in the toolbox to help things along. After what seemed an eternity Stan was finished. Seth gave him the beer as they headed out the door.

Seth jumped on the Harley and sped down the road to the condo. He didn't see her car in the upper lot, so he went on downstairs to the underground parking area. The car wasn't down there either. A million thoughts were swimming in his head. Where was she? Why was he going after her? He had a right to his life too. What would he say if he found her? Jesus, he wondered if she was on her way out of town on her trip. He had no idea where she was going, other than "out west". He decided to go upstairs and see if she had packed already. Maybe he would find some sort of clue of where she was, or where she was going.

He looked for her duffel bag. It was still in the closet. None of the toiletries seemed to be missing. Everything seemed the same as when he left this morning. Where was she? He went to the balcony and stared out at the ocean, looking for answers. She wasn't close to anyone here. She had casual relationships with their neighbors, but she didn't have any true friends in Daytona besides him.

Seth started thinking of the places she liked to go with him; maybe she went there to think. He decided to start at the lighthouse and then he would go north from there if he didn't find her. He decided to take the beach, maybe she was parked out by the ocean. After he reached the lighthouse and hadn't found her he decided to go to the boardwalk. Sterling always liked to go there on the weekends when it was really busy and just watch the people. Even though it was the middle of the afternoon on a weekday he gave it a try. He looked at all the parking lots and still didn't see her car. He parked at one of the "biker" bars and left on foot. He roamed up and down the boardwalk and still didn't find her.

He decided to go to the pier to think, and collect his thoughts. As he paid the fee to get on the pier he had the feeling he was being watched. He stopped and looked out at the ocean, but the feeling wouldn't go away. Who was looking at him? He turned around and rested his back against the side of the walkway. He knew he had found her, but where was she? He looked up at the beer garden and there she was, staring down at him. Their eyes met and she turned and walked away. He ran into the building. He had to talk to her. Had to make her see his side of things.

When he got upstairs she was sitting at a table alone, looking out at the ocean. When he approached he could tell that she was crying. He put his hands on her shoulders, but she pushed them away. She turned around and yelled that he had hurt her more than she could stand. He tried to calm her down, but she only seemed to get angrier. The few people that were there were starting to stare.

"Baby, I'm sorry."

"Don't you call me Baby again! Don't you talk to me like you talk to that whore!"

"Sterling, be reasonable, she is not a whore. She is one of our newer dancers. You know I have a life too. You've made it clear that..."and his voice trailed off

282

again.

She was shaking her head and still crying, as she brushed passed him and told him to go to hell. He followed her out all the way to her car. Neither of them spoke as she got into the car. Finally, he told her they needed to have a talk. She told him she was going to the park on the river. So many times they had packed a lunch and gone to this park to watch for the manatees. He ran back to his cycle and hurried after her. He knew that if he didn't get there right behind her she would be gone again. The next time he might not find her.

She was waiting down by the water. In the distance he could see a manatee floating lazily along. On the way over, he had been rehearsing what he planned to say, but kept wondering how she would respond, or if she would even listen. He knew he couldn't just rush up to her, she'd let him know that earlier. She was mad, and hurt, he knew that too. He knew that the instant he heard her leave the bar.

As he approached the water's edge, she turned to him and he noticed she was no longer crying. She actually looked quite calm.

"Seth, I know this isn't how things should be between friends, and I know I can't give you all you need, but I'm terribly hurt."

Before she could utter another word, he said, "Sterling, I do need more than you have been willing to give. I haven't pushed and I won't, but I am a man and curling up with you at the end of every day and living as man and wife without the touching is driving me crazy. We weren't together before we left, but we have grown much closer. I have wanted you since the first time I met you. That feeling has never left my heart. I didn't give up a lot to come with you, and I had no expectations when I left, but I can only take so much. First we had to deal with the Ahmir situation, and all I could do was hold you and listen. Then, the abortion, and against my objections you became a high class whore." At that she started crying, but she knew he was right.

"Baby. I love you and I told you a long time ago I would never push myself on you, or hurt you intentionally. I have kept my word. I never meant to hurt you today when you saw me with Michelle. I have been with other women since we came here, but you made it perfectly clear in Bristol that we were never going to be more than friends. I accepted that, have you?"

Sterling told him she had wanted him over the years she has known him, but in her position she could never cross that line. And, she told him she had been in love with someone else, so she thought maybe she was just lusting after him and she would put it out of her mind. She admitted that she didn't think of his feelings when she was working, because he seemed content with the arrangement.

She said, "Maybe I just wanted to believe you were content so I could justify my behavior as not hurting anyone. I know you love me, but I don't think I can love you back in the same way. I can't just let you believe I love you and things will work out, that wouldn't be fair either. I'll understand if you want to move out, but I'm begging you to please continue being my friend. I am so screwed up right now and I truly don't know what to do. I have no one else. The only person I can trust is you, I have no other friends here, and my friends at home think I'm dead. Please say you will be my friend and please just give me some more time."

"Baby, I will always be your friend and I'm not going anywhere right now. Michelle and the others are just a diversion. A diversion from the way I want to be with you. I know you were in love with someone back home, but he left you, or have you forgotten that? I'm here. I've always been here. Why can't you give me a chance?" Sterling just shook her head, both of them very sad right now.

They stood for a long time not saying anything, just watching the sun go down. Finally he stated, "Why did you come to the lounge this afternoon?"

Sterling replied, "I didn't understand the note that you left and I wanted to talk to you about it. When I couldn't reach you on the phone I decided to drive over since I was going to be out anyway. I had stopped off at the travel agency before I came to see you."

"But, Baby I told you I would be home late tonight in the note. Why didn't you just wait?"

"Seth I want you to go with me, and from what the note said I thought you just wanted to know where I was going and when I would be back. Don't you understand I want you to be with me?"

"Baby, don't you hear what you're saying? First you want me to be with you wherever you are, to be your friend, your protector, your bedmate. But secondly you want me to just go along not having feelings for you, follow wherever you lead and still not be able to have my own life. I cannot go on like this. You have to make a decision about us."

"Seth please give me more time."

"Baby you've had nine months with just me by your side. You've been out with others, I've been out with others, but you are the one person I truly want to be with."

"Seth, I do love you, but I know I can't love you the way you love me. True, I was in love with someone back home and he left me, but my feelings for him didn't just disappear. I can't let myself love you the way you want me to. I wasn't in love with you when we left. I cared deeply for you, but not like a lover. If I let myself go I could love you now, but what would happen to us when all this is over and I go back home?"

"Who says we have to go back home Sterling? We've been happy here. If you don't want to stay here we can go somewhere else. I'll do whatever you want me to do just to be with you."

"Seth, is that fair to either of us? I miss home. I miss my family and my other friends. I'm happy here most of the time, but this isn't where I belong. You know I'm only here to escape the problems back home and to keep everyone safe. I called you because I knew I could trust you, and because no one would connect the two of us. No one knows that our friendship continued after you were off probation. I doubt if anyone you know ever knew of our friendship either. I have to go back home someday. Maybe you don't. But, I'm telling you now I will not hurt you by saying we can be more than friends while we're here, but it has to end when we go home. You have fallen in love with Sterling, but you don't know anything about Marisa. You have been with Sterling too long. I never let you know Marisa. I couldn't cross that line and jeopardize my career, or my personal life. I always wanted to remain your friend, and I'm sorry I couldn't tell you more about me, but I wasn't sure if you would fit into the life I had. I know how bad that sounds. I hate myself for even thinking that way, but it's the truth."

She could tell Seth was hurt and she wished she could take it all back, but she couldn't. Somehow she just felt relief. She really didn't have anymore secrets from him. Oh, he still didn't know who her family was, or where she lived, but at this point he probably didn't want to know much else. Seth sat there quietly for a long time. Sterling was crying softly because she knew she had hurt the only person she could trust right now, and she wished it would all just go away.

Finally Seth turned to her and said, "How long are we going to be gone so I can let the boss know?"

Sterling was shocked. She had just unloaded on him, and he was still willing to help her. He was a true friend, probably the best she had ever had. "Well, I wanted to go to Wyoming or Montana, and I planned to see the country, so probably a couple of weeks if you can swing it."

"You know the Sturgis Rally is coming up. South Dakota could be our destination," Seth replied.

Sterling thought this would be great fun, and she knew this was a place he had always wanted to go, she agreed that this is where they should go.

"I'll call the boss when I get back to work and see if we can take off tomorrow. Hopefully I'll have a job when we get back."

She was glad she had called him a long time ago, but she hated the way it had turned out. Maybe calling him had not been a good idea, at least on his part. She truly appreciated his friendship and all he was willing to do for her, but she just couldn't let it go where he wanted it. She knew she did love him in her own way, just not the way he loved her. She felt badly about this, but she still longed for what she had with Elliot. This was something else that was never going to turn out the way she wanted. She wondered if she and Seth would ever find their true soul mates.

She went to Seth to hug him. He wasn't hugging her back the way he usually did, she knew she had really wounded him. She told him she was terribly sorry for all the things she had just said, but she told him she had to be honest now. She had been lying too long. He bent down and kissed her head. She knew then that he still cared very much for her. He told her he had to get back to work, but he wanted her to pack a small bag for him. He reminded her to pack light as they were going on his Harley.

Sterling wanted to make up for the hurt she had caused, but she knew that was impossible. She wanted him to have a small token of gratitude before they left. As she started home she realized they would need outerwear for their trip even though it was August. She knew Seth had his eye on a jacket in the Harley store down by the club. She decided right then that she was buying it for him, and if they had one in her size she would buy it too. She went home and grabbed a thousand dollars from her hiding place, and headed out for the store.

The store was just about to close, but she waved the cash at the clerk and he came and unlocked the door. After she went in he re-locked the door and put out the closed sign. She told him that she wanted to buy the jacket in the window, and wondered if they had a matching jacket in her size. The clerk told her that a shipment had just arrived in the back but it wasn't unpacked yet. She told him she had to have the jackets now, because she and her "boyfriend" were leaving for Sturgis in the morning. He told her that he had been there the year before, but due to some surgery he wasn't able to go this year. He also said he understood she was in a hurry, but if she would wait a few minutes he would go look for the smaller jacket.

After about fifteen minutes, the clerk came back with a jacket that looked as if it were made for Sterling. He grabbed the jacket out of the window display and rung both jackets up. The total came to $900.00. Sterling gave him two $500 bills and told him to keep the change for all the trouble he had gone through. As she started to leave she told the clerk told her to have a great time, but to be careful.

Once back at the condo, she grabbed her duffel bag and stuffed it full of both of their clothes. She threw in a small bag of toiletries. She decided that she should split up some of the money, so in case of theft or an accident all of it wouldn't be missing. Then she grabbed a couple of blankets and some garbage bags and wrapped up everything. She was now exhausted; it had been a very tiring and emotional day. She decided to run a hot bubble bath and just relax to some music and candlelight. The tub filled with hot water and she poured herself a glass of wine and entered her large whirlpool tub.

As she started to relax and unwind she started thinking about the day. Within a few minutes she started crying again. What was she doing with the rest of her life, she thought? Would things now be different between she and Seth? She missed everyone so much at home, and wondered if things were any closer to being resolved with Wanda and the others. She knew she couldn't go home until people were arrested and her family was safe. As long as she was gone and they couldn't find her, no harm would come to her family or friends. Or at least she didn't think so. After she had refilled the tub with warm water several times and was becoming quite tired she decided to get out and go on to bed. She didn't know what time Seth would be home, but she knew at least that he would be coming home. With any luck they would be leaving in the morning.

She went to bed around 9:00 p.m., and she didn't

hear Seth come in at midnight. He came into the bedroom and watched her sleep for a very long time. He wondered if he had been wrong all these years. He truly believed they were kindred spirits and would eventually find each other. After today, he wondered how he would ever go on without her. He knew he was fighting a losing game. She had told him today how she had always felt.

Deep inside he always knew she was out of his league, but he wanted to believe that he could make her see that he was one of the good guys. The guy she belonged with now and forever. Admittedly, the things she told him today hurt him, but he knew that she was hurt by it too. She was emotionally drained. Too much had gone on in her life in such a short time, and she had to let some of it out. He knew she didn't mean to hurt him, she was just being honest. Honesty. That was what he had always been able to count on her for. And today, he didn't want her to be honest about their future.

He went into the bathroom, pulled off his clothes and took a shower. It was a long shower. Today had not been good to him. In the shower, Seth cried. He cried for all that he knew would never be his, and for all that he ever wanted--Sterling. As the tears stopped, he realized that tomorrow one of his dreams would be coming true. Sterling was going with him to Sturgis. This was something he had wanted to do for a long time. This was just what they both needed right now-another diversion. After drying off, he pulled on a pair of shorts and climbed into bed with Sterling. He put his arms around her, as she cuddled close to him. He wanted to be with her so badly now. But, he knew that this was one dream that would never come true.

Chapter Twelve

Around 9:00 a.m. Seth awoke to the smell of bacon and eggs frying. He could even smell coffee. He rubbed his eyes and wondered if he was still dreaming. Sterling was never awake before he was, and she never cooked a big breakfast. He climbed out of bed and looked out at the ocean. It was a beautiful morning. Sterling told him she was serving breakfast out on the balcony. He went to her and kissed her good morning. She seemed in such a happy mood. He knew she wanted to get away from everything, but he thought she was just along for the ride. Maybe she really was going to enjoy herself too.

She told him that she had a little present for him, but he needed to go outside and close his eyes. He went out without question and watched the surf. A few minutes later she came outside wearing her favorite bikini and his new leather biker jacket. She sat down on his lap while his eyes were still closed. He could smell the leather and feel her soft legs. It was not going to be a bad morning he thought. He opened his eyes and looked at her with disbelief. Sterling stood up and modeled his new jacket for him.

He said, "Baby what have you done? This jacket costs a fortune!"

She told him she had another surprise for him, but he could put on his jacket while he waited for the other surprise. He gladly took it from her and put it on. He looked at it with amazement. No one besides Sterling had ever done anything this nice for him. A few minutes later, Sterling came out with a tray full of food, and she was wearing a matching jacket.

"Baby if you look like this in Sturgis we might get arrested!" Sterling giggled.

She told him that he better hurry and eat his breakfast before it got cold. He could hardly believe his day. From a terrible beginning yesterday, to a great beginning today. He wished that this moment could last forever. He also hoped that they would have a great time on their trip.

"So when do we leave?" Sterling asked.

He asked if she had packed everything and she told him she had. "Well Baby, we can leave whenever you're ready."

Although they both had different ideas about this trip and why they were going, Sterling knew that her life could only get better. Seth wondered if anything on this trip could change Sterling's mind about their relationship, or lack thereof. He wasn't going to push her to be something she wasn't, but he wanted her to see him for what he was, a man that was totally in love with her.

After breakfast Sterling cleaned up the kitchen and called the manager to tell her that she would be gone for a couple of weeks. The manager asked if anyone else had access to the apartment besides Seth. Sterling told her they were traveling together. The manager told her she would collect the mail for them, and she would see them when they got back. After the phone call, Seth told her he was going downstairs to pack up the cycle and look at the atlas. She would be ready shortly, she told him.

She left on her bikini, but pulled on a pair of oversize denim overalls, and her leather boots that Seth insisted she have when he bought the Harley. She put on her leather jacket and took a look in the mirror. What a cutie, she thought to herself. She removed the jacket and put on her fanny pack underneath the overalls. She also grabbed her sunscreen and sunglasses. Sterling wanted to take a camera but decided just to buy a disposable one when they arrived. The scenery would be going along too fast to get any good pictures. Besides, she wasn't sure if she wanted pictures of her life as it was now to follow her into the future.

Seth returned and seemed quite exhilarated. He was talking a mile a minute. Finally, Sterling asked him if he was ready to go and he laughed and said "yes ma'am!" She told him to put some sunscreen on and not to forget his jacket. He told her he would never forget the jacket. They grabbed up the remainder of their things and double checked the locks on the patio doors, windows and made sure the stove was off before leaving. Seth was almost running to the elevators. She laughed because she knew he was having a hard time containing his enthusiasm. He may not have a job to return to, but he was happy about this trip. It seemed to her as if he had forgotten all the things she said to him only the day before. For this, she was thankful.

Seth told her he was just going to head north and west on the highway, and go wherever the road took him. The rally didn't actually start for another week so they may as well enjoy the ride and take their time. With no destination in mind for the day's end, they started on this new journey. A journey that seemed so familiar to Sterling, just like the one she began only a few months ago. So, off they rode. He could feel her hands around him, and she was just so glad he was there with her. Both in different worlds right now, but at least they were together.

They drove for several hours before stopping. Sterling finally told him she had to get off the cycle as her butt was numb and she had to use the bathroom. He laughed and stopped at a rest area. They walked around for a little while then went under some shade trees and stretched out on the cool grass. Sterling told him she was having a great time already. Many times they had taken rides on the cycle, but never a ride this long before. The trip thus far had been spent just listening to the hum of the road and loud music blaring from the radio. Finally, Sterling told him she was ready to go. Seth was up before she had finished the sentence. Back on the cycle she held him close to her and thanked him for going with her on this trip. He nodded. He was just as happy that she had insisted he go with her.

Late in the afternoon, nearly dinnertime, they stopped at a little roadside diner. Neither of them were very hungry. They had eaten a big breakfast and had not really worked up an appetite sitting there on the cycle. He told her he would like to drive past dark this evening just to watch the setting of the sun and see the stars come out. He described it so well to her that it sounded heavenly. He told her that the sky was going to blaze with colors of orange and pink. And as the sun went down past the horizon it would fade to lavender and blue. Finally when the sun was completely down and the clouds had moved out she would see the twinkling lights of a million stars. Sterling couldn't wait to see this panorama. She knew he had seen this view before, but she wondered with whom.

Back on the cycle just before dusk they decided to put on their new jackets. The air on the road was getting a little chilly. They had no idea where they would stop, or even if they would stay in a motel. They had blankets with them, and Seth had mentioned it might be nice to stay out under the stars somewhere. Sterling couldn't help but like this idea. It sounded so rejuvenating and full of freedom. She was a little afraid of the creatures of the night, but Seth assured her they would be in no danger. She also worried about the legalities of staying outdoors, without a permit or in a specified area, but Seth told her she was worrying too much and acting too much like Marisa.

"Baby, sometimes you just have to take chances. Life isn't any fun if you don't take risks. Lighten up, we'll be fine. I won't let anyone or anything hurt you," Seth told her.

She knew he was right. She had decided not too long ago that from now on she was going to listen to Seth. He hadn't steered her wrong yet. She had managed to get into trouble on her own; he had merely bailed her out when she needed help.

Sterling realized the sun was beginning to set for the day. The sky lit up like a blazing fire. The clouds were swirled with pink and orange as the sun started to set in the western sky. Gradually the orange faded to a muted shade of pink and the pink turned purple. It was all happening so quickly, but she wanted to remember every instant of this sunset. As the sun sunk lower in the sky, the colors continued to change. It was now more lavender, blue and a darker purple. Finally the sun was gone and the sky became darker. She could see the clouds start to dissipate, and slowly the stars started to shine. She told him it was the most beautiful sunset she had ever experienced. He shook his head in agreement and leaned into her. The sky grew darker until it was a midnight blue. A million stars twinkled overhead. Seth had been right once again. This view gave her a feeling of freedom and bliss. Right now she wasn't thinking of anything else.

Neither of them knew where they were, only that they were somewhere in Alabama. Seth told her if they got off the main highway, they would have better luck in finding a place to sleep. She had no better idea so they got off at the next exit. It was pretty well deserted. They bought some gas and went to the bathroom. They were out in the country in no time. As they drove he told her to watch for a wheat field or large, hilly field. He explained that they would get off the cycle on the road and walk it back with them. He told her he wanted to be a long distance off the road so they wouldn't be easily visible by any passing motorists. She thought it sounded risky, but she was ready for this adventure.

Finally, Seth spotted the perfect area. It looked like a lot of hilly acreage, but there was no house in sight. Only the moon and stars lighted their way. They walked back a long way from the road. Sterling guessed it was at least a quarter mile from the road. He parked the cycle and unpacked the blankets. He told her she might want to put on a sweatshirt in addition to her jacket. She told him she needed to take off her bathing suit. She had worn it on the road in order to work on her tan. He just smiled as she put on the sweatshirt and then started tugging at her bikini top. She took off her overalls and removed her bottoms. Then she put on a pair of sweatpants. He was making a bed for them, using the duffel bag as their pillow. Sterling told him she was really tired, and she guessed they would probably wake up with the sunrise. He told her she was probably right.

As they sat alone in the dark, she again thanked him for coming with her. Then, she reached for him and gave him a kiss on the cheek. He pulled her close to him and kissed her neck. She didn't pull away from him or tell him to stop. He then turned her face to his and he kissed her passionately. He could feel her kissing him back. This was his dream. To have Sterling love him the way he loved her. They kissed for a long time, and he started to lay her down. She resisted slightly, but he didn't stop kissing her. They lie side by side kissing and caressing each other. She could feel that he wanted her. Thoughts of the others ran through her mind. Thoughts of Elliot were there too. What is she thinking? Although she doesn't want to hurt Seth, she knows she can't give into this passion. Not now, probably not ever.

"Seth, we have to stop this. I didn't mean to lead you on, I don't want to hurt you, but I got caught up in the romance of this evening and I'm just not thinking clearly. I'm sorry baby."

Seth knew his luck was too good to be true. He understood. He wasn't going to push her to do something she didn't want to do. He did want her. He just wished she could want him the same way. Another time, another place, he thought.

They held each other as they drifted off to sleep. The sounds of the night echoed all around them. The crickets chirped, and the locusts buzzed. An occasional sound of an owl could be heard in the distance. Sterling awoke in his arms briefly during the night. She sat up and looked around. Everything was still in place, nothing to worry about. Seth pulled her back down and whispered that they were all right. She knew he was right. She snuggled close to him. She could feel the dew on her skin, and on the blankets. She fell back to sleep in his arms. Her protector, her friend.

As the sun started to come up they both started to stir. Seth kissed her awake. He told her that she needed to experience this beautiful country sunrise. Sterling opened her eyes to see the most brilliant colors. The lush green of the landscape and dew was sparkling all around. The sky was just starting to blaze with color. The dark blue was turning lighter and lighter with hues of pink running through it. As the minutes rolled by the sky became more orange and yellow. The birds were chirping and a light breeze was blowing through the trees. This place looked like paradise to them both. Sterling thought that if she ever lost her sight, this would be a scene she would always remember. And, the sunset last night would be forever ingrained in her memory as well. She had an overwhelming feeling of peace right now.

She wondered if she would have felt this way if Seth hadn't been with her.

They lay there together wrapped in each other's arms. He told her there was no hurry to get up. The blankets needed to dry out and they should just take in the beauty of nature while they waited. Sterling had no problems with this. She liked to sleep in late. She stretched and turned toward him. She apologized again for leading him on last night. He told her it was his own fault; he shouldn't have kissed her like that.

"Baby you made it clear to me the other day that you weren't interested in me as a lover, just your friend. I'm the one that was out of line. I hope you can forgive me. It's just that you're so damn cute, and I don't think I'll ever get over you."

"Seth I'm sorry I can't be all that you need me to be, but I will always be your friend, please remember that. I don't think you were rude. We both got caught up in the moment. It was beautiful and romantic. I will always treasure this time together."

Seth hugged her to him and they both closed their eyes again. Somewhere deep inside himself he was content with her on this level. He just wished it could be more. Having her by his side now was going to have to be enough he told himself. A short time later Sterling got up and started to change her clothes. Seth heard her moving around, but she didn't know he was awake. She had her back to him as she took off her sweatpants and put on the bikini again. He watched her with desire. She took off the sweatshirt and put on her bikini top. She did have a beautiful body. She turned toward him while she folded up her clothes and looked to see if he was awake. After believing that he was still asleep she quietly placed her clothes by the cycle. She combed her hair and put on some sunscreen. She then sat down and looked out at the view all around her. He slowly sat up and watched her.

Finally, she turned to him and asked if they could be on their way because she had to go to the bathroom. He laughed and told her she better learn to use what nature had given her. Trees and bushes were all around. She told him she would do that if she had too, but she knew of a gas station not far away. Seth got up and went to a clump of trees while she folded the blankets and put them back in the garbage bags. He felt relieved and refreshed he said. She told him she needed to feel relief too, so they better get on their way. He laughed as he loaded everything back on the Harley. While Sterling was freshening up in the bathroom, he planned to consult the atlas. He thought they could probably get through at least three more states today.

They went back the way they came, but it looked so different in this light. She told him she was glad they had taken in the outdoors last night. It was beautiful and serene. She also told him how peaceful she felt in his arms. He wondered if she was beginning to feel more for him than she did just a few days ago. He wouldn't question her about this. He knew everything would have to be on her terms.

As they drove off down the road Sterling thought about how quickly the night sky turned into day. It seemed as though her life had changed just as dramatically over the last few months. She hoped that one day she could forgive herself for all the mistakes she had made. She also hoped that if anyone else ever learned of what she had done they too would forgive her.

Once they were back on the road he told her they could probably get all the way to Illinois today. She asked if they could go more or less than just to Illinois, she explained that it was just too close to home for her to feel comfortable. He said they would just see where the road took them, and how they felt at the day's end. She agreed with this plan. He told her that they would probably be on some rolling hills today because of the terrain of the land. Although she had traveled a lot as a kid she had never been through this part of the country. She was excited to see all the sights. She laughed and told him that she was hoping her butt got used to the vibration of the road, or it was going to be a long trip. He laughed too.

They stopped for breakfast after about an hour on the road. The people in the south were charming and very hospitable. Many of the people they met on the road asked where they were headed. When they said they were going to Sturgis, South Dakota many said they wouldn't want to ride that far in a car, let alone on a motorcycle. But, they said they would definitely see the beautiful scenery of the land. Back on the cycle they listened to the radio and the hum of the road. The sun beat down on them and made them feel alive and refreshed. Both of them loved the heat and wind in their face. Sterling found it amazing that most of the day they didn't really talk to each other. They pointed out sights to one another, but for the most part it was a time of quiet reflection for Sterling. Seth was just happy that he was with the woman he loved, on his bike, and on his way to a place he had only dreamed about.

Late in the afternoon they pulled off the interstate and drove as near as they could to the Mississippi River. Neither of them had ever seen such a large river before. They ate lunch on a boat on the riverbank. After lunch they got back on the road and headed for St. Louis. They both wanted to see the Arch. Sterling remembered that she had been inside the Arch on a family vacation. He told her he was content to look at it from the ground once he saw how tall it was.

They found an inexpensive motel to stay in for the

night in St. Louis. Seth stretched out on the bed while Sterling took a long, hot bath. When she came out of the bathroom, he was asleep. She debated for a long time whether she should wake him up, but finally decided to let him sleep. He would probably want to get a shower and go out to a bar if she woke him up, and she really just wanted to watch TV. and listen to him sleep. After the news went off she crawled into bed next to him. He was still wearing his leather jacket laying on top of the covers when she got into bed. She figured he would wake up early, so she didn't bother placing a wake-up call with the front desk.

Neither of them had awakened by the time the maid knocked on the door at 10 o'clock. Seth answered the door, but said they would need another thirty minutes or so. The maid said she would come back later. As he walked back to the bed, Sterling was starting to wake up. He sat on the edge of the bed and asked her why she didn't wake him up last night. She just said she thought he looked like he really needed the rest, and she was too tired to go out. He told her he was going to take a shower, and they could be on their way. She told him she wanted a quick shower before they left since she didn't know from one day to the next when she would get another one. He laughed and offered to share his shower with her, but she declined stating that she would get their things together while she waited. They rode by the office, dropped off the key, and started the next phase of their journey.

Sterling told Seth that last night she had looked at the atlas and saw some pretty interesting tourist spots she would like to see if he was interested. Although he was not much of a traveler, he knew it would mean a lot to her, so he asked her where she wanted to go. She told him she wanted to see Mt. Rushmore, and Badlands National Park if he didn't mind. She also told him that she really wanted to go to Devil's Tower, but it was farther than they had planned. He asked her how far out of the way it was, but she wasn't sure. She told him it was in Wyoming, one of her original destination spots. He told her she could go wherever she wanted and he would be there right by her side. Although he couldn't see her face, he knew she was smiling. He knew that she cared deeply for him, although it wasn't a romantic love. But, he loved her with all his heart and soul.

Seth was thinking about the differences and similarities between them as they rode. He wondered if this would turn out to be the love of his life, or if he would live with this part of his life unfulfilled. He knew when he left home so long ago to help her that she didn't love him. But, he had hoped in time that she could see how wonderful they were together. He also thought that maybe another reason she had left so abruptly and had called him was because she felt the same way about him, but couldn't face it as long as she was Marisa. As the miles rolled by he became lost in his thoughts.

About noon they decided to stop and eat. They were sweltering under the hot, summer sun. After eating they decided to just drive around this sleepy little town and find a park. The park was small but there was a huge oak tree they could rest under. He unpacked the sleeping bags and opened a bottle of water.

"Seth, do you think it's safe just to be here like this? I mean, do you think anyone will try to steal anything if we fall asleep."

"Baby this place is Mayberry. Barney is probably out here on patrol as we speak." She just smiled.

Within a few minutes a police cruiser went by, and the deputy smiled and waved at them. Seth just nodded his head to the deputy, and closed his eyes. Although Sterling didn't really sleep she was resting.

302

About an hour later Seth woke up and said they had better get back on the road. They stopped by a soft drink machine and grabbed two sodas for the road.

As the two headed farther west the sky was turning dark gray. Sterling was worried that they would be caught in a tornado. Seth told her she had just watched "The Wizard of Oz" too many times. He pulled the cycle off the side of the road though and brought out the rain gear. He told her she might want to put on some heavier clothing as well because if it did start raining it would be cold tonight. It was nearing dinnertime but neither of them were very hungry. They got back on the bike and headed out again. It was getting windy, but still no rain. They were not far from Badlands National Park. Of course neither of them knew if the park would even be open this late, but they really didn't have another alternative. They had stopped at several motels along the way but they were all completely booked. The rain started, no lightning, but lots of thunder. Sterling held Seth tightly.

They both saw the signs along the road telling about the park. He told her they might not have any other options tonight besides camping. She said she had never camped in a storm, but she would do whatever she had to do. He reminded her that this was a new adventure, and risks are part of every adventure. They got off the highway at Cactus Flat and followed the signs to the park. They were both surprised to see that the park was actually open twenty-four hours. The ranger gave them directions to the campground, and wished them well. He reminded them that they could not have a campfire. Seth did not find that amusing. The ranger laughed as they rode off.

They made their way to the campground, and learned that there were only a few spots open. But for this they were grateful. They paid the camp fee and went where the ranger told them. Along the way they saw many tent campers, RV's, and vans. Several of the tent campers had pick-up trucks with motorcycles in the bed of the truck. They were probably on their way to Sturgis too.

They finally arrived at their campsite, and Sterling was trying not to be miserable. She knew when she left that the weather would be unpredictable, and she knew that they probably would be camping most nights. Seth was trying to position the bike beside a tree and put up a tarp for shelter. She asked him how she could help and he told her to just stay out of his way for a few minutes and he would have camp set up. He didn't seem to be mad at her or the weather; he was just glad that they were nearer to one of his dreams. He finally had a shelter fixed up, but they would be sleeping much closer than normal tonight. Sterling was a little worried about lightning striking and them being positioned right next to a tree, but he tried to assure her that they would be fine. She knew she would be clinging onto him tonight because she was really scared. He knew she was scared, but they didn't really have any other alternatives.

He zipped the sleeping bags together and told her to take off her rain gear underneath the shelter. Moving around would be rather difficult because the shelter was very low to the ground. Sterling pulled off her rain suit pants as she sat down on the edge of the bags and then took off her jacket. He took them and put them in a garbage bag and placed them under the sleeping bags. She slid into the bag and waited for him to do the same thing; however, as he pulled off his rain suit pants he pulled off his jeans too. He rolled up his jeans and stuffed them inside the sleeping bag down near his feet. He told her he would get too hot in the bags tonight if he left on his pants. She was surprised that he had on a pair of boxer shorts. He kept on his long sleeve tee shirt in case his arms needed to be out of the bag. He put out his arm for her to lay her head on, and they lay there and talked for awhile before she finally drifted off to sleep. He listened to her breathe and he rubbed her hair.

Seth looked out into the night sky and wondered how he could be so unlucky in love. He wanted her so badly now, but he reminded himself that she was not interested in him sexually. She just wanted a friend. He wondered how she could be so comfortable with him like this and still not feel anything remotely romantic about them.

Sterling awakened to a loud clap of thunder. She was terrified, and Seth had a hard time convincing her to just stay where she was, in his arms. He told her that there was less chance of them being hurt if they just stayed under the shelter instead of being in the open air without any protection. She told him she was getting too warm under the canopy of the tarp, and she needed some air. He partially unzipped the bags, and she said she had to take off some of her clothes. She then informed him she only had on her underwear under her sweatshirt. He told her he would close his eyes and she could take off her sweatshirt and he would give her his tee shirt to wear. That left him in only his boxers. He said he would be fine as long as she would stay next to him for warmth. She reluctantly slid out of her clothes and kicked them down to the bottom of the sleeping bags and put on his shirt. She did feel a lot better now.

The thundering had subsided and the rain was starting to slow down. She cuddled up next to him and thanked him for being so patient with her. He laughed and said he was enjoying just watching her react to everything. He told her she was being a real sport about the whole thing. She then kissed him lightly on the lips and told him goodnight. It really was a pleasant night for Seth. He didn't give the weather another thought.

Morning came too quickly for the wet campers.

The rain had stopped sometime in the night, but the edges of the sleeping bags were rather wet. The ground was muddy all around their campsite, and it was getting warm. Seth told her they would have to get up as soon as possible and hang the bags up to dry. She grabbed her sweatpants and pulled them on while still inside the bag. He had stood up outside the tarp still wearing only his boxers. He didn't care who could see him. She came up from under the tarp wearing his tee shirt. He liked this look on her too. She had all the clothes from inside the bags and was hanging them on some bushes until they could get the bike dry enough to put the clothes away.

Seth put on his jeans and wandered around the campsite. It was a beautiful place. It was wide open country with rolling prairies all around. Some other campers walked by and said hello. He asked them about the park. They told him there were a number of nature walks throughout the park and a variety of organized activities if they were interested. He was only interested in finding someplace to eat. The campers told him there was a lodge nearby that served meals. He told Sterling that as soon as they were dry enough to pack he wanted to go check out the lodge and eat. She liked this idea, but told him the first thing she was going to do was find the restrooms.

After they packed up the cycle and cleaned up at the restroom/bath house they finally got to eat a big breakfast. They planned to drive around the park then head over to Mt. Rushmore toward the end of the day. He had heard of a place called Wall, South Dakota, and he wanted to go there too. Sterling had no objections. She was just glad to be away from everything and seeing some beautiful parts of the country. She was also just thankful that Seth was so good to her. He was more than a friend, she knew this more than ever last night. She was so afraid last night during the storm, but he was right there trying to calm her and being very protective. How could she have ever said all the things she did to him just a few short days ago? Sterling felt terrible about that tirade now, and although it was how she felt when she said it she didn't think how it might affect him later.

Sterling was anxious to go sightseeing today, but she was really tired. Seth told her she had tossed and turned all night, so she probably didn't get a very restful sleep. She said if she was tired, he must be too, since he knew how little sleep she actually got. He laughed and told her it didn't matter how tired he was, he was seeing things he had never even dreamed of and he didn't want to waste time sleeping. He talked to some people at the lodge and got directions to Wall, and some tips to see the Badlands and other area tourist sights. Sterling had paid the check by the time he was ready to go. They hopped on the cycle and headed further west. No destination in sight for tonight, just going wherever the cycle and their imaginations took them.

They drove across the grasslands, and prairies, and looked with wonder at the spires and mountains all around them. They passed some archaeological digs, but neither were interested in that. They arrived in Wall and laughed to see that the big attraction was the Wall Drug Store. It had a huge sign that said free ice water. Sterling said she just had to have some free water, so they went in and looked around. There were other things to see in Wall, but nothing that really knocked their socks off, so on they went toward Mt. Rushmore. Seth didn't really care about any of these tourist sights, but Sterling was telling him how massive this structure was, and how long it took to carve it. Of course along the way they passed many other cyclists, and many people towing their motorcycles. They waved at every cycle that they passed. There was a real camaraderie on the road between people that rode motorcycles.

On the drive to Mt. Rushmore Sterling placed her

head against Seth's back. He told her to put her arms around him if she was sleepy because he didn't want her falling off the bike. She complied, and drifted off to sleep. While she was sleeping Seth thought about staying out on the road with her forever. She seemed content holding onto him and riding with him now. The road was unending and as long as they were out there, somewhere different every night, no one could hurt her or take her away from him. If only she could see in him what he saw in her. As she started to stretch and move his thoughts went back to the road.

"Hey how long did I sleep? I feel much better now."

"I don't know Baby, maybe an hour or so, I kinda lost track of time."

"What were you thinking about?"

He lied, "Nothing really, I've just been watching the scenery change."

Seth had driven through the park and all around Wall and just took his time getting to Mt. Rushmore. Finally they arrived there in the late afternoon. Seth was more interested in finding them a place to stay since all the motels and hotels along the way laughed at him when they tried to rent a room. Apparently the Sturgis Rally really brought a lot of people into this state. Although it was a big state, it wasn't really heavily populated, but for now, all the rooms available for rent had already been reserved. Sterling was not going to be too happy about this, but he knew they would be fine camping all week if they had to. He would make sure they would find a room somewhere near before the Rally started just to make her happy.

Mt. Rushmore was an awesome sight. It was

massive, and unbelievable. The pair stood and stared at it for what seemed an eternity. Both of them were mesmerized by the detail and the time and dedication it took to complete this wonder. After about an hour at this spot they moved to get a different perspective of the mountain. Just a small change in movement brought out another nuance of this magnificent work of art. Neither of them spoke for a long time, but finally they had absorbed all they could and decided to drive around just looking at the rest of the scenery. Later in the day they went to the Crazy Horse Monument. They spoke to several people along the way, inquiring about a room. Most people just laughed at them, stating with the upcoming rally there was probably not a room to be had anywhere near here. Sterling hoped that someone could offer them good news soon, she didn't know how long she could really last while "roughing it".

Their journey continued today in a higher elevation and with lower temperatures, with just the hum of the road, the wind hitting their faces and the radio playing loudly.

The mountainous views were breathtaking. The freedom of the road and the scenic countryside balanced the colder air they were feeling today. It certainly didn't feel like August. Sterling liked the picturesque views, but she longed for the warm weather of Florida and the sound of the rolling waves at the beach.

Camping another night was hard for Sterling, but she remained quiet. She felt like this was a modest price for the freedom of the open road and beauty she was seeing. And, more importantly, Seth was so happy. Devil's Tower was certainly an odd sight to them both. They both remembered the movie that was filmed near there, and it seemed many of the other tourists were discussing the same thing. Back on the bike they headed toward Sturgis. No plans, and no accommodations in sight, but they were having a good time. As they came closer to their destination Seth was beginning to feel bad. He had not yet been able to keep his word about finding a place for them to stay. He was about to give up on the rally and head back to Florida. But first, he decided to stop and eat, and to fill up with gas.

Seth struck up a conversation with the lady running the register after stopping for gas. Sterling could see her laughing at him, and he was grinning. The lady looked in Sterling's direction, then back toward Seth. She then sternly pointed her finger at him and Seth was shaking his head. Sterling continued to be amused by what she was witnessing, though she didn't know what they could be discussing. Just after Seth paid for the gas he shook the woman's hand. He jogged out of the building and told Sterling he had great news.

"Baby, you wouldn't believe our luck. That woman is gonna let us stay with her a few days. Says she is living near Sturgis in a big, old house all alone and she wouldn't mind the company. But, she warned me that you better behave yourself. She said that over the years she has brought home strays, as she called us for not having reservations before getting here, during the rally. What do you think?"

"Well, Seth you know I don't trust easily, but if you think this is a good thing I guess we'll be okay. And, don't forget we better pay her something."

"I have to go back in and tell her we'll take her up on her offer. She said she is just about ready to get off work, so we can follow her back. Are you sure you're okay with this? Really Baby I want you to be alright with it."

"Seth, go back in there now, before she changes her mind, and hurry up about it," she laughed. He jogged back to the cashier and said he and his girl would be pleased to stay with her for a few days.

The ride to Betty's house was a pretty good distance. She lived in a place called Bear Butte. Of course both Seth and Sterling laughed about how it could pronounced differently than it was supposed to be.

Sterling decided that people out in these parts apparently have to drive some distance to civilization, or to their chosen jobs. She realized though that the scenery and peaceful atmosphere probably made it all worthwhile.

Betty's house was rambling, and on several acres. She warned them that if they were out late at night they should beware of all the wildlife, some of which are not friendly. She showed them to their room, and their bathroom. She told them they could have the run of the house, but to stay out of her private bedroom.

Sterling said, "Betty, you'll not have a problem from either of us. And, if you don't mind I'd like to cook for all of us. If you could tell me where the nearest grocery store is Seth can take me there now."

"Well Sterling, the grocery store is a long way back. I have just about anything you might need in the cellar or the pantry in the kitchen. Help yourself."

Sterling looked at Seth and let him know with her glance that she wanted help in the kitchen. As she walked down the hall, Seth called out, "Right behind you Baby! Betty, I will return with a drink."

As they entered the massive kitchen Sterling acclimated herself to the surroundings, and asked what she should fix for them tonight.

"Baby, anything you cook will be a welcome treat from the roadhouse food we've been eating. Now get busy, I'm starved!"

Seth poured a tall glass of bourbon for Betty, just as she had instructed. He took a shot of it himself, but then grabbed a beer.

A little while later Sterling called them to the table where she brought in a pot of chili, and a large salad. They all ate quietly. It had been a long day for all. Sterling cleaned up the mess in the kitchen while Seth cleared the table. Betty went back to her chair and started reading the mail. It was obvious that she did not mind having houseguests, especially the kind that cooked and cleaned. Afterwards, Sterling said she really wanted to take a long hot bath, and then she was going to bed. Seth said he would be up in an hour or so.

Seth sat and talked to Betty for some time about the rally, and some of things that he shouldn't miss. He was looking at some information that he had picked up and he noticed that Betty had drifted off to sleep. He covered her, turned out the lights, locked the door and went upstairs to get a shower and go to bed. He went into the bathroom to start the shower, and as he passed the bedroom he noticed that Sterling had already fallen asleep. He took a quick shower and climbed into bed next to her. She didn't even move. He watched her sleep for a long moment before turning out the light. Sleep came easy for Seth too.

When he awakened in the morning Betty had already gone to work. Sterling was still asleep, so he slipped downstairs and fixed something to eat. He hated to wake Sterling up, but he really wanted to go to Sturgis this morning. He decided he would fix her something to eat and try to wake her easily. As he came into the room he noticed that she was really in a deep sleep.

"Baby, are you alright? Baby, wake up, the rally has already started, come on get up."

"Seth would you be terribly hurt if I stayed here today, or maybe you could come back and get me later?"

"Sterling, you're still asleep. Don't you wanna go with me to Sturgis today?"

"I really just want to sleep in a bed Seth. I want to just sit around here and read or watch television. Would you be terribly hurt if I stayed here today? Besides you will have more fun without me."

"Okay, look I will take the phone number here with me, and I will call you in a couple of hours. If you want then I'll come back and get you. Deal?"

"Yeah, sure that would work. Thanks. Nighty night Seth, and be careful."

Seth grabbed his things and looked at the directions that Betty gave him and off he went. Sterling turned over and went back to sleep. Several hours later, she finally got up and took a shower. She made some breakfast and decided that she would look around outside. She grabbed the newspaper from last night and sat on the wraparound porch for another hour or so. When the phone rang it startled her. She ran to it and heard Seth on the other end. He was so excited about everything he was seeing. She couldn't match his enthusiasm about motorcycles, but she was glad he was having so much fun.

"Seth I don't want to be a stick in the mud, but would you mind if I just hung out here today?"

"Baby, I would really like you to be here, but I understand that you want to just lounge today.

313

Tomorrow we will do this together. When should I be back?"

"Seth, you're a big boy. You need to decide when you need to be home. Besides, I have no idea about all the things and times of events. Don't worry about me, have fun and be careful."

"Will do Baby, but I'll be thinking about you. I'll be home before you go back to bed."

"Yeah right Seth. Have a good time and don't be stupid." When she hung up she was smiling. He was like a kid at Christmas.

Seth finally rolled in about 4:00 a.m. Of course Sterling was back in bed, but she was a bit worried. He climbed into bed and she could smell liquor. Seth wasn't usually a drinking man, but he was in a totally different atmosphere. When she awoke the next morning Seth was still sleeping soundly. She grabbed a quick shower and talked to Betty before she left for work. Seth came into the brightly-lit kitchen and kissed Sterling. He was smiling. He asked her how long it would be before they could leave.

"Well, I'm already showered, I can be ready anytime."

"Let's go, I don't want them to start the party without me!"

Betty laughed. She and Sterling had already discussed the rally events.

"Oh Betty, before I forget, Seth keeps some pretty late hours, should we be in by a certain time so we don't disturb you?"

"No babydoll, you kids have a great time, and don't worry about me."

Seth talked incessantly on the ride to the rally. He told her he went to this one bar last night and he really liked the atmosphere.

Sterling laughed, "Yeah, what does she look like?" Seth just grinned.

They walked around, drove around, and talked to hundreds of people it seemed. There were all kinds of bikes from everywhere and no two were alike. Later, they went to the bar where Seth had gone last night. He saw some familiar faces and they joined the group. Laughing and talking Sterling was introduced as his "woman". She just smiled, not knowing what to say. These people reminded her of so many of the people she had supervised over the years. She also noticed there were many professional people that were dressed in leather. They tried to blend into this culture, but there was still something about them that looked out of place. She wondered if she looked like she belonged here, or did she stick out too?

Later in the evening, Seth was having difficulty concentrating on the conversations. She noticed he was having a hard time keeping his eyes off the bartender. She was cute, and she noticed Seth too. After watching more women parade nearly naked for yet another contest, Sterling was becoming restless. Seth, of course, was taking it all in and having a great time. He could tell however that Sterling was ready to move on. They bid farewell to their new friends and decided to walk up and down the sidewalk looking at all the bikes and their owners. There were mobile tattoo artists, all kinds of T-shirt and paraphernalia vendors. It was like a carnival, but without the corny rides. Finally, Seth asked her if she had seen enough for one evening. When Sterling said yes, they jumped on the bike and headed back to Betty's. It was past 1:00 a.m. now; Betty would probably be asleep in her chair.

In their room, Sterling told Seth she was sorry she wasn't as excited as he was, but before she could finish he put his fingers to her lips and told her he understood.

"Baby, your idea was to come out west, my idea was the rally. Bikes and pretty girls are pretty a much guy thing, but I'm glad you're sharing it with me."

"So you aren't mad that we came home earlier than you had planned?"

"No, of course not. Besides I left with the prettiest girl at the party." Seth definitely had a way of making Sterling smile. "Oh by the way, I bought you something yesterday," he said as he handed her a sack.

Sterling peered into the bag, and pulled out an oversize black Harley Davidson rally T-shirt. She told him to close his eyes while she changed. She hurriedly threw off her top and pulled it on, then she tugged off her jeans.

"Okay, open your eyes!"

"Mmm, lookin' good girl!"

"Do I look as good as your favorite red-headed bartender?"

"What bartender?" he said with a smile.

She climbed into bed, pulling the covers up around her while he undressed. Just for her, he pulled on a pair of shorts then he climbed into bed beside her. Snuggled like spoons, they quickly fell asleep.

The next few days blended together for Sterling. She was seeing a different side of Seth here. He was among his peers, and his personality really came through. It was different with him back home. She was always an authority figure, even after he was off probation. Then in Daytona, she didn't really like the people from the bar where he worked. This was Seth. He felt at home here. She wished she could too.

Toward the end of the week, they were sitting at their now "regular" bar. The music was good, the drinks strong and the crowd was rowdy. Sterling had found out the bartender's name was Jasmine, but Seth said he wasn't interested. He went back to his conversation, and suddenly a man approached Sterling and asked, though it sounded a bit like a command, "Come dance with me sugar? I've been watching you for an hour. I want to dance with you."

Sterling looked at Seth, trying to impart her lack of desire to be held by this man. Seth was lost in conversation with his buddies and said, "Go on Baby, dance for me."

Sterling tried to speak; her voice was gone. But if she had, no one would have heard her anyhow. Sterling was afraid. Her past was coming into her present, and she didn't know what to do. This man, his name she had long forgotten, took her arm and pulled her onto the dance floor. He was an ex-probationer.

Not sure he recognized her; she decided to stay calm, and silent. She could disguise herself, but her voice would always be the same.

"You're very beautiful. And, you look so familiar to me, but I know I've never been with someone like you."

He had been drinking, but he had recognized something about her. She kept trying to get Seth's attention to no avail. As the song ended, the man said, "Let's just stay out here, your old man doesn't care."

She nodded her head, but then whispered, "Well just this one, I can hear my drink calling me."

About midway through the song she caught Seth's eye and motioned to him to cut in. Reluctantly, Seth came out to the dance floor.

He started to take her arm while saying, "Okay man, my turn."

"No man I don't think so, the lady is staying right here with me. You don't give a damn about her!" His grip tightened around Sterling's waist. She was truly frightened, but she knew Seth could take care of things.

"Come on Baby, this dance is over for Bubba."

Just at that time the guy took a swing at Seth, missing. Seth punched him in the kidney, and kicked him in the face as he started to double over. Seth grabbed Sterling and headed for the door. As they hit the sidewalk they could hear the rumble of the rowdy crowd in a large brawl. Sterling was crying as they ran down the sidewalk.

"Seth please get us out of here. I know him! I'm scared."

They jumped on the bike and headed out of town. Sterling was hanging onto Seth still sobbing. They didn't speak for a long time. Once they were away from the city lights, safely out into the countryside Seth pulled the bike over off the road. He stepped off the bike and held her as

318

she too climbed off the bike. He pulled her to him and hugged her tightly.

"Baby I'm sorry. I never thought anything like this would happen. I didn't mean for you to get hurt. I never even thought that this could jeopardize your safety. But know this, I will always take care of you, as long as you let me."

"Seth this isn't your fault. But thanks for getting us out of there."

"We can leave now or wait until the morning?" This caught her by surprise. The rally wouldn't be over for a few more days.

"No Seth, you can finish out the rally and I'll hang out at Betty's."

"Baby, we're leaving. The only decision to be made is when we leave?"

"But Seth you're having so much fun here."

"Baby, I won't be having any fun if I have to worry about that guy figuring out who you are, or having his buddies try to exact some revenge on me. I've had a blast, but now we're going home."

"Okay. Let's wait and leave tomorrow. I can't tell you I'll sleep peacefully, but we need some rest, and to sober up."

They drove back to Betty's silently. When they got there the door was still open, the lights on, and Betty was asleep in her chair. Sterling tidied things up in the kitchen and picked up the papers in the living room. She would clean the bathroom and their bedroom in the morning before they left. She told Seth she felt very dirty

and had to shower. He just hoped this shower wouldn't
be as traumatic as one he remembered before.
Nonetheless, he would stand outside the door and listen
to her cry as the water poured over her.

About thirty minutes later the water went off. He
quietly went back into the bedroom and got into bed. The
lights were out when Sterling climbed into bed in her new
nightshirt. She reached out to him. He put his arm
around her, and a tear fell from his cheek. He loved her
so much. Sterling was crying softly. Her protector, her
friend. Why couldn't she love him like he loved her?
She did feel closer to Seth here than she ever had. But
she couldn't make love to him tonight. There were too
many things swimming in her head. And, making love
with Seth tonight would only complicate her thoughts and
complicate his life now. She knew he had a thing for the
bartender. How would she ever fix that for him? She had
stopped crying. She drifted off to sleep in his arms. He
too was wondering many things tonight. Tonight would
not be a restful night for either of them.

Seth had awakened from a restless night and had
packed up his things on the bike. He knew Sterling
would be ready quickly, but she would want to say
goodbye to Betty. He told Betty they were leaving the
rally and heading home. She could tell something had
happened; but he didn't offer, and she didn't pry. She
told him she would miss having them around, and told
him he should make an honest woman of Sterling.

Betty said, "Seth I don't like mushy good-byes,
and although I'll probably never see the two of you again,
you're welcome anytime. I'm going to leave before Miss
Sterling gets up. I just can't stick around and watch you
ride away. Please tell her I'll miss her, and thanks for
coming into my life."

"Betty, thank you so much. We felt very at home

here. Sterling just has some things on her mind, and we need to get on back."

As he started to extend his hand to shake hers, she gave him a big bear hug. She didn't utter another word. She left the kitchen with her coffee thermos and drove away in her big, rattling truck. Seth just watched her leave. She didn't even look in the rearview mirror, or wave. He walked back into the house as Sterling was entering the kitchen.

"Where is she going so early?"

"Baby, I told her we were leaving today, and she said she didn't like goodbye scenes. She told me to tell you that she would miss you, and that I should make an honest woman out of you."

"Is she going to work? I mean, I wanted to personally thank her for her hospitality. We had nowhere else to go and she made us feel like family."

"Baby, you can write her a note when we get home. She made it clear she didn't want to be here when we left. Let's just get on the road Darlin'."

Sterling left the room. She went back upstairs and took a shower. A short time later she came downstairs with her bag and a bundle of towels and sheets. She told him she had already cleaned up the bathroom and bedroom, so they could leave whenever he was ready.

"Let's go Baby. Let's get back to the fun in the sun!"

They rode along silently for about a half an hour. He told her they needed gas, but he didn't want to stick around long. He didn't know if the police would be looking for them, and he didn't want to run into anyone that he had met this past week. They pulled into a gas station and she told him she was going to use the restroom. She was still trying to figure how she was going to hook him up with the bartender. She had about five minutes to find a way.

As she entered the station, she asked the clerk for a phone book and the directions to the restroom. He didn't say a word. He pointed to the rear of the store and handed her a tattered phone book. She just took it and headed for the rear of the building. Hurriedly she paged through the book and found the name of the bar. She didn't have a pencil or paper with her, so she ripped out the page and tucked it into her back pocket. She wasn't sure how she would handle this tidbit of information, but at least she had the number and address. She was sure she had seen sparks between Seth and the bartender.

Back on the road they listened to the music loudly. They were on the same highways and byways that they used on their journey north. Things looked different somehow. Everything had changed in Sturgis. Seth had blossomed right before her eyes. She thought of him now in a different light. He had always protected her, taken care of her, and been her friend. But now she was feeling differently, and it scared her a bit. Now, she felt closer to Seth than she ever had. Something else that scared her more now was wondering if that man would ever remember who he was dancing with last night. She really hoped he was too drunk to remember any part of the evening.

They stayed in motels on the way home. Time seemed to fly. She knew that on the way north they had taken their time and stopped at tourist destinations, but Seth just seemed in a hurry to get home. She wished she knew if he was mad at her, or just eager to get back to work, and some cash flow. They did talk of the rally and the bike he would buy if he had unlimited funds. He didn't really seem to mind that they were leaving, but he was distracted in some way. Sterling had a feeling that he was bothered by the fact that he hadn't been able to say goodbye to his new friends, or the bartender. Somehow she would find a way to help him find her again.

They pulled into Daytona during the middle of the night. Once they had gotten close to home they decided to drive straight through. Why stay in another motel room when they could be on the beach in their own place just a few hundred miles away? Instead of driving on the road when they got back close to the condo, Seth broke the law and drove out to the beach. The tide was precariously close, but he knew what he was doing. The smell of the salt and sand was intoxicating to them both. He knew that Sterling needed to be on the beach before going to bed tonight. He also knew that he was so tired he wouldn't feel like going down to the beach with her, so this would do until the morning. She squeezed him tight, hugging him, letting him know that this really made her happy. Although she couldn't see his face, she knew he was smiling. If only she could make him as happy as he made her. Something was changing for Sterling. Perhaps she could be what he wanted if she would only hang onto what he was now, his potential, and not their pasts.

The condo was hot and stuffy when they got in. Sterling opened all the windows while Seth crawled into bed fully clothed. She was happy to be back. She knew too, that he was exhausted. She took a quick shower and crawled into bed beside him. She could have played the drums in the room and not disturbed him.

The next few weeks passed without anything of significance happening in their lives. They reminisced about their trip, but no talk of what took them there. Seth got back into the grind at work, and Sterling went back to

323

her life of leisure at the beach. Seth had changed, and after only a few short days back in town she realized that she did love him.

Chapter Thirteen

Two weeks after returning from Sturgis Sterling awakened to the sound of rolling waves and the constant pat-pat sound of two very tanned, well-oiled muscle boys playing volleyball on the beach. Stretching lazily she wonders if she can stand one more morning at the beach. Of course she could; she could stand a lot more days at the beach. But those haunting thoughts of the other person she was before return. As the sun filters through the lace at her window, she drifts away again. Those faraway thoughts are happening more frequently, and she cannot forget everything she's done. The smell of the ocean brings her back. If things weren't so peaceful here, would she have gone back sooner? Could she ever really go home? Those are the questions she does not want to think about now.

Even though they had been gone for nearly ten months, Sterling had never told Seth the whole story about why she left everyone and everything so abruptly. She had told him enough that he knew she was in danger. He never pushed her about telling him the whole long cycle of events that lead to where they were now. He had no idea who or how many were chasing her, only that she was in trouble and asked for his help. He knew that one day when she was ready she would tell him everything. Sterling knew that it wasn't a boring story, and although Seth had been in the system a long time ago, he might not understand all that she had gone through to uncover information.

Seth had been gone for three days, but some of his friends kept an eye on her for him; a small detail he didn't bother to share with her. She had no idea where he went, or if he was alone. She was ready for him to return; she needed someone to talk to about her thoughts the last few days. After her shower and a light breakfast, she grabbed a book and a towel and started for the pool. Just as she closed the door she heard the phone ring. She knew it was Seth; she didn't answer it. Seth was her only true friend in Daytona, and without him she would never have survived. He knew this too. She also knew that if he didn't get her on the phone he would be over shortly to check on her. For her safety, and his peace of mind, she never went anywhere without telling him. Frankly, she didn't like being accountable to anyone, but she knew he only wanted what was best for her. She just wished he would offer her the same courtesy. He was never gone for more than a few days, but he didn't always tell her he was leaving, or for that matter where he was going or with whom. She knew; however, that he was never far away. And, he was always there to rescue her.

When he returned to the condo he watched her from the balcony. Down by the pool in her regular chaise lounge, she was engrossed in the newest Grisham novel and had forgotten about the rest of the world. About fifteen minutes later, Seth stood there, dripping on her pages. He dove into the pool completely unnoticed by Sterling.

Seth reminded her he could be one of the bad guys, but she just laughed. "Well, almost ten months have gone by and they haven't found me yet. Grab a towel, you're getting me wet."

"That's just what I hoped you would say, now why don't we go back up to your place so we can take care of that," Seth muttered.

Sterling giggled, and flung her towel at him. "Always a kidder, huh Seth?"

"Why do you always think I'm kidding, Sterling?"

Sterling knew he wasn't kidding. She knew Seth was something she might like to experience if they had met under different circumstances, but she never let him in on that secret. They could both feel the sexual tension, but he knew not to push her, and she knew she couldn't give in to him. Not yet anyway. Seth knew one day he would have her, he thought she knew it too.

Although, Sterling's perception of Seth had certainly changed after their trip out west she knew that Seth wasn't the commitment type, at least he never had been. These past few months he had spent more time with her than he ever had with one of his previous girlfriends. He had taken care of her, been her friend, and unquestionably she had been thinking of him in a different light lately, but she was unsure if he was the person she needed to be with now, or ever. During the trip and over the last few months she had seen a side of Seth she had really never seen before, and though he often told her he loved her, she knew she had seen sparks between Seth and his favorite red-headed bartender in Sturgis.

They went for a swim and a long walk on the beach. He told her he had gone on a ride with some friends, and was certainly glad to be back. She didn't bring up what had been troubling her the last few days. After they had finished lunch she asked if he had time tonight to talk. She indicated that she would like to tell him about the bad guys and the series of events that led to her own disappearance. And she wanted to discuss what options she had at this point.

Seth turned to her and sweetly said, "Baby, I've always got time for you. Would you rather talk now, or do you really want to wait until this evening?"

"No, let's wait 'til dinner to start talking about it. I've thought of little else since you've been gone, but I want to go over some information before I let you in on all of it," she said.

"Is that all you've been thinkin' about?"

"We can talk about that later too, you better get on to work."

For the past three days she had been thinking a great deal about Wanda, and everything she had uncovered. She knew it was time to tell Seth all about this big mystery. She also knew that it was about time to do something else, but she put that thought out of her mind for the time being.

Seth told her he had some errands to run and he needed to run by work to check the schedule, but he promised to be back around 4:30 p.m. so they could walk on the beach for a while before dinner. As he grabbed his keys, he pulled her close to him and gave her a very steamy, passionate kiss. He told her there was more of him for her to experience later. Sterling blushed; he laughed.

Sterling started looking through all the papers she had brought with her about this case, and she looked over the notes she had made about it since she left. The images then started flooding through her mind, and as she began recalling the information, one thought came to her: Wanda Newton was a miserable woman. It was time for someone to take a stand and put an end to it once and for all. Sterling knew it was time for Marisa to reemerge. She didn't know if she would ever be the same, but she had to draw on her inner strength now and get back to her past.

It would be tough going back and facing uncertainty. And it would be hard focusing on what started this tailspin, but she had to remember why she was here. Her first thought was her own mortality.

Although not all of her clients disliked her, nor did she dislike all of them, one of them wanted her dead! Wanda Newton was that person. Wanda and her boyfriend had harassed and threatened her, and she knew they would kill her if given the chance. She was close to exposing Wanda's web of deceit, and Wanda knew it.

Even though Wanda had always tried to come off as this syrupy sweet, middle aged woman to anyone she met, Marisa's instinct allowed her to look right through this impersonation. Marisa really wondered if Wanda actually believed she was convincing. Never once did Marisa trust anything that Wanda told her. It was a gut instinct for Marisa to be untrusting of this woman. She would definitely watch her back when dealing with Wanda. That is why she left, and now no one knew where she was, or even if she was all right.

Only Marisa's family and a handful of friends could be trusted, and if they knew of her whereabouts they too could be in danger. So, when she decided to leave, it was a difficult decision. What would her family do? How would they react? She only knew that she couldn't stay and jeopardize anyone else. It was better this way she had decided. She decided this a long time ago, a time when she was Marisa Spencer. Now, she was a lifetime away, and someone that they would never know. She is the free spirit she had always longed to be. Marisa never really thought she could be anything but a good person, a good student, and a professional. Many things had happened in just a short time, but all those qualities are still in her, just at a new and different level. Maybe not everyone could see it, but it had taken all those things to create the new self. She didn't think she could ever go back to being that other person again. Would they ever understand? Could they ever forgive her? Could she ever forgive herself?

Marisa Spencer has become Sterling Summers, a girl with only one real friend, a beautiful condo on the beach, plenty of free time, and a very empty existence. Only one person really knew her now, but he still didn't know about Marisa's private life. How could he know so much about her, and yet know so little? He was her only confidant, the only person she could trust right now. This was something she thought about often. Would she ever tell him about Marisa? If she did, he would always be a part of her life, and if she didn't she would always feel she had lied to him.

The sound of the crashing waves brought reality back to the surface. Maybe she should go for a long walk on the beach alone, or maybe just sit by the pool soaking up some sun. The beach was pretty deserted today, just those boys playing volleyball. What a life, she thought. Looking down the beach she could see a few more of the vendors pulling up and setting up shop. The motorcycles, dune buggies, golf carts and go-carts were already out in full force. The endless stream of cars full of tourists that just had to drive on the beach would be here until dusk.

She remembers when she first arrived at the beach how she too had to drive on the beach; it was such a release, and yet it seemed so forbidden. She felt a freedom she never knew existed when she was driving along with the windows down, the wind flying through her hair, and the surf just beyond the edge of the tires. Of course the beach was like an obstacle course, trying to dodge the tourists, sand castles, and other kinds of motorized traffic, and still look cool. She loved this place! When she and Seth first arrived in Daytona, they stayed a few nights at the various motels near the Boardwalk. The Boardwalk was the place for action. Many nights Sterling still went there just to watch the people.

Seth returned a few hours later and took her for that promised walk on the beach. While they walked, she asked him about his trip. He only admitted that he had had a good time, but he missed her. She didn't press him for any details, and he didn't offer any other information. She then began the long, tortuous story of why she had left town so abruptly and why she lived in fear even now. Seth listened intently as the story began to unfold.

When Sterling finished telling Seth the whole sordid story he was amazed that she had been able to keep all this inside her for so long. He had sat for over four hours with rapt attention. He watched her movements and hand gestures. She seemed more serene now than when the story began. Afterwards they went out to the balcony and sat quietly. She had finally shared all the pain that she had bottled up for nearly a year. Maybe now she would find some measure of peace. They had been safe and he had protected her from the unknown danger. But he knew she would start working on the case again.

Somehow she knew that the warrant was still outstanding on Wanda. He was worried that she would want to go back. He had to make her understand that she needed help from home if she started investigating again, but he didn't want her to go home. He had to make her understand that she would never be safe as long as Wanda and her boyfriend were alive. If either of them went to prison it would only be a matter of time before they were released and come after her again. He thought to himself that he had not thought of Marisa for a long time. For so long now she had been Sterling, and he was truly in love with her.

While sitting on the balcony, he noticed how calm Sterling seemed, but how totally exhausted she looked. He took her hand and led her to bed. She was asleep, peacefully, before her head hit the pillow. Seth watched her breathe, touching her hair, lightly touching her face while she slept snuggled close to him. Finally he allowed sleep to take him too.

They slept peacefully until almost lunchtime. Seth went down to the beach and rented go-carts for the two of them to ride after lunch. And, although motorized traffic was not to travel over 10 miles per hour, they had to have a race. Sterling crashed into a sand dune and fell out of the cart giggling. Seth of course raced to her rescue, and as he was helping her up she pulled him down on top of her. No one was there to see them as she started kissing him. He kissed her back, but then decided against it. As he struggled to control himself she wouldn't let go of him.

He was confused and getting angry when he asked her, "Sterling why are you teasing me like this? You know how I feel about you."

Sterling replied in a very hurt tone, "Why do you think I'm teasing you?"

Seth just shook his head as he turned to pull her go-cart upright and put it back on the beach. When he was back in his cart he called to her but she didn't answer. He drove around to look for her. He saw her sitting behind the sand dune crying. He went to her, but now he couldn't seem to console her. She told him she was so lonely. He assured her that he would always be there for her. She told him she knew how he felt about her and now the feeling was mutual, but when she tried to give herself to him, he pushed her away. Seth apologized for hurting her feelings. He told her that he just didn't want their lovemaking to be a tool to get her through the depression. He stated that when and if they ever made love he wanted it to be spontaneous and real. As they hugged he noticed that she was not letting go of him like she usually did. And, she was no longer crying. When they finally walked back to the go-carts she told him that she really missed home and her family, and she was so glad he was there with her.

Sometimes he wondered why he ever took this wild ride, but he knew he was the only one that could protect her. Seth spent the whole day with Sterling, laughing and talking and just being great friends. He had a way of getting her to let go and have a good time. He always knows when she is contemplating her future. He also recognizes that as long as she stays in Daytona she would stay with him. If she returned to the old life, he understood there was no place for him in her world. He couldn't let her go.

Many times Sterling was so lonely she would walk on the beach and just cry until she couldn't cry anymore. Somehow Seth would always be there on the sea wall when she returned. All he could do was hold her and remind her of the reason she was there, and why she involved him. She knew that when she was truly safe and secure, after her tormentors were arrested and sent to jail, she would call her family and let them know she was fine. They would want her to come home, but she wondered if she could ever give up the life she and Seth had now. How would she ever explain how she survived? She hadn't spoken to her parent's for over three months, and now was not the time to make a call. Just a little while longer she thought.

Sterling was fascinated by Seth, and his devotion to her. He did make her happy, now. But, she wondered if they could really ever have a future together. She had great fun with him, and he always was there when she needed him. When she needed someone to hold her, he was there. When she needed someone to talk to, he was there. And, although she knew he wanted more from her, he never pushed her. He was too afraid of losing her.

Thinking back she remembers that the day she left she was not consciously aware that she would contact Seth.

After dinner, Seth and Sterling rented a movie and went back to the condo. The movie was what Seth referred to as a "chick flick," but he knew Sterling wanted him to watch it with her. After the movie ended and he was about to leave, Sterling asked him to stay with her tonight.

Seth replied, "Sure Baby I would be glad to spend the night on one condition."

"And that would be what?"

"That we take a midnight swim in the ocean?" Seth had no idea that she would ever change her mind about swimming after dark, so he was astonished to hear her say that she would go.
"Sure why not."

"Baby, are you feeling okay? I thought you didn't swim after dark."

Sterling replied, "I suppose there's nothing in there tonight that isn't in there during the day, so I should just get over that fear. What better time than now?"

"Well okay, let's get going before you change your mind."

She and Seth had initially rented the two-bedroom condo together, but more recently he had been spending only about four or five nights with her each week. Since he spent a lot of nights away from home she believed he must have been seeing others. Many nights when she was really afraid, or lonely, they did share a bed, but nothing more. Sometimes she just needed him near her. Tonight something was different. He went into the bedroom and grabbed his trunks. When he was finished changing, Sterling was coming out of the bathroom in a new, very revealing bikini. He knew she had a nice figure, but this suit was made for her. He didn't let on that he had noticed. She grabbed a blanket and a couple of towels. He grabbed what remained of the bottle of wine they had been drinking during the movie.

Once they were down by the pool, Sterling tried to get Seth to agree to swimming in the pool. He told her a deal was a deal, so reluctantly she left the pool deck and headed for the blackness of the now deserted beach. The moon was full, and there was a cool breeze. The tide was out so there was a large expanse of beach before reaching the surf. Sterling laid out the blanket and threw the towels on top of it. Seth dug a hole in the sand and placed the bottle of wine in it. They sat down for a minute just listening to the surf. Realizing they had forgotten the wine glasses they both laughed and drank from the bottle. She leaned into him and he kissed her on the forehead, thanking her for being there with him. Finally he told her it was time to go swimming.

Sterling walked on down to the water's edge waiting to go in until he was right there beside her. As he glanced around, he knew he should just run toward her, throw her over his shoulder and run into the water. He thought she might be a little shocked at first, but he knew she would get over it. As he took off toward her she knew what he had planned and she started yelling and giggling, and off she ran. He caught up with her about 100 yards down the beach, and gently tackled her. Her hair was full of sand and she was still giggling when he scooped her up in his arms and ran straight into the water.

At that hour the wind had a chill in it, but the water felt enticingly warm. Seth pulled Sterling out into the very deep water, until she was begging him to go closer to shore.

"Seth, please let's go back to more shallow water, I'm terrified. This water is too deep for me. Please Seth let's go back!"

"Baby, we always swim out this deep during the day. It's okay, really Baby. I won't ever let anything, or anyone hurt you. I'm right here."

"Seth, hold me, don't move away."

As he swam close to her, she grabbed him and wrapped her arms around his chest and back. She held him closer than she ever had, and she was shaking with what he assumed was fear. They clung to each other, treading water, but Seth could sense a subtle change in her mood. He noticed that her touch had changed on his skin. At first she held him tightly, but now her touch was softer, caressing him he thought. She moved around him and nuzzled close to his neck. She kissed him softly on his ear. He was nearly overcome by this sudden change in her behavior, but he said nothing for a time. He held her as she kissed his cheek, and then his lips. This kiss was soft, playful, but it quickly turned more passionate. Seth had to kick hard, still treading water, just to keep them both afloat. After the kiss ended, he took her hand and swam with her to more shallow water.

They were both now standing, and she came to him again. He kissed her and held her wet hair in both of his hands. He reached for the tie of the bikini at the nape of her neck, watching her eyes to see if she was going to stop him now. As he untied it, she did not remove her gaze from his. She watched him intently. Then she reached to untie the back of the bikini. As the bikini top started to fall away, she grabbed it and threw it up on the dry sand of the beach. He had never seen her like this. Her breasts were exposed, and she wanted him to look at her. He could barely breathe as he looked at her with such desire.

"Baby," his voice unsure, "I do want to be with you now, and I have for a very long time, but if you're not sure, if you might regret this in the morning, we need to stop now. I'm not sure I can stop if we wait much longer or go much further."

She smiled, putting her index finger to his lips, as if telling him to not speak. She stepped back and in answer to his question, her hands trailed down her body to her bikini bottom. She slid her hands down her hips, and she stepped from the small piece of cloth. She watched his eyes as she reached down into the water to grab the bottoms. She threw it up to the dry sand next to where they stood.

"Does that answer your question Seth?"

Seth could only watch her, the moonlight sparkling on her wet body. The lights from the pier danced on the water and made the drops of water shimmer on her skin. He reached down and pulled off his trunks, throwing them up towards where her suit had landed. In an instant they were holding each other again, and wildly kissing each other. He had waited for this moment for many years. He walked backwards, still holding her close to him, going back out into deeper water.

He led her into the deep water slowly, knowing that she was genuinely afraid. He kissed her softly as she clung to him. After they were mostly submerged in the deep, warm water he felt her legs wrap around him instantly, and she began to rub his back. She pressed her hips against him, their bodies bobbing in the water. His hands were roaming hungrily over her body as he held her tight.

The waves washed over them as they began to make love. He was so full of passion and desire for this woman that had eluded him so often. Her passion surprised him as she kissed him hard, and pressed her hips harder against his. She moved away from him for an instant and slid her hand down his stomach until she touched him. He moaned with pleasure and anticipation as she guided him into her and wrapped her legs around him once again. Pulling him closer still, whispering to him in a low husky voice, "Seth, I do want you. Now."

His prayers had been answered. Finally he was loving her the way he had wanted to for a very long time. Passionately they made love; no one in the world mattered at this moment to either one of them. No fears, just she and him. He whispered over and over again how much he loved her and how good she felt. Afterwards they swam toward shore and walked out of the surf hand in hand. They snuggled together on the blanket under a million stars shining above. They drank from the bottle, but sat in silence for what seemed like eternity to Seth. He wondered if she already regretted what they had just done. He looked at her, but she seemed content, and at peace.

"Seth," she whispered softly, "I don't regret what just happened. It was so intense, the passion, the desire was so strong I think because we waited so long. I feel incredible, and it isn't hard to tell that you felt the same way."

"I'm glad you're okay. I love you Baby."

A short time later he pulled her to her feet and kissed her again. "You know, we should go back in," he said. I'm getting cold."

He wrapped the towels around him, and the blanket around her, and quietly re-entered the condo.

338

They both fell into bed a little drunk from the wine, and romance. Holding each other close, he kissed her again as they drifted off to sleep. He prayed that everything would be fine in the morning. In a few hours the sun would be up, and life would go on.

Seth awakened before Sterling. He watched her sleep, and wondered if she wanted to go on as if nothing had happened. That isn't what he wanted, but he would do whatever she wanted in order to keep her with him. As he started to get out of bed, still asleep she snuggled close to him. He put his arms around her and went back to sleep. Sterling awoke with a terrible nightmare. She said she was afraid of everything anymore. This nightmare was about her family being terrorized by the criminals that were after her. She told him she couldn't stop thinking of what was going on at home. She was too afraid to go back, but she was also too afraid to stay here. As he was rubbing her back she turned to him and they began kissing. The kind of kissing that seems like no one else exists in the world. Again, they made love.

She was still so filled with emotion, but she could not let herself tell him she loved him. She was still confused after all this time about how she really felt about Elliot. She wondered if Elliot missed her now, so much time had passed. Was he still in love with his wife, or was he with someone different now. She felt like she was using Seth. During their lovemaking he constantly whispered that he loved her. Afterwards all she could say to him was that she cared deeply about him. Did she love him? Did she still love Elliot? What really mattered now was someone was taking care of her in every way and she truly felt loved by that person. That person was Seth.

Even though she missed Elliot, her feelings of love for him had not surfaced until making love with Seth. She did feel guilty, but she could never tell Seth. Seth knew about her relationship with Elliot, but he believed that when they broke up, she was really over him. He would feel betrayed if she told him her most recent thoughts. She wouldn't blame him. She had never even asked if he left anyone behind when he decided to help her. And, for this too, she felt guilty. Seth told her he needed to get a shower and get to work. He asked her if she wanted to join him, but she declined.

When Seth finished with his shower he called to her, but she didn't answer. He walked into the living room and the other bedroom, but he couldn't find her. With just a towel wrapped around him he went out to the balcony to see if she had gone to the pool, but she was not there either. In the distance he could see a girl walking alone on the deserted beach. The sun hadn't been up long, he knew that it had to be Sterling.

He pulled on his jeans, grabbed his keys and took off to the beach. The girl was some distance away from him and didn't respond when he called to her. He knew it was Sterling. He wondered what was wrong. He was certain it had to do with what had happened last night and again this morning. He had to get her back, had to take care of her. Finally the girl sat down. She had something draped around her as she looked out at the horizon. As he got closer, he could see that it was Sterling. She didn't even seem to notice him as he approached her.

He sat down behind her and put his arms and legs around her. She was crying. He leaned into her hoping he could take away the pain. Finally, she told him she had so much going on in her mind. She was feeling overwhelmed and she didn't want to scare him. He told her he was only afraid of one thing and that was losing her. She smiled with tears rolling down her cheeks. She knew she felt something for Seth, but was it genuine romantic love, or something else? She wondered if she would ever figure that out. And her feelings for Ian surfaced too. She missed him desperately, and knew that he could have stopped all this a long time ago if only he hadn't died. She wondered now if she and Ian would have ever came together romantically if he had lived. So many suppressed emotions came flooding back. She just had to let them go now or she was never going to be okay again.

As they sat there, him holding her, she told him he was only the second man she had really cared enough about to make love too. She stood, looking out at the ocean, and he could hear her start to cry again. She was whispering, "Those other men meant," and she paused. She was starting to shake and she fell to the ground; Seth rushed to her. He told her he knew the others meant nothing.

"Sterling, put them out of your mind, no one ever has to know. You got caught up in something that was bigger than you were and you couldn't get out. Remember Baby I got you out. I took care of you. It's over. It's in the past. Please Baby, stop thinking of that time in your life or you'll never get over it."

He knew about her long love affair with Elliot, and he could never forget about Ahmir. He knew she had no real feelings for Ahmir. And although he wasn't sure of all the others when she worked at the escort service, he knew she was just doing a job: those other men meant nothing to her. She had told him she had never actually had sex with any of her clients, but he would never know if that was the truth. He asked her if she had loved Elliot. Sterling couldn't speak; she just shook her head yes. Seth sat with her for a long time. Neither of them spoke. She was grateful he didn't ask her if she loved him, or if she still loved Elliot. Finally, she told him she was fine, and he should go to work.

He came back later in the evening to see her, and to tell her he would be gone for another few days. He assured her as soon as he got back he would come home. As he started to leave he kissed her gently. He told her that when he returned home, he was moving back into the condo on a full time basis. She wondered if he had to break off another relationship and that is why he was going to be gone those few days. She never asked him where he was going or if he was going to be with anyone.

She had been gone just less than ten months when she finally let Seth love her the way he wanted too. The passion they shared on the beach the first time they made love was something that would stay in her heart forever. Unfortunately the next morning would be with her forever too. She had so many emotions going on in her mind afterwards, but she knew making love with Seth was the right thing to do. Seth was aware how hard this had been for Sterling, but the passion they shared was what he had always hoped and dreamed it would be. He would never push himself on her, but he truly thought they could love each other forever. To him their love and passion was extraordinary.

As their sexual relationship grew, their friendship deepened too. She shared everything with Seth. But, there was still loneliness inside Sterling, and he knew he could never make that go away. He knew she would never feel whole living away from those that she cared about, but he tried so hard to make her happy. The nights he went out alone, she always knew where he was in case she wanted to join him. She never did.

Seth and Sterling were happy together as a couple for just less than two months when Seth began to grow angry because she wouldn't extend herself to his friends. He wondered how two people could be the best of friends and so in love, but still a small piece was missing.

"Look Baby, we're a couple. I want to show you off to my friends."

"Seth, am I just a trophy to you? Why do I have to be with your friends to be with you? I just don't have anything in common with them."

"You have me in common with them Baby. And, you're not a trophy. I just get tired of going to parties alone, to dinner or a bar without you."

"Seth, maybe what we share isn't enough for either of us."

"Baby, don't say that! You know how much I love you."

"I know you love me. Things are just really complicated, and it's all my fault. Please Seth just give me time."

"Baby, you have had almost a year. I've been patient, but this is not the kind of relationship that either of us want it to be." With that said, Seth shook his head and headed for the door.

"Seth, please don't be mad at me," she cried.

"Baby, I'm not mad at you. I don't like the situation. Sometimes being with you just hurts too much. I don't like to feel this way. I just need to get out of here for awhile. I'll be back later."

Tears were streaming down her face. She was hurt by all of this too. She hated the situation she had caused. No, she hated the situation that Wanda caused!

Sterling sat on the balcony for a long time. She was heartbroken. She knew she should have never become intimate with Seth. He was a fantastic lover, but she knew they had no future together. This break-up would be hard on both of them. It would be hard to go back to being roommates, but she knew that Seth would take care of her as long as she let him.

Chapter Fourteen

Nearly every day since leaving home Sterling walked alone on the beach. Contemplating her future, and her past, she would walk thinking of nothing else. Many days she would walk for miles. Sometimes she came back refreshed; other times she was terribly depressed. Once in a while she crossed paths with the same people, and other times she saw no one. The few people that she did see regularly always spoke or smiled cordially. There were never any lengthy conversations, just an exchange of pleasantries, or talk of the weather.

There was one man however, that Sterling was always glad to see. She didn't know his name, and thankfully he had never seen her in one of her blue moods. She thought he was quite handsome. He had the look of an athlete, quite tall and muscular. She wondered what his story was; was he here just for the exercise, or was he exorcising his demons too? Although she didn't walk at the same time every day she knew there was a pattern to his excursions. He probably worked a day job and walked every afternoon after work.

She wondered if he was married, or had a girlfriend, even if he was happy, but of course, she never really talked to him. Initially, she had suspected he was there following her, but then she decided she was being paranoid. If he had wanted to harm her, or threaten her in any way he had had many opportunities. She decided by his appearance that he was a gentle man and probably a gentleman. She always felt this urge to ask him to have dinner, but she couldn't let herself drag anyone else into her web of deceit. Foolish notions, foolish dreams. This was all her life seemed to be anymore.

Several days later, Sterling was thinking about everyone she has hurt at home by her absence, and how

she had hurt Seth by being there with him. She missed
her life desperatcly at times--the family get-togethers, her
sister, and her friends. Sometimes she even missed her
job. Most of the time though, she just missed being
Marisa. When thinking of her family she remembered
how they had a way of making fun from nothing at all.
They were such a close knit family she didn't think
anyone or anything could ever tear them apart. Today
she realized Wanda had destroyed her life. Wanda had
torn her family apart.

Sterling was crying and walking slowly, and not
paying attention to the passersby. Suddenly approaching
her was the tall, handsome stranger. He was rushing to
her. He knew something was wrong. Did he sense it, or
could he see her tears? She didn't even know whether he
had passed by her and noticed and came back to help her,
or if he could see from a distance that she was troubled.
Sterling felt so foolish. She was in her own little world
during these outings; now she would have to explain her
behavior to him. She didn't want to tell him a lie, but she
couldn't risk telling him the truth. She hoped he would
be satisfied with whatever came to mind, and not ask her
a bunch of questions.

"Miss, hi. Are you okay? Is there something I
can do for you?" the stranger asked her.

Sterling was wiping away her tears, and tried to
smile. "Oh no, I'm fine. Just have a lot on my mind
today."

The stranger put out his hand, "Hello, my name is
Jake. I see you a lot out here. I've always been a little
shy, and haven't introduced myself. I'm sorry, but I
didn't want to be too forward."

Sterling demurely shook his hand. "Hi, I'm
Sterling. Glad to meet you Jake."

He grinned, and again asked if she was okay. She told him she was just thinking of her family back home and how much she missed them. This was not a lie. He told her that he was originally from North Carolina but had recently relocated here too for his job. He told her he really liked living at the beach, but he was homesick too. He admitted to her that he really liked seeing her on the beach, and he hated it when their paths didn't cross. She smiled, and told him that she too looked forward to seeing him, if only for an instant.

She apologized for not ever introducing herself to him, but explained that she didn't want to intrude into his life. She didn't want to appear forward either, and since she never saw anyone with him, she didn't just want to assume that he didn't have a significant other. He laughed and said his only significant other was his job. She told him she knew all about that, because she had recently walked away from a high stress position. Luckily for Sterling he didn't pry. She wasn't sure what she would have told him. She didn't ask him what he did either. For now she was just happy to have a new friend: a person that probably wouldn't ask too many questions, or have to know about any of her past.

"Sterling, what a beautiful name. A beautiful name, and a beautiful woman. Please don't be mad at me for stating the obvious," he said.

Sterling was a little embarrassed. Men had always given her compliments, but it seemed like she received more now as Sterling than she ever did as Marisa. Maybe it was the hair color, or her new attitude. She blushed, and said, "Thanks Jake, you sure know how to make a girl smile."

"Would I be too forward in asking you to have dinner with me tonight?"

"Well, uh, tonight I already have plans with a friend, but maybe."

Jake interrupted her, "Oh how presumptuous of me. I'm sorry. I don't mean to put you on the spot. I completely understand, I didn't even stop to think that you might be involved with someone else."

"No Jake, you don't understand. I would like to have dinner with you, just not tonight. And, I have a male friend, a roommate so to speak, but nothing serious. If the offer is still open I'd like to have a rain check," Sterling replied.

Jake was smiling. He asked her when it would be convenient for him to cook dinner for her. Sterling was surprised. A man was going to cook dinner for her. She was flattered. She told him she could come to dinner the next night if that was okay.

He said, "Well the maid has the day off then, but I think I can scramble some eggs and fry some bacon for us to eat as the sun sets over the river." They were both now laughing.

She was really excited by this new prospect, but a little frightened as well. They continued walking back toward her condo and making arrangements for the next night. He told her he only lived about four blocks from her, so he could come and pick her up, she could drive or they could meet for drinks at the pier and walk back to his place. Sterling liked the idea of drinks on the pier, so it was settled. He touched her hands as they parted, and asked her if she was happier now. She told him she was fine and he better go home and start working on dinner. She thought to herself as he walked away that he was truly a kind person.

The next day seemed to take an eternity. Sterling was nervous about her "date" with Jake. She had not told Seth about it. She didn't want him to get his feelings hurt, nor did she want him to be jealous. She kept telling herself that she was just having drinks and dinner with a friend. Hopefully she would be back before Seth got home from work, and he would never know she had been gone.

At 5:00 p.m. Sterling left the condo and went out onto the beach. To her surprise, Jake was waiting for her at the seawall. He told her he didn't know which unit she lived in, and since it was a security building he just decided to wait for her on the beach. Sterling was delighted. They walked down to the bar at the pier and ordered a couple of drinks. Over drinks they discussed the weather, how their days had been, and the dinner he had prepared for her.

"Well I have made quite a feast for us. I've been slaving all day over the stove. I decided to fix my specialties: peas and carrots, lima beans and liver," he said jokingly.

"Oh that's too bad. I forgot to tell you that I started fasting today for religious reasons," she teased.

They both laughed, and he put his hand on hers. Sterling held his hand. Suddenly this seemed very romantic. They continued to sit and laugh. Talking of favorite movies and television shows from the past that they both enjoyed. She was having such fun. She had always had fun with Seth, but this seemed more grown up to her. Jake asked for the check and told her they should get back before dinner was ruined.

On the way back to his condo, they held hands. She liked his company, but wasn't sure where this was going to lead. She knew her time in Daytona was coming to a close at some point soon, and she was sure that when she left no one here could be a part of the life she would lead back home. Back at his condo, she could smell the aroma of spaghetti sauce and bread. He told her he wasn't a gourmet cook, and it would be hard to screw up lasagna and garlic bread. She told him that she loved to cook, and maybe she could fix dinner for him one day.

The table was set for two. He lit candles and poured wine. The stereo was playing soft music. She knew he was a very romantic guy. She could really learn to like this. Jake was in the kitchen. He told her to go out on the balcony and he would be there shortly. He told her he was finishing with the salad and warming the bread. She let herself out on the balcony. He had a view of both the ocean and the river. He had a bouquet of fresh flowers outside and he brought out a glass of wine for them both. They sat at the deck table on the balcony and watched the setting sun. Sterling was at her happiest when she was watching the sun set over the horizon. Somehow Jake noticed this. He watched her as she watched the setting sun. Just as it went out of sight he asked her if she would like more wine.

"No, one glass of wine before dinner is enough for me."

Jake asked her what she was thinking about while she watched the sunset tonight. She talked to him but kept her eyes on the sky.

"Jake, I could sit here all night and watch a million sunsets. It is the most spectacular thing I have ever watched. I truly don't think of anything else except how magnificent it all is," Sterling told him.

"I'm quite fond of sunsets too. In fact, the most beautiful sunset I ever watched was back home on a vacation once," he told her.

He went to her to help her out of her chair. They went inside where he held out her chair. She realized he was truly one of the nicest men she had ever met. You could just tell he was from the south and was a very chivalrous man. This evening was turning out quite nicely. A very handsome man was treating her like a lady and he seemed to really enjoy her company. This evening was bringing back fond memories of the way Elliot had always treated her, and there were also memories of another man and a few "dates" she tried hard to repress. Right now she needed to keep this thought to herself and put it out of her mind if she intended to enjoy Jake's company.

The lasagna was delicious, and the rest of the meal was perfect too. They laughed at silly things and just talked like two old friends, but they hadn't known each other really more than just a few hours. Sterling decided this was what people must mean when they were "fast friends" with someone. She had felt this way with one other person in her whole life and that was Ian. She decided she couldn't think about Ian now, it would definitely make her sad. She missed him so much.

After dinner they went back out on the balcony and looked out at the darkened ocean. There seemed to be a million stars out and the moon was bright. She pointed out the Big and Little Dippers to Jake, and he showed her Orion's Belt. There was a brisk breeze, and the night air was a little cooler than normal. They were standing next to one another, and he put his arm around her shoulders. She leaned her head against him and told him she was having a wonderful time. He looked down at her and told her he was enjoying this evening as well.

They stood for a long time just looking out at the ocean. Finally, Jake suggested a moonlight walk on the beach. She told him she would really like to do that, but perhaps he should just walk her home. She could tell by the look on his face that he was disappointed, but assured her he understood. She told him that she really just needed to get home, but she would like to do this again sometime. She told him she didn't want to overstay her welcome. He laughed and said that if she had stayed any longer he would make her clean up the mess in the kitchen. She appreciated his humor, and diffusing the awkward situation she was causing by leaving now. It was nearly 10:00 p.m. but she didn't want Seth to worry if he got home early.

They strolled leisurely on the beach, walking toward her condo. They stopped periodically to listen to the surf, or just to look at something that had washed ashore. Finally they reached her security gate. He told her again that he had a lovely evening and hoped that they would see each other again sometime. She told him that he should give her a call. Neither of them had a paper or pen, so she told him her phone number several times. She hoped he would remember it. He turned to leave without even attempting a good night kiss. Sterling was a little disappointed, but realized he was just being a gentleman. He waited for her to get inside the gate, and then into the building safely before he walked away. Sterling watched him disappear down the beach.

When she entered her condo she realized Seth was not yet home. She checked the voice-mail only to learn that Seth wouldn't be home for several more hours. She was mad at herself for not telling him she had plans and then she could have stayed a little longer with Jake. Just as she was about ready to pull on her nightshirt the phone rang. Only Seth's friends called this late.

Before she could even say hello the caller said, "Hello, Sterling?"

Sterling recognized his voice right away, "Jake, is

that you?"

"Yes, please forgive me for calling you this late, and so soon after I just left you, but I was afraid I would forget the number."

Sterling was laughing and told him it was not a problem at all. She was quite happy that he called. She knew now that he would try to call her again.

Jake and Sterling were spending more time together as the days passed. Now they walked together, instead of just running into each other on the beach. Seth had pulled away from her, but he wasn't really ready to let her go completely. One night when she returned home Seth was already home from work. He had questioning eyes, but he wasn't going to ask something he wouldn't like the answer too.

"Seth, we need to talk about this. I don't want the hurt to continue. I've been seeing someone I see on the beach just about every day. I never talked to him until the day after we had that argument I swear that to you. When I was with you, I was with you only. But, in my heart, and probably in yours too, we both know we don't have a future together. We come from two different worlds. As much as I have tried to become a part of yours, I can't. And, I don't think you would be happy in my world at home either. I do want to go home. I have to go home."

"Baby, as much as I want you to stay, I know I can't make you completely happy. But promise me one thing?"

"Anything Seth, just tell me what I can do."

"Baby, don't go home until you know you're safe. And don't fall in love with someone from here. He probably can't go back either."

"Seth, I'm not falling in love with anyone. And I promise you that I'll be safe when I go home." He came to her and held her. She knew he was crying because she was too. It had been a great romance, but she knew when it started that it could never last.

The days turned into weeks with Jake and Sterling. Sterling spent a lot of time at his condo, even while he was at work. He had shown her his love of computers. She had grown quite fond of surfing the Internet. When he came home from work they walked on the beach, ate dinner, and most nights just played on the computer. They visited chat rooms and talked to anonymous strangers. Sterling thought to herself that she had been an anonymous stranger to most of the people she had met since leaving home. She couldn't keep this from Jake anymore. She trusted him. She could easily fall in love with him, but it was true what Seth had told her. She couldn't ask anyone else to give up their life, job, or family for her. And, too, she was still in love with someone from home. Even though she and Elliot had broken up over a year ago, she still carried a piece of him in her heart.

"Jake, I need to tell you something."

"Sterling you sound so serious. What's wrong?"

Tears welled up in her eyes, and her voice cracked. "Jake, my name isn't Sterling. My name is Marisa. I know this sounds crazy, and if you throw me out of here now I would completely understand."

"Ster, uh, Marisa, tell me what? I would never throw you out. Please tell me who you are."

"Well, it's a long story, and I hate myself for

lying to you. I just couldn't trust you, trust anyone. I had to hide. I ran away from my life about a year ago. But, I have to go back one day, and I can't lie to you anymore."

Jake was puzzled. He was sitting rigidly, not sure what she was talking about. Not sure he wanted to know what she was running from. But he was starting to fall in love with this girl he knew as Sterling.

"Jake this is very hard, and I haven't known you for very long, but lying to you all this time has been pure torture for me. You have a right to know what I'm all about, who I am."

Jake said, "I'm listening now Sterl, I mean Marisa. I'm not sure what to think and why you think you can't trust me. I don't know what has happened in your life, but I want to help you. I want to be with you."

Her voice cracked, and the tears fell from her eyes. "About a year ago, a person was trying to kill me, all because of information I was gathering. Jake, I was a probation officer. No one but Seth knows where I am. I left everything, my life, my family and friends, and my job to save myself and not let anyone else get hurt. In the process of all that, I became someone I don't like very much. I've done things I would have never done as Marisa. The person I'm running from is probably running too. She is a suspect in whatever the world thinks happened to me. She doesn't know where I am, but she knows if she comes forward, her life, as she knows it will be over quickly. She has done a lot of illegal things, and I can prove it. Before I could get it taken care of, she and her boyfriend started making my life a living hell. They threatened me night and day, and hurt people I was close too."

She paused, but she was crying much harder now. Jake was unsure whether to interrupt her, listen to her, or hold her. She didn't even seem to be in this realm now.

"Jake, I started making plans to leave and as it all came together I had one opportunity to do it. I took that opportunity and ran as fast as I could. My parents don't even know where I am. I called them about a month after I left, just to tell them I was okay, and not to look for me. I've only spoken to them a few times since I left. I was scared when I left, and didn't know where to turn once I was gone. I called someone that is a friend. Someone that had nothing to do with my life, except that he used to be on probation with me. That person is Seth, my roommate. No one at home would connect the two of us. He was just a casual friend to me after his discharge. He knows virtually nothing about Marisa; however, he has always loved me. He and I came here as friends, and just recently we became lovers. That too, is over. I've broken his heart, yet he still takes care of me."

She started to speak again, but the words wouldn't come out. She sat there sobbing, her head hung down. Finally, she spoke, "Things have happened that I won't talk about now, but Seth has done his best to take care of me."

Jake moved to be close to her. He put his arms around her, not knowing what is beyond what she has told him, not caring now. He would help her any way he could. He saw Marisa now, a woman child--so vulnerable, so afraid, and so innocent.

A few minutes passed before either of them spoke. She held onto him and told him she knew she could trust him with her secrets, and she was sorry for lying to him.

"Darlin', you'll be fine. I won't hurt you, and I'll protect you just as Seth has."

"I feel terrible about how Seth's life has come apart and all because of what I dragged him into."

"Darlin', you didn't force Seth to help you, he helped you because he loves you."

"Yes, but even that is coming apart. I have hurt him, by pulling away from him and by being with you. I can't love him like he loves me. Before I left I was with someone, but we had broken up. I always knew Seth would be my friend, but he wanted more. He never took more than I was willing to give, but now I can't continue with that either. Being with Seth brought those old emotions back to the surface. Now, I'm starting to fall for you, but I know I can't let those feelings continue either. I have a home to go back to, a life before this that I need to reclaim. And, being one step away from Seth means being one more step closer to home. I have to go home, and I have to see what is back there for me. I can't drag this life back into that one. I have to use this opportunity to go home just like I used the last opportunity to run away."

"Marisa, I'll help you in any way you ask me. I, too, feel very close to you. And as much as I don't want to lose you, I guess I never had you. I had Sterling. I don't even know Marisa, but I would like to meet her one day."

She was smiling now, tears still rolling down her face, but she was smiling.

"Until I leave here, and I don't know when that will be, will you still call me Sterling?"

"How about if I just call you Darlin' instead, that way neither of us will be confused."

"Darlin' is nice, it suits me fine."

"Tell me Darlin', is Marisa anything like Sterling?"

"Well, we both like you," she laughed. She said, "Marisa is very sure of herself, while Sterling is less confident. Marisa is a professional but Sterling is a beach bum. Both of us like the south, and southern gentlemen. But you have to realize that Sterling has just gotten into some things that Marisa would never have been involved in. I had to change a lot to be what I am now, but I need to get back to who I was before."

Jake hugged her and kissed her on the forehead. "I think you'll be fine. You want to go for a walk?"

"Sure Jake, a nice long walk."

Chapter Fifteen

On the beach she had questioned Jake about using the Internet safely to contact someone at home to help her. They discussed several options, but the only one she would agree to was going out of town and using a computer at a computer cafe or library. She didn't want anyone finding her before she was ready to return. Jake offered to go with her to various other cities on the weekdays after work or on the weekends. They decided that they would go about an hour or so away the first time.

The first thing she needed to do was make a plan. The next thing would be making an anonymous phone call to her old friend's office to find out his e-mail account. Clay Watson was a friend from college that was now an agent with the Bureau of Alcohol, Tobacco, and Firearms (ATF). This was going to be the simple part. The hard part would be writing the e-mail letter, and waiting for his response.

The next morning she went to a pay phone at the boardwalk and called the local ATF office and asked if they could give her an e-mail address for an agent in another state. Upon checking, the receptionist indicated that it wouldn't be a problem and requested the agent's name. Sterling gave her Clay's name and field city. A few moments later she was given the e-mail address from the receptionist. She thanked her and hung up.

Sterling drove home and made list of things she needed to tell Clay, and a brief plan of how it all should come together. She would trust Clay to pull her plan together, working with whomever he felt he could trust. She knew he would have to contact Elliot and Dani. Hopefully he would be able to handle the rest himself.

The phone rang as she finished her "to do" list.

"Hi Darlin', are you ready for some dinner and a little road trip?"

"Hi Jake, yeah, I can be ready by the time you get here. I'll be in the lobby waiting for you."

She left a note in case Seth came home and wondered where she was. Though he still worried about her, he knew that Jake was taking care of her. She grabbed the e-mail address and her notes and stuffed them in her bag. She then fixed her make-up and headed downstairs for the lobby.

When she got in the car, Jake gave her a kiss and told her she looked beautiful.

"Thanks Jake. I called and got my friend's e-mail address without any problem. I think I know what I want the first note to say. It will be very cryptic, but I think I'll get his attention. He usually works late, so if he gets this note before he leaves we might just get an answer tonight. Do you have a place picked out to use the computer?"

"Darlin' don't worry about anything. I have it all figured out. You'll be in control. No one is going to find you until you're ready for that to happen. I think that maybe we should post the message first, go out and grab some dinner and check back for a reply later. Does that sound okay to you?"

"That sounds great. I'm scared you know, but very excited. I might just get my life back pretty soon."

They made small talk and looked at the scenery, and finally arrived at their destination about ninety minutes later. When they got out of the car they were at a computer cafe. Jake talked to the manager, indicating they were new at this, but wanted to try out some chat rooms and set up an e-mail account. Jake talked to him as if he were a novice. Sterling indicated that they wanted to insure privacy and security so no one could "stalk" them. The manager indicated that if they wanted anonymity there were various free e-mail sites and gave them a list. He told them to just fill in the information with fictitious information. He also told them to use a log on name that was different from their own. The manager told them if they needed any help to just get his attention and he would take care of them. They headed to the computer station he had set up for them, and brought them the drinks they ordered.

Initially they went to the first e-mail service provider and set up a phony account for Sterling. Jake used "runaway" as her log on name. She smiled.

Jake said, "Darlin' time for you to pick a password, and I don't want to know it. Pick something you will always remember."

He turned the screen toward her, and let her peck out the password on the keyboard. She chose "Jake1995" as her password. She could never forget that without his help she wouldn't be here now.

"Okay Darlin' I think you're ready for your first e-mail. Get out the address and go to the compose section." Sterling did as he said and started typing:

Clay please read this brief note in its entirety. You must keep all this information to yourself and it must stay anonymous. I need your help, and have no one else to turn too. You will learn my identity if you agree to my terms. My terms: 1) Do not try to find me, and 2) Do not try to find out who I am before I'm ready to tell you. I'll be fine, and I will be home soon. Can you do as I ask? Please respond promptly and if you agree I will tell you what's going on. Love, an old

and dear friend

She had Jake look over the note before sending it. The time at home was almost 5:30 p.m.

"It looks fine Darlin'. Just push the send button and let's be on our way. We'll come back after dinner and see if he responded. And let's remember to log off this terminal."

As they started to leave they told the manager they were going to dinner and would be back a little later.

They ate dinner, but Sterling had a hard time concentrating on anything but what she had just done. Jake could tell she was nervous and tried to keep her mind off of it, but it was a daunting task. Finally they finished and he paid the check. They drove back to the cafe in relative silence.

As they entered the building Jake said, "You know Darlin', we may have no response tonight. He may not be at work today, or on vacation, so don't get disappointed. We can come back everyday or access it from my computer at home."

"No! We will not access anything from your computer. This has to be done this way. Please understand I just need to do this my way," Sterling snapped.

He knew she was under a great deal of pressure and said, "Okay Darlin', fine. We'll drive back everyday if we have too. Don't worry please. Calm down."

He put his arm around her and they went to another terminal. Jake logged them on and she put in the password. To their surprise they had a response. Sterling opened the response and said a little prayer. Clay's note said:

I agree to your terms for now. I'm trusting that this is not a joke, and that you are an old and dear friend that needs my help. I will stay here until 8:00 p.m. working and awaiting your next transmission.

Sterling had less than fifteen minutes to tell him what she needed. Jake could detect how nervous she was, and offered to type the next note. As she told him what to say he typed it out. The note said:

I'm fine. I will be fine, but I want to come home. People will need to be contacted, and charges will have to be filed before I can return safely. People need to be in jail before I will return. Can you help me?

Before he sent it she wanted to type something of her own. Sterling then typed, **"Never look back, and have no regrets."** If Clay had a good memory he would remember her always saying that in college. She pushed send and waited.

Within minutes they had a reply. Sterling felt great. She knew that on the other end of this computer was a person that knew she was fine, and would help her. The note said:

I will not use your name in any of the transmissions and I will do as you ask. I trust that you are safe, and in control of this situation. I knew when your name was in the media and read the whole story that you had to be fine. I have prayed many nights that you would come home safely. I will do all I can to help you. Can I call you? I can make the contacts as early as tomorrow and let you know my progress. This is a good time to contact me. The

363

office is virtually empty. **I will delete all transmissions. You know my phone numbers. I will await your next reply.**

Sterling told Jake to send a reply that said all phone calls at this point were unacceptable, and that she would continue to monitor this e-mail account daily. She then gave him the details of what Clay would need to do. Jake sent the following note:

You will need to contact Dani Taylor. She needs to make sure that Elliot Green still holds the key to my heart. I gave it to him a long time ago, put on his keychain. He has no idea what the key goes to. Make sure Dani knows that she cannot slip up, and they must not talk of any of this. After the key is obtained, Dani can take you to the bank where I put some rental papers in a safe deposit box. Elliot will need to go, as his name is the only other person on the box. He doesn't know this. Inside the box you will find the information you need. It's all marked and labeled. I know this is a lot to ask. Take your time, I'm fine. I'll continue to monitor this account regularly. I will not call you; you cannot call me. Please remember my rules. I can disappear again.

Clay's next note was short and to the point. The note said:

I understand, and will do as you asked. I'll be here at 6:00 p.m. tomorrow. Love, me

Sterling was nervous but she felt like a weight had been lifted. Jake said they better get back to the beach. Before they left he sent her a message to his e-mail account at home. When they got back he would show her what her outgoing messages looked like. He knew this would calm her down.

During the drive back Sterling talked incessantly. She was raw nerves. Jake knew that she would calm down eventually, but right now they both knew that she had set the ball rolling and her life was going to be in turmoil again until everything was resolved. As much as she was ready to go home, she knew her life had changed drastically. She also knew that she couldn't take Jake home with her. She had a lot of things to think about now, and later.

Jake told her they needed to stop by his condo first because he had something to show her. He booted up the computer and got ready to go online. Once he was connected he went to his e-mail account and said, "Look Darlin' you sent me a note." Much to Sterling's surprise she saw a note that indicated she had sent something to him from the new e-mail account.

"Jake, I didn't send you anything. What is that about?"

"Darlin' I sent it to me. I wanted you to see what your outgoing mail looked like." She just smiled and looked on in wonder. The note said:

Darlin' thanks for coming into my life. I know one day you will have to leave. I won't be prepared for that, but I know it's something you have to do. I hope you don't disappear forever. Thank you for trusting me, and allowing me to help you. Your forever friend, Jake.

As Sterling read the note, tears filled her eyes; however, she was smiling.

"Jake, you have been the best friend I've been missing. As much as I don't want to lose you, I can't take you back with me. The girl you know is here, the girl that leaves is someone else entirely. I do trust you with my heart and soul. I don't know what my future holds and maybe one day things will be normal again. Maybe one day you will find me again. Maybe one day I'll find myself too."

She bent to kiss him, and sat on his lap. Resting her head on his shoulder she started to wish she had never gotten him involved, but then she realized, if he hadn't talked to her that day on the beach they may never have evolved to where they were now. She would have to be thankful that at least he was in her life, for whatever time they had to share.

"Well Darlin', it's getting late, and some of us have to work tomorrow. I'm going to get you home, before I try to get you to stay with me tonight."

Those were words Sterling had longed to hear, but this was not something she would allow to happen. She would find leaving him too hard if they shared intimacy. As it was, leaving Jake and Seth was going to be one of the hardest things she would ever have to do.

As they got back to her condo, she told Jake she would be hanging out at his condo more while he was away.

"Jake, while all of this is going on, I need a diversion. Those chat rooms we play in will be my diversion. We sometimes lose track of time while we're there. I have to have something to put my mind too, only if it is talking to anonymous strangers. I hope you don't mind."

"Darlin' I don't care how long you stay at my place, or what you do while you're there. And, if being in the chat rooms keeps you occupied and happy while all this is going on around you then have a great time. I'll see you when I get home tomorrow."

He kissed her and turned to leave. He didn't look back, but she had to watch him leave.

Chapter Sixteen

"Hello, Criminal Division Probation. How may I direct your call?"

"I need to speak to Dani Taylor please, and may I have her extension for future reference?"

"Sir I'll connect you. Ms. Taylor can decide if she wants you to have her direct number. Please hold."

"Probation, Ms. Taylor."

"Ms. Taylor, this is Agent Watson with the Bureau of Alcohol, Tobacco and Firearms. We need to discuss one of your cases immediately. Would it be possible for you to meet me in my office in oh, say an hour?"

"Well, let me see. Which case is it Agent Watson? I have some appointments, but I think I can move them around, or have them seen by another officer."

"Ms. Taylor, I'd just like to meet with you initially and talk. It may be nothing with this guy, I would just like some feedback from you now."

"Well that sounds a little different, but yes, I can meet with you. Tell me where you're located exactly." Clay gave her the address to his office, and told her he would see her in an hour.

About an hour later, Dani left the building and walked the three blocks to her meeting at the ATF agency. She was perplexed and wondered why this agent wouldn't tell her the name over the phone. Then, just as she was getting ready to head into the Federal Building, she realized it just might be a top-secret operation and the phones weren't secure as Marisa had always told her.

"Ms. Taylor I presume?"

"Yes, hello. I guess you must be Agent Watson?"

"Yes, how are you? I hope this hasn't been too inconvenient for you. Would you like something to drink?"

"No, it's kind of nice to get away, but I'm at a loss. What case are we going to discuss?"

"Oh, and please call me Clay. Do you mind if we walk? I have a mess in my office."

"Uh, sure we can walk, and call me Dani."

As they started down the hall, Dani was becoming acutely aware of everything around her. She began wondering why they couldn't go to his office, why he couldn't talk on the phone, and why he didn't need a file.

"Ms. Taylor, Dani, I need to talk about something very important to both of us. I'm sorry I wasn't completely truthful with you earlier, but what I have to say must stay between us. The ramifications could be detrimental to another life. I'm not willing to risk a life because one of us can't keep a secret. Do you understand how important this is?"

Taken aback she answered, "Sure. I completely understand that someone must be into something deep. How can I help? And, who is in such trouble that I know?"

"I won't speak the name, and will ask that you never mention it either. But I will assure you that she is safe."

Dani stopped walking. First looking at the floor, choosing her words cautiously, she started to speak but stopped. She looked up at him, and with great concern on her face, her muscles tense in her jaw, she said, "I hope you are telling me about a friend. A friend that has been gone for a very long time. Please tell me where she is and why she left?"

"Dani I have a lot of questions myself, and I can't answer either of yours. Do you understand the gravity of this situation, and what could happen if word leaked out before we can get to her?"

"Certainly I understand the situation. How long have you known she is okay, and how can I help you?"

"She contacted me only yesterday. She made me make two promises. The first promise was that I would not try to find her, and the second was that I could not try to determine her identity before she was ready to tell me. I knew within hours who she was, but only because of a hint she gave to me. I will keep my promises. She is an old friend and I'll help her any way I can. She asked me to do some things here and they involve you. Let's go on down to the cafeteria."

Tears filled Dani's eyes, but she smiled as they walked. "Can I ask you if she is with anyone? How has she survived, and do her parent's know she's okay. Can we please just tell them?"

"Look, she has contacted me to help her. I will not breach her trust. If she wants her parents to know anything she'll let me know. I have an idea that they know she's fine. Now, can you keep this to yourself, and more importantly can you act as if you know nothing?"

"I don't know anything but what you've told me. I can't tell people something I don't know. But I think you're wrong about her family. I've been with them, been with her sister, they don't know where she is, or even if she's okay. Don't they at least have a right to know that?"

Angrily Clay said to her, "Look, if you can't handle this situation within the parameters she has set I'll go it alone. I will not let you compromise her safety or her plan. Now can you put all this aside and help me to get her back here?"

Stunned by his anger Dani replied meekly, "I'll do as she asked. I'll do anything I can to help you, and her."

"Good, welcome aboard. Now you need to know that I'll probably from time to time call you at work. I will choose my words very carefully, and you must too. There may be times when you need to read between the lines so to speak. Listen to what I say, think about what I say, and proceed carefully. It's obvious to her that someone at work caused all this, either a client or a co-worker, or both. Watch your back and do as I say. I can get her home, but I must be able to count on you."

"Just tell me what you want me to do."

"Okay, she was brief and I couldn't ask too many questions. She indicated that we needed to involve someone else, an Elliot Green. Is there any reason you would have to speak with him?"

"Sure he's a D.A., and he and Ma, uh, our friend, used to date."

"Well she said she gave him something, but she never told him what it was really for. I need you to see if he still has it, possibly get it back from him. Can you do that and tell him I will be in contact with him?"

"Sure, but what is it that he has that we need?"

"She said that she gave him a key, and told him it was the key to her heart. She said she put it on a keychain he had. There were no other details about it, I just hope he kept it after they broke up."

"The key to her heart?"

"Look, don't try to analyze that, just go to him and ask him about it. If he remembers it, get it from him somehow and tell him nothing else except to say that I'll get in touch with him. Can you do this?"

"Yes, I'll get it, somehow, some way. He'll have a lot of questions, I'll just tell him I know nothing but that you will enlighten him."

"Good, keep it simple. Talk to him today or first thing tomorrow. I think you should just wait for my call. Talk to no one of this, and most importantly, think of her safety, her rules. The last thing she said was that she could disappear again."

"I can do this for her. I miss her terribly. I, I thought the worst. I will do this for her," Dani stammered.

All the way back to the office Dani was trying to think of the best way to approach Elliot. She kept coming up with a plan then it would turn too dramatic. Once back at the office she picked up the phone and went with plan B, just say whatever came out of her mouth. Surprisingly, things went well.

"Elliot, Dani Taylor here. I have a huge favor to ask of you about a case we share. Can I come up?"

"Sure Dani, who's it about?"

"Oh, I'll just tell you when I get there. Be right there." And she hung up the phone.

Elliot was waiting in his doorway as Dani approached. "Do you mind walking over to the market while we talk? I have court in half an hour and need some caffeine?" he asked.

"No problem, things are so stuffy in here anyway. Let's go."

As they walked they talked about the day they had had and everyday problems within the justice system. No time, little pay and big headaches. Once at the market Dani said, "Elliot, what I'm going to ask you is going to come out of left field. Please don't ask me any questions. I need something from you that Marisa gave you. She gave you a key or a keychain a long time ago. Do you still have it?"

"She told me it was the key to her heart, and all things important."

"Elliot I need the key."

"Dani, do you realize the only thing I have left of her are my memories and this keychain?"

"If you give me only the key, you will still have your memories. Please Elliot I need the key."

"Do you know what the key unlocks?"

"I think it will unlock the future Elliot. Please let me have it."

"Tell me why you need the key Dani, or you can't have it. It's all I have left of her."

"Elliot I can't tell you anything, but an agent with ATF will call you. His name is Clay Watson. Elliot please give me the key."

Elliot pulled out of his breast pocket a keychain with a single key on it. He looked at it longingly. Holding it tightly he kissed it and gave it to Dani.

"Please take care of it. I have kept it with me, near my heart since the day she gave it to me. Whatever it unlocks, it can't bring her back. I lost her twice you know."

"Elliot, talk with Agent Watson. I don't know what he'll tell you, but he may answer some of your questions. Thank you, I will protect this as you have. And, if anyone wants to know what we were discussing just tell them I had some procedural questions on a case." Elliot wistfully just shook his head.

Dani went through the rest of the day but didn't hear from Clay. She guarded the key as if it was a precious stone. She wondered what this key opened, but decided to put it out of her mind. She was certain she would find out soon enough.

Later that evening, when the office was empty Clay sent a note to the e-mail account Marisa would monitor from wherever she was. The note simply said:

Contact with D made. D to contact E for retrieval of item. I will contact D in the morning. D understands the situation. I think it will be hard for her, but she'll be fine. Love, me.

374

Clay waited at his computer terminal for a response from Marisa. Just as he was about to leave, the system message center indicated he had new mail. He opened his mail and the note said:

E will be difficult to convince. You will need to remind D constantly of my terms. Contact with family was made long ago, don't worry. All is well. Miss home, miss my life. Thank you. Talk again soon. Love, me.

Convincing Elliot was going to be difficult she thought. Perhaps he would just tell him the truth. If Elliot still had any feelings for Marisa he would understand and keep his mouth shut. Frankly Clay was more worried about Dani being able to go on as if she knew nothing.

First thing in the morning Clay called Dani's office. "Good morning Ms. Taylor, Agent Watson here. Did you get that matter taken care of that we discussed?"

"Sure did, right after I got back to my office. Mission accomplished," she laughed.

"Good, hang onto it and I'll be in touch. Stay together. See ya."

The next call was to the D.A.'s office. He identified himself to the receptionist and his call was connected. Elliot seemed a bit preoccupied when he answered the phone.

"Mr. Green, this is Agent Watson with the ATF. I have a matter we need to discuss, can we meet sometime today?"

Elliot had thought of nothing else since yesterday afternoon. "Say what you have to say, I'm a busy man

Agent Watson."

"Fine, I wouldn't normally discuss such an important matter on the phone, but someone we both know needs a favor." Elliot sat straight up, concentrating on what this man had just said.

"What someone?"

"Look we're both busy people, but I think you and I should discuss this face to face. Is there somewhere between your office and mine we can meet briefly?"

"I have a trial about to start in under an hour. Meet me at the coffeehouse on Plymouth. I'm leaving now."

With little time to think Elliot called to his secretary and told her to stall the court if he wasn't back in thirty minutes. Both arrived at the coffeehouse within minutes of each other.

Clay had no idea what Elliot looked like, but when a well-dressed man looking rather flustered came through the door he said, "Elliot Green?"

"Yes. Look something you said on the phone really stunned me. Tell me what all this is about, and don't think you can lie to me or pacify me with half-truths."

"Fine, we both have a friend that shall remain nameless for the time being per her request. I believe Ms. Taylor spoke to you briefly yesterday about a certain item. I have talked with her today and know that you gave it to her. I thank you for that. The person that gave it to you has made contact with me, but has indicated that if we don't play by her rules she will disappear again. Do you know what friend I'm talking about Mr. Green?"

"You mean she's alive?" Elliot seemed to be in a stupor at this point.

"She's alive and well she says, and is in control of this situation. She only asks that you cooperate with me, that we don't try to find her before she is ready to come home, and that we do not discuss this with anyone else. Can you live with that?"

"Knowing she is alive I'll do anything she wants me to do. Please tell her that. Please tell her I miss her desperately. Ask her to contact me, or how I can contact her."

"Look, she is only in contact with me at this point. I'll relay the message, but you must get a hold of yourself. Something big has been brewing, and it is all about to come crashing down."

"I'll help you anyway I can, please just make sure she's not harmed. I'll be fine. Knowing she is alive will give me a reason to be happy again."

"I hope to hear from her again soon, but I'll relay to her what I can. Do you understand that I'll need more help from you shortly, but that I'm running the show on this end? Don't try to go any faster, or do anything to jeopardize what she wants us to do."

"I understand completely. I would go to the ends of the earth for her. Tell me what you want me to do."

"Right now I want you to go on about your life as if nothing has changed. Tell no one of any of this. Right now I don't trust anyone but whom she tells me to trust. The three of us can get her home, safely. But right now I don't even know why she left. I don't want you asking any questions, or go poking around. Wait for my calls, or do as Ms. Taylor tells you. I'll be in touch."

Each grabbed a cup of coffee, paid and walked away as strangers.

Later that evening after most of the staff had gone, Clay went to his computer. He wasn't sure if anyone was with her, reading his thoughts, or if she was alone. He was methodical in his transmissions to her. Stating only necessary information, and in a way she would understand. The note said:

D retrieved item without incident. I contacted E this morning. He was not hard to convince. He knows situation, misses you, will do anything we ask. Due to weekend, will go to place early next week. I expect no problems. What now? Love, me.

Clay waited in his office on this Friday night for over an hour. No message was returned. He would try again tomorrow, but he wondered all night how the key and Elliot went together. He wondered if that relationship had been over months or weeks when she left. He also wondered why it ended. Clay and Marisa had lunch occasionally, but he never knew about Elliot. He also wondered about this.

Jake had been keeping Sterling busy during his off hours with miniature golf, long walks on the beach, dinner, movies, and when she was alone she kept herself occupied by reading or playing on the internet at his place. Sometimes he would log on at work and see if he could find her. Many times he would trick her into thinking he was someone else just to see what she would say. Usually though he just had time to say hello and tell her what time he would be home.

Since the first transmission was sent she and Jake

had gone to various cyber cafes to retrieve and send her e-mail. Even though the account was anonymous she was wary about someone being able to tell the city from which the messages were generated or retrieved. They always went at least an hour away, and in a varied pattern of locations. She didn't want anyone to look on a map and figure out they were staying in a general area. She knew how to cover her bases. If anything was amiss in any of Clay's transmissions she would cease sending them, and wait a little longer.

Because it was a Friday night and she thought that Elliot would put up a fuss, she decided to wait until Monday to check her accounts. She surprised Jake with her patience. If he only knew the truth, she was surprising herself too. She knew that once everything came together the train would be speeding out of control again. She would have little time to be patient then.

Finally Sunday night she decided to go to check her e-mail account. To her surprise Jake had also sent her notes during the week. They contained nothing serious, just anecdotes or little tidbits of his day that he wanted to share but said he might forget if he didn't write them down. She finally opened the one from Clay. She read the note and laughed. She showed the note to Jake and said that Clay was just so serious in these transmissions.

"Well Darlin', he is worried about you, and he is a professional. He has no idea that you are well taken care of. Don't be too hard on him."

"I know what you mean, but neither of us are giving any unnecessary details of what's going on. I guess that is a good thing, but it might be nice to hear how things are at home. It has been a long time since I called home. And, when I do, I don't say too much, just in case."

She typed out a note to Clay that stated:

Wonder of wonders. He misses me after all this? Nevermind that. Tell him I'm sorry I missed our lunch. Stay in control and remind others to as well. You're in charge. Have D take E to bank. Number on key. Access with E only! E may only look at papers with you present. Keep D clear of all else. Her part is minimal now. I, too, have copies. E will know what to do with them. Everything we need is there. Tell him to do what he has too. Tell no one about me yet!! I like where I am and don't want to hide again. Will check in tomorrow. Love, me

The next morning Clay was happy to find the note from Marisa. He read it through three times before calling Dani. He knew she was not going to like being left out of the loop, but he figured that Marisa was trying to protect her. From what, he did not know. He called Dani's direct number.

When she answered he said, "Hi there, your friendly ATF agent checking in. I received a new directive from our mutual friend. Can we meet at lunch time to go pick up some incriminating paperwork?"

"Well certainly. I can be ready at 11:30 a.m., but I need to be back by 1:00 p.m. for violation hearings. What?"

"What, what?"

"I heard a noise, and couldn't hear you. Are you on a car phone?"

"No, probably just a glitch in the wires. Okay, I'll see you at 11:30 downstairs. I'll be driving a federal car from the pool. I'll honk the horn a couple of times so you know it's me. See you at lunch. Oh, and be sure to check your facts before you leave."

"Okay, see you in awhile. I'll be on the lookout for a cop car and listen for the honks," she laughed.

Just as soon as she hung up she wondered what his last comment was about. She had no facts to check. They were going somewhere to pick something up. She then started thinking about their first conversation. He had told her something important, but what was it? She knew she couldn't call him. Now she was really thinking. And, if he wasn't on a car phone what was that noise?

Just as she started to turn her attention to the files of the day, Monika walked out from the empty office next door. Eyeing her she wondered why she was in there. There was something about Monika that Marisa had never liked. Marisa had often said that she was sneaky and underhanded. Dani didn't know what it was about Monika that got under Marisa's skin, but more recently she was starting to dislike her too.

The morning wore on, and just as she was getting ready to leave the receptionist called to her and said, "Hey there, Dani! I just got a call, but haven't had time to write it down."

"Yeah, what is it?"

"Well it was a guy that didn't identify himself, but he said before you go to your important meeting just remember to get all your ducks in a row and check your facts before proceeding. Oh and he said it was real important that I tell you exactly what he said."

"Okay, sure and thanks." Puzzled, she decided to go back to her desk and check her voice-mail.

Dani went back to her desk. She had five minutes before she needed to be downstairs. Just as she went back to her office she noticed that Monika was leaving. Monika never went outside the building for lunch but she had an umbrella and her purse. Dani thought about what the receptionist had said and then remembered the words Clay had used when he called this morning. He had told her to check her facts. What did he mean? An idea struck her like a bolt of lightning! She now remembered more of that first conversation. She needed to read between the lines, and that she would need to listen carefully to what he said and proceed carefully. Maybe he said fax and not facts. She ran to the fax machine and in the tray waiting was a facsimile paper from the ATF. There was no indication from whom it was sent, but it was sent to her two hours earlier. The printing was garbled and fuzzy, but in between a message that meant nothing to her, the words **FORGET THE MTG TODAY-I WILL BE IN TOUCH** were bolded so she could see them. She decided to stay in for lunch. Hopefully he would call her later. If he did show up and she wasn't downstairs he would call her from his car phone she was sure.

Dani didn't receive any calls regarding the meeting, or lack thereof the rest of the day. The next morning she still had no messages. Finally around 10 a.m. she got a call from Clay.

"Sorry about yesterday. I guess you figured it out. Something just wasn't right, so I called it off. Can we go today? Same time, same plan?"

Not taking any chances, she simply said, "Sure, no problem."

"Oh, and see if you can get that other friend of ours to go with us. Just tell him it won't take too long."

"Okay, I'll see what I can do." With nothing left to be said both just hung up. She decided to pay Elliot a visit, rather than using the phone. As she started to leave the office she was stopped at the front desk.

"Dani, you're one of the first people to get into the office right?"

"Yes, why?"

"Well Monika didn't show up for work today, and she has some people scheduled. We let some of them just sign in, but wondered if maybe she called in sick to you and you just forgot to tell someone."

"Nope. No calls to me from her. Sorry." She proceeded to Elliot's office not giving it another thought.

She stopped at the front desk in the D.A.'s office and asked to see Elliot. They buzzed his office and he told them to send her back.

As she went down the hall he met her and said, "Good, yes we have some things to discuss."

"Umm, yes we do, can we do it over lunch? A friend wants to take us out at about 11:30 can you make it?"

"Well, sure, I just can't be gone long. It will have to be a quick lunch, I have bond hearings later."

"Well, just meet me downstairs at 11:30, and we can go on a little field trip. I'll talk to you then okay?"

"Sure, a field trip," he said excitedly.

"Oh, I don't think it will be anything exciting."

"No, of course not. Okay then, I'll see you in a bit downstairs. And, thanks."

"Sure, no problem."

Lunchtime didn't come quickly enough for any of the players in this game. Finally at 11:25a.m. Dani left her desk and told the front desk she was going out to lunch. She gave them instructions what to do if anyone came in for their appointment and she wasn't back yet. She got into the same elevator that Elliot was in already. They smiled at one another and made small talk.

"Hey Dani, I'm meeting a friend for lunch, I think you might like him. Would you like to join us?"

A little embarrassed, she said, "Well I was just going to grab a quick sandwich but I guess that would be fun."

"Good, he's waiting for me downstairs."

When they got into the car, Clay turned to Dani and said, "Well, where to?"

"What do you mean? I thought you were taking us somewhere."

"I am, but you're the only one that knows where that key will work. You do have the key don't you?"

"Of course I have the key. But I have no idea what it opens."

Elliot interjected, "Can I interrupt a minute here?" They both turned to look at him. "That key probably goes to a safety deposit box, or a post office box. What did Marisa tell you about it Clay?"

"She indicated that Dani would know the bank where the documents are held. They both looked at Dani. Dani sat stunned, thinking.

"I know where she deposits her checks, but it's just across the street from here. Do you think that's where we need to go?"

"No, she said something about rental papers, but I can't remember any more about it? Does that mean anything to you?"

Dani said, "Well awhile before she came up missing I remember we went to put some papers belonging to her parents in their safe deposit box, but I don't remember what they were about. However, her parents do have rental properties."

"Well, tell us where you went and we'll start there."

Dani tried to remember where they had gone to eat lunch that day. Finally, as Clay started driving, she remembered and directed him to the bank.

As they pulled into the lot Clay told Elliot he needed to go into the bank alone, and get out whatever was in the safe deposit box. When Elliot started to question him about the legalities of it, Clay assured him that his name was on the box as a co-owner. Dani gave the key back to him. As he started to get out of the car, Clay told him that he was not to open the contents until they were all together. Elliot said he understood, and went into the bank.

Elliot told the girl at the desk that he needed to get into his safe deposit box to retrieve some paperwork. She told him to follow her to the vault and sign his name on the logbook. She then took his key and located the box.

She inserted her key, he inserted his key and she turned them both, unlocking the box. She pulled it out of its location and handed him the whole thing. She escorted him to the antechamber where he could be alone. He looked at the thick envelope on top of the stack. It was marked: Newton evidence. It was Marisa's handwriting. He thumbed through the remaining items. Finding nothing else that he needed he put the envelope in his suit jacket and went back to the hallway. He told the girl that he was finished and thanked her. They locked the box back up and he signed out. He then went back out into the parking lot with a smile on his face.

When he got into the car he said, "Well let me look at what we have."

Before he could get it out of his jacket Clay cautioned him that Marisa gave specific instructions and for the safety and integrity of the investigation he would like to honor them.

"She indicated that you and I need to look at these documents alone, that Dani's job is done for the time being. I'm sorry, but I think you understand. She is trying to protect you. I respect that, and I'll do as she asked. I hope you can both live with that. Let's get together tonight and look at what she has given to us. I'll hang onto the envelope, as I'm the person she has asked to get you both involved. I won't open it until we are together. Agreed?"

Elliot just shook his head as he stared at the handwriting on the envelope.

Dani was a bit hurt, but of course she knew that Marisa wanted only the best for her, and safety was of the utmost importance at this point. "I understand. I'm curious of course, but I'll respect her wishes too. If at any point though you decide you can share this, please call me."

When Dani arrived back at the office she could sense the tension. She asked one of the typists what was going on.

"Well, Monika seems to still be missing."

"No great loss there. I'm sure she'll turn up."

"Well the interesting part is, her husband called in to talk to her. He was a bit concerned when she didn't come home last night. Now the whole office is buzzing. Wonder what to make of it?"

"I wouldn't make anything of it. Monika is a strange bird. She's sneaky, and she's probably cheating on him."

The typist just laughed and said, "Yeah, you're probably right. And now the whole darn place knows!"

When Monika didn't come home again after work, her husband called the police. She had now been missing for over twenty-four hours. The questions would center on their marriage, and why he had not called any sooner. They also asked if she liked her job. He said that she never brought her work home with her, and that they should probably talk to her friends at work.

The police decided to question her superiors at work to find out more about her and her friends there. Charles informed them that she pretty much stuck to herself. In the nicest way he could he told them that she was a very private person, and this did not lead to many friendships within the office or cooperative departments. Charles was with them, as was her husband, when they looked at her car. Her car was in her parking spot, and her desk was left as it would have been if she were just going out to lunch. She was listed as missing at that time.

Chapter Seventeen

"Look Mister, I think you and I got off on the wrong foot. I thought I was meeting someone that had information about a friend of mine. You seem to think I have more information than I do. So, why don't you just let me go, and we can both forget that this ever happened. I'm tired, hungry and have to find something to tell my husband about why I've been gone for so long." Monika said this to the menacing stranger with all the confidence she could muster.

"Look Bitch, I'm tired of messing around! Can't you see that I am in control of this situation, and you're not leaving here until you tell me where Ms. Spencer is!" As the stranger said this he slapped her hard across the face as she sat tied to a kitchen chair. Her lip was bleeding and her hair was a mess from all the rough treatment over the last several hours.

"I told you! I don't know where she is!"

"You lying Bitch! You were on that phone, and said you would meet with someone and that you were going to pick up some papers from somewhere. Now tell me where she is, so I can take care of some unfinished business."

"I have told you a hundred times, I met with you in the place of someone else! I got downstairs before they did. I thought you could tell me something. I was only calling your bluff. I'm not the person you heard on the phone!" Monika was crying. She was becoming hysterical, and she just wished that Marisa had never caused all these problems for her.

"Well I guess you must be into pain. I think that maybe you'll like what I have in store for you, then maybe we can get some answers." As he said that he pulled out a switchblade knife. When he came toward her, twisting the handle of it, the light danced on the blade. He had a sick gleam in his eye as he watched Monika squirm. Slowly he walked toward her and caressed her cheek and neck with the knife.

"I told you I'm not the person you heard on the phone!" she yelled.

He got a steely glaze in his eyes. His face more menacing than before and he quickly took the blade away from her face and ripped the front of her dress all the way down to the waist, cutting also her slip and bra. "Do I have your attention yet?"

"Fuck you! You've had my attention for as long as we have been in this godforsaken dump. I cannot tell you something I don't know."

He slapped her hard again in the face. Her ears were ringing and her lip was busted. She could feel the blood trickle down her nose. "Tell me what the papers were about. Tell me where I can find her. Now!"

She sat there in silence. Her voice hoarse from yelling all night that she didn't know what he was talking about. He took the knife out again where she could see it. He walked closer to her and acted as if he was going to cut the wrist restraints. She wiggled both wrists and started to thank him, just as he sliced her left arm from the wrist to the elbow. She screamed in terror.

"Is that what you like? Does that feel good to you? Now tell me what I want to know before your whole body looks like a jigsaw puzzle."

"Please, please I'm begging you. Let me go. I won't tell anyone about you. I'll make up a story that I was mugged and taken out to the country and dumped. Please don't hurt me. I don't know what you need to know. I'd gladly help you. Marisa only wants to destroy my life too. I came to meet you in hopes I could find her first. I'm begging you to believe me. Please?"

"Don't waste my time. You aren't going anywhere until you tell me what those papers are for, and where you were supposed to meet her."

She just cried and shook her head. He came toward her and as she started to scream again, he sliced her face with the shiny blade. The cuts were not deep but they stung horribly. He slapped her again and again.

"I was not on the phone when you heard that. I have been eavesdropping on Dani Taylor for months trying to find out about Marisa's whereabouts. I only heard that she would meet you downstairs. I left the building before she did. I swear to you I don't know anymore than you do apparently."

"Are you calling me stupid?" The rage was building in him and he was tired. He, too, had been listening in on some phones in Marisa's office. He needed a break, and this bitch was trying to thwart his attempts to rid his life of Marisa. He began hitting Monika so hard, and when she appeared to be unconscious he slapped her a couple of times to bring her around. She was messing up his plan, and setting back his agenda. He picked up the phone and began smashing it into her head. Finally, when he had worn himself out he threw the phone across the room and looked at the mess this lying bitch had caused. He went to the back room to sleep. Maybe in the morning she would be ready to talk.

Several hours later he awakened and went back to his victim. Her head was slung down at an odd angle, and her body was more slumped over than it had been when he was finished with her last night. Her body was covered in dried blood, cuts and bruises. He called to her, but she didn't respond. As he got closer to her he noticed that her eyes were open and glazed over. Her skin was blue and cold to the touch. He realized then that she was going to be no help to anyone. He went to the garage and found a big canvas tarp to wrap her in. Now he started to wonder what he would do with her body. He needed to show her as an example to the rest of them what could happen if they got in his way again. And, he wanted Ms. Spencer to realize wherever she was what was in store for if she didn't leave everyone alone and mind her own business.

He waited several more hours until most everyone would be asleep and he could dump Monika's body and make a point. He was somewhat concerned about the shape she was in. She certainly didn't look like she did when he picked her up. He decided to burn her purse and most of its contents and he took what little jewelry she was wearing. He didn't want them to have much to go on to determine her identity before he was back safe at home. He then decided to work on her fingertips. He figured that since she was employed in the field of law enforcement she would be fingerprinted somewhere. The best thing he could think of was to cut off her fingers, but that would take time, and leave more blood behind. He settled on something quicker and less risky. After about an hour of work he rinsed away the blood and remaining evidence in the tub.

Finally, he loaded her into the trunk of the car and drove to Marisa's old apartment complex. Leaving her body here would send a message if the detectives working the case were very smart. He decided a long time ago though that the police were not as smart as he was. If they were as good as the Police Chief indicated they would have found Marisa a long time ago. He drove around the lot several times checking to make sure no one was out and about. He parked the car and opened the trunk. He decided to sit back in the car for a few minutes and just watch the complex like he used to when Marisa lived there. When he finally decided the coast was clear, he moved swiftly, carrying the heavy load in the blanket. He deposited her on the lawn in front of the building where Marisa had lived. Hurriedly he got back into the car and drove carefully back to his real home several counties away.

The next morning on his way into work, Detective Matheson heard the dispatcher notify Homicide of a body found at Lake in the Woods Apartments. It wasn't far from where he was so he decided to stop by to see if he could be of any assistance until Homicide arrived. He arrived and saw the flashing lights of the district cars near the back of the complex. Just about the time he reached the officers near the crime scene he saw the detective car pull up. He spoke to them, joking what a way to spend the morning. He could see the body propped near the building, but it was in pretty bad shape. The officers told him that this woman must have really pissed someone off. They informed the lead detective that they could find no identification in the area and the body was pretty badly destroyed. Because of what the corpse was wearing they were pretty certain she was a female. Detective Matheson decided to head on into work and let his buddies do their job.

He got into work about thirty minutes later than normal. His partner, Detective Konjesky was giving him a hard time about being late. "Yeah, well when you help out your fellow officers then someday you might be late too."

"Helping out who with what," Konjesky questioned.

"Oh I was on my way in when I heard dispatch tell Homicide of a body being found out there at Lake in the Woods. I thought since I was in the area I would go out and assist the district guys until help arrived."

"Lake in the Woods huh?"

"Yeah, something on your mind?"

Konjesky pondered and then said, "Well you know it was about a year ago we were out there ourselves. Wonder if there is any connection?"

"I doubt it, coincidence probably. We can check with Miller later though when he gets in, see what he finds out."

"Yeah, you're probably right. Besides I don't want our body turning up dead. I would just as soon find her and get her back to work."

Neither of them had given much time to finding Marisa after about six months of her disappearance. They both hoped for the best, but knew the trail was cold by the end of the week when she first disappeared. Now, however, they were both wondering about her again.

It had now been two days since Monika had been heard from, and everyone around the department was starting to gossip and speculate. Looking at the calendar people soon realized it was almost a year before that Marisa had turned up missing. Jansen called a meeting with the supervisors to tell them to talk to their units and let them know that the gossip was not going to be tolerated. The department had to pull together and not let this out to the media. She was too late however.

Detective Miller returned to the office after lunch. He was perplexed by the damage to the body, and yet nothing else had been left at the scene. He knew from the crime scene that the body had been dumped there, but he wondered why the perpetrator had picked such a high profile area unless they were trying to make a statement. Several of the local news stations had been to the scene, and it made the lunch hour broadcasts. The local newspaper had their crime reporter on the scene as well. It would make it in tonight's evening news too. Perhaps, some good would come of the exposure.

Miller decided to call missing persons to see if they had any recent Jane Doe descriptions matching the body that was found today. There were eight close matches. The body was in the morgue being readied for the autopsy, but he could tell them basic information regarding size and hair color. The woman's body was too badly beaten to give any better description. Printing her was useless too. Someone had taken the time to remove most of the flesh from her palms and fingertips.

Dani had seen the news broadcast at lunch across the street. She watched intently when they talked about the body that was found in Marisa's old apartment complex. She felt a chill run down her spine, and she couldn't finish her lunch. She rushed back to the office and called Clay, even though she had always let him call her, she needed to talk to him now and be reassured.

"ATF, Agent Watson speaking."

"Clay this is Dani. I, uh, just watched the noon news and I'm getting sick."

"Dani calm down. Why are you getting sick?"

Her voice cracked, and she said, "A woman's badly beaten body was found at Marisa's old apartment complex. They didn't list the address, but I recognized from the shot that it was her building!"

"Oh my God! Okay, look it isn't her, I'm just sure of it. Can you meet me somewhere now?"

"Uh, yeah, come over here and meet me out in the court corridor on fourteen. Please hurry, I don't know how long I can keep this together."

"Look, it isn't her. Calm down and I'll be there in five minutes."

Before he left he fired off a short message to Marisa's e-mail account. The note said:

You have been rather quiet. Please respond so I know things are still okay. E and I are still going over items from box. Love, Me.

He ran the few blocks over to Dani's office and quickly took the elevator to the fourteenth floor. He walked down the hall like he was on his way to an office and just bumped into an old friend. "Dani, hi how have you been?"

Dani looked around and motioned for him to sit on one of the benches outside the court offices. "This is all getting really creepy. What was in the envelope, and how do you know if she's still okay?"

"Look, you're just going to have to trust me. I don't think she is anywhere around here, and what was in the envelope is still under scrutiny. If it makes you feel any better I sent her a note just before I left my desk. I'll call you as soon as I hear from her. Now tell me what makes you think this body had anything to do with her?"

"I don't know, gut instinct maybe. It was her building, I know that. It was a white female body. That's all they would say. And, one of the reporters for the evening paper is hinting at a connection because of the timing. Oh, and one more thing. One of our other officers has gone missing."

"What? Who's missing and why haven't I heard about this?"

"Well, her name is Monika Garza, and she is a bit of a flake. Marisa couldn't stand her. She always said she was sneaky and underhanded, just like Jansen, our Chief. Of course there has always been some speculation that she and Jansen were having some torrid affair, but it could just be idle gossip. Jansen is a bit shaken over this one though. She didn't act this way when Marisa disappeared. You haven't heard about it because there is little to report except to say that she is missing."

Clay sat for a moment lost in thought. "Did you ever mention to the detectives about this Garza woman?"

"What was there to tell? She and Marisa didn't

like each other, but I doubt she had anything to do with Marisa disappearing."

"Look, if I go to the detectives they're going to start asking way too many questions. I think we have an opportunity that we can't let pass. You need to call the detective you spoke with initially. Tell him that you were just thinking about Marisa, and now that this other officer is missing you thought he should be made aware of it. Don't screw this up. Keep it simple. Just tell him you heard about the dead body on the news, and that you were wondering if it's all just coincidental. Let him take it from there, but I'm warning you now, do not let the cat out of the bag that there has been any contact with her!"

"Yeah, I'll call him now. Maybe he can lay these fears to rest. Thanks for coming over. I feel better just talking to you. And, please call me as soon as you hear from her."

"Well dear it has been nice seeing you, we've got to get together sometime soon and have lunch or something." Clay said this loud enough for anyone around them to hear.

"Ok, we'll talk soon. Call me."

Dani went into the court office and dialed Detective Konjesky's number. "Konjesky," he said when he answered the phone.

"Detective Konjesky, this is Dani Taylor from Probation. Can I come over in about thirty minutes and talk to you about something?"

"Well, Ms. Taylor I was about ready to step out, can you make it any sooner?"

"Uh, well it's really important. Sure, I'll be right over," she said as she hung up the phone.

She couldn't risk being seen going over to talk to him so she left the building from the west entrance and re-entered the building on the east side. She took the elevator to his floor and walked right to his office.

"I don't know if you remember me, but I was a close friend of Marisa Spencer's. I have some information that may help you, or it may just be useless. I'm still so overwrought with emotion about her, but something happened today and I don't know if it's related to her disappearance."

"Sit down. Let me get my notes on that case. Do you need a drink or anything?"

"No, I'm fine. I can't be here long, but I just needed to talk to you."

"Okay, go on."

"Well today at lunch I saw on the news that there was a woman's body found at the same complex where Marisa used to live. Well, to say the least, it shook me up. And, then there's the other issue that we have another missing officer, and the timing couldn't have been more eerie. Maybe these things aren't connected, but I really didn't know if you knew any of this."

"Well actually I did know about the body being found today, and I had heard something about the other officer being missing. However, I talked to Missing Persons and they wonder if this other officer isn't just hiding from her responsibilities. Was she linked to any of

Marisa's cases that you know of?"

"Marisa hated Monika. Monika Garza, the missing officer. No, they weren't connected except they were on the same unit in the department."

"Well, my partner, Detective Matheson, was out at the homicide scene briefly this morning. He was a little concerned about the location of the body, but we really think it's just coincidental. I'll check it out though. Is there anything else? Anything at all besides what you've told me?"

"No, really I just want to know that it isn't Marisa that you found out there this morning."

"Look the body was in pretty bad shape, but as soon as it's cleaned up and the coroner can rule on the cause of death they'll start working it against any missing persons that match the description. Let's just keep thinking positively that it isn't Ms. Spencer."

"Okay, please let me know what you find out."

"Sure, but I imagine you'll read about it in the paper tonight or see it on the evening news before I hear anything. But thanks for the additional information. I'll keep it in the file."

Dani didn't feel much better when she left, but at least they had more information than they did. She went straight back to her office and started seeing her backlog of clients.

Konjesky called Matheson on the radio to tell him about this new tidbit of information. "What do you say you meet me in the morgue in twenty?"

"Yeah, maybe we can get more information from the coroner. You better call Miller too since it's his case."

"Right on that. I'm gonna see what Missing Persons can tell me about this Garza chick, maybe get a picture."

Konjesky talked to Miller by phone briefly. He still hadn't heard from the coroner, but was pretty sure it would be blunt force injury to the head on cause of death. Her face was pretty well destroyed and there were not going to be any fingerprints. Konjesky told him to meet him in the morgue in fifteen minutes and to bring his Jane Doe photos that he had obtained from Missing Persons.

When the trio arrived at the morgue the coroner was just about to begin the autopsy on this morning's first arrival. The technicians had done their best to clean the body and had taken the necessary pictures. It would be a sad sight for a family member to have to identify this Jane Doe, but the detective's and the coroner's staff would do what they could to expedite the process.

Miller had eight photos matching the brief description he had given to Missing Persons. Three of the photos were tossed out immediately due to obvious scarring and identifying marks that were not present on this body. The technicians had determined the eye color was a greenish brown. That information tossed out three more photos. They were down to two photos of missing women. One of them belonged to Monika Garza.

Jake and Sterling made a trip to the computer cafe during his lunch break. Today they had just stayed in town, figuring anyone that may be looking for them would decide this was just another note from another city. When Sterling pulled up the account she was surprised by what she read. Although Clay had said nothing out of the ordinary, Sterling felt odd about what he wrote. Jake didn't read anything into it. She knew this was her sixth sense, her intuition. Sterling sent back a note that simply said:

Of course I'm fine. What's happened at home? Don't lie to me, I will find out the truth. Respond ASAP! Love, me

Sterling tried to tell Jake about her experience with her instincts. He just laughed, thinking she was just making too much out of what Clay had sent her. Just as they were about to leave, her account indicated she had new mail. She opened it, and read:

I won't hide anything from you. Another P.O. has been missing for a few days. This morning a body was found at your old complex. There may be no connection. The missing P.O. is someone you do not like or trust. I'll be here monitoring this account until I hear from you again. You're safe I know. Love, me

Jake read in disbelief. Sterling was silent for a long time; tears filled her eyes as she turned to Jake. "Do you see? I knew something was wrong. I have an idea who is missing, but it's only a matter of time before they start looking for me again."

"Darlin', you need to send him a note. He's sitting there at his desk and he needs to hear from you. And, you need to find out who's missing."

Sterling just shook her head and turned back to the computer. Slowly she typed out her thoughts.

**Has her body been identified yet? Tell me
what you know, briefly. Get with E and do something
before they find me! I'm here waiting. Love, me**

Clay read the note, and wondered what she would
be able to find out from wherever she was hiding. He
decided to tell her about the phone call to Dani first.

**D and I were discussing our meeting place.
Something happened during the call, so I called off the
meeting. That other person must have been
monitoring the calls and she must have met the person
that was obviously bugging the phone. If, and I
repeat, if, the body that was found is indeed her, we
have trouble. D has given the detectives info about
your relationship with other P.O. An autopsy is
scheduled for today. We think it's her. Did she know
anything? Love, me**

As much as Jake needed to get back to work there
was no way he was leaving Sterling now. She was really
shaken up. Jake took over the keyboard and asked her
what she needed to tell her friend. Looking rather numb,
she told him to tell Clay that her co-worker was nosy, and
she knew nothing about anything on Marisa's caseload.
Jake typed quickly:

**She knew nothing of my life, or my caseload.
Is D alright? Please find out about autopsy now. I
need to be more alert now. Love, me**

Before Clay received the next note he called
Dani's office. "Ms. Taylor, this is Agent Watson. Could
you make a call to the detectives and find out what they
know? And, everything is fine."

"Uh, yeah I'll do that now. Give me a few

minutes, and call me right back. And, you're sure that everything else is fine?"

"Yep. Fine. I'll call you back in a few."

Dani called Det. Konjesky's office and learned he was over at the morgue. "Well, this is urgent, could you patch me through please?"

"I suppose, hold please."

"City Morgue, can I help you?"

"Um, yes, is Detective Konjesky anywhere that he can be reached? This is Dani Taylor."

"Hold on a minute and I'll page him. If he's here he should pick up."

Dani could hear the page in the background of the receiver. She wasn't sure what she would say, or how she would respond if she knew before anyone else that Monika was in fact the body that was found.

"Konjesky here. Who's calling?"

"Detective, this is Dani Taylor from Probation. I just wondered if you could tell me anymore."

"Dani, I really can't tell you anything before the family is notified, but I think you can read between the lines."

"Oh my God!" Dani whispered.

"Dani, get a hold of yourself. You cannot say anything to anyone. I'll be calling your Chief just as soon as the family is notified. Now pull yourself together and I'll be in touch."

Dani sat there. What if Clay hadn't sent her that note calling off the meeting? The body that was found could have just as easily been hers. Stunned and speechless she sat and waited for Clay to call her back.

The phone rang, but she just sat and stared at it. Finally, she picked it up, but didn't say anything. "Dani, is that you? It's your friendly ATF agent."

"Yeah, it's me. I, uh, just spoke with the Detective. He said he couldn't tell me anything before the family is notified. I guess you know what that means, don't you?"

"Well, yes. Hang in there. She'll be fine. I'll do everything I can to protect her, and you. I'll be in touch."

Knowing that Marisa was going to be shocked he just sent a simple note.

Identification is positive. Be careful! I'm calling E now. Things will move faster now. Hang on tight, and stay in touch. Love, me

She couldn't even look at the computer screen. Jake read the note to himself. "Look, Darlin' you need to stay with me, or call Seth. You cannot be alone now. Things are going to start happening at home and it's obvious that someone wants you found."

"I want Seth to know what's going on. I know you want to protect me, but I have to let him do this. He knows everything and has taken care of me so far. I promise to be careful. And, I promise I'll keep you apprised of what's happening."

As they headed back to the car, Jake handed her

his cell phone and told her to call Seth now. Slowly she dialed the number. One of the waitresses went to get him once they finally answered the phone.

"Seth here, whatcha' need?"

"Seth, we need to talk. Can you meet me at the condo now?"

"Baby, what's up? Are you okay?"

Sterling began to cry. She was confused about everything now. No one was supposed to be hurt by all this. But now someone that was a known troublemaker was dead. Sterling was crying so hard that Jake took the phone from her and said, "This is Jake, and she's gotten some bad news from home. Could you just meet us back at her place?"

"I'll be right there."

Jake knew that Seth would take care of her, and he knew he couldn't leave her alone until Seth got there. Though they had never seen each other or spoken until just now, they both loved Sterling, and would do anything to help her.

When Seth walked in, Jake kissed her lightly on the cheek. As he passed Seth in the hall, he told him, "I won't get in your way, but don't you let anything happen to that lady."

"I'll always take care of her. She'll call you I suppose."

Jake left and headed back to work. He would not be able to concentrate for the next few days.

Seth went out to the balcony where Sterling sat

silently staring out at the ocean. "Baby, talk to me."

"Seth, someone died at home because of me. I never liked her, but I didn't wish her any harm." She had tears in her eyes now.

Seth knelt beside her and wiped away the tears as they fell. "Baby, it isn't your fault. You've tried to get that probationer off the street, but you aren't responsible for everyone or everything that happens. Why don't you just tell me what you know, and we'll try to figure this out."

Sterling told him what she had learned, and about the contacts she had made at home. Although he wasn't pleased, he knew that Jake wouldn't let her do anything foolish. Seth asked her what would happen now.

"All I can think is that the media will put two and two together and they'll start looking for me again. I've given people the information they need to find her, but that just started when this happened. I suppose now that the bullet train will be on a fast track and there will be little or no control. I just have to be ready. Ready for anything that happens, and be willing to run again. I won't go home until I know my family is safe, and that I can return safely."

"We've talked of this day, and you know how I feel. I'll follow you anywhere, and I'll always be there for you. I know you love him now, but you know that I can protect you better than anyone."

"Seth, I love you, but you know it's not romantic love. I love him too, but that won't keep me here, and it's not enough for him to follow me. He has no idea how I feel about him. We date, we're friends, but we haven't been intimate. I have to control that part of our relationship because I know I'm leaving one day soon."

They sat out on the balcony until dark and just watched the tide and the cars pass by beneath them. Although Sterling wasn't very hungry Seth made her try to eat some salad. They watched a rented movie, and she fell asleep on his lap. He dared not move her. She was peaceful now. He shifted his body and leaned back into the sofa, closing his eyes. About 4:00 a.m. she awakened with a scream. He calmed her down telling her it was just a bad dream. Then he took her hand and led her into the bedroom. He told her he would sleep on the couch, but he would be right outside the door.

"No, sleep with me. Seth, I'm scared, please don't leave me now."

"Okay Baby. I'm right here. Right here for you, just go to sleep."

Chapter Eighteen

The late news back home had picked up the missing Probation Officer as the lead story on all three local stations. Only one had alluded to the fact that this was the same complex that another Probation Officer had been missing from only a year before. Clay and Elliot had discussed that it was only a matter of time before all of the media got a hold of that information.

Elliot had reviewed the information contained in the sealed envelope with Clay. They discussed that all that was needed now was to verify again that what Marisa had discovered was still in fact accurate, and then file charges against Wanda. It would take the better part of the day to make the necessary contacts and verify the information. Clay told Elliot to do whatever had to be done, and to move on it as soon as possible. Marisa had left them good notes, phone numbers and each person she had spoken with regarding Wanda's alleged activities.

The next morning Elliot called in sick to work. He told his secretary to rearrange his court hearings if possible and if things couldn't be continued to find someone to cover for him. Right now he had more important business to attend to, and helping the county prosecute the various lawbreakers was not on his agenda.

He started his list of phone calls with the State Unemployment Compensation Board. That Board's central record division showed that checks were still being issued to Cynthia Reynolds; however, Wanda Newton stopped receiving checks almost a year ago. Cynthia Reynolds checks were still being sent to an out of county address. The records clerk indicated for more detailed information he would have to call the regional office where the claims originated.

Elliot then called the numbers Marisa had written

down in the notes. The first call was made to Debbie Meyers, the caseworker assigned to Wanda Newton.

"Hi, this is Debbie. Can I help you?"

"Hello Ms. Meyers, this is Elliot Green. I'm a deputy district attorney for the Central region of the state. Some time ago, a friend and colleague of mine called and discussed with you a former client by the name of Wanda Newton. Do you remember that call?"

"Oh sure. I don't recall the woman's name that called, but she just wanted to verify that Ms. Newton was indeed receiving benefits I believe. Is that right?"

"Well, yes and no. How long did Ms. Newton collect those checks, and can you tell me why she stopped receiving benefits?"

"Well let me look at her file. Hold on just a second. Okay, here it is. She received benefits for nine months, but then indicated she had taken a job out of state and would be leaving. I put in the necessary forms and stopped any further benefits from being generated. I haven't heard another word from her, so I assume things are finally going well for her."

"Okay, so she didn't need to tell you where she was going or come in to sign anything after that?"

"No, really it's a relatively simple, painless procedure to stop benefits. But, starting them is something different."

"I will need documentation of all checks issued to Ms. Newton and any applications that were filled out in her behalf. If you could, please fax copies of that to me at your earliest convenience, but put a hard copy in the mail and send it out in the next day or so. It seems that your department and the State have been bilked out of some money. Ms. Newton has been running a scam and we intend to prosecute her."

"Oh my gosh. Are you sure you have the right person? Wanda, er, I mean Ms. Newton was always so kind and gentle."

"Yes, Ms. Meyers, I'm quite sure I have the right person. Ms. Spencer is a probation officer. She was merely verifying information she had, and was attempting to get charges filed when Ms. Newton disappeared. Please get that information out at your earliest convenience."

"Oh sure. I'll do it as soon as I hang up. You should have the hard copy in a day or so. Call me again if you need anything further."

"You've been quite helpful. Thank you."

Elliot called Dan Burris next. He wondered if Wanda was still at the address listed on both files in this office. Quickly he dialed the number.

"Dan Burris."

"Hello Mr. Burris, I'm Elliot Green. I'm a deputy district attorney for the Central region of the state. Some time ago, a friend and colleague of mine called and discussed with you a former client by the name of Cynthia Reynolds. Do you remember that call?"

"Yeah vaguely. Is there something going on that I should know about?"

"Well yes. We have reason to believe that the person claiming to be Cynthia Reynolds is indeed someone else. Our records indicate that she is Wanda

Newton; however, recent information indicates that her true identity is actually Velma Harris-Reynolds. Is she still receiving benefits?"

"Yes. What can I do? I already gave her a description and she has the address where the checks are mailed."

"I'd like you to make a kind of sting operation with the okay of your supervisor. We want you to call her and indicate that records need to be updated or something along that line and get her in the office. We'll have someone down there take her into custody whenever you set up the appointment, or we can have the local sheriff arrest her and we can get her transported after she's in custody."

"That sounds easy enough. She hasn't been into the office in some months, always calling about car trouble, or health problems and this being a small county we just let things slide."

"Well exactly how long has she been receiving checks?"

"Let me look. It appears she's been issued checks weekly for the past eighteen months. Boy, do I feel stupid about this. I guess because of her age and all I really thought she was having a tough time finding work."

"Well, don't beat yourself up over this. At least we're on to her and I'm going to put a stop to it. Fax me a copy of anything pertinent, but put a hard copy in the mail and get it out to me at your earliest convenience. And, as soon as you have an appointment with her, notify me so we can get the warrant down to your sheriff."

"Hey, this is the first thing on my list of things to

do. I'll call her now, and get something set up. You should have the fax within the hour and the hard copies in the next day or two. Call me if you need anything else."

"Sure, and be casual, we don't want her to suspect anything. Thanks for your help."

Elliot felt pretty good about this. Now if only Ms. Newton would be cooperative and come in to sign some 'paperwork'. He decided since Marisa wasn't here to write up the amended violation report, he would look at her rules and do his best. He also started looking in the criminal code book to write up the affidavit and warrant. Of course it would still have to go through the felony screening division of his office, but if he could have it all done up for them it would be a mere formality. He decided to call Clay and tell him the good news.

"Clay Watson, ATF."

"Clay, it's Elliot. I made some calls and have pretty much verified enough information to get the case screened tomorrow and get a warrant for Newton. Have you heard from our friend?"

"Well, there has been a glitch in some stuff. Have you heard the news or read the paper lately?"

"No, is she okay?"

"She's upset, but things are going to be moving quickly I believe. Another one went missing. The news is she turned up dead. I don't think this is a coincidence. I'll meet you in the usual spot. Oh, and order mine to go. See you in about thirty minutes."

Elliot was in a rush to get to the coffee shop. Clay had no way of knowing that Elliot wasn't at work today. He just hoped they could talk, and figure out what was going on. And he hoped that no one from work would see him.

Clay got to the coffee shop first and was about to leave as Elliot rushed in. "I thought I told you to order mine to go?"

"I was off today. I'm sick can't you tell? Now tell me what in the hell is going on."

"Briefly, you should keep up on current events, or perhaps office gossip. Another P.O. went missing a few days ago. Well, a body was found yesterday morning. Badly beaten, and appears to have been tortured. Although it hasn't been in the news yet, I'm sure it will make it by this evening. Dani called me when she heard about the body; it was found near Marisa's old building. We decided that she would have to contact the detectives and let them know about the missing P.O. It seems that the one that went missing had a grudge or something against our girl. She may have intercepted one of my phone calls to Dani, and the rest as they say is history. Dani called the detective who happened to be over at the morgue yesterday afternoon. All he would say was that he couldn't say anything to her until contact was made with the family. Any questions?"

"Yeah, just one. Does Marisa know?"

"I have messaged her, so she knows. I'm sure she's upset, but she assures me she's fine. She also knows that she must be more careful now, and that things are going to start happening quickly."

"Okay. Well I need to write up an affidavit with a request for a warrant in order to get some new charges filed. It seems that Newton stopped receiving those checks about the same time as Marisa left; however, she is still collecting them at the same address under her

414

daughter's name. The caseworker is going to help me with a sting type of operation once I have the warrant on the system. He's going to call her and arrange for her to come in and sign some documents, and hopefully we can just grab her up. Of course, I'm not holding my breath or anything, but she has to slip up sometime."

"With all that's going on, I doubt she will slip up. You better get someone on that address as soon as you have the warrant, and grab her at home. Anyway, our girl is safe now. Let's get moving on this. I'll be in touch."

As usual, they parted at the exit as strangers. Both had things to do, and they didn't need anyone getting in the way or asking too many questions. On the way home Elliot decided to do one more thing. Clay headed back to his office. He wanted to send Marisa a note telling her what he had just learned. He also needed to contact Dani to see if she was staying calm. It was going to heat up again, and she would need some encouragement. Hurrying back to his office Clay called Dani.

"Probation, Ms. Taylor."

"Hi Dani, Clay here. I just spoke to our mutual friend and things are going to start heating up again most likely. You need to stay calm, deny everything, and just remember what you told them a year ago if they question you again. Everything and everyone is fine. Just keep it together, okay?"

"Yeah, sure. I just keep thinking of her, and that keeps me sane. I'll be fine. You know the whole office is abuzz with the recent development. There's all kinds of speculation. Of course most officers don't believe it has anything to do with the other. They think it's just one of her clients getting even. She really didn't have too many friends here, and she was not a very nice person to anyone on her caseload. Do what you have to do and just get our friend home. Don't worry about me. I'll be fine."

"Okay, good to hear. Take care and I'll be in touch."

Afterwards he sent a note to Marisa. The note said:

Things at home will be fine. E has made verification calls. Charges/warrant are pending. Stay calm. We have good address on person. Questions will probably begin again tomorrow. Stay tuned. Love, me

Elliot decided to use the other names for Ms. Newton and run criminal record checks on her in as many jurisdictions as he could. He had been thinking about this since reading the information initially, but until now he had not acted on his suspicions. There had to be a reason for her use of all the scrambled names and numbers.

Jake called Sterling everyday from work several times. She was okay under the circumstances, but he knew she was terribly shaken. He wondered how she would have ever gotten through this alone. He was glad for the friend she had in Seth. She had never really told him anything about Seth, but he could see that they came from different worlds. He wondered what Seth was running from, if anything. Today when he called, Seth answered and told him she had had a bad night. She was not doing much sleeping in the darkness, but she would sleep once daylight shined through her windows.

"May I speak to her please?"

"Yeah, hang on she's in the shower."

A few minutes later, Sterling came to the phone.

"Hi babe. Yes, Seth is taking good care of me, but he won't let me go anywhere out of his sight."

"Well, it has been a few days since you checked the account. Should I get you for lunch and we can check it? You know there has to be some news from home, and you really should stay on top of it. I know you're afraid, but Seth and I are here for you."

"Uh, yeah, sure. He really needs to get out of here and so do I. Maybe we can eat, check the account and then you can drop me off at the bar. He can just bring me home when he comes."

"Whatever you want Darlin'."

"Hey, to save time I'll have him drop me at your car in about thirty minutes okay?"

"Yeah if he doesn't mind that would be great."

"No, he'll do it. I'll see you shortly."

When they hung up Jake thought she sounded a lot better. Now if only she could stay in such a good mood when they checked her e-mail account. He had been scanning several daily newspapers, but he had seen nothing of a missing Probation Officer. Sterling had never even told him what city she was from, so he had no idea what papers to check. He knew only that she was from the Midwest. She didn't have a discernible accent, so he couldn't really pinpoint even the state. Apparently it slipped her mind to tell him, or it was to protect her in case he decided to try and help her without her knowledge. All he knew was that he had fallen in love with a girl that had a lot of problems right now, and he hoped she didn't disappear from his life forever.

Back home Elliot was having some interesting

responses from his calls to various criminal justice agencies. It seems Ms. Newton first started her criminal career as soon as her first husband, Henry, went off to war. She was arrested in various little burgs around her hometown for Prostitution and Lewd and Lascivious Acts. Later, out west while the in-laws were caring for her daughter, she began getting arrested for Petty Theft, Shoplifting, and a few Drunk and Disorderly charges. At that time she was using her infant daughter's name when she was arrested. It seems that there was never a long period or lull between her forays into crime. This information indicated to Elliot that she probably never served any lengthy jail time.

As the years passed her record moved all across the United States. Although Elliot could pretty well track her arrest record he could not find out much else about her because so much time had passed, and records were destroyed. Finally, there was a three-year period when there was no activity anywhere. Elliot presumed either she was locked up or had given up the criminal lifestyle. Then all of a sudden she was arrested in another fictitious name, Barbara Harris.

Her crimes were getting a bit bolder. Now her record consisted of Grand Larceny and bad check charges. However, because she appeared to be a first time offender, she was not given any jail time. Just after being released from a short probationary term she moved again. Her next offenses were Pandering, Prostitution, and various other offenses that indicated she was running a brothel. It was during this time that she had her daughter living with her. No one else was named as a co-conspirator on any of her arrests.

Elliot was having a hard time believing that she was acting independently. On these various offenses she was slapped with a three-year prison term and released to parole after her incarceration. Records did not indicate what was done with her daughter, whom she was now calling Simone Harris. Parole records had been destroyed, but it appeared she served a year on probation without incident, and then moved on.

For the past eight years there was no trace of Wanda Newton, or any of her known legal or alias names. Nor, was there any trace of her daughter, Cynthia Reynolds AKA Simone Harris, from the time Wanda was sentenced on the Prostitution charges in 1983 until Cynthia reached legal age in 1988. Although she was young, school records should be available in the areas where Wanda was supposedly living, but there were none. Elliot presumed that Cynthia was made a ward of the court and was quite possibly in foster care much of that time. Perhaps this is why Cynthia had no use for her mother at this point in time.

Unfortunately Elliot found only the outstanding violation warrant on Wanda, but he knew that this old background information would be used against her when she was arrested and later sentenced on the new charges he was having filed. With any luck, Wanda was in for a lengthy prison term on the additional charges and for the violation that was pending against her. Though there was already a violation of probation warrant pending, a warrant for new charges was a higher priority to most police agencies.

Elliot made one last call for today. As he dialed the Felony Screening Division of his office he said a little prayer. As soon as the receptionist answered he told her to check the computer to see if the charges had been screened today. "Yes, Mr. Green it looks like the charges have been filed and a warrant is active. Can I do anything else for you?"

"No, sweetheart. Well wait a minute, maybe you can do one more thing. Could you print a hard copy of all the charges and the warrant and give them to my secretary before you close up shop today?"

"Sure, no problem. I'll do that right now. Anything else?"

"No, that should do it. Thanks. Bye."

After hanging up Elliot then called Clay. He wanted to celebrate, but there was little time to waste now.

"Clay Watson, ATF."

"Clay, I'm glad you're still there. Let our friend know that a warrant has been issued. It's only a matter of time before we lock Wanda up and our friend can come home."

"Well I already informed her that a warrant was pending. I think I'll save the celebrating until we actually have her in custody. You need any help?"

"No, I'll notify the Sheriff's office down there, and I'm calling that caseworker back after I hang up with you."

"Keep me updated, and get busy. Talk to you later."

Elliot thought Clay was being too pessimistic. Wanda would have no idea when she came in to sign some papers at the unemployment office that she would be arrested. He dialed the number to Dan Burris' office.

"Dan Burris."

"Dan this is Elliot Green, regarding that Cynthia Reynolds case. We have the warrant."

"Great! I called her yesterday and set something up for tomorrow afternoon. I figured you would get those charges filed and I wanted her to think that it was a 'no hurry' paperwork situation. She whined and cried the blues a few minutes, but I just told her that she had a few days to figure out the transportation problem. I told her that I had let it slide so many times, and now my supervisor was breathing down my neck so I couldn't mail the forms to her. She seemed okay with that, and said she didn't mean to cause me any trouble."

"Okay, well I'll notify your Sheriff about the warrant. What time is her appointment?"

"It's at two o'clock. If I were you I'd tell the Sheriff to come in an unmarked car, just so she doesn't get spooked."

"Yeah, good idea on the car. You call me as soon as she gets to your office before you see her. I want to know every detail."

"Sure, no problem. This will give the office something to talk about probably for the next few months."

"Well, I have to go, but will be looking forward to your call tomorrow afternoon. See ya!"

Elliot called his county Sheriff's office warrant division and had them fax a copy down south. He also requested that they make sure the warrant was active on the NCIC computers and any other regional or national crime computers. He didn't want her slipping through the system this time. He had made sure to include all known alias names, social security numbers and most recent address.

It was getting late, but Elliot decided to make one more call to the Sheriff down south in Webster County. He spoke to one of the warrant officers, but this deputy was going to be off for the next few days. The deputy indicated he had written all the information down and would make sure the next day's duty officer would make the day shift sergeant aware. Elliot thanked him and hung up. The next twenty-four hours or so were going to seem to take an eternity for Elliot. He tried to watch television, and work on some case notes, but he just couldn't focus on anything but Marisa. He was so glad she was safe. He had nearly given up hope of ever seeing her again. Now he just hoped that when she returned things could go back to what they were before. He had so much to tell her, to ask her.

The next afternoon came and went without a phone call from Dan Burris. Elliot waited until three o'clock and then he called Burris. "Dan Burris."

"Dan, this is Elliot Green. Did she come in?"

"No, she missed the appointment, the Sheriff is sitting over at the diner across the street waiting for my call, but I think she is onto me."

"Why would she be onto you?"

"Well she called this morning and said she would be in town early and wanted to come in at 7:30 a.m., but I knew the warrant division didn't even open up 'til around nine. I figured that no one would know what was going on, so I told her I just couldn't see her any earlier."

"Okay, and what did she say?"

"Well, she said she didn't see why she couldn't just come in and sign the papers and be on her way. I told her that she needed to sign them in my presence. I think I've screwed up the whole operation. I'm really sorry."

"Look, I'll just have the Sheriff's office head out to her place and scoop her up there. I'll be in touch."

"Okay. I'm really sorry. If I hear from her again, I'll get in touch with you. Let me know something."

"Sure, no problem. Hey, it was a long shot. Thanks for trying anyway."

Elliot was steamed now. He called the Webster County Sheriff's Office and spoke to someone in the warrant division. They told him that they had a car in that area and would go right out. The deputy told him to stay by his phone and they would be in touch shortly. Elliot just had a hunch this was not going to be as easy as he had initially hoped. He was glad that Clay had insisted on not telling Marisa anymore until Wanda was locked up. At this point he blamed himself for the problems in Webster County. Now the waiting game began again.

About an hour later, Elliot received word from the warrant division that no one was living at the address on the warrant. They did say that it looked like someone had been there very recently, but there were no clothes left in the closets, and only a few personal items were scattered around. Neighbors indicated that the couple had been renting there for years, but in the past week or so they had been moving things out of the house slowly. No one seemed to know where they were from, or where they were going. Elliot decided he had to tell Clay right away.

"Clay Watson, ATF."

"Clay, Elliot here. I have some disturbing news."

423

"Yeah, what is it?"

"Things didn't go as planned down at the unemployment office today. So, I had the Sheriff's office go out to the address we had on her, and it appears she has vanished into thin air."

"Damn! Now what?"

"Well, I've done some research on her. She moves effortlessly around the country. She started getting arrested in the late 60's and she really hasn't slowed down. I don't know what to do at this point. Our girl did an extensive amount of investigating, but there are no other leads at this point."

"Do you think her daughter would be of any help?"

"As I see it, either her daughter is as devious as she is, or she truly wants nothing to do with her mother."

"Well, if we call the daughter and she is in on this with her mom, we tip them off that we are looking. If we call and she really does hate her mom, then maybe she would help us."

"I don't know. Our girl may be able to help us here. I think you should tell her what's going on. She needs to know anyway since Wanda is on the move again."

"Yeah, I'll get back to you on that. Soon, hopefully. I have to go."

It was time to tell Marisa the bad news. Clay gathered his thoughts and sent an e-mail to Marisa. He hoped she held some answers.

Bad news. E set up a sting with caseworker, but she didn't take the bait. Sheriff went to address; she was gone. Neighbors were no help. We think daughter may hold the answer, but need input from you. ASAP! I'll be here all night waiting for your answer. Love, me

Jake was reading the most recent e-mail from home over her shoulder. She no longer wanted total privacy when things came in from home. They both finished reading it at the same time, and looked at each other pensively.

"Well Darlin' I think they want some insight. You know this woman better than they do, probably better than anyone. What do you think they should do?"

"Well, I hate dragging an innocent person back into something they tried to leave behind, but I don't think we have any other choice. They have to call her, find out what she knows. If she really despises her mother I think she should be willing to help. I guess we'll find out soon enough."

Sterling wrote a brief e-mail to Clay and hoped he would act quickly before anymore harm came to anyone.

You need to call daughter. I believe she hates her mom. Something or someone needs to reach her, make her understand what her mom is capable of doing. Be gentle. If no luck, there is another way. I'll come back tomorrow to check your progress. Be careful. Love, me

Clay read the note through three times before calling Elliot. They decided that Elliot was the one that should call her. He was the one filing the charges, and he knew the questions he needed to ask. Clay just reminded him not to push her, Marisa had indicated there was another way to reach her if their call didn't do the trick. Elliot decided he would call her tonight from home. Hopefully she would be responsive to him, and even if she weren't maybe he would learn something about Wanda that would help him in his search for her.

About 8:00 p.m. he called the last number that was listed for Cynthia Reynolds. As the phone rang, he hoped that she had not moved and the number had been reassigned to someone else. He didn't need any other obstacles at this point. On the fifth ring a young woman answered the phone.

"Hello."

"Hi, may I speak to Cynthia please?"

"Speaking. Who's this?"

"Cynthia my name is Elliot Green. I hope you will talk to me a minute. I'm a deputy district attorney, and I am investigating your"

"Look, before you go any further. I know you aren't investigating me, because I have done nothing wrong. If you want to know about my mother call someone who cares!"

"Wait, Miss Reynolds. Please let me explain. Don't hang up. Please."

"You have three minutes to tell me why you people keep bothering me!"

"Okay, look. About a year ago your mother's Probation officer disappeared. Your mother disappeared about the same time. Although a body has not been found, her family and everyone else presume that the officer is dead and that your mother killed her. Your mother had been making threats against this officer, and now both of them have vanished. Just when we thought things were going our way, and we were close to apprehending her, she vanished again."

"Before you waste anymore of my time or yours let me make this clear to you. I have nothing whatsoever to do with my mother. As far as I'm concerned my mother is dead. Do you understand that?"

"Yes ma'am I do. It's just that, and what I am going to tell you I hope remains between us. I have it on good authority that the officer is not dead, but is in hiding from your mother. She believes if she stays away, no harm will come to anyone else."

"Look Mr. Green, I'm real sorry about your officer and all, but I can't help you. I'm sorry. Please don't call me again."

The next sound was a dial tone in Elliot's ear. "Damn it!"

Elliot called Clay at home but there was no answer. He dialed him at work, still no answer. It wasn't worth paging him now. He would just wait until the morning. He wondered what else Marisa thought could work. He didn't push Cynthia, and hopefully she would think about this phone call all night like he was doing right now.

The next morning when Elliot got into work he already had two messages from Clay. He called him before even checking the court dockets.

"Clay Watson, ATF."

"Clay, Elliot here. I hope you have some ideas. I called the daughter last night. She really blasted me, and said she had nothing to do with her mother. I didn't push her. I did try to reason with her, briefly, before she cut me off. She told me she was really sorry but that she couldn't help me. Now what?"

"Well, now I e-mail our mutual friend and let her tell me the other idea she has. Calm down. We're going to get nowhere by getting excited. That's how mistakes get made. I'll get back to you as soon as I know something."

Clay sent a message to Marisa and hoped he wouldn't have to wait long.

E called daughter. After chewing him out she indicated she could be of no assistance. What is your other idea? He says he didn't push. Love, me

Sterling had Seth accompany her to Jake's condo to use the computer. She decided that everyone at home could probably be trusted by now. She had called Jake at work and he agreed there was probably no sense in traipsing around town at this point, and things were getting down to the wire so she needed a quicker response since she refused to use the phone.

She typed out a note to Clay that said:

Hang tight. The ball is in my court now. I'll keep you posted. Things will be fine. Love, me

Clay was surprised by the quick response, and he wondered what she meant by this cryptic note. He called Elliot and told him she had taken the lead and they would just await her further instructions. Elliot questioned whether this was the smartest thing to do, but Clay told him, "Look, she has done a great job of staying on top of this for this long, why question her judgment now?"

"Okay I agree to a point. But, we don't know where she is, if she is safe, or where the other person is at this point?"

"You're right about all of it, but I'm not going to second guess her and possibly screw something up. You agreed from the start that you would let me handle this, now back off and let her do what she thinks is best."

"Alright. You're right about my commitment to this project. She has been right about a lot of things. Just keep me posted. If I'm not here, just tell my secretary you called and I'll get back to you as soon as I can. I have a bunch of hearings today, so I'll be in and out."

"Fine. Talk to you later."

Seth and Sterling went to the pool. She told him what had happened at home. Seth asked her if she really wanted to move forward on this, or if he could just persuade her to stay in Daytona forever. He knew the answer before she gave it.

"Look Seth, I told you a long time ago, this was not a permanent situation. I have to do what I have to do. The time is right. Things are happening at home, and I want to go back to my family, to that life I had before. This has been a great adventure, but I don't belong in it anymore."

"Baby, I know how you feel about me, about us, but I'll always worry about you. How do you think you can fix things from here?"

"Maybe I can't fix things, but I can set things up so that when I do get home everyone will be fine."

"You know, that's what I always loved about you. Your determination in all you do. It sets you apart from everyone."

"Will you take me to the boardwalk? I need to make a phone call."

"I guess you don't want to use our phone huh?"

"You guessed right babe."

"Yeah, when do you wanna go?"

"Now would be good. The sooner the better for everyone I think. Let me run upstairs and get the number."

"I'll meet you out front."

A few minutes later they roared off on Seth's Harley. She knew she wouldn't be taking many more of these rides with him. She hugged him as they rode. They got down to the boardwalk, and she asked him to go get a place on the pier where they could have lunch. She didn't think the call would take very long. He agreed, but told her he would be watching her from his perch above the water.

She stood for a moment and silently said a little prayer. Slowly she dialed the number. Just as she was about to hang up a woman answered. "Hello."

"Hi, is this Cynthia?"

"Yes, who wants to know this time?"

"Cynthia, please hear me out. A friend of mine called you yesterday I believe. He was calling about the person that calls herself your mother."

"You listen to me! I have nothing to say to you or

her, or anyone else. That person died a long time ago in my mind. I would like to go on with my life and pretend she doesn't exist, why won't all of you just leave me alone?"

"Cynthia, my name is Marisa. I was your, um, uh, Wanda's probation officer. I have been hiding from her and everyone for over a year. It's time to put this thing to bed and let you and me get on with our lives. I don't want to torment you. I just want your help. Will you please just talk to me for a minute?"

"I don't know what you think I can help you with. I have no use for Velma, or whatever name she is going by these days. She still tries to contact me from time to time. I finally gave up trying to hide. She has been relentless in pursuing me, now I just hang up on her."

"I know she must have done some pretty horrible things in the past for you to feel this way, but I really have no other place to turn. Can I ask you just a few questions, and I promise no one will bother you again."

"Yeah let's get this over with. And you don't know the half of it, why I hate her so bad."

"Look, I'll listen if you want to tell me. Or I can just state my case and promise not to call you again."

"You know, you people are chasing a ghost. She lost herself a long time ago. She uses people, she hurts people, and she even kills people to get what she wants. I'm the only person, aside from you apparently, that she hasn't totally destroyed. I try to think of myself as an orphan, not a victim. I have no idea who my real father is, and I doubt that she does either. I know what my birth certificate says, but I also know her husband was out of the country before I was even conceived. I found that out when I was about ten. You see I was left with strangers

431

to be raised while she ran off and did her thing. Then when she finally found her calling I was raised by whores. She ran a bunch of whorehouses before she finally got busted when I was thirteen. You don't know how many times I wished her dead before that. She put me to work when I was eleven years old. Yeah, miss probation officer, my own mother turned me out to make a buck." Cynthia's voice quivered, but Sterling could tell this girl was not going to cry.

"I'm listening. I'm really sorry. I had no idea."

"Well you know Velma is a real class act. Of course she was laying down with anything that paid her price. She charged a bit more for me though. And, she claimed to protect me; she stayed right there in the room and watched, making sure they weren't too rough with me. And do you know who my first customer was? It was her boyfriend, Mr. Randolph. Said he wanted to get the best I had to offer, and "break me in". I was 11 years old! Do you have any idea how humiliating it is for someone to take something like that away from you and then to have your own mother watch and encourage you to do something that you know is wrong? You have no idea how hard I have worked to turn my life around and forget the past, but as long as she is still alive I guess I'll have no peace. You can't imagine just how happy I was when she finally got busted, and I got sent off to yet another foster home. Of course to make it easier for me she said she called me a different name during the time she put me to work. I was Simone then. I guess it has a classier sound than my given name. So you see, as soon as I was old enough to slip from her grasp I took the first bus out of town and never looked back. She found me though, every time. For that past few years I've been here. I'm tired of running. I know she has used my name in her life of crime, and she's called me a million times and tried to apologize, but you know, you can't go back. She is a detestable creature. I hate her, and I wish she was dead. I might go to hell for all the horrible things I have thought about her, but I can't think even one good thought about her."

There was a brief period of silence before Sterling spoke. Finally she said, "You know I can't tell you how sorry I am for bringing you into this, but there is a chance that I can get her out of your life for a very long time if you help me set a trap for her."

"How long?"

"Only a guess, but you said something earlier that may add to it. You said she had destroyed people, killed people. What did you mean by that?"

"What names do you have for her?"

"Well, Velma Harris Reynolds, Barbara Harris, Velma Higgins, and your name."

"Barbara Higgins was her cousin. It was one of the first names she started using. Barbara was killed in an unexplained accident. My mother told me once when she was drunk that she and her boyfriend killed her and made it look like an accident. No one was ever arrested, but it's a safe bet one of them killed her."

"I don't know if you are aware, but another probation officer was found murdered recently there. Velma threatened me many times. I believed she was capable of following through and that's why I left."

"Well, there was a reason that person was killed. I bet when someone finds Velma she will have already started using that person's identification. Velma is not a stupid woman. She is a cold, heartless bitch, but she is not stupid."

"Cynthia, if she did murder Barbara, or was involved in anyway, she can still be tried for that. There is no statute of limitation on murder. Will you help me catch her?"

"I don't know what more I can do. She knows how I feel about her."

"Yes she does, I suppose, but you said she still calls you. She must think that her twisted version of love will conquer all. If you're right about Barbara's death and they convict her, on top of all the new charges that have been filed in the last few days I think that your, Velma, is looking at a life sentence at least."

"Tell me what you want me to do."

Sterling thought a moment, and said, "Do you have any children?"

"God no! There is no way I would ever have a child with the bad blood I have running through my veins."

"Does she know how you feel about having children?"

"No. I never talk to her."

"Do you suppose she would be interested if you did have children?"

"Yeah, I guess maybe she would. One more person she could use."

"When does she call you, or is there any pattern to her calls?"

"Well she hasn't called in a month or so. She

usually calls me if she has moved or if she is in some more trouble."

"Well then I guess she'll be calling you soon."

"Oh? What now?"

"Well my friend tried to serve a warrant yesterday, but she had moved quietly and no one knows where she is. She has to know they are getting close to her."

"Okay, so how do I get in touch with you?"

"At this point I would like you to trust one of my friends. He is in town with you and can talk with you about what to do so they can arrest her. Will you talk to him?"

"Did I already talk to him last night?"

"Actually you talked to one of them, there are two working together. I believe you talked to Elliot Green. The other guy is Clay Watson. And again, I'm Marisa Spencer, but please don't tell anyone besides either of them that you have talked to me."

"I think I scared Mr. Green off. I doubt he'll want to talk to me again."

"Right now Mr. Green will do whatever I ask. I would really appreciate anything you can tell them, or do for them."

"Okay Marisa, I'll help you on one condition."

"And what is that?"

"Get her convicted and out of my fucking life

forever!"

"I swear to you I'll do my best. Thank you again.
I'll have my friends call you soon. And, someday soon I
hope that maybe we can meet. I have information I think
you might be interested in learning more about."

"You know my number. Just do what you have to
do with Velma."

The dial tone came on quickly. Sterling took a
chance and made one more call. "Clay Watson, ATF."

"I don't have much time, so don't ask any
questions. Don't try to trace this call. Okay?"

"Yes, okay. God I'm so glad to hear your voice!"

"I called Cynthia. She told me the whole sordid
story, but there may be one more murder that needs to be
re-investigated. It seems Barbara Higgins was not really
in an accident all those many years ago, so work on that.
But, Cynthia will talk to you and Elliot. I think the way
to go here is that she is pregnant or just had a child and is
having some life threatening difficulties and she needs
something medical from her mother. She said she would
do whatever she could to help you as long as we
promised to get Wanda out of her life permanently. She
also said that Wanda usually calls her when she moves or
when she is in some kind of legal trouble. You better call
her now, and figure something out before Wanda beats
you to the punch. I'll be in touch. Oh, and thanks. I love
you, bye."

Before Clay could utter another word, she was
gone. Quickly he called Elliot. "I just spoke to our girl.
We need to contact Cynthia now. Our girl called her and
Cynthia agreed to help us. We need to get her now
before she has time to think about it and change her mind,

and before Wanda calls her. Can you make the call?"

"I'll call her now. Stay put, we may need to meet her or something. I'll get right back with you."

Elliot frantically searched through the papers in his briefcase looking for Cynthia's number. Once he found it, he dialed it quickly.

"Hello."

"Cynthia, this is Elliot Green. I was told by a friend that you want to talk to me."

"No, Mr. Green you misunderstood. I want Velma the hell out of my life. I'll do what you need me to do, but I would really like to be left alone."

"Okay, I'm sorry. My friend indicated that perhaps we should tell your, I mean, Wanda, or Velma that you are having a problem pregnancy and that you need something from her medically. Do you think she would do that for you?"

"I think for a price Velma would do something for me."

"A price?"

"Yeah, she wants me to love her. She wants me to send her money. She uses people and discards them like garbage."

"Okay, I believe I understand. Do you think you could tell her that you need medical information or blood perhaps and we could meet you at the hospital and arrest her?"

"And, what do you suppose I can give her?"

"Do you think you could lie to her as she has lied to you all these years and tell her that you finally realize the sacrifices she made for you, and that you want her to be able to save your baby so you can all be a family again?"

"Mr. Green, if it means getting this person out of my life for good, I would go to hell and back. Give me your number and when she calls I'll set something up. Just realize you get one chance at this. Like I told your friend, Marisa, Velma is not a stupid woman."

"I know Cynthia, and I promise I'll do whatever is necessary to get her off the street and out of your life forever. My office number is 555-1889, and my home number is 532-9043. Call me anytime, day or night. I'll leave the details to you, just don't wait to call me when you know something."

"I'll take care of it Mr. Green. You just hold up your end of the deal. I'll have one more request when this is all said and done. Goodbye Mr. Green."

Elliot called Clay to report how things went with Cynthia.

"Clay Watson, ATF."

"Clay, Elliot here. I called her. Man, she must have ice water running through her veins. She says she will manage to get Wanda to a hospital under the impression Wanda needs to donate some blood to help save her dying, unborn grandchild. She expects a call soon since our girl told her that Wanda had moved within the last day or two. She sternly warned me that we have one chance to do this, because Wanda isn't a stupid woman."

"I hope you gave her all your phone numbers. You call me anytime, day or night. When she tells you where the meet is, I want to know. I think we should be there, in addition to any uniform officers that you think are necessary.

"Oh I agree. I'm going to call the warrant division now and put them on alert. I imagine she'll go to the hospital nearest her, which is Community General. I don't think I'll notify their security department yet though. I don't want some gung ho officer getting in the way. Well I have a hearing in about ten minutes. My secretary has been instructed to page me with a 911 in case she calls. I'll keep you posted. See you later."

As soon as Clay hung up he sent an e-mail to Marisa.

Whatever you said to her worked. She talked with E. Things will probably happen in next day or so. It was great to hear your voice. You know I would never betray your trust. You can call me at home or here if you want. I just wish this was all over and I could look at you while we talk. Love, me

After she and Seth had eaten lunch, they walked around the boardwalk and went into some of the shops. They dropped over at the bar and picked up some inventory lists and order sheets that he needed to look over before the day was over. Before going back to the condo though she asked him to go back to Jake's condo so she could check her e-mail. He agreed, but didn't think she would have anything so quickly. She, however, knew just how fast things were happening.

She logged on with Jake's password and opened up her e-mail account. To Seth's surprise there were two notes. One was from Jake just telling her to have a nice day. The other was from Clay. Both made her smile.

Seth waited while she responded to Clay's note.

Not surprised she will work with us. She has had it bad. Unbelievable things have happened to her at the hand of Wanda. Will tell you when I get home, I'm sure she won't talk to you about it. Keep me posted. Be careful. Neither of them are stupid. Love, me

The next three days passed without word from anyone. Finally about 10:00 p.m. one evening Wanda called Cynthia. "Hello."

"Hello Doll, it's momma."

"Momma? Why are you calling me so late?"

"Well Doll, I just wanted to tell you things didn't work out with the place I was staying, and I moved again. I don't know exactly how long I'll be here but I haven't talked to you for some time."

"Mommy, I'm so scared. I don't know how to tell you this, but I need something from you."

"What is it Doll? You know I would do anything for you. I just wish we could get past all that stuff you want to believe about me."

"Mommy, I'm pregnant."

"Oh Doll! I'm gonna be a grandma?"

"Well Mommy I don't know about that. I have been having some really bad problems. They aren't sure if I can carry it. I guess she's got something wrong that I can't fix."

"She? My baby's gonna have a doll of her own?"

"Yeah, Mommy I'm having a baby girl if she makes it. I thought I could show you how much I really love you. I wanna name her after you, but I am afraid she's really sick."

"What can I do? And, I don't like my name that's why I never use it. Why don't you let me pick her name? That would be nicer for me? Please?"

"Oh Mommy, I'm scared. I have to go to the doctor all the time. They want information I can't give them. I know you sacrificed so often when I was a kid because my dad ran off and left us. Mommy I don't think I can do this alone. I'm so glad you called me Mommy."

"Well Doll where's the father? You know I can't tell you too much about your Daddy. He knocked me up and didn't stick around to even see you. Got himself shipped off overseas, then they claimed he was killed. You know, I think he's still over there."

"Well Mommy, I guess I don't have much better luck in picking a father for my girl either. I just hope she is nicer to me than I've been to you. Oh Mommy, I never knew how you must have loved me to take such good care of me."

"Well, what does the doctor want to do? What things have they already done? And Doll you need to stop crying, you're gonna make yourself sick and lose that baby for sure."

"They just keep running blood tests. Telling me that she needs some kind of transfusion, but my blood will kill her. They want me to have my parents to give blood to see if they match. I told them my Daddy was dead, and I don't have any other blood relation besides you. I just told them you were out of the country on a long trip. But they keep telling me if they don't find a match soon she can't live."

"Well, will it take long? I mean if I go and give them the blood and I match, how long will it take?"

"Oh Mommy would you?"

"Well, of course. But I can't be held up there too long. I have things going and I need to find some permanent place to live. Do we have to have an appointment?"

"No, he told me as soon as you get in to rush right to the hospital lab and get the test. It won't hurt you Mommy I promise."

"Well, how about I meet you at the hospital emergency room tomorrow about noon? Then we can just walk over to the lab."

"Oh yes Mommy. Oh Mommy I'm so glad you called me. I've been worried sick. And, you be thinking of a name for your little girl. I'll see you at noon at Community General, in the ER. Maybe after we can have lunch?"

"Well one thing at a time Doll. I'll see you tomorrow."

Before calling Elliot tonight Cynthia went to the bathroom and threw up. She detested Velma and she detested the things she had to say with such sincerity. Velma was a vile person, and talking to her for any length of time made Cynthia sick. She dialed Elliot's home number. He picked up on the third ring.

Groggily he said, "Hello."

"Mr. Green, Velma just called me. She took the bait and is meeting me tomorrow at noon at the Community General's Emergency Room. Don't be obvious, and don't delay. Remember, you'll only get one chance with her."

Before he could utter a word she had hung up. He jumped out of bed and called Clay at home.
"Hello."

"Clay, it's me. Cynthia just called. Wanda is meeting her tomorrow at noon in the Community General ER. That's all I know. She called, stated the facts, and I didn't utter one word after saying hello."

"Okay let's not screw this up. I'll be there in the ER around 10:30 a.m. just in case they decide to come early. I think it would be wise for you to be there as well, but stay in the shadows. We need to call the Sheriff's warrant division or talk to the night duty sergeant and let them know what's going on. I think things will be fine. We just need to grab her as soon as she is inside the doors. If we do it outside we don't know who else will be with her and watching."

"I agree. I'll go over early and see if I can't pretend to be a doctor, wear a lab coat and blend into the scenery. I'll have the hard copy of the warrant, but I won't tell security until just before noon. I'll take one of the female undercover deputies with me. She can handle the arrest and transportation. Afterwards you find Cynthia. She said she wanted one more thing when this was all over."

"Fine. I guess I'll see you in the ER tomorrow morning."

Neither of them would get much sleep the rest of the night. Cynthia was anxious too. She had not spent any time with her mother in the past five years. Trying to overcome the look of hate she had for her was going to be difficult. She also needed to look a little pregnant when she arrived at the hospital, just in case Elliot wasn't ready for her.

The next morning Elliot went into work and picked up some things to take with him to work on just in case he had extra time. This was all so clandestine he hadn't even told Michael. He knew Michael had been involved earlier, but things pretty much had settled on the back burner. He had also neglected to tell the detectives working the missing person case on Marisa that he had a warrant for Wanda. He figured any outside help at this point could just screw things up. For now, he and Clay would work things out. Once Wanda was in custody they would both have some explaining to do, but by then Marisa would be on her way home.

Chapter Nineteen

Elliot arrived at the hospital about ten o'clock; Clay walked in just minutes after him. They decided to walk around the emergency room waiting area checking for a good view of the door. Clay would sit away from Elliot and closer to the exit just in case he needed to block her from leaving. Elliot had spoken with the duty nurse and the triage nurse telling them briefly what was going to happen if all happened as he thought it should. They decided that the chief resident should be informed as well. None of them wanted to involve the security department. The resident looked at the paperwork and felt they could handle it. He did require them to call the security department as soon as they had her in custody though just for the record. Of course Elliot understood that the resident and nurses wanted him to make it look like they had no idea what had just happened. Elliot had no problem with this little area of deceit.

Both men blended pretty well into the hospital waiting room scenery. Pretending to read papers and magazines and keeping an eye on every person, male and female, that walked in or out of the door.

About twenty minutes before noon a young, attractive woman walked through the doors and glanced around the waiting room. She appeared to be a few months pregnant. Neither Clay, nor Elliot had ever seen Cynthia, but both thought this had to be her. Clay caught her eye and nodded his head slightly. She gave him a faint smile and looked at her watch. She looked back around the room and Clay nodded his head toward Elliot, who by now had made eye contact with her. She nodded to him slightly. The duty nurse was watching and winked at Clay. Now they all waited for the last player of this game to arrive. All glanced at the clock at once. Only ten more minutes until Wanda should arrive.

Cynthia sat toward the back of the waiting room where Clay had pointed out some seats. This gave the men the advantage of sealing Wanda from the exit and gaining control of the situation. As she walked past Clay a small piece of paper fell from her hand. Clay waited until she was seated; he then bent to pick up the paper. He opened it up and read what it said, *Do Not Forget-one chance! Be fast, I hate her and don't want to be with her any longer than necessary!!*

Clay nodded his head affirmatively to Cynthia when he caught her eye. Cynthia flipped through a magazine, finding it too difficult to concentrate on anything but the people walking in and out of the room. She knew she had to look numb, and she may be forced to cry when she saw Velma. The clock ticked by minute after minute. Wanda was late. Cynthia expected no less from her. Elliot was about to give up hope when he noticed Cynthia start to grimace and thought he saw her cry. Slowly he turned his head and saw Wanda saunter through the main doors, glancing about as she walked. She didn't appear to be looking for her daughter, but rather looking for someone to pop from the shadows and arrest her.

Wanda was guarded as she walked toward Cynthia. Clay waited until she was closer to her daughter and some distance from an exit. Cynthia stood to greet her mother, hoping that it would be the last time she ever saw her.

"Well Doll, I don't have much time, so let's get to the lab."

"Oh mommy! I'm so glad you can help me."

Just as Cynthia spoke those words Elliot was behind Wanda and Clay had stepped between her and the exit. Both men and Cynthia knew she would have no

446

place to run. As Wanda put out her arms to hug her daughter, a gleam grew in Cynthia's eyes.

"Wanda Newton, Velma Reynolds," Elliot questioned.

Wanda did not respond she just stared at her daughter. Cynthia gave her mother an evil grin, and said, "Velma, you have helped me more than you can imagine. These men have something to talk to you about."

"I have no idea what you're talking about. Cynthia what have you done?"

"Me? What have I done? I have done nothing but try to get away from you my whole life. Hopefully this will end it. I hope you rot in prison because that's where these men are taking you! Don't ever try to contact me again!" With that said, Cynthia pulled a cushion from under her top, threw it in the trashcan and walked away.

As Clay was handcuffing Wanda and Elliot was reading the warrant, Cynthia didn't even look back as Wanda screeched, "You little whore, you'll pay for this!"

Clay instructed the admitting supervisor to contact the hospital security department. Wanda was cursing at both men, at Cynthia who was already gone, and at Marisa. Elliot had paged the undercover officer that was sitting in the parking lot. Neither man wanted to deal with the paperwork, or the hassle of transporting her. Once the transport deputy came inside she did a pat down search of her and found she was carrying a concealed weapon. This was a crime in itself, which would be added later to her list of offenses already filed. Also, in her wallet the officer found identification belonging to Monika Garza, but the picture and identifiers were of Wanda.

Wanda refused to answer any questions about the identification, or how she arrived at the hospital. They assumed she had arrived by taxi, but she would not confirm or deny that assumption. Once she was en route to the lock-up the two men went out into the parking lot looking for a clue. What they didn't see was her friend, Mr. Randolph, sitting at a meter on the street, not in the hospital parking lot. He had seen her being taken away in handcuffs. He waited until both men had left the lot before pulling away. He had not noticed when Cynthia left before all the commotion started.

When Elliot got back to his desk he called Detective Konjesky to inform him that Wanda Newton had been apprehended. Konjesky asked him if he had asked Wanda any questions regarding Marisa's disappearance, but he had not. Elliot alluded to the fact that he believed Marisa had something to do with Wanda's apprehension. When Konjesky pressed him for more details, Elliot indicated he had some other things to do, but he would keep in touch. Konjesky radioed Matheson and told him they needed to get to the lock up and talk to Wanda.

Clay immediately sent Marisa a note:

Wanda is in custody--no bond! She had a concealed weapon when apprehended. Cynthia left before anyone could talk to her. Thank you, you're safe now. Please call. Please come home. Love, me

Elliot called Michael to inform him that Wanda was in custody. Michael then asked Elliot to contact Tom Roberts and meet in his office in fifteen minutes. Elliot hung up and asked his secretary to find Tom and relay the message. Elliot then called Clay.

"Clay Watson, ATF."

"Clay, great work today! Man, I feel like a weight has been lifted. Did you tell our girl?"

"I sent her a note, but she hasn't responded. Yes, good work. Now, I just wonder what we should do about Cynthia."

"Well I have an idea Cynthia will be in touch with us. She said there was one more request when this was all over. I think it's all over at this point."

"Well, just let me know. I wonder what she wants besides for us to never contact her again."

"Do you think she wants money?"

"Nah, not really. Probably more than money, peace perhaps."

"Well I have a meeting with the D.A. in less than five minutes. I need to update him on everything. Do you think it's safe at this point to tell him that Marisa's okay?"

"NO! We made a promise to her that she was calling the shots. She hasn't indicated to me that she's ready to come home or for her secret to be revealed. You keep your damn mouth shut! Do you hear me?"

"Calm down! Alright I'll keep the secret, but you need to find out when we can let everyone know she's okay."

"You just tell the D.A. what you know from today, and from your research or whatever you want to call it. You let me handle the other stuff. I'll let you know when the time is right, but you figure out a way to keep her secret."

"Fine Clay, I'll keep my promise to you and to her. But you let her know we want her home, now. I'll talk to you later."

Elliot reached Michael's office just as Tom was sitting down. Both men looked at him as he entered. "Michael, Tom, nice to see you both. I have some extraordinary news."

"Yes, so you said earlier," Michael stated.

Tom said, "Okay, I'll bite. What news?"

"Well today I had the audacity to apprehend one of the probation department's fugitives. Let me tell you, Ms. Wanda Newton was not a happy camper. I'm not sure either of you know this, but I've been doing some homework on dear Wanda. And, with what I found out I was able to file additional charges against her. Also, I think there will be more charges forthcoming, but I need to contact some other jurisdictions and our own homicide department."

Michael stated, "Wait a minute! Back up just a bit. Who told you to go out and investigate this person without authorization from me?"

"Well, no one actually. I was acting on a tip. So, I just started with a little shred of information and soon I had enough for more charges here and down south in Webster County."

Tom sat perplexed by the conversation swimming around him. Finally after about forty-five minutes Elliot had replayed the whole story to both men's satisfaction. Of course the obvious question was; who gave Elliot the tip? Elliot just said he had an anonymous phone call, and decided to look things up on his own after that information panned out. Michael indicated that he needed to call the detectives looking for Marisa and let them know.

"Yeah Boss, I already did. I told them what they needed to question Wanda, but I doubt they have any luck. However, I do believe Wanda just may have some information on the other P.O. that was killed."

"Well we need to stay on top of this thing. Tom I want you to get this in front of Judge Taylor immediately for the violation. We can let the other things wait a bit, but I don't want her out of jail any time soon. Understand?"

"Sure Michael, I'll get right on it! I'm sure the Judge will have no problem making room for her on the docket in the next day or two."

Elliot informed them, "You guys realize that there is a two week hold on her, due to the new charges, and there is no bond. Also, because she had a weapon on her when she was arrested she will have some federal charges pending as soon as I get paperwork to the ATF. That alone should add an additional five years to whatever sentence she receives."

Tom stood to leave, telling them both he would be in touch as soon as he knew anything. Michael asked Elliot to stay. Michael then closed the door and came back around the table and sat down. "Look Elliot, the media is going to jump on this as soon as one of the crime reporters sees her name on the docket. What can you tell me about your source?"

"Michael, I promised I wouldn't reveal my source, and I won't. I will tell you that Wanda's daughter was instrumental in letting us apprehend her however. That will have to be enough for you right now. In the next few days or perhaps weeks you'll learn the source.

That's all I can or will tell you right now.

"Is Marisa your source?"

"Marisa? Yeah right, I wish."

"Look, you can play dumb if you want. I know, as did most of the office, that you two were an item. Has she been in contact with you Elliot?"

"No Michael, she hasn't been in contact with me. Though if she is okay I'd love to hear from her." Elliot was telling the truth now. Marisa had not contacted him, and he would love to hear her voice.

"Fine, but believe me when the Judge starts breathing down my neck you better hope you have a better answer for him. And, you have no comment on any of this if anyone else starts asking questions. Understand?"

"Understood Michael. And, if you hear from her, tell her to call me."

"You know at the beginning of all this I really did believe she was dead, but the more I thought about it I just came to the conclusion she was watching all this from afar. I hope I'm right Elliot. For all of us, I hope I'm right."

"Me too Michael, me too."

Elliot left Michael's office and went right to his own office to make a call.

"Clay Watson, ATF."

"Clay, it's Elliot. The D.A. has told Wanda's original A.D.A. to get this on the court docket as soon as possible. He wants to get the violation settled, and let the other charges pend until they come up for hearing. Also, your office needs to get the paperwork started to file federal weapons charges on her."

"Great, let me know when it comes for hearing. I'll get the paperwork started and I'll serve them at the violation hearing. Also, I'll want to inform our girl of the hearing date. She should be able to return safely after Wanda is sentenced on the violation."

"Let me know something as soon as you know. I really miss her Clay."

"Will do. See ya'."

Clay typed out a note to Marisa, wondering just how she would respond. He also wondered if she could come home as easily as she seemed to disappear.

Wanda is in custody, your problems seem to be solved. E indicates that it should be on the docket very soon for violation. Other charges will pend as scheduled. She is off the street, and I will notify you of hearing date, and outcome. Get ready to come home, we all miss you terribly! Love, me

At the computer terminal in Jake's condo all alone Sterling read the note. She cried, knowing all she had given up in order to capture this horrible woman had to be worth it. And, she cried too because now she had so much more to give up in order to go home. She knew that the violation would probably come up within the next week, and she needed to be ready when it was over. How would she tell Jake and Seth goodbye? She realized she had fallen in love with Jake, and she already knew that Seth had fallen in love with her. Oh what a mess she had made of three lives by trying to save herself a long time ago. She did miss home and her family, but leaving the first time seemed so much easier.

Finally pulling herself together she typed out a note to Clay.

Thank you for everything. Words cannot express my happiness. I hope all are safe. How is Cynthia? Keep me posted I'll be home sometime soon. Keep the secret! Love, me

Just after she logged off, and checked herself in the mirror, Jake walked in from work.

"Hi Darlin'!"

"Hi baby! Well I got some news from home."

"Good news I hope?"

"Well I guess it depends on who you are," she laughed.

"Okay, are we going to play a guessing game, or are you going to tell me? The suspense is killing me." He bent to kiss her on the forehead as he put his briefcase down on the desk.

"Well I made a call the other day to Wanda's daughter. She reluctantly helped my friends set a trap for her mother so they could arrest her. Well, the trap worked, and Wanda was arrested sometime in the last few days. I don't know exactly when, but I just got an e-mail that indicated she is locked up."

"Well you must be feeling pretty proud of yourself. A great stress has been removed from your life, right?"

"Yeah it sure has. I can sleep peacefully again."

"Well what now? Did you call your parents or anything?"

"No, you're the first person to know about this besides me and my co-conspirators at home. I won't do or say anything until after the violation hearing is over."

"Oh, and when will that be do you think?"

Sterling lied, "Well the court dockets are pretty full and it is just a violation hearing. She has no bond, due to new pending charges so she isn't going anywhere."

She couldn't tell him the truth just now. She didn't want to have to worry about saying goodbye until she knew she was leaving. She didn't even want to think about good-byes.

"Well how about let's celebrate? We could go for a walk on the beach and go out to dinner if you want."

"Sounds great to me! Let's go."

He changed his clothes and they headed out to the beach. They held hands and walked their usual route. Watching the sun sink in the western sky made Sterling realize her time at the beach, and with Jake, was coming to a close too. He was talking of his day, but Sterling was in another world. She got tears in her eyes, silently streaming down her face. Jake finally realized something was the matter when she didn't respond to a couple of questions.

"Darlin' are you alright?"

"Yeah baby, just thinking about home. I'm sorry, what were you saying?"

"Never mind that. Things are going to be fine, you'll see."

"Oh yeah, I know. It's just that I have to tell Seth too."

"Well he'll be happy too I'm sure."

"Jake, don't you understand? With all this over, I have to go home."

"Darlin' let's not worry about that now. You just said it could be awhile for things to get straightened out. Let's just cross that bridge when we come to it."

"You're right. It's just a lot to think about. When I left I guess I didn't think I would be gone this long. So much has happened in my life, since I left. Some good, some bad. Most of it I can't even share with anyone. Only Seth knows it all. I guess it's best that way."

"Darlin' things will work out the way they're supposed too. Stop worrying. And, just remember this, you have people here that love you very much, and you have people at home that love you very much too. You just need to focus on that and you'll be fine. We'll all be fine. Now c'mon and let's go eat."

Sterling smiled. Jake always knew just what to say to make her smile. She knew he was right. She had always believed in fate. Things would work out the way they were supposed to and everyone would be fine.

A few days later she received word from home. She wasn't sure if she was ready to read the note, but again she had chosen a time that both Seth and Jake were at work.

Hearing is tomorrow at 9am. E states the Judge has ruled there will be no continuances, or other motions to halt this hearing. Stay tuned, and I'll let you know the outcome. Love, me

When she read the note, the hearing had already taken place. Her stomach was in knots. Just as she was about ready to log off, the sound let her know she had more mail. Gripped with uncertainty, and perhaps some fear she opened the note. It stated:

Big surprise, Judge found her in complete violation and ordered all original suspended time to now be served as an executed sentence. I filed federal firearm violations on her, which adds an additional 5 years without "good time", and she now has other charges which we are sure she'll be convicted of and given maximum executed time. They consolidated checks she received into three felony cases, in addition she has also been charged with Conspiracy to Commit Murder, which carries 60 years. And, they have re-opened the death investigation of her cousin over twenty years ago. You're safe, call me and we can arrange your return. Love, me

Sterling was shocked. All she had waited for had come true. Wanda was locked up tight. She had no worries now. She could go home. She knew she couldn't wait. She would have to leave Daytona as swiftly as she had left home. Telling Seth was going to be hard, but saying goodbye to Jake was not going to be any easier. She did love this man, probably as much as she had loved Elliot. Leaving him just to go back home didn't seem quite right. But, she knew she had to get her life back. She left home without a man in her life; she needed to return the same way. Just then Jake walked in.

Chapter Twenty

"Hi Darlin' I tried to call you earlier but I got the voice-mail. Have you been online?"

"Yeah, checking e-mail and surfing. What did you need?"

"Oh just checking on you. I couldn't reach you at your place, so I figured you were here."

"Yeah, I got a little bored at the pool today, so I decided I needed a change of scenery and to play in the chat rooms."

"Hey, I'm going to take a shower and then I thought we could go out. How's that sound?"

"Sounds great. Can I go like this, or should I run home?"

"No, you look fine. I was just crawling around on the floor today hooking up some computers and I have dirt and dust all over me."

"Okay, well I'll be right here waiting patiently."

"Great. I'll hurry."

Sterling thought for a moment and realized that while she had the nerve she needed to make a decision. She knew just how she was going to say goodbye to Seth, but she still hadn't told him any of the recent happenings back home. She could hear the water running, so she grabbed the phone book and found the listing for airlines. Just as she dialed the number and a voice answered she heard the water shut off.

"USAir reservation desk. This is Tammy how may I assist you?"

Quietly she spoke, "Hi Tammy, I need to know if you have flights out of Myrtle Beach going to Indianapolis, Indiana in the next few days?"

"Yes ma'am we sure do. We have daily departures from there. Can I get your information and we'll see what we have available?"

"Umm, yeah. I need a one way ticket from Myrtle Beach departing on Friday. Early afternoon if possible."

"Well we have a few seats still available on our 12:20 flight. Can I talk you into a roundtrip though, it's much more economical?"

"No Tammy, but thanks. Book me on that flight, one way. My name is Marisa Spencer. And, can you hold that ticket and I'll pay for it at the gate?" It had been a long time since she had said that name.

"Well do you have a credit card that I can use to guarantee it? I can only hold it for twenty-four hours without one, and then you have to go to one of our ticket counters and pay for it. They will issue it then, or hold it for you at the departure gate in Myrtle Beach."

"Umm, put a twenty-four hour hold on it. I'll go to my airport tomorrow and pay for it in cash, just make sure I'm booked on that flight."

"Okay, you are booked on flight 167B out of Myrtle Beach for Friday at 12:20pm. Your total is $284.00. Your confirmation number is 16ZWY4289-035. Have a great trip, and remember that ticket is only on hold until tomorrow by 5:15pm. Thanks for flying

USAir."

Sterling quietly hung up the receiver. Jake had heard every word. He was stunned. He knew he couldn't say anything to her; she had to be the one to bring it up. He finished getting ready and came into the living room. He noticed she was putting a piece of paper in her purse as he walked into the room.

"What are you doing Darlin'?"

"Oh, you scared me. I just put a recipe in my purse that I got off the internet today. Maybe one day I'll try it out on you."

"Oh okay, well try it out on Seth first. If he makes it through then I'll try it. Hey, I need to check my e-mail before we leave do you mind?"

"No, go ahead. I need to fix my hair and refresh my make-up. I'll only be a few minutes."

Jake sat down at the desk where she had called from and noticed the notepad she had used. He grabbed a pencil and lightly colored over the indentations she had made from the other piece of paper she had torn off. He could barely read it, but he had enough information to see what he wasn't able to hear from the other room. She was flying USAir to Indianapolis from Myrtle Beach, flight 167B leaving in just three days. He folded the paper and put it in his drawer.

"Darlin' are you about ready to go?"

"Coming baby. Where are you taking me tonight?"

"Oh the regular if that's okay?"

"Any place is okay as long as I'm with you, you know that."

They ate dinner and played a game of Putt-Putt before calling it a night. After he dropped her off at her place and returned to his own condo he picked up the phone book and got the number for USAir.

"Hello, and thank you for choosing USAir. My name is Jennifer, how can I help you?"

"I need to book a roundtrip ticket from Daytona International Airport to Indianapolis for Friday, early morning if you have it."

"We have flights leaving at 8:32am, 11:27am, and then several afternoon and evening flights on Friday. Will either of those work for you sir?"

"Book me on the 11:27 flight. What time will it reach Indianapolis?"

"You will have one stop over in Atlanta, and you will arrive Indianapolis at 3:48 p.m."

"Can you check something for me first?"

"Sure what is it?"

"I need to know what time flight 167B arrives in Indianapolis from Myrtle Beach."

"Okay, that flight arrives in Indianapolis at 3:16pm."

"Oh wow! Then I need to be on an earlier flight. What time is that earlier one out of Daytona and when will it arrive Indianapolis?"

"Okay the 8:32 am flight arrives in Indianapolis at 12:53pm. Of course these are expected times, weather can mess up our arrivals and departures."

"Sure, okay book me on the 8:32 am flight. And, for the return trip, make it for Saturday night back to Daytona. Oh, and if I need to change the return time or day will that be a problem?"

"Changing the return shouldn't be a problem as long as we have seats. Okay, can I have your name and a credit card to put this in the computer?"

He gave her the information and received his flight confirmation number. He just had a feeling that Sterling wasn't going to tell him she was leaving. For the rest of the night and the next day Sterling didn't mention a word about leaving. He wondered if perhaps she was just going to go home for a bit and return to Daytona.

When Sterling decided to tell Seth she was going home she knew it had to be very private. She knew he had a few days off on Thursday and Friday, so she had gone by the bar on Wednesday night and asked him if they could take a road trip on his days off. She asked him to take her back to Myrtle Beach for a long weekend. He loved that idea. He thought it sounded great that she wanted to spend some time with him. Lately she had been spending most of her time with Jake.

On Thursday morning she was out of bed early and packed for a trip on the bike. She asked him if they could go up the coast and go back to Myrtle Beach. She suggested that they stay at the Sea Mist Motel again. He loved all of her most recent ideas. They arrived at the motel in the evening, and both were very hungry. They went to the Red Lobster for dinner, and afterwards headed back to the motel.

Sterling told him she would like to take a long walk on the beach. He worries about what is going on, but he loves all of her ideas thus far. He has no idea why they are here, but he doesn't care as long as she is with him. Sterling changes into her bikini and puts on one of his sweatshirts. He has on some trunks and his denim jacket. "It's a pretty chilly night for a stroll," says the desk clerk as they pass through the lobby. They both just nod their heads affirmatively.

Down by the water's edge, Sterling takes off her sweatshirt and tells him she wants to go swimming. "You know I made you a promise a long time ago and I didn't keep it then. I'd like you to remember that I'm a woman of my word," Sterling told him.

Seth replied, "Baby, the water and the air's a bit cold this evening, how about another time?"

Sterling just shook her head no. She didn't want him to hear the crack in her voice, because she was starting to cry.

Because she didn't say anything he knew something was wrong. He took off his jacket and held her hand as they walked slowly into the icy water. He picked her up and started running into the deeper water until they both couldn't touch the bottom. He knew when he picked her up that she was crying. "Baby, tell me what's wrong. Are you pregnant?"

"Seth, you know in my own way I do love you and I trust you with all my heart, but I'm not in love with you. You've always known that, I know. You also know I haven't been myself lately, and I miss my family terribly. There's something I haven't told you." She was really sobbing and his eyes filled with tears too. "Baby the bad guys are in jail now and there's no reason for me not to go home. I love this place and you've made me so happy, but I really need to go home."

"How long have you known this?"

"Seth I just found out a few days ago. I didn't know how to tell you. I didn't even tell Jake goodbye. But I have to leave. I have to leave now."

"I love you and I know you love me in your own way. I know I can't keep you here any longer. I wish I could, but I can't. You need to get back, but I have nothing to go back too. I'll see you home safely, but I can't stay there. Hell, I don't know if I can stay in Daytona either. But I'll do what you want me too."

Sterling told him, "I brought you here because this is really where our journey started, and this is the place where you first saw the ocean. This is where I promised to swim with you and I didn't. Seth, I'm not going back to Daytona. I can't right now, maybe sometime down the road but not now. I'm leaving here in the morning. I have a one-way plane ticket home. This is where I wanted to say our good-byes."

He pulled her close to kiss her on the cheek, she was crying, but she let him know she wanted him; just like their first time. He removed her bikini and his trunks and threw them onto the dry sand. They made love with all the passion and tenderness of two newlyweds, but this couple would probably never see each other again. Afterwards they dressed and ran back to the motel. Sand was everywhere, so they decided they needed to shower. It was after midnight when they finally fell into bed. When Sterling awakened she had a lot of emotions welling up inside her. She was terribly sad that her life with Seth was ending, and the life she had wanted with Jake was over too. But, she was tremendously happy about going home. She knew she would have a hard time going back to work, but she had her whole life to decide what she wanted to do.

Seth woke up and asked if he could make love to her again. She told him he needed to remember what they had shared, and if she said yes they would just be delaying the inevitable. He understood. She told him she had packed a lot of her clothes and personal stuff and left it in her closet. She said he could take whatever he wanted, and donate the rest to charity. She told him not to send it back to her. She had brought with her what she wanted to take back home to remember their adventure, and she would always have her memories. He said he understood.

"You know we've been through a lot together, and I hope you'll do one more thing for me," Sterling asked.

"Baby you know I would do anything for you. Name it."

"When we were in Sturgis there was someone there you really liked besides me."

"Yeah, we had a great time there didn't we?"

"We did. And I want you to have a great life. I just know there is someone that you need to call."

"Baby, I don't even remember the name of the bar."

"When we stopped for gas before we headed out of town, I got that and the number. I want you to call it and ask for Jasmine."

"C'mon. I'm sure she doesn't remember me. I'll be fine."

"You remember her don't you? I know you talked to her. Call her when I get on that plane. It's the last thing I will ever ask you to do. Promise me you'll do it?"

"Yeah sure," he laughed.

Her plane left a little after noon, and as they said good-bye for the last time they both held each other tightly and said, "I love you". Seth called to her as she started to board the plane, "Baby, thank you for sharing this adventure with me."

Chapter Twenty-One

When Marisa made her plane reservation she knew someone had to be at the airport to pick her up, so she had called Dani from the plane. Dani was instructed to tell no one, especially Marisa's family about her surprise return, Dani agreed. However, Dani had a little plan of her own. Dani did not know much about Marisa's life in Daytona; she just knew that Elliot still loved her.

Marisa had only a carry-on bag and her purse. She had neglected to tell Dani of her new hairstyle, so she knew she would really have to be on her toes to find Dani. Upon arrival at the airport back where this life had started she realized she no longer even felt like Sterling. She didn't feel like Marisa either. She wondered if everyone else would notice all the changes she had been through.

At the arrival gate she looked everywhere but she couldn't find Dani. She even went to the baggage claim area, but no one was there either. She went back up the gate to look again. Finally, she called the probation department to see when Dani left; however, the receptionist indicated that Dani was at her desk. Marisa asked to be connected to Dani. Dani said, "Oh I'm sorry, I made other arrangements for you, just look around." Then the phone went dead.

There were still a lot of people milling about, and she had no idea what Dani was up to. When she turned around, she saw a man with a huge bouquet of lilies; he was the only person looking out the window near the, arrival gate. She thought it must be her father, so she ran toward him yelling "Daddy, Daddy, I'm right here." About that time the man took the bouquet away from his face. It was Elliot.

"Baby, I missed you!"

Marisa had tears in her eyes; there was only one other person that had ever called her Baby. He never called her that while they were together. "But I thought you and Tess were," she didn't get to finish her sentence because he was kissing her like he truly loved her. She kissed him back. She never noticed Jake sitting there watching her.

Jake dared not move. He had come to see that she got home safely. He was quite surprised when she disembarked the plane, alone. He wondered if she had told Seth she was leaving. And, he wondered why she had routed herself through Myrtle Beach. These were questions he would probably never have answered. He wanted to talk to her so badly, but he knew there wasn't room for him in her life right now. He never realized that the man she left so long ago would be at the airport waiting for her too. He knew he had to stay in the shadows.

Marisa was crying thinking about how much she loved the man that was holding her now, and for what she had left behind just days and hours ago. But no one here could ever know of that life, or that these tears were for anymore than happiness as she began to walk back into her life with Elliot by her side.

Jake stood, and watched Marisa walk out of his life with another man. His only hope for her now was happiness and many more shared sunsets with a man that loved her. All his hopes for himself vanished, as she became lost in the crowd. He would only pray that one day their paths would cross again. He blinked back a tear, and hung his head.

As they walked to the car Marisa had a lot on her mind, and she told Elliot that she wanted to tell him things before they went anywhere.

"Elliot a lot of things have happened to me in the past year or so, and I'm not the naive young girl that left here. I guess things have changed significantly in your life, but I may not fit into the life you have carved out. I want more now. I've become a very independent person, someone that you may not like. I'm not the old Marisa anymore. I loved you a long time ago, and perhaps I still do. But you have to know that I wasn't alone. We both have a lot to think about, and a lot to do. I had to come home and finish what I started. Someone from my other life helped me make that decision. He was someone I dated for the past few months, but I didn't even tell him goodbye. He has no idea about this life; he knows the other me. No one here was aware of my life there, not even my family. They only knew that I was safe."

"Is it over with the other guy?"

"It has to be. He doesn't even know I left, and he had no idea where I was from."

"Do you, or did you love him?"

"I was never with him intimately. But yes, I think I did. But he has a life there, and I have a life here that I need to reclaim. It's over with him Elliot. It has to be."

"Let's just start from here Baby. I never stopped loving you, never. I've been divorced and alone for months. I'd really like to have you back in my life."

"Elliot let's start slow. I just want to get my life back and see my family. Will you help me?"

"I'd do anything for you Baby."

On the ride back being with him seemed so normal, so comfortable. She really had missed him. And then she knew she still loved him. When they pulled into the driveway her parents, Kate and Dani were right there. She was so happy to see them all. Everyone was filled with such emotion. Everyone was hugging Marisa and telling her how much she had changed. She said changes on the outside were not really as significant as the ones on the inside. Elliot just stood back and smiled. Finally Cliff came to him and shook his hand and thanked him for all he had done. Just a few minutes later, Clay pulled up.

"Girl I've missed you. Thank God you're safe. I can't stay long, but Elliot called me just before your plane landed to let me know he was picking you up. I have to get back, something came up and they need me at the office. We have to do lunch, and I want to hear all about your hiding place, and Elliot. Call me." She hugged Clay and kissed him on the cheek just before he pulled away.

Her parents decided on taking the newly assembled group out for dinner. Marisa worried that people might wonder about her while they were out, but Elliot convinced her to go. After dinner Elliot asked if he could drive Marisa home. Marisa had only one request: to drive around the city and see how things had changed. Elliot agreed and escorted his date to the car. As they drove he said, "Marisa there is so much I want to say to you. Let me first start with the day you presumably left town."

"Sure Elliot, but let me apologize for missing our lunch. I just couldn't call you."

"I know that now, but there are some things you need to know. I was devastated when you stood me up, because I had something so important to ask you. I know a lot of time has passed and many things have happened in the course of a year, but what I had to say then is still very important to me. I know you have a lot to think about, but even though you disappeared, my love for you did not."

"Wait Elliot. I'm not the girl you used to know."

"Marisa please, hear me out. Shortly after Tess and I got back together I found out she had not ended her affair. I was miserable, and confronted her. She told me I could leave. I left for work the next morning a broken man. I didn't leave. She was unhappy with me, and there were the kids to think about. About a week of silence ensued, and one day I came home from work to an empty house. She had packed everything and moved out without a word. She took the kids out of school, filed for divorce and moved a few hours away. Then the call from you came. I had so hoped you would call me. I couldn't be the one to call you, not the way I had left you before. Marisa I love you. I finally realized it when I went back home. Marisa, I know a lot has changed in your life. A lot has changed in mine too, but I do want to be with you. I have wanted that for so long."

"Elliot I have loved you since the first time we were together. A lot has changed in both of our lives, but I know I still love you. So much happened while I was away, but I never felt as close to any man as I did to you all that time ago."

"Baby, when you're ready I want you to be my wife."

"Elliot? You don't even know some of the things that happened while I was away. There is so much I need to tell you."

471

"Look Marisa, I don't care about the other men you may have been with. I don't care about the relationship you had with that guy. I love you. I have for a long time. We belong together. All I want to know is if you feel the same way?"

"Yes Elliot. I do love you."

When they pulled into the driveway they sat and kissed a long time. Just before they got to the door, he pulled out a small box from his jacket pocket. It was dark now, but under the moonlight he placed the ring on her finger and said, "Whenever you're ready, please make me the happiest man and be my wife."

Marisa was crying softly and she held him tight. He held her in his arms and stroked her hair. Kissing her head and telling her things were going to be all right now. She looked up to him and said she knew when she was with him things would always be okay. She opened the door to find both of her parents, Dani and Kate playing a game of cards. Marisa was beaming when she walked to the table and showed everyone the ring.

Chapter Twenty-Two

The day after she arrived home she called in to work. She spoke to Jansen first about coming back to work. She told her she needed a week or so to decompress, but she was ready to get back to work. She told her that her office would be waiting for her when she returned. She had so many people to talk to she barely had time to think. The press was calling around the clock wanting her story. She kept up the 'no comment' routine until she could barely stand it. It didn't matter whether she had a comment or not, it was the top story for several days after she arrived home.

Although her parents wanted her to stay with them she just couldn't. She had changed so much in her time away. It was just too difficult being under their roof twenty-four hours a day. On her third day back she and Elliot started looking for apartments with a short-term lease. After looking at several she decided on one near his house. She figured she wouldn't be spending every night with him, and her parents would have thrown a fit if she had moved in with him and was not married. Her things from the old apartment were still boxed up in her parent's basement. Moving in was not a huge problem, but she was anxious to get settled again.

Finally, she convinced everyone she just needed some time alone. After everyone left she sat and tried to imagine the sounds of the surf, but it just wasn't there. She looked around at the small apartment, and wished she had the space she had had at the condo. The walls seemed to be closing in on her. She finally allowed herself to cry. She worried about Seth, and Jake. She wanted so badly to call them, but she knew she couldn't, not yet. She had to make this life work. She knew that it was supposed to be this way.

Clay called her and asked if he could stop by, but she told him she just really needed to be alone tonight. He asked if she was okay, and she told him she was just really tired, and overwhelmed by everything going on around her. He told her he would be in touch, and to take care. He was a little worried though when he hung up.

Elliot called to tell her good night, but she let the machine pick up. She just didn't want to ask him to come over tonight, or have him offer when he heard the pain in her voice. She tried to get her mind off of everything, but she kept thinking about returning to work in the morning, and eventually having to face Wanda in court once again. Elliot had told her that she would be called as a witness in the new cases since she had done all the preliminary work on the investigation. Oh how she dreaded seeing her again.

Just as she was about to go to bed the phone rang again. As the voice came over the machine she hurriedly picked it up.

"Hello, hold on just a minute."

"Hi, I'm glad you made it home safely. I told your friend that I would have one more request when Velma was finally locked up. Do you think you can help me with it?"

"Cynthia, of course I'll try to help you. What is it that you want?"

"I want to disappear just like you did. I don't want her to ever find me again. I want to become someone else."

"Cynthia what I did was very difficult. Coming back has not been easy. Besides, Velma is locked up and she will be for a very long time."

"Look, I'm not planning on coming back. I want to be someone else. I don't want her or that boyfriend of hers ever finding me again. I want to start a new life, without ever thinking of her again, or looking over my shoulder."

"Let me talk to my friend, but I think I can help you. But you realize you'll have to walk away from everything you have here. Everything. Do you really think you can do that, and never look back?"

"Trust me Ms. Spencer I will never look back."

"Call me tomorrow at work in the afternoon. Let me work on this."

"I'll be in touch. And don't forget, Velma still has him on the outside."

The dial tone clicked on before Marisa could say another word. She wondered if she really had anything to fear from Velma or her friends now. Oh how she detested this woman and all she was capable of doing.

The next morning Marisa went to work pondering the request made by Cynthia. She knew she could help her but wondered if she should involve anyone else. She also thought a lot about Velma's boyfriend, Mr. Randolph, or whatever his real name might be. The day flew by as every co-worker had talked to her at length about her time away. She preferred to tell them that she had just gone out west and stayed up in the mountains, not interacting with anyone. She had no desire to tell anyone what she had really done over the course of the last year to remain anonymous. Telling Elliot would be hard enough. She was glad her family hadn't pressed her for more details. She knew they trusted her to do the right things. They would probably be ashamed and astonished to find out otherwise.

Only Dani had asked about Seth. When Seth's name was mentioned Marisa got tears in her eyes, and told Dani that without him she would never have made it. She told her that she needed some time to heal before she could discuss any more about him or the relationship they had shared. Dani realized that a romance must have blossomed, but she also knew he didn't return home with Marisa.

Late in the afternoon she got a call from Cynthia. "Ms. Spencer, have you had time to decide if you can help me with my only request?"

"Yes Cynthia I have. I'll tell you everything I did to hide. I suggest you follow my advice if this is really what you want to do, and don't even tell me what name you will be using or where you want to go."

"Great. Can you talk now, or should I meet you somewhere?"

"Why don't you meet me tonight at a little restaurant near here? We can have drinks and some dinner, and I'll tell you everything I know."

"Fine. How about Farley's on Norman Ave. about five o'clock?"

"That sounds good to me. See you then."

Before leaving work Marisa called Elliot to tell him she was meeting a friend for dinner, but she would call him when she got home. As much as he hated sharing her with anyone, he knew she had a lot of catching up to do. She walked into Farley's a few minutes before 5:00 p.m. She noticed a woman standing at the bar watching her. She walked to the bar and ordered a drink. The young woman looked her over and said, "Are you Ms. Spencer?"

"Yes, Cynthia?"

"Let's get a table."

After they sat down Cynthia told Marisa she had closed all of her bank accounts and was making sure all of her bills were caught up. She indicated she had decided against giving notice at her place of employment.

Marisa told her all about getting a fake identification, which should only take about two weeks, then it would be up to her to feign a really good excuse to get a real identification card with her new name. She also stated she would be without a real social security number, but if she could make good money in her chosen field she might not need to worry about that money when she was retirement age. She also indicated that leaving town anonymously might be the way to go as well just in case anyone started looking for her. Marisa gave her the number to Auto Mover's and explained how that service worked. Afterwards, Cynthia thanked her and gave her a hug.

"You know, I've never told anyone the things I told you over the phone about my past. Please keep that secret for me. I don't have any real close friends, but I would consider you a friend now."

"Cynthia, your secret is safe with me. I'm glad you think I can help you. I have told no one that you contacted me. I suppose it's best if we don't talk again. You can get on with your new life with no strings attached. Just remember, pick a name that she would never consider, and a name that you like hearing."

"I've been thinking of names since the other night. I just hope one day I can find happiness as you did."

"Cynthia, out there somewhere is someone for you. Just get away from here and be careful."

They ate their meal in relative silence. The waiter brought the checks but Cynthia picked up both of them. When Marisa tried to get both checks Cynthia stated, "It's the least I can do. You've helped me tremendously. I won't let you down. Now don't you let me down either, see that she gets every minute she deserves. And, you be careful too. He is still out there lurking somewhere." With that said, Cynthia quickly excused herself from the table, paid the check and walked out of the restaurant. Marisa just sat there stunned and thinking that she had just had dinner with a very nice person that deserved a better shot at life than Velma had given her.

Chapter Twenty-Three

Jansen and Charles thought it would be best to ease Marisa back into a caseload slowly. Although most things had not changed in the office it would still be beneficial for her to shadow another officer or two to review programs, policies, and general office procedures. By the third day Marisa was bored stiff. She discussed her predicament with Charles, but he indicated she just needed to be more patient and get cases slowly. The whole building was buzzing about her. She was like a celebrity everywhere she went. Marisa hated the attention. She wished that things could return to the way that they were before she left.

She met Clay for lunch one day. He could see that she was still rather anxious. He tried to get her mind off of her problems by congratulating her on her recent engagement, but even that didn't help. Finally, she decided to tell him that Cynthia had said something to her about Velma's boyfriend. Clay knew that Mr. Randolph wasn't done with Marisa. And, he knew he had to protect her. No one would know that he would be keeping Marisa under surveillance whenever he could.

Clay watched the lot this night as he had the past week. Tonight though, something just felt different. He could feel the electricity in the air. The lights went off in Marisa's apartment, and he saw her watch the lot through the curtains. He wondered if she sensed something different tonight too. He also wondered if they were watching for the same unknown predator.

From the corner of his eye he noticed a large shadow lurking beside Marisa's building. The shadow disappeared, but no lights came on inside any of the apartments. Silently he slipped from his car and walked through the darkness. As he approached the building he heard a gunshot. He burst through the side door and noticed a female figure hurriedly walking to the other exit door. He yelled to her to stop, but she ignored his request. He sprinted down the hall and up the stairs to Marisa's apartment. The door was ajar and he heard a scream.

With his gun in hand and ready he entered the dark apartment. He reached for a wall switch but it seemed the power was out. Unsure of the layout of the rooms he cautiously stepped around furniture. He could see a figure in the hall near a bedroom. Marisa then yelled, "STOP! I'll shoot!"

"Marisa, it's me, Clay. Put down your gun. Are you okay?"

"Clay? What are you doing here?"

"Dammit Marisa, it's dark in here. Who in the hell is that?"

"Umm, I guess it's someone that wanted me dead. Let me get a light."

"Jesus Marisa, you shoot first and ask questions later? Someone besides us must have heard that shot, hurry up!"

"Dammit Clay, I'm nervous wreck, shut up! And I didn't fire my weapon."

Marisa had grabbed a flashlight, and was lighting a candle. When she shined the light toward the doorway she gasped. Blood was everywhere, and Mr. Randolph lay face down in her hallway.

"Oh Clay, Oh Clay! Now what do we do?"

"What do you mean? Who is this scumbag?"
And as he started to pick up the phone he noticed the gun behind Mr. Randolph toward the living room. He looked down at it, and then to Marisa for an explanation. He knew then, the Marisa had not fired the shot that killed Mr. Randolph.

"Marisa, who else was here with you tonight?"

"Clay I was asleep. No one was here with me that I knew of. And, this scumbag is Wanda's boyfriend, Mr. Randolph. And as far as anyone needs to know, I killed him!"

"It was that woman that I saw leaving. She did this. Why would you take any responsibility for it? I yelled to her to stop but she wouldn't. Who was she Marisa?"

"Clay why are you here tonight? You don't have to be a part of this. Please just leave now, and I'll make the call."

"Dammit Marisa I've been here every night for a week, and I can't leave now! What's going on? Tell me who killed this scumbag. NOW!"

"Look, the person you saw leaving is going to remain a mystery to us both. I killed him do you understand that Clay?"

"But Marisa, the gun is over here, he was shot in the back and you were asleep in bed."

She stepped around Clay and over the heap on the floor, and picked up the gun. With a steely glaze in her eyes she stated, "I was standing here when he tried to kill me. I was hiding in this closet because I saw him in the parking lot. I didn't have time to call the police, so I picked up my gun and hid."

"Marisa, when they check you for residue you won't have any on you. And, that isn't your gun. You're not thinking clearly. We'll just tell them that I saw a woman leaving and they can start looking for her."

"NO! I had no idea this was going to happen, I had no idea you were even watching me, but I'm not going to say that I know who killed him and ruin another life. Now I'm telling you, I killed him, and I bought this gun in Florida from a guy in a bar, do you understand what I'm saying? And my real gun is going back to a safe place."

"It was Cynthia wasn't it Marisa? They will never believe us Marisa. They'll keep looking for her, and you'll be in trouble for not telling what really happened."

"They won't find her Clay. Now let's get it straight. You were here watching, but didn't see anything initially. You heard a shot and ran in here. The apartment was dark and you heard me crying in the hall. When you finally got me calmed down, we called the police. End of story. They may not even test me for residue since I'm going to tell them I shot him, and the gun has been fired."

"Ok Marisa, Jesus I can't believe I'm going to lie. This is serious shit!" He picked up the phone and dialed 911, as she went to put her own weapon away in the back of the closet.

Still holding the gun that killed Mr. Randolph she returned to the hallway and sat down. She then got a glazed look in her eyes and huddled into a ball on the floor. Clay wasn't sure if this was an act, or if she was in shock. He knew though that he couldn't let her down, and he would tell them the story just as she had told him. He only hoped she knew what she was doing.

The police arrived within minutes of the call. When the police arrived, they found Clay in the doorway to the apartment, and Marisa was still huddled in the hallway, holding the gun. The first officer to arrive immediately took the gun from Marisa, and led her to the couch in the living room.

Clay had lit some candles in the living room, but it was still very dark in the apartment. The power had been cut for the whole building, but the police were able to get some auxiliary power going and began working the crime scene. Once the detective arrived Marisa identified the victim as Mr. Randolph. It was noted that he was struck in the back of the head by 'her' gun. Blood and gray matter were splattered all over the walls and carpet. He had fallen face down and was still holding the piano wire he undoubtedly was planning to use to strangle Marisa in her bed.

Clay had spoken to the detective as soon as he arrived. He learned that no one else had reported hearing a gunshot. He then told the detective the story just as Marisa had recited it to him before he called the police. When the detective spoke to Marisa, she told them she didn't realize Clay was in the lot, but she saw someone lurking about after she had turned out the lights and was looking outside. She grabbed the gun she had brought back from Florida and hid in the hall closet. She indicated she was so nervous when she heard him enter the apartment, and walk down the hall. Once he passed the closet door she popped out and shot him, knowing no one she knew would come into her apartment at night and startle her in the dark. She explained that once she shot the subject she heard someone else enter, but soon realized it was Clay coming to her rescue. She indicated that Clay calmed her down for a good long while, and when they finally found the flashlight they learned that it was Mr. Randolph she had shot and killed, and it was at that time that they called the police.

The detective took notes, and allowed her to call Elliot. Elliot arrived just minutes later and was allowed to comfort her. Both Elliot and the detective told her that charges would most likely not be filed as she had shot in self-defense, but they did relieve her of the gun and told her it was probably best if she find someplace else to stay for the next few days. The detective told Elliot he should probably make arrangements to have the apartment professionally cleaned. Elliot stepped over the body in the hall and grabbed a few things for Marisa. He told the detective that if he needed to reach her in the next few days she would be at his home, and he gave him the phone number. The detective took the information and told her to try and get some rest.

Clay walked out with them, but never got a chance to talk to her alone. He knew she was still shaken up about it. Clay hugged her and told her if she needed to talk to call him. He then got into his car and drove away knowing that they would never talk of this night again.

There were several people milling about in the parking lot wondering why there were so many police cars around at this hour of the night. Marisa didn't really know any of them, and didn't feel that she needed to give any of them an explanation. They would probably hear all about it on the morning news. Most of the people were standing near the building and let her pass without a second glance.

However, just as she started to get into the car she saw a glint of light, and a click. Two cars away a woman was standing, smoking a cigarette. Quietly the woman said, "He won't bother you again." Marisa then realized it was Cynthia, but she couldn't speak, she just nodded her head. Elliot was putting the bag in the trunk and didn't hear or see the other woman. Cynthia got into her car, but waited until Elliot was out of the lot before she left. Although Marisa couldn't tell Cynthia or anyone, she was quite thankful that Cynthia had been there watching over her tonight.

As they drove away, both lost in their own thoughts, Marisa was thinking that her life was still on hold. She had been back in town less than two weeks and she was in the middle of a media circus. She knew she would be cleared if any charges were filed against her, but the media would get a hold of this and her life would once again be back in the papers, on the radio, and on the television news once again. She could not stand the attention. And she finally spoke, "Elliot, how do you feel about being married to a woman who doesn't work for a living?"

"Baby, do what you need to do. I can take care of us both, and would enjoy doing just that."

"I think I'll call work in the morning and tell them I have bigger plans to deal with right now. I need to focus on being Mrs. Elliot Green. Besides I was never cut out for a life in the limelight."

EPILOGUE

Six months later, on the eve of her wedding, Marisa called the bar where Seth was working when they left Daytona. Desiree answered the phone.

"May I speak to Seth Anthony please," Marisa said.

Desiree asked, "Sterling, is that you?"

"Yes, is Seth there?"

"Honey I don't like being the bearer of bad news, but after Seth came back to town things just weren't the same for him. After you guys broke up, he left this place and went to work at Cheater's in Ormond Beach. He was the manager, and was making some big money. He hired this bartender with red hair. Her name is Jasmine, and they fell in love. They packed up about a month ago and moved to Myrtle Beach. He didn't give anyone any other information. I'm sorry."

"Hey that's okay. I just wanted to let him know I'm getting married tomorrow. If you ever see him again, please tell him I called."

Marisa made one more phone call. She slowly dialed Jake's number only to hear a recording come on that indicated that the number was no longer in service. She hurriedly dialed directory assistance and asked for a new listing for him. She learned there were no listings for this man she had called her friend. She took out a piece of stationery and wrote him a note. The note said:

Dearest Jake, my forever friend,

I know this isn't the way to treat your friends, but good-byes are just too hard for me. I couldn't bring you into my world and I couldn't stay in yours. I just want you to know that leaving was the best thing for me, and my family, and I'm sorry I couldn't tell you about it. There is so much I want you to know, so much I want to share with you, but I had to come back here to reclaim my life. There is one thing that I want you to know: I love you. I fell in love with you the first night you fixed me dinner, and we watched the sun set over the river. You are the most gentle, loving man I have ever known, and I'm truly sorry for the way I left. It was very cowardly of me. I want to be your friend, but with all that has happened since I returned I don't know if you would still want to be mine. One day I know our paths will cross again, and I thank God for the time we had together. I hope this finds you well. I will one day be on the "net", and maybe we can chat and be friends again. I will always remember your e-mail address and log-on name. I hope you remember mine--it describes me now, and then. Love, me xoxo

She sealed and addressed the envelope, but she didn't put a return address label on it. If he was no longer at that address she didn't want to know it. And, if this letter did reach him, he would not be able to contact her. Hearing his voice, or seeing his words now might just be too difficult.

Marisa had tears streaming down her face. She was very happy with the life she was about to begin with Elliot. She was so happy for Seth too, but she would always wonder what would have happened if she had stayed with Jake. But then she decided: never look back, and have no regrets.

ACKNOWLEDGEMENTS

There are many people I wish to thank and/or acknowledge for their help while I wrote this book. Without the help and encouragement of many I would never have accomplished what I set out to do.

First and foremost I would like to thank my children, Alex, Kelsey and Alaina, for their patience and understanding while I lost myself writing. Without their love and support I would never have finished writing this story that had floated around in my head for so many years. I wish that Kelsey was here to join me in my joy, but I know she's watching over me from above.

Secondly, I'd like to thank my husband, Oscar, who has encouraged me to finish what I started, and been behind me whispering loudly to get it published for the past 12 years. He was not even a presence in my life while I wrote this story, but he was one of the first to read it when it was done. He is the one that begged me to get it off the shelf, work on it and get it out there.

I would also like to thank my parents and sister for bearing with me while I was often online chatting with people, and researching for this novel and was unavailable to them. I know they don't share the same love of the internet and books like I do, but without any of it, this novel would never have even gotten off the ground.

I owe a huge debt of gratitude to the few people that read this book before I had even found a way to publish it. They were looking not only at the forest, but at the trees too. Thank you very much for your help in proofing the manuscripts, and helping to make this novel better. Thanks Lisa Brueggeman, Michelle Smith, Amy Sitzman, Harry and Kyle Morris, Cheryl Dubay, and Oscar Jones. And, Andi Taylor, for her help in scanning the manuscript back into the computer when I lost everything, and for her help whenever I called about computer problems. Thank you all so much!

I also wish to thank some people that helped with motivation, and character development. John "Jake" Meares was with me all the way. He heard me rumble, grumble and jump with joy with my minor setbacks and great triumphs. He was surely the person that I based the character of Jake on, and for that I am eternally grateful. Without Jake in this book, Marisa may never have made it home. To my best friend, Chad Wilkinson, we met long after I had finished this manuscript and put it away. You were there reading it and encouraging me for years to get it published! You started writing your own novel and got it published before I even pulled my manuscript out again. You helped me with your constant praise and encouragement more than you can ever know. Thank you, and may you have continued success with your writing and publishing. And to another writer friend, Dan Brown, or D.P. Brown as his readers know him, thank you so much for always encouraging me, answering my questions, and making me laugh with your sarcasm and wit. Much luck to you with your books.

Thank you to "Micky" on Flikr and Wikimedia for her amazing photography and what I used as my cover art.

I may never have gotten in the mood to write certain scenes, or stay motivated while writing if I had not had great music to listen to. So, a huge thank you to The Eagles, Trace Adkins, Santana, Smokey Robinson, and Neil Young. Thanks for making great music, and keep it coming, I have more books to write!

And, I would like to thank John Grisham for writing such griping stories. The author's note in A TIME TO KILL was the impetus I needed for putting pen to paper and writing my own novel. Whenever I got discouraged, or had a writer's block, I read that note and got back to what I set out to do—write my own novel. And, to quote Mr. Grisham, "This one came from the heart. It's a first novel, and at time it rambles, but I wouldn't change a word if given the chance.

490

Lastly, to the readers...Thank you for taking time to read this story.

Made in the USA
Monee, IL
06 January 2022